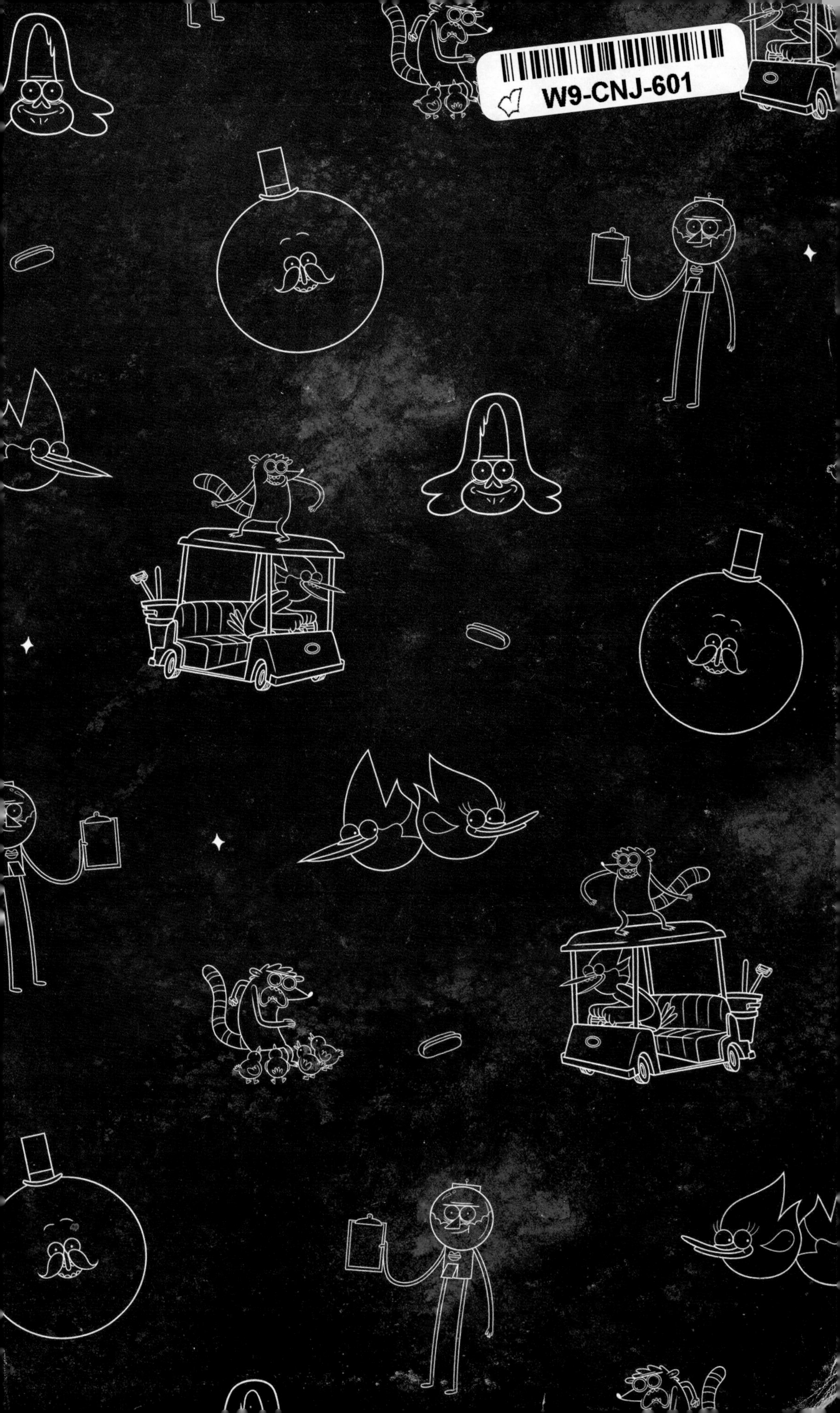

ROSS RICHIE CEO & Founder • MATT GAGNON Editor-in-Chief • FILIP SABLIK President of Publishing & Marketing • STEPHEN CHRISTY President of Development • LANCE KREITER VP of Licensing & Merchandising
PHIL BARBARO VP of Finance • ARUNE SINGH VP of Marketing • BRYCE CARLSON Managing Editor • MEL CAYLO Marketing Manager • SCOTT NEWMAN Production Design Manager • KATE HENNING Operations Manager
SIERRA HAHN Senior Editor • DAFNA PLEBAN Editor, Talent Development • SHANNON WATTERS Editor • ERIC HARBURN Editor • WHITNEY LEOPARD Editor • JASMINE AMIRI Editor • CHRIS ROSA Associate Editor
ALEX GALER Associate Editor • CAMERON CHITTOCK Associate Editor • MATTHEW LEVINE Assistant Editor • SOPHIE PHILIPS-ROBERTS Assistant Editor • KELSEY DIETERICH Designer • JILLIAN CRAB Production Designer
MICHELLE ANKLEY Production Designer • KARA LEOPARD Production Designer • GRACE PARK Production Design Assistant • ELIZABETH LOUGHRIDGE Accounting Coordinator • STEPHANIE HOCUTT Social Media Coordinator
JOSÉ MEZA Event Coordinator • JAMES ARRIOLA Mailroom Assistant • HOLLY AITCHISON Operations Assistant • MEGAN CHRISTOPHER Operations Assistant • MORGAN PERRY Direct Market Representative

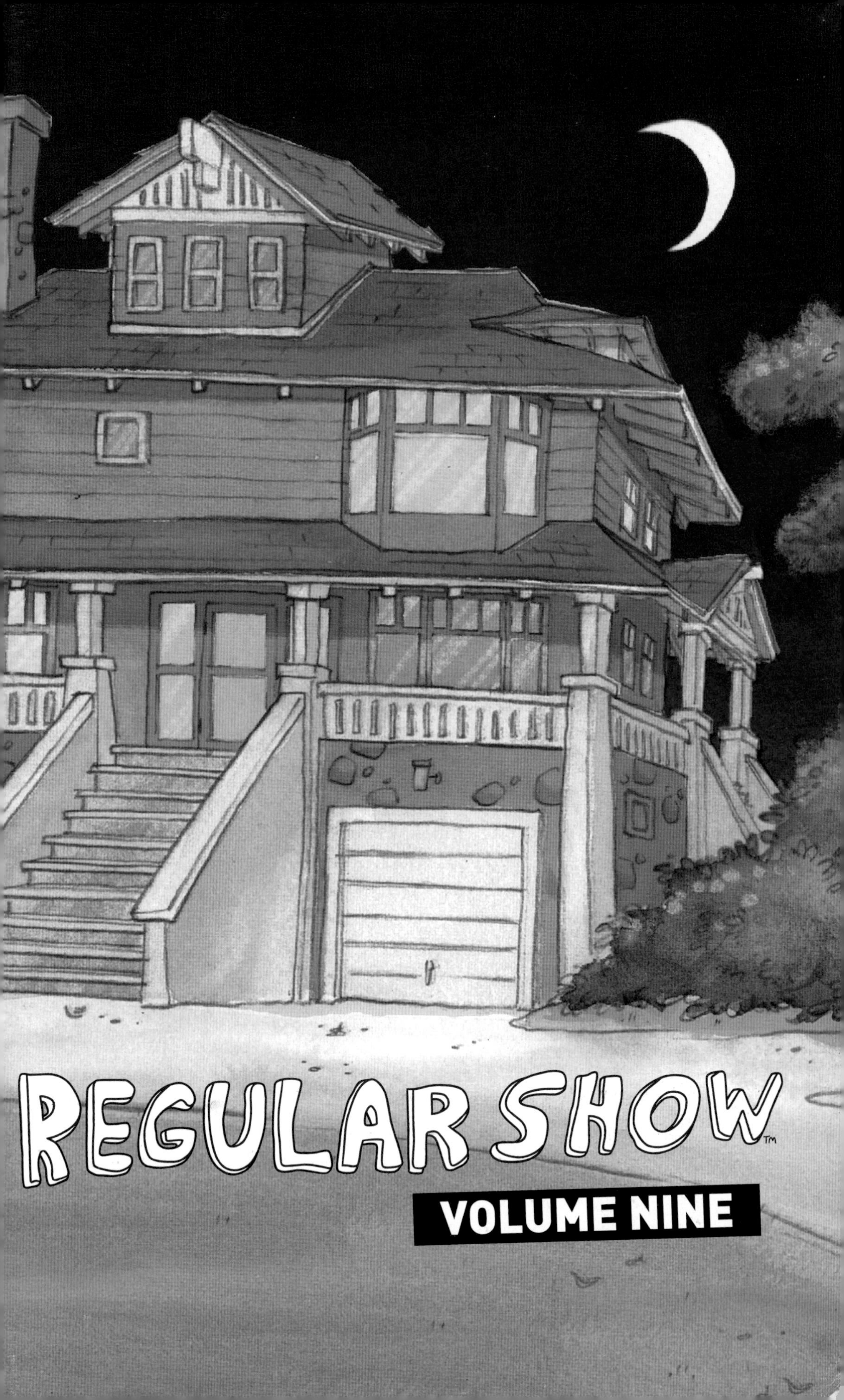
REGULAR SHOW™
VOLUME NINE

REGULAR

CREATED BY **JG QUINTEL**

"REAL DEAL HEROES"

SCRIPT BY **ULISES FARINAS & ERICK FREITAS**

ART BY **LAURA HOWELL**

COLORS BY **LISA MOORE**

LETTERS BY **STEVE WANDS**

COVER BY
PHILIP MURPHY

DESIGNER
MICHELLE ANKLEY

ASSISTANT EDITOR
MARY GUMPORT &
SOPHIE PHILIPS-ROBERTS

EDITOR
SIERRA HAHN

SHOW™

"KAIJU EX"
SCRIPT BY **SHANNA MATUSZAK**
ART BY **WILL KIRKBY**
LETTERS BY **STEVE WANDS**

"TEA FOR ONE"
SCRIPT AND ART BY **LAURA HOWELL**

"BIG BAD BULLY BABY BIKER BEEF"
SCRIPT BY **RYAN FERRIER**
ART BY **MATTHEW SMIGIEL**

"I LEFT MY HEART AT CHEEZER'S"
SCRIPT AND ART BY **BOX BROWN**

"EARTH B"
SCRIPT BY **DEWAYNE FEENSTRA**
ART BY **JENNA AYOUB**

WITH SPECIAL THANKS TO
MARISA MARIONAKIS, JANET NO, CURTIS LELASH,
CONRAD MONTGOMERY, MEGHAN BRADLEY, KELLY
CREWS, RYAN SLATER AND THE WONDERFUL FOLKS AT
CARTOON NETWORK.

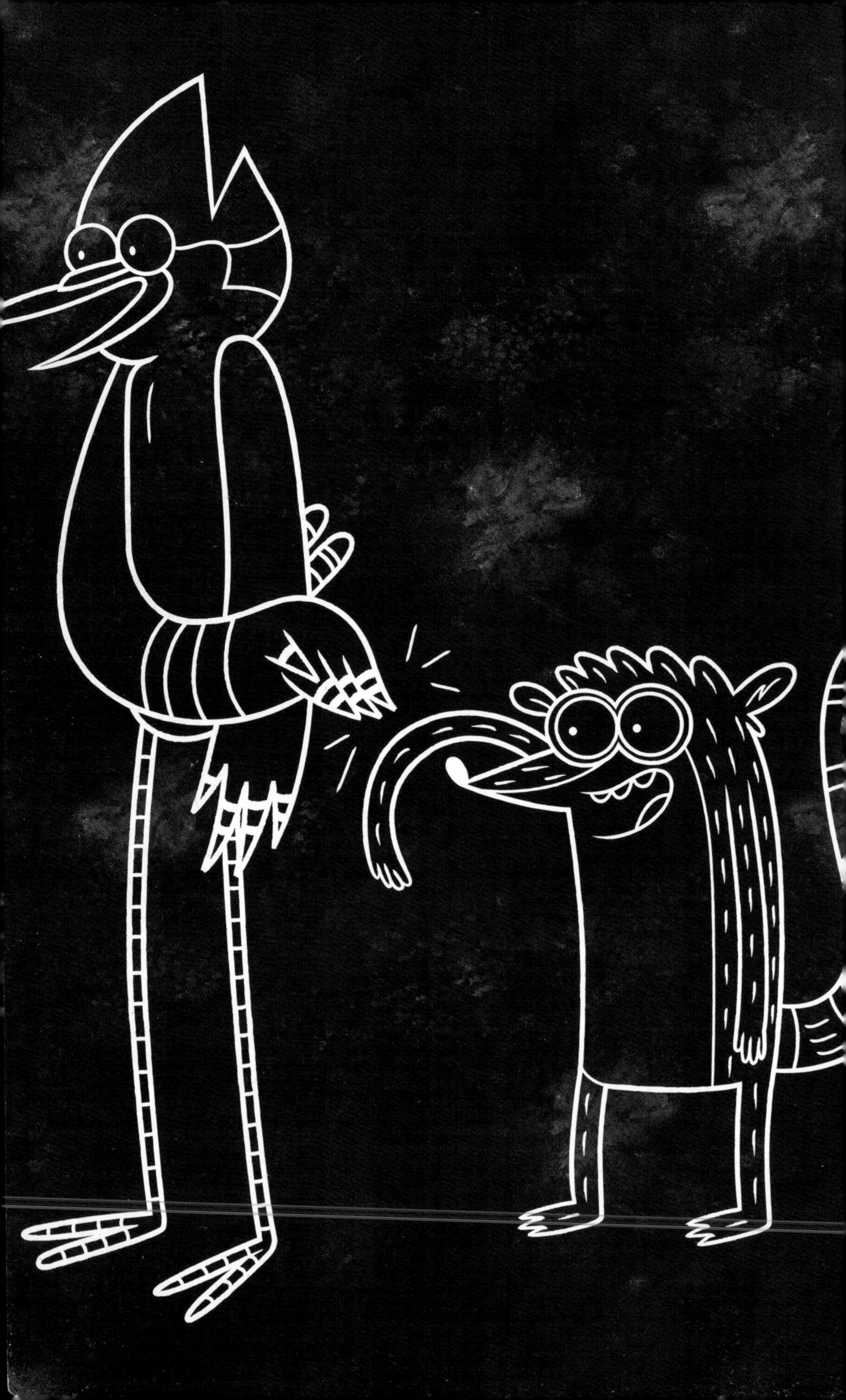

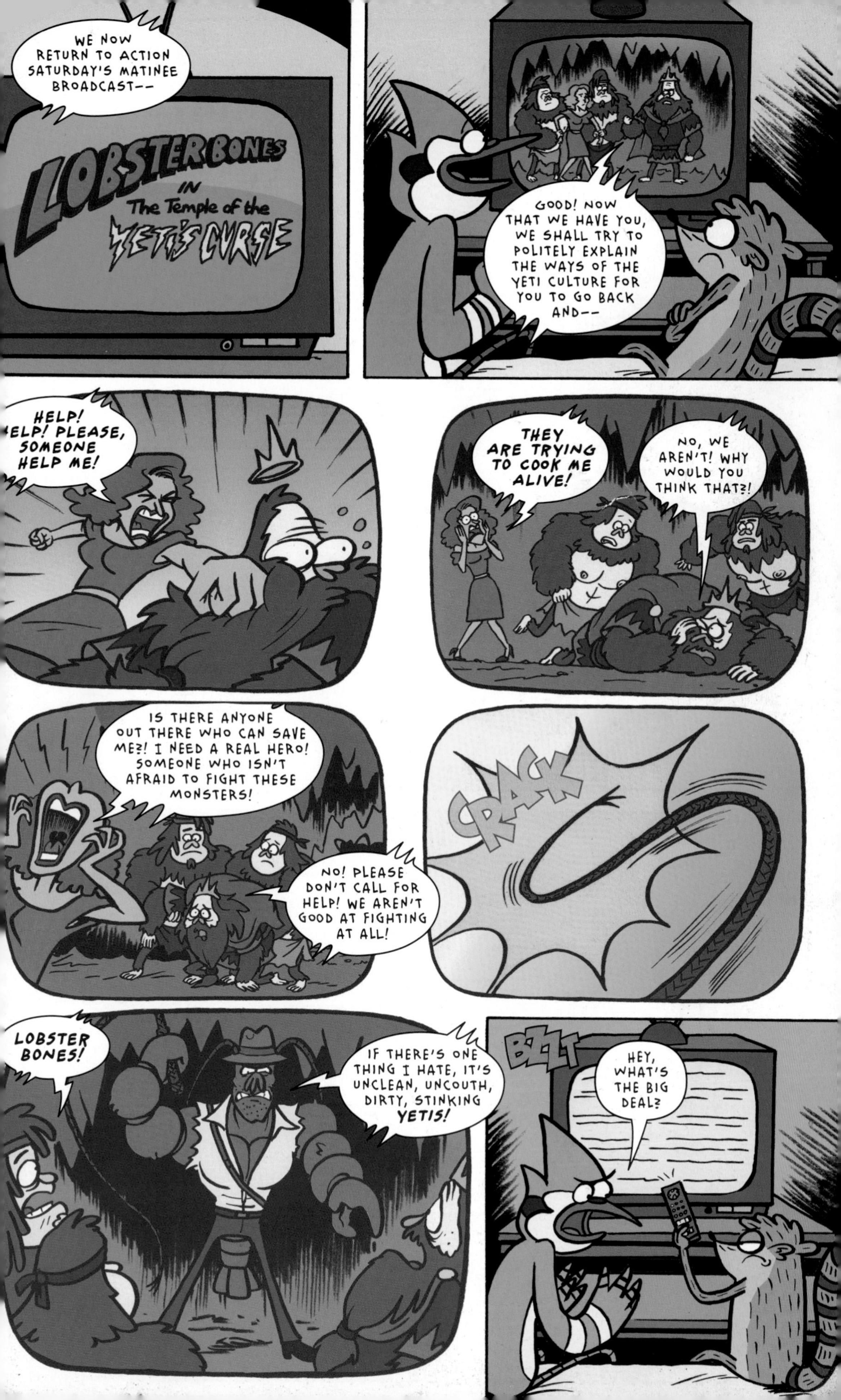
WE NOW RETURN TO ACTION SATURDAY'S MATINEE BROADCAST--
LOBSTER BONES IN The Temple of the YETI'S CURSE
GOOD! NOW THAT WE HAVE YOU, WE SHALL TRY TO POLITELY EXPLAIN THE WAYS OF THE YETI CULTURE FOR YOU TO GO BACK AND--
HELP! HELP! PLEASE, SOMEONE HELP ME!
THEY ARE TRYING TO COOK ME ALIVE!
NO, WE AREN'T! WHY WOULD YOU THINK THAT?!
IS THERE ANYONE OUT THERE WHO CAN SAVE ME?! I NEED A REAL HERO! SOMEONE WHO ISN'T AFRAID TO FIGHT THESE MONSTERS!
NO! PLEASE DON'T CALL FOR HELP! WE AREN'T GOOD AT FIGHTING AT ALL!
CRACK
LOBSTER BONES!
IF THERE'S ONE THING I HATE, IT'S UNCLEAN, UNCOUTH, DIRTY, STINKING YETIS!
BZZT
HEY, WHAT'S THE BIG DEAL?

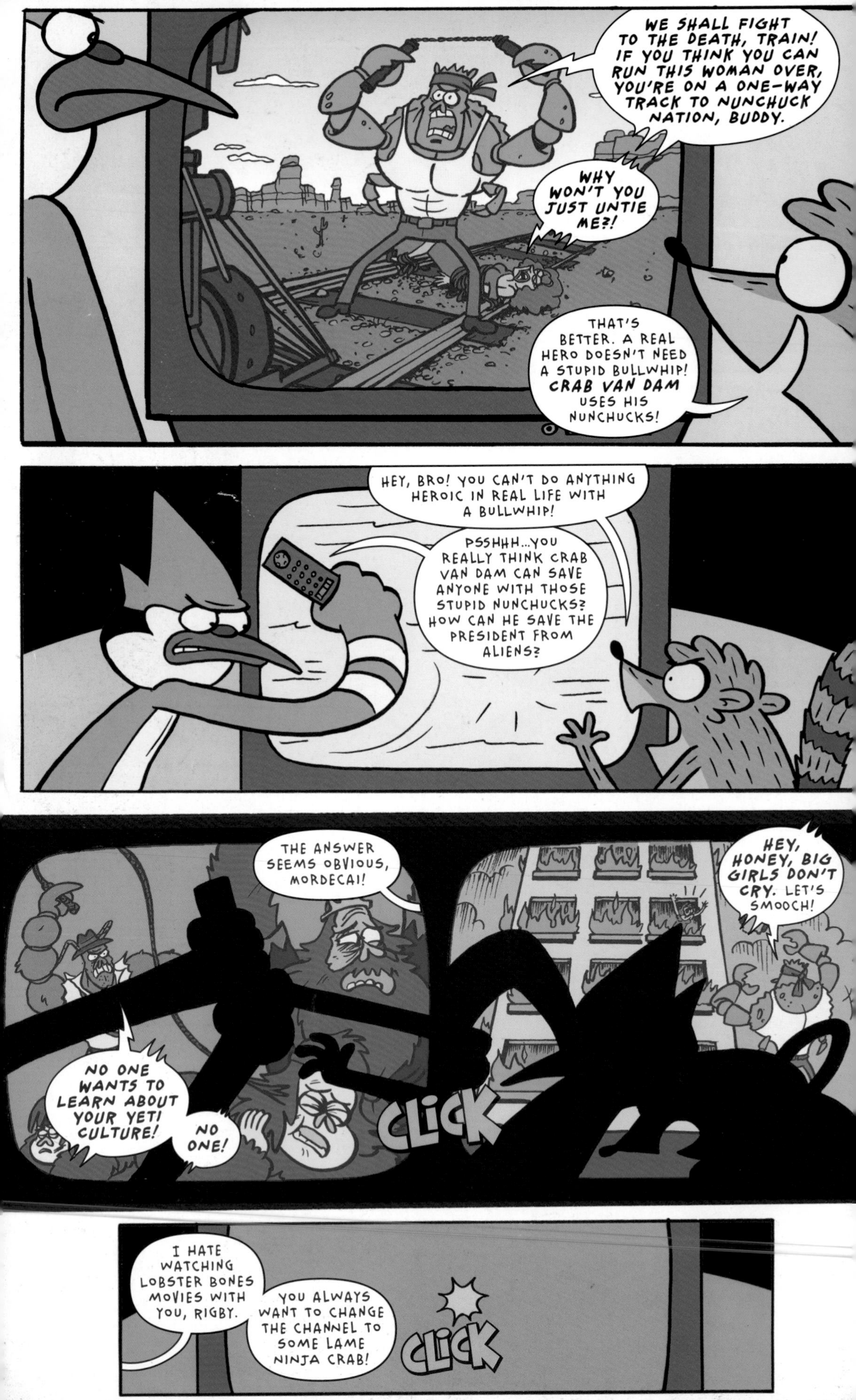
WE SHALL FIGHT TO THE DEATH, TRAIN! IF YOU THINK YOU CAN RUN THIS WOMAN OVER, YOU'RE ON A ONE-WAY TRACK TO NUNCHUCK NATION, BUDDY.
WHY WON'T YOU JUST UNTIE ME?!
THAT'S BETTER. A REAL HERO DOESN'T NEED A STUPID BULLWHIP! CRAB VAN DAM USES HIS NUNCHUCKS!
HEY, BRO! YOU CAN'T DO ANYTHING HEROIC IN REAL LIFE WITH A BULLWHIP!
PSSHHH...YOU REALLY THINK CRAB VAN DAM CAN SAVE ANYONE WITH THOSE STUPID NUNCHUCKS? HOW CAN HE SAVE THE PRESIDENT FROM ALIENS?
THE ANSWER SEEMS OBVIOUS, MORDECAI!
HEY, HONEY, BIG GIRLS DON'T CRY. LET'S SMOOCH!
NO ONE WANTS TO LEARN ABOUT YOUR YETI CULTURE!
NO ONE!
CLICK
I HATE WATCHING LOBSTER BONES MOVIES WITH YOU, RIGBY.
YOU ALWAYS WANT TO CHANGE THE CHANNEL TO SOME LAME NINJA CRAB!
CLICK

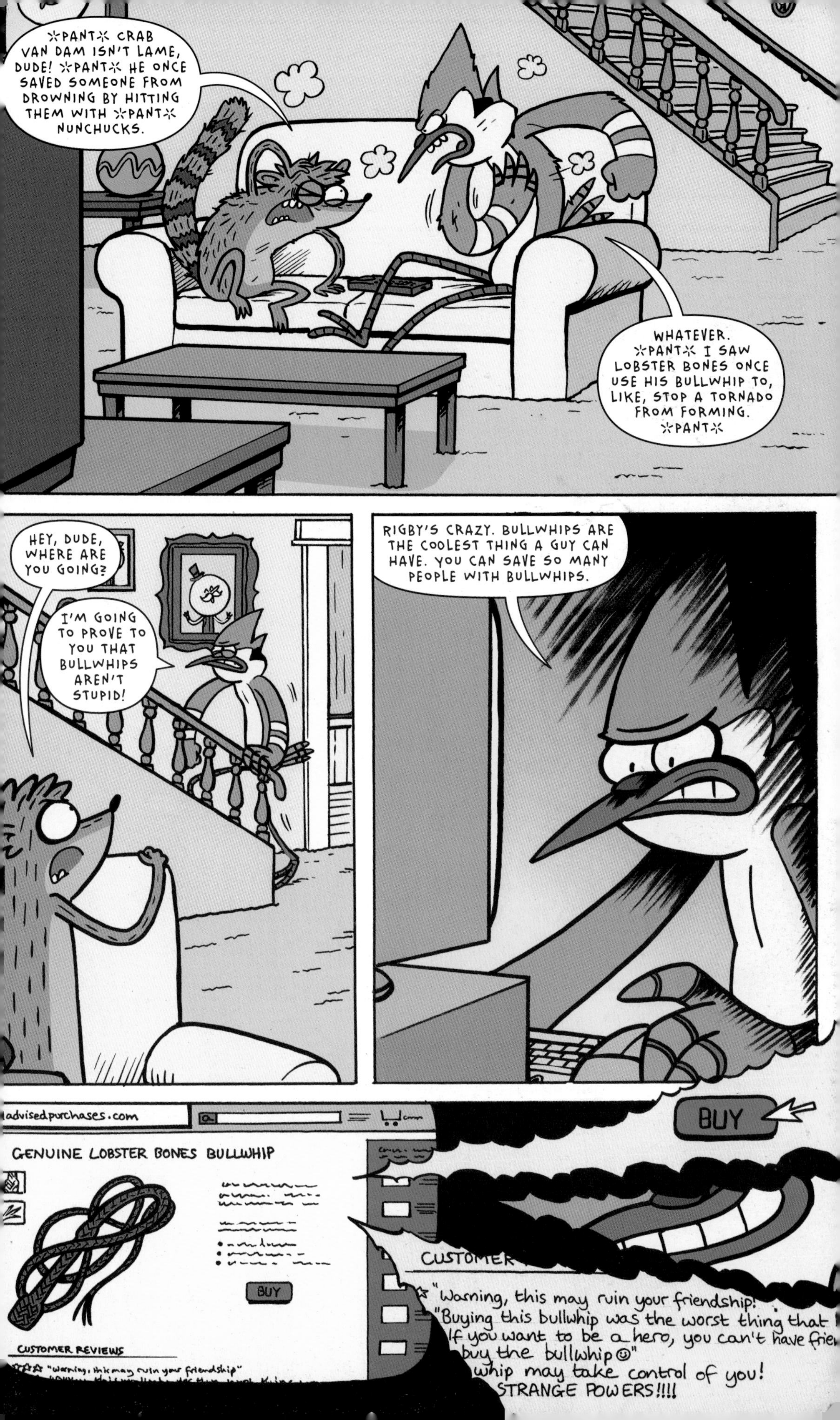
⁜PANT⁜ CRAB VAN DAM ISN'T LAME, DUDE! ⁜PANT⁜ HE ONCE SAVED SOMEONE FROM DROWNING BY HITTING THEM WITH ⁜PANT⁜ NUNCHUCKS.
WHATEVER. ⁜PANT⁜ I SAW LOBSTER BONES ONCE USE HIS BULLWHIP TO, LIKE, STOP A TORNADO FROM FORMING. ⁜PANT⁜
HEY, DUDE, WHERE ARE YOU GOING?
I'M GOING TO PROVE TO YOU THAT BULLWHIPS AREN'T STUPID!
RIGBY'S CRAZY. BULLWHIPS ARE THE COOLEST THING A GUY CAN HAVE. YOU CAN SAVE SO MANY PEOPLE WITH BULLWHIPS.
advisedpurchases.com
GENUINE LOBSTER BONES BULLWHIP
BUY
CUSTOMER REVIEWS
"Warning, this may ruin your friendship"
BUY
CUSTOMER
"Warning, this may ruin your friendship!
"Buying this bullwhip was the worst thing that
If you want to be a hero, you can't have frie
buy the bullwhip ☺"
whip may take control of you!
STRANGE POWERS!!!!

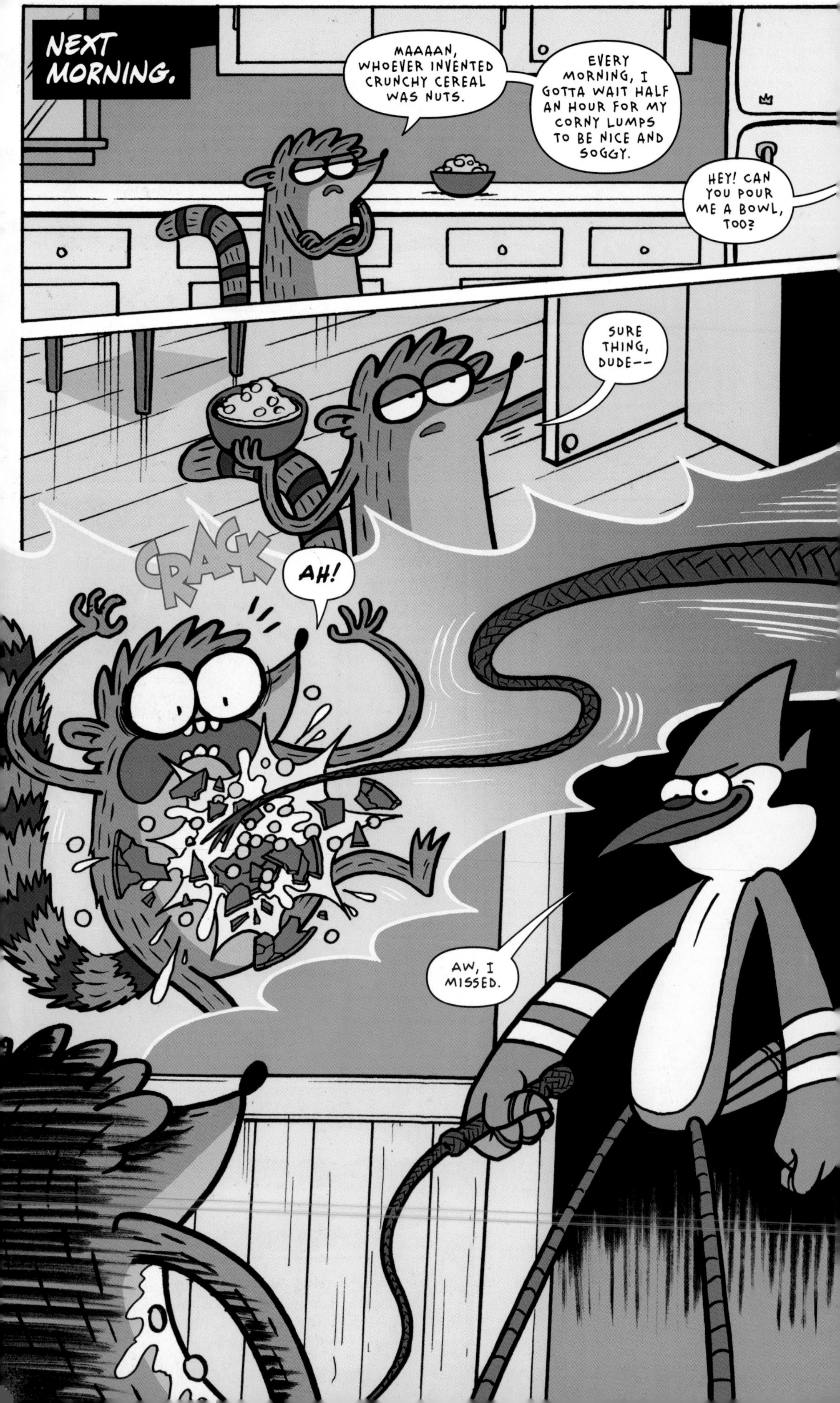
NEXT MORNING.
MAAAAN, WHOEVER INVENTED CRUNCHY CEREAL WAS NUTS.
EVERY MORNING, I GOTTA WAIT HALF AN HOUR FOR MY CORNY LUMPS TO BE NICE AND SOGGY.
HEY! CAN YOU POUR ME A BOWL, TOO?
SURE THING, DUDE--
CRACK
AH!
AW, I MISSED.

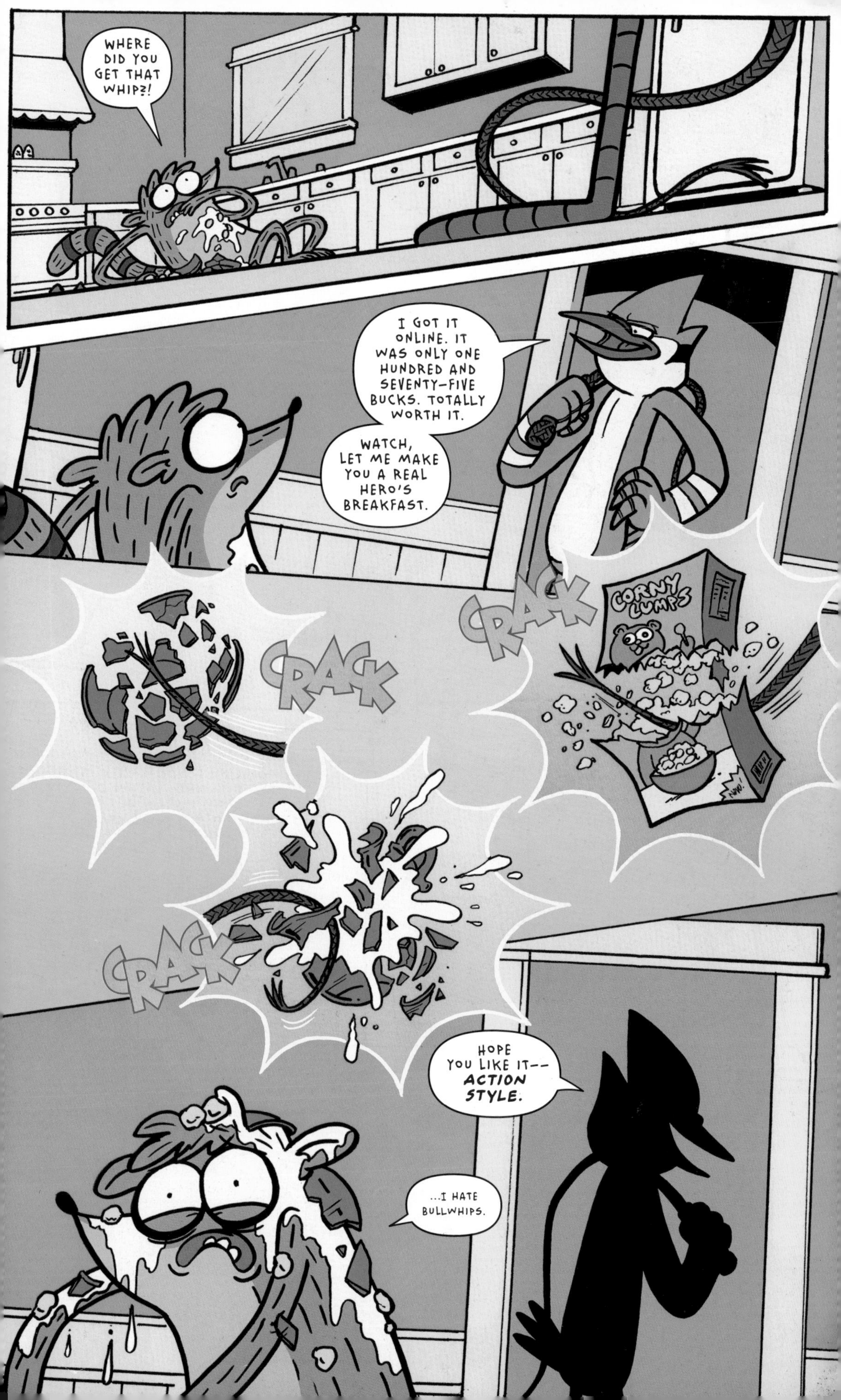

WHERE DID YOU GET THAT WHIP?!
I GOT IT ONLINE. IT WAS ONLY ONE HUNDRED AND SEVENTY-FIVE BUCKS. TOTALLY WORTH IT.
WATCH, LET ME MAKE YOU A REAL HERO'S BREAKFAST.
CRACK
CRACK
CORNY LUMPS
CRACK
HOPE YOU LIKE IT-- ACTION STYLE.
...I HATE BULLWHIPS.

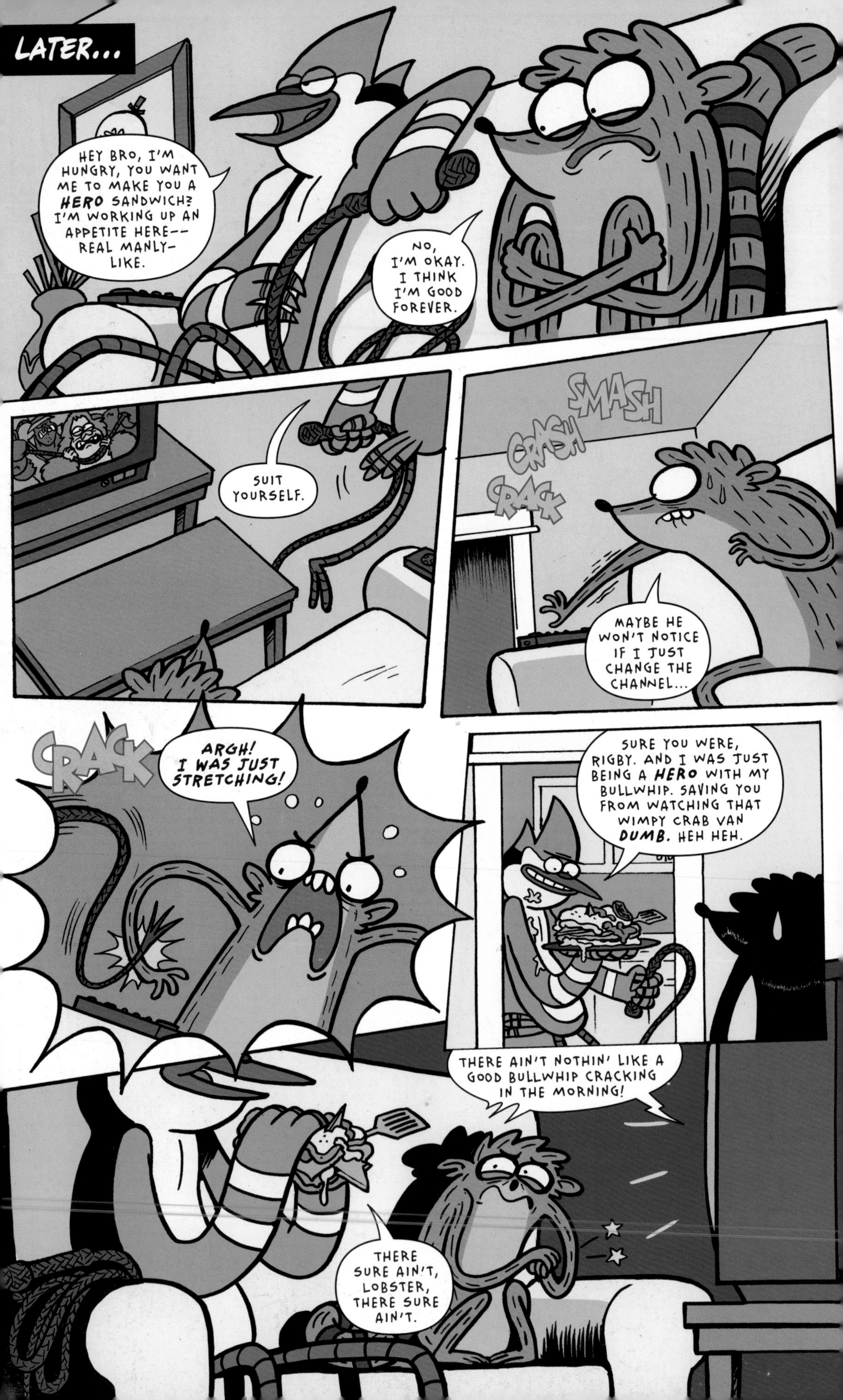
LATER...
HEY BRO, I'M HUNGRY, YOU WANT ME TO MAKE YOU A HERO SANDWICH? I'M WORKING UP AN APPETITE HERE-- REAL MANLY-LIKE.
NO, I'M OKAY. I THINK I'M GOOD FOREVER.
SUIT YOURSELF.
SMASH
CRASH
CRACK
MAYBE HE WON'T NOTICE IF I JUST CHANGE THE CHANNEL...
CRACK
ARGH! I WAS JUST STRETCHING!
SURE YOU WERE, RIGBY. AND I WAS JUST BEING A HERO WITH MY BULLWHIP. SAVING YOU FROM WATCHING THAT WIMPY CRAB VAN DUMB. HEH HEH.
THERE AIN'T NOTHIN' LIKE A GOOD BULLWHIP CRACKING IN THE MORNING!
THERE SURE AIN'T, LOBSTER, THERE SURE AIN'T.

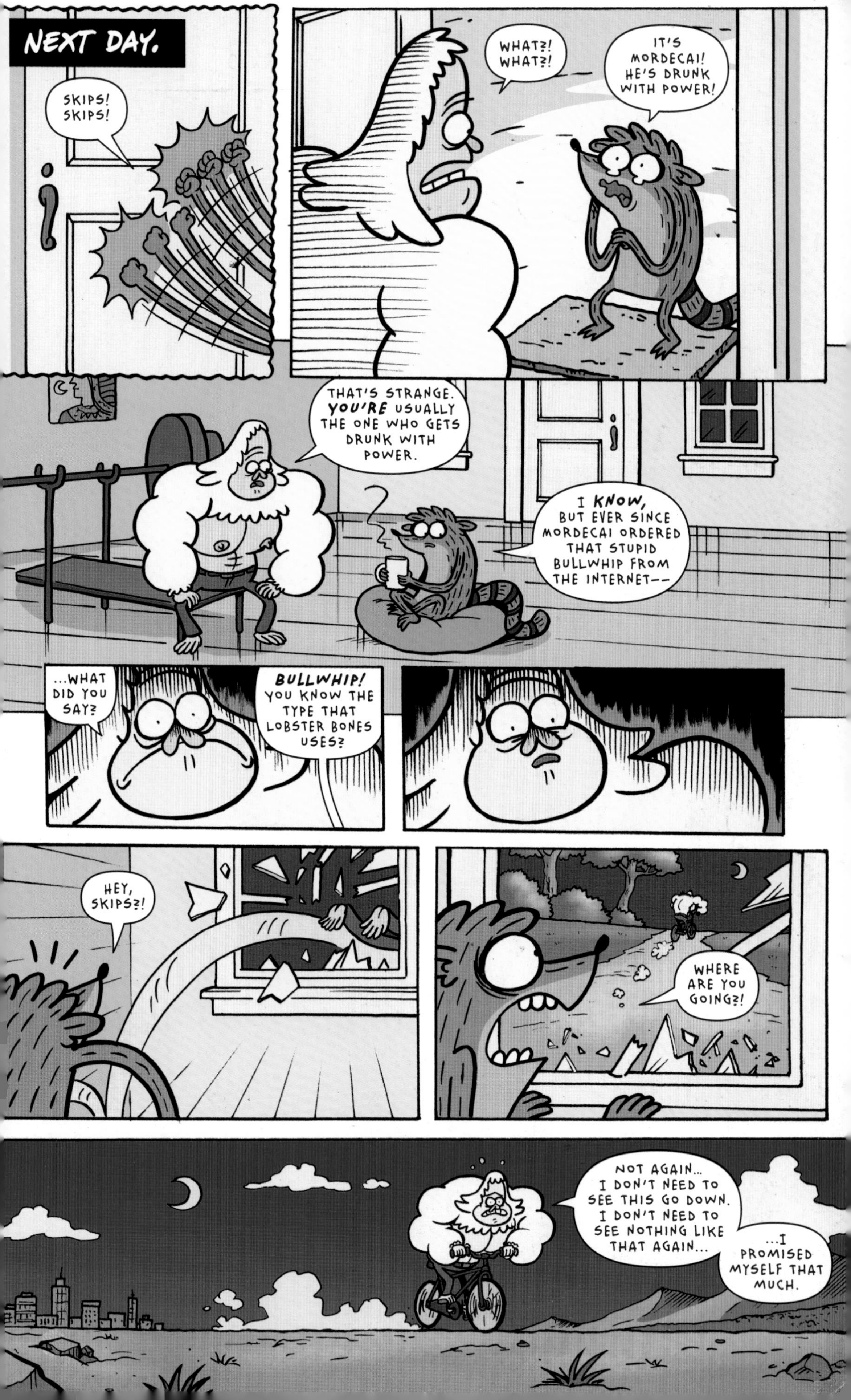
NEXT DAY.
SKIPS! SKIPS!
WHAT?! WHAT?!
IT'S MORDECAI! HE'S DRUNK WITH POWER!
THAT'S STRANGE. YOU'RE USUALLY THE ONE WHO GETS DRUNK WITH POWER.
I KNOW, BUT EVER SINCE MORDECAI ORDERED THAT STUPID BULLWHIP FROM THE INTERNET--
...WHAT DID YOU SAY?
BULLWHIP! YOU KNOW THE TYPE THAT LOBSTER BONES USES?
HEY, SKIPS?!
WHERE ARE YOU GOING?!
NOT AGAIN... I DON'T NEED TO SEE THIS GO DOWN. I DON'T NEED TO SEE NOTHING LIKE THAT AGAIN...
...I PROMISED MYSELF THAT MUCH.

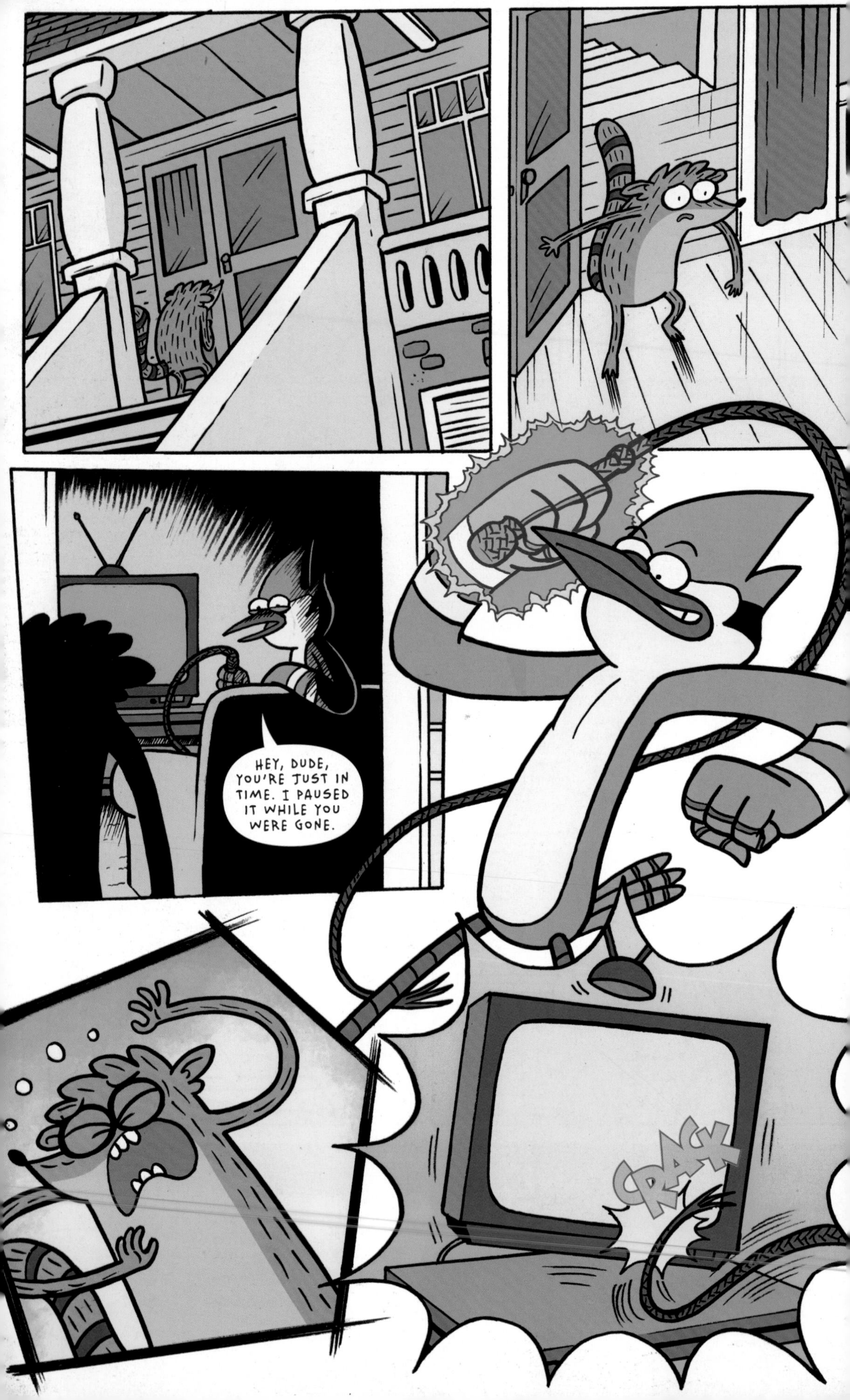
HEY, DUDE, YOU'RE JUST IN TIME. I PAUSED IT WHILE YOU WERE GONE.
CRACK

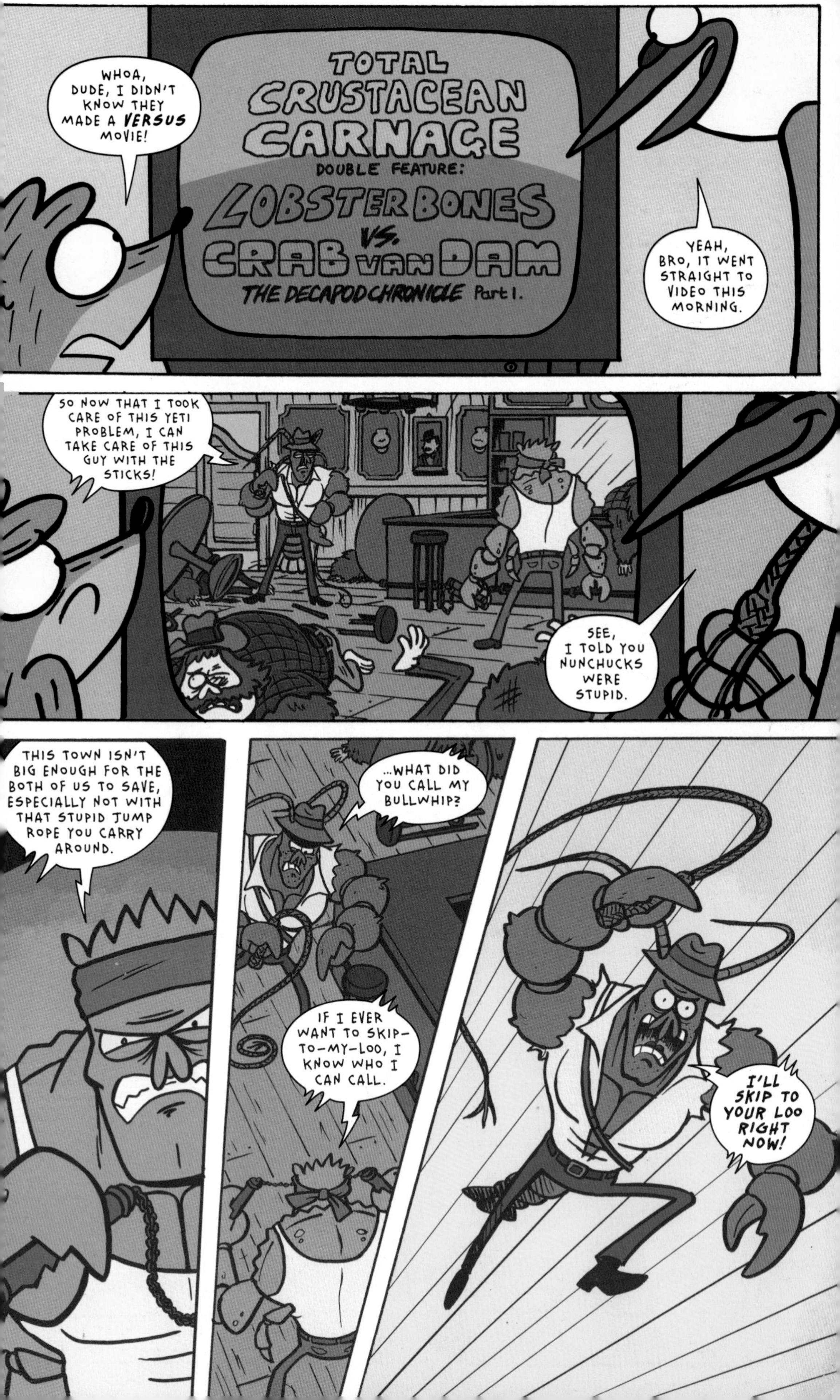

WHOA, DUDE, I DIDN'T KNOW THEY MADE A **VERSUS** MOVIE!
TOTAL CRUSTACEAN CARNAGE
DOUBLE FEATURE:
LOBSTER BONES VS. CRAB VAN DAM
THE DECAPOD CHRONICLE Part 1.
YEAH, BRO, IT WENT STRAIGHT TO VIDEO THIS MORNING.
SO NOW THAT I TOOK CARE OF THIS YETI PROBLEM, I CAN TAKE CARE OF THIS GUY WITH THE STICKS!
SEE, I TOLD YOU NUNCHUCKS WERE STUPID.
THIS TOWN ISN'T BIG ENOUGH FOR THE BOTH OF US TO SAVE, ESPECIALLY NOT WITH THAT STUPID JUMP ROPE YOU CARRY AROUND.
...WHAT DID YOU CALL MY BULLWHIP?
IF I EVER WANT TO SKIP-TO-MY-LOO, I KNOW WHO I CAN CALL.
I'LL SKIP TO YOUR LOO RIGHT NOW!

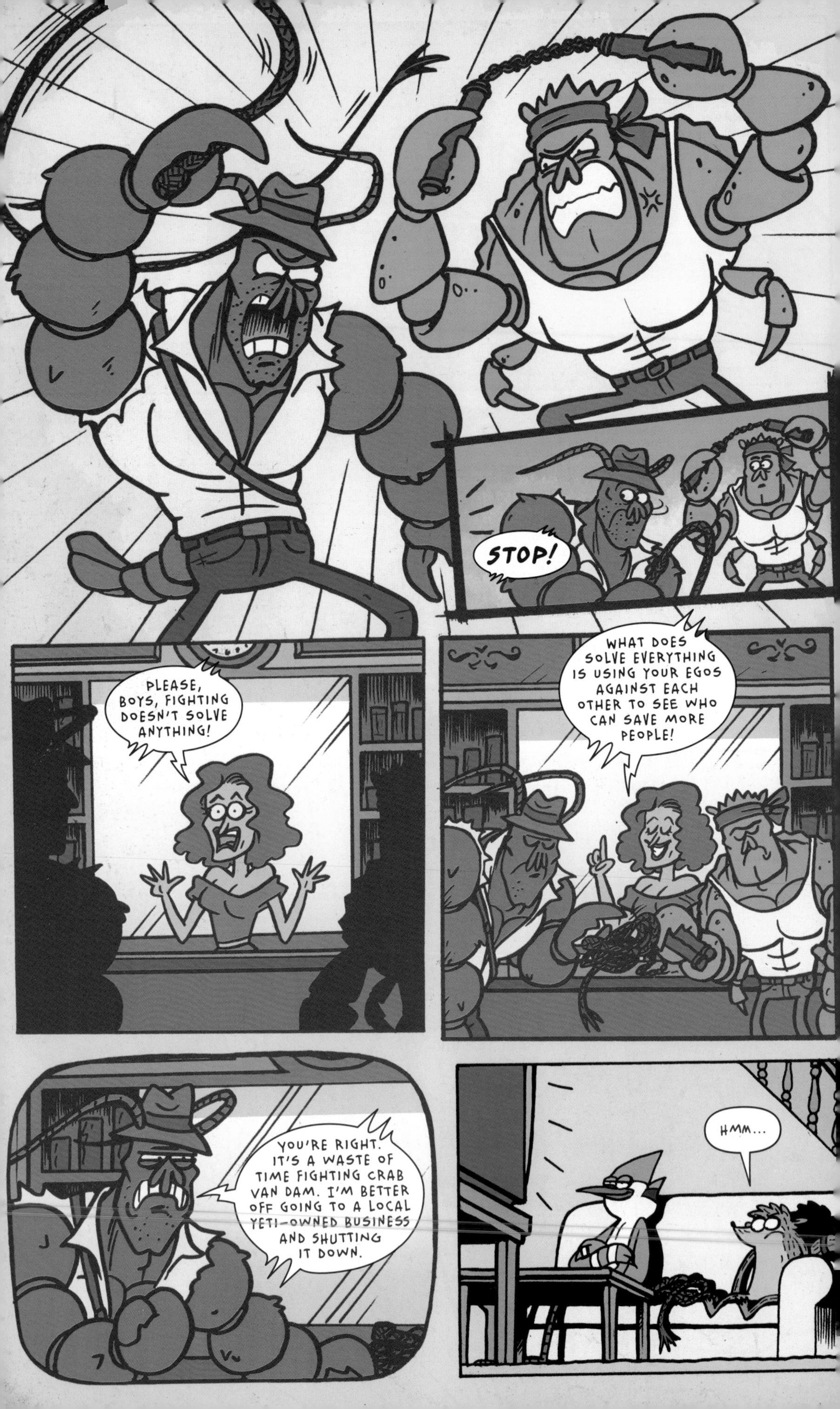
STOP!
PLEASE, BOYS, FIGHTING DOESN'T SOLVE ANYTHING!
WHAT DOES SOLVE EVERYTHING IS USING YOUR EGOS AGAINST EACH OTHER TO SEE WHO CAN SAVE MORE PEOPLE!
YOU'RE RIGHT. IT'S A WASTE OF TIME FIGHTING CRAB VAN DAM. I'M BETTER OFF GOING TO A LOCAL YETI-OWNED BUSINESS AND SHUTTING IT DOWN.
HMM...

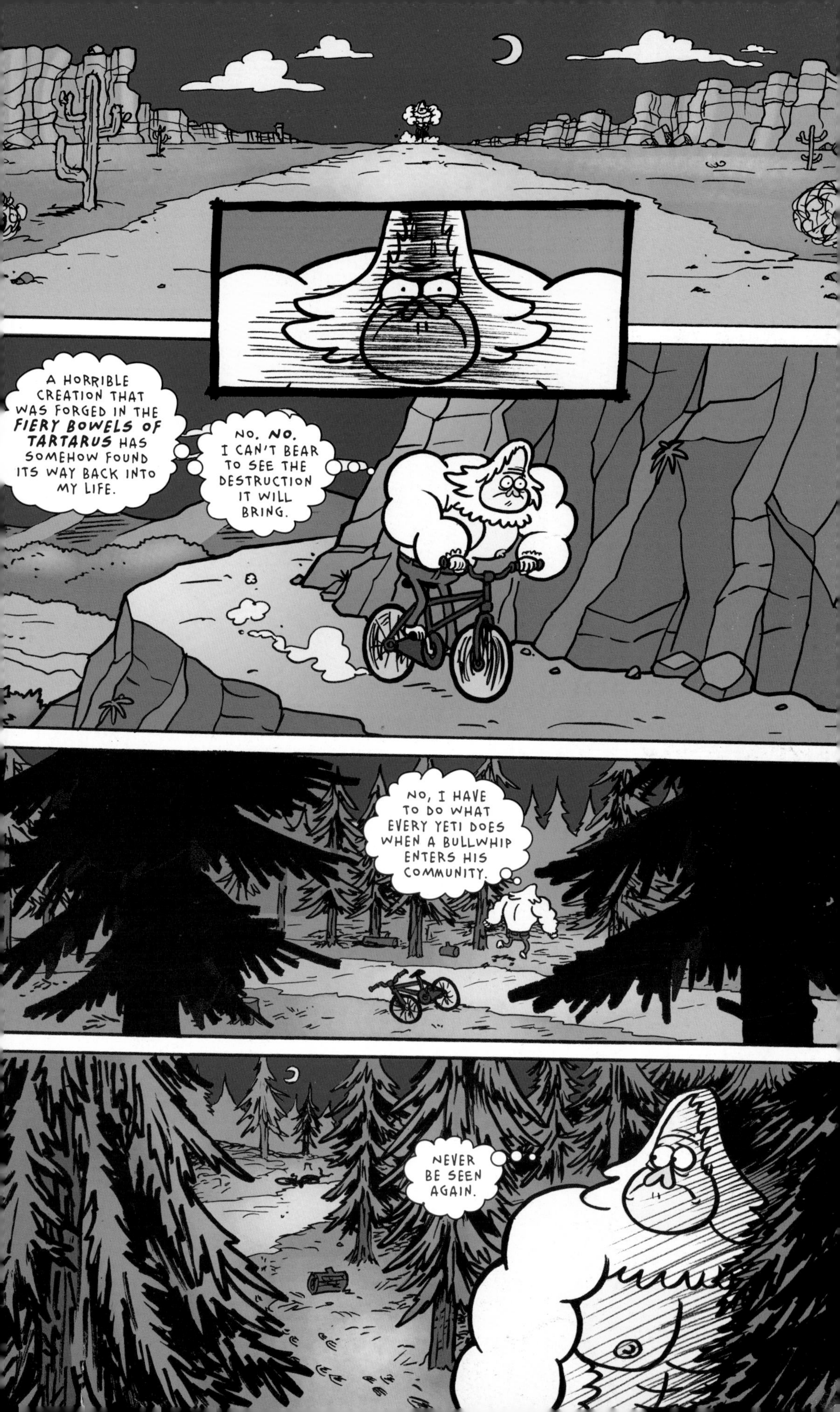
A HORRIBLE CREATION THAT WAS FORGED IN THE FIERY BOWELS OF TARTARUS HAS SOMEHOW FOUND ITS WAY BACK INTO MY LIFE.
NO. NO. I CAN'T BEAR TO SEE THE DESTRUCTION IT WILL BRING.
NO, I HAVE TO DO WHAT EVERY YETI DOES WHEN A BULLWHIP ENTERS HIS COMMUNITY.
NEVER BE SEEN AGAIN.

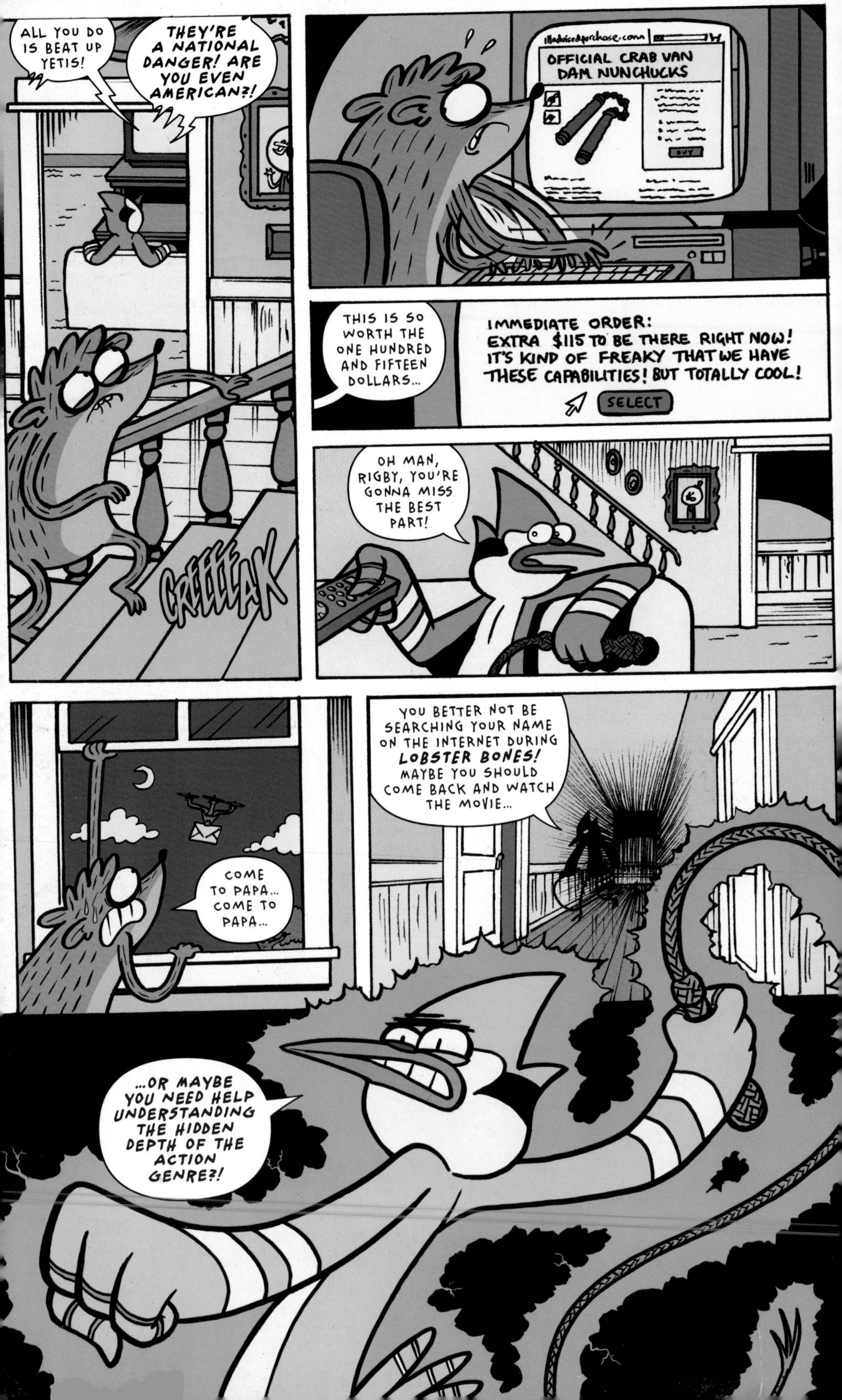
ALL YOU DO IS BEAT UP YETIS!
THEY'RE A NATIONAL DANGER! ARE YOU EVEN AMERICAN?!
OFFICIAL CRAB VAN DAM NUNCHUCKS
BUY
CREEEEAK
THIS IS SO WORTH THE ONE HUNDRED AND FIFTEEN DOLLARS...
IMMEDIATE ORDER:
EXTRA $115 TO BE THERE RIGHT NOW!
IT'S KIND OF FREAKY THAT WE HAVE THESE CAPABILITIES! BUT TOTALLY COOL!
SELECT
OH MAN, RIGBY, YOU'RE GONNA MISS THE BEST PART!
COME TO PAPA... COME TO PAPA...
YOU BETTER NOT BE SEARCHING YOUR NAME ON THE INTERNET DURING *LOBSTER BONES!* MAYBE YOU SHOULD COME BACK AND WATCH THE MOVIE...
...OR MAYBE YOU NEED HELP UNDERSTANDING THE HIDDEN DEPTH OF THE ACTION GENRE?!

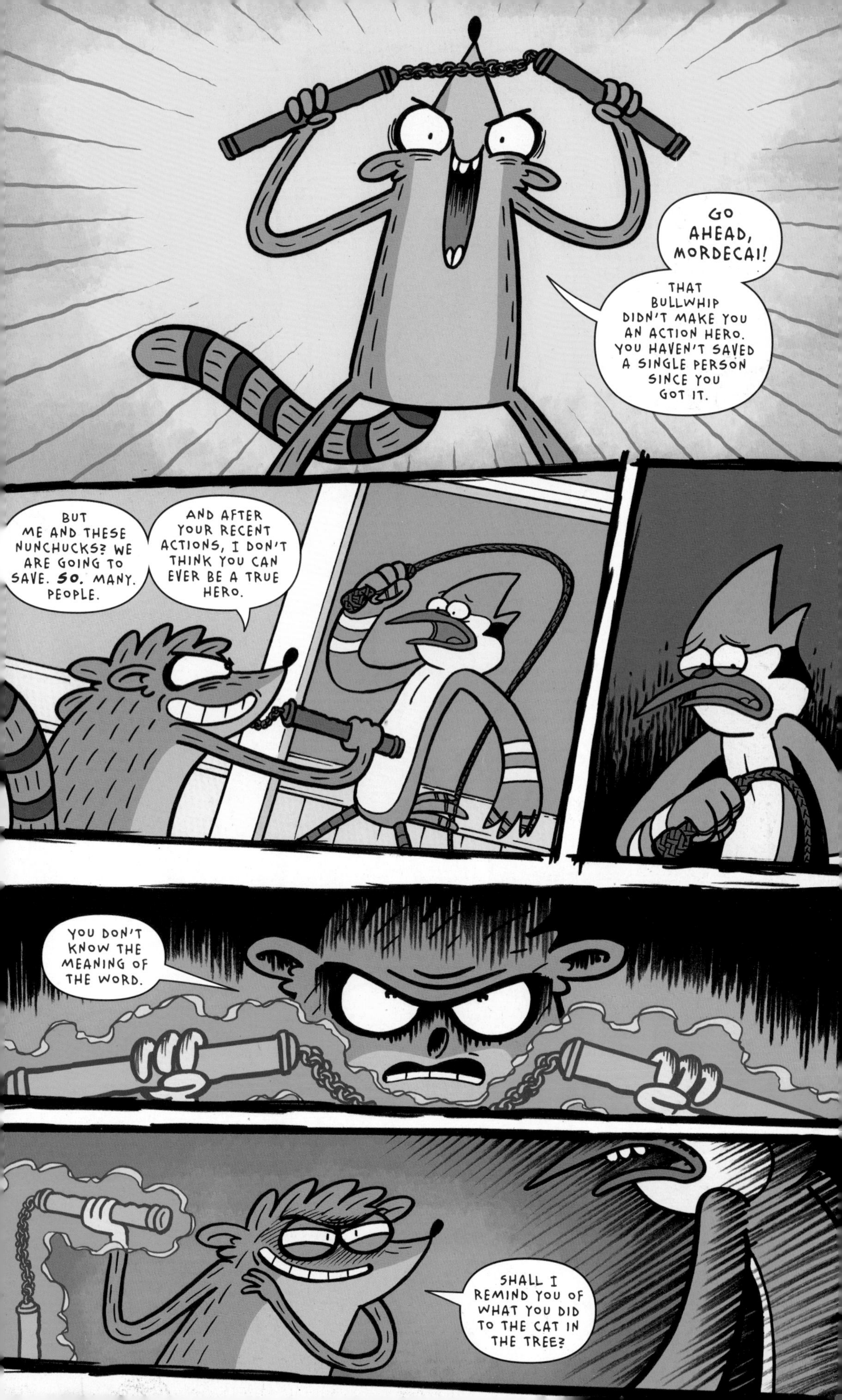

GO AHEAD, MORDECAI!
THAT BULLWHIP DIDN'T MAKE YOU AN ACTION HERO. YOU HAVEN'T SAVED A SINGLE PERSON SINCE YOU GOT IT.
BUT ME AND THESE NUNCHUCKS? WE ARE GOING TO SAVE. SO. MANY. PEOPLE.
AND AFTER YOUR RECENT ACTIONS, I DON'T THINK YOU CAN EVER BE A TRUE HERO.
YOU DON'T KNOW THE MEANING OF THE WORD.
SHALL I REMIND YOU OF WHAT YOU DID TO THE CAT IN THE TREE?

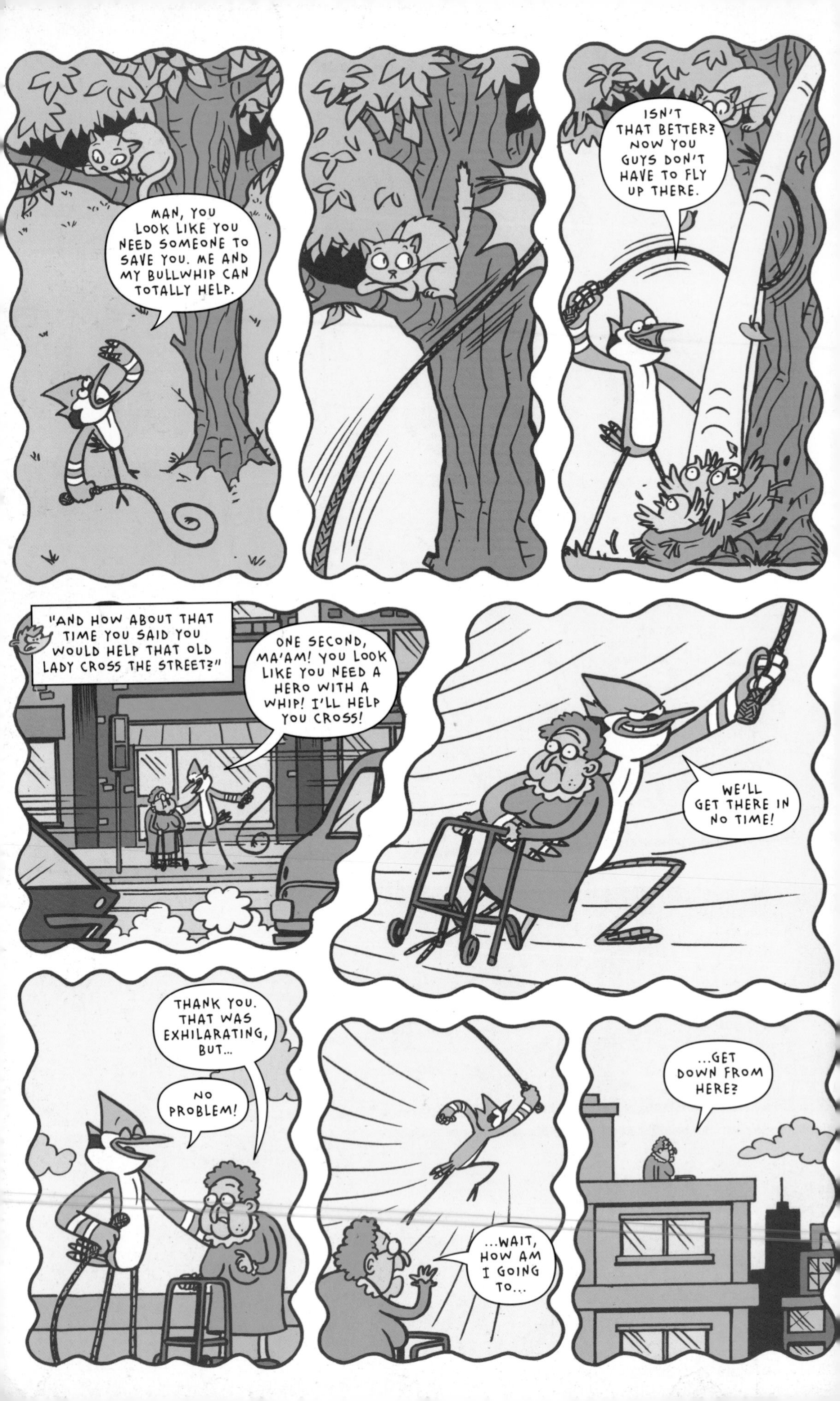
MAN, YOU LOOK LIKE YOU NEED SOMEONE TO SAVE YOU. ME AND MY BULLWHIP CAN TOTALLY HELP.
ISN'T THAT BETTER? NOW YOU GUYS DON'T HAVE TO FLY UP THERE.
"AND HOW ABOUT THAT TIME YOU SAID YOU WOULD HELP THAT OLD LADY CROSS THE STREET?"
ONE SECOND, MA'AM! YOU LOOK LIKE YOU NEED A HERO WITH A WHIP! I'LL HELP YOU CROSS!
WE'LL GET THERE IN NO TIME!
THANK YOU. THAT WAS EXHILARATING, BUT...
NO PROBLEM!
...WAIT, HOW AM I GOING TO...
...GET DOWN FROM HERE?

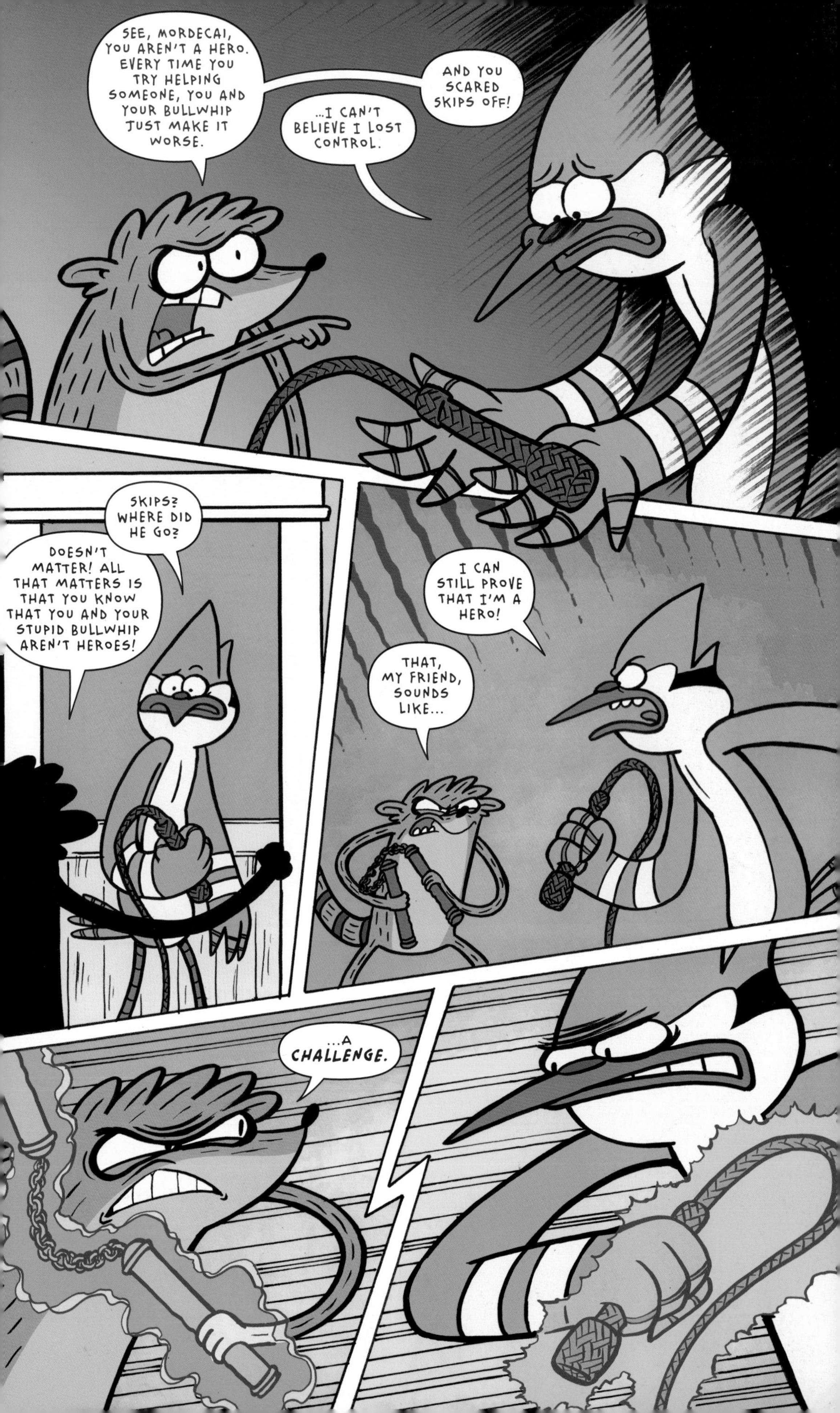
SEE, MORDECAI, YOU AREN'T A HERO. EVERY TIME YOU TRY HELPING SOMEONE, YOU AND YOUR BULLWHIP JUST MAKE IT WORSE.
AND YOU SCARED SKIPS OFF!
...I CAN'T BELIEVE I LOST CONTROL.
SKIPS? WHERE DID HE GO?
DOESN'T MATTER! ALL THAT MATTERS IS THAT YOU KNOW THAT YOU AND YOUR STUPID BULLWHIP AREN'T HEROES!
I CAN STILL PROVE THAT I'M A HERO!
THAT, MY FRIEND, SOUNDS LIKE...
...A CHALLENGE.

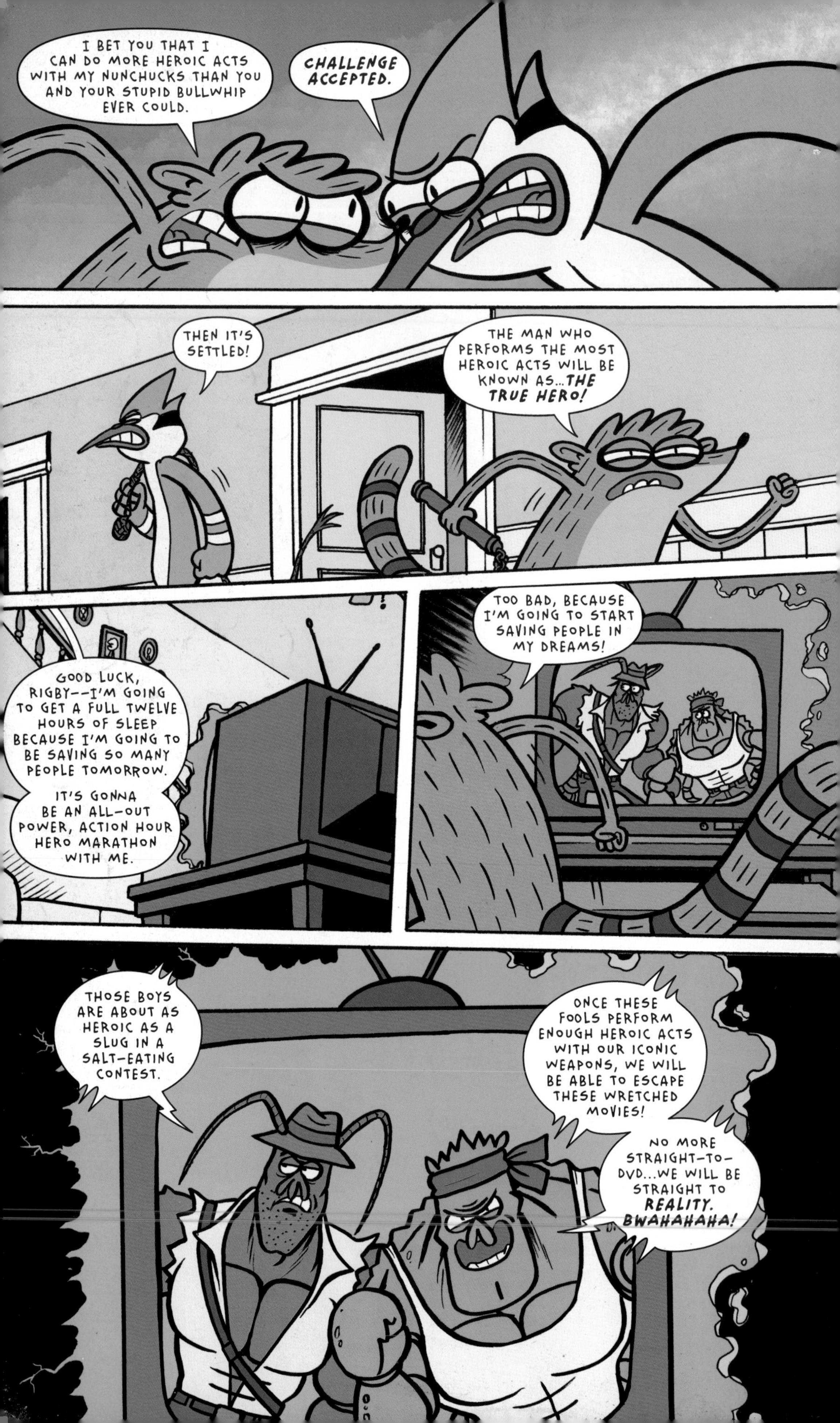
I BET YOU THAT I CAN DO MORE HEROIC ACTS WITH MY NUNCHUCKS THAN YOU AND YOUR STUPID BULLWHIP EVER COULD.
CHALLENGE ACCEPTED.
THEN IT'S SETTLED!
THE MAN WHO PERFORMS THE MOST HEROIC ACTS WILL BE KNOWN AS... THE TRUE HERO!
GOOD LUCK, RIGBY--I'M GOING TO GET A FULL TWELVE HOURS OF SLEEP BECAUSE I'M GOING TO BE SAVING SO MANY PEOPLE TOMORROW.
IT'S GONNA BE AN ALL-OUT POWER, ACTION HOUR HERO MARATHON WITH ME.
TOO BAD, BECAUSE I'M GOING TO START SAVING PEOPLE IN MY DREAMS!
THOSE BOYS ARE ABOUT AS HEROIC AS A SLUG IN A SALT-EATING CONTEST.
ONCE THESE FOOLS PERFORM ENOUGH HEROIC ACTS WITH OUR ICONIC WEAPONS, WE WILL BE ABLE TO ESCAPE THESE WRETCHED MOVIES!
NO MORE STRAIGHT-TO-DVD... WE WILL BE STRAIGHT TO REALITY. BWAHAHAHA!

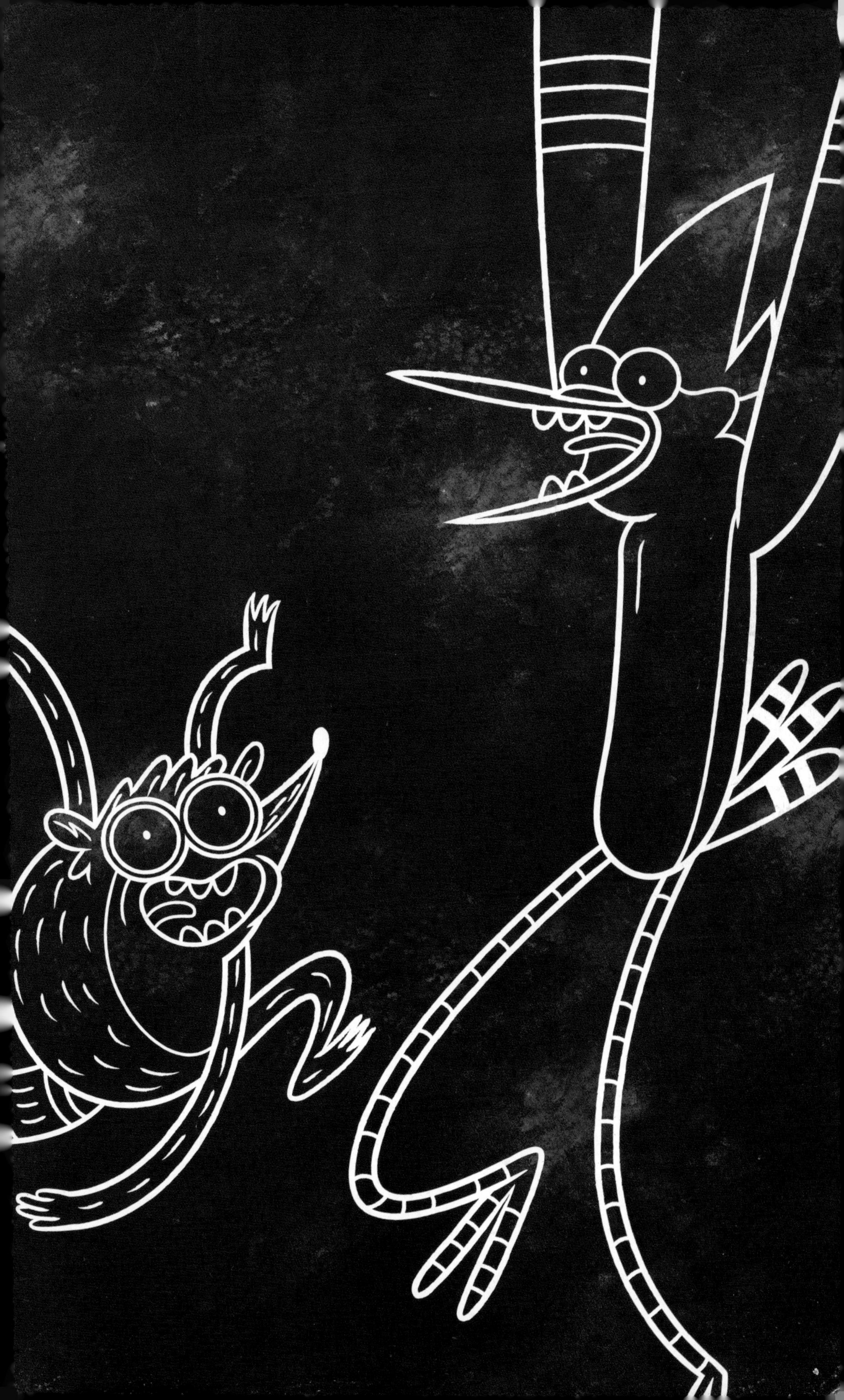

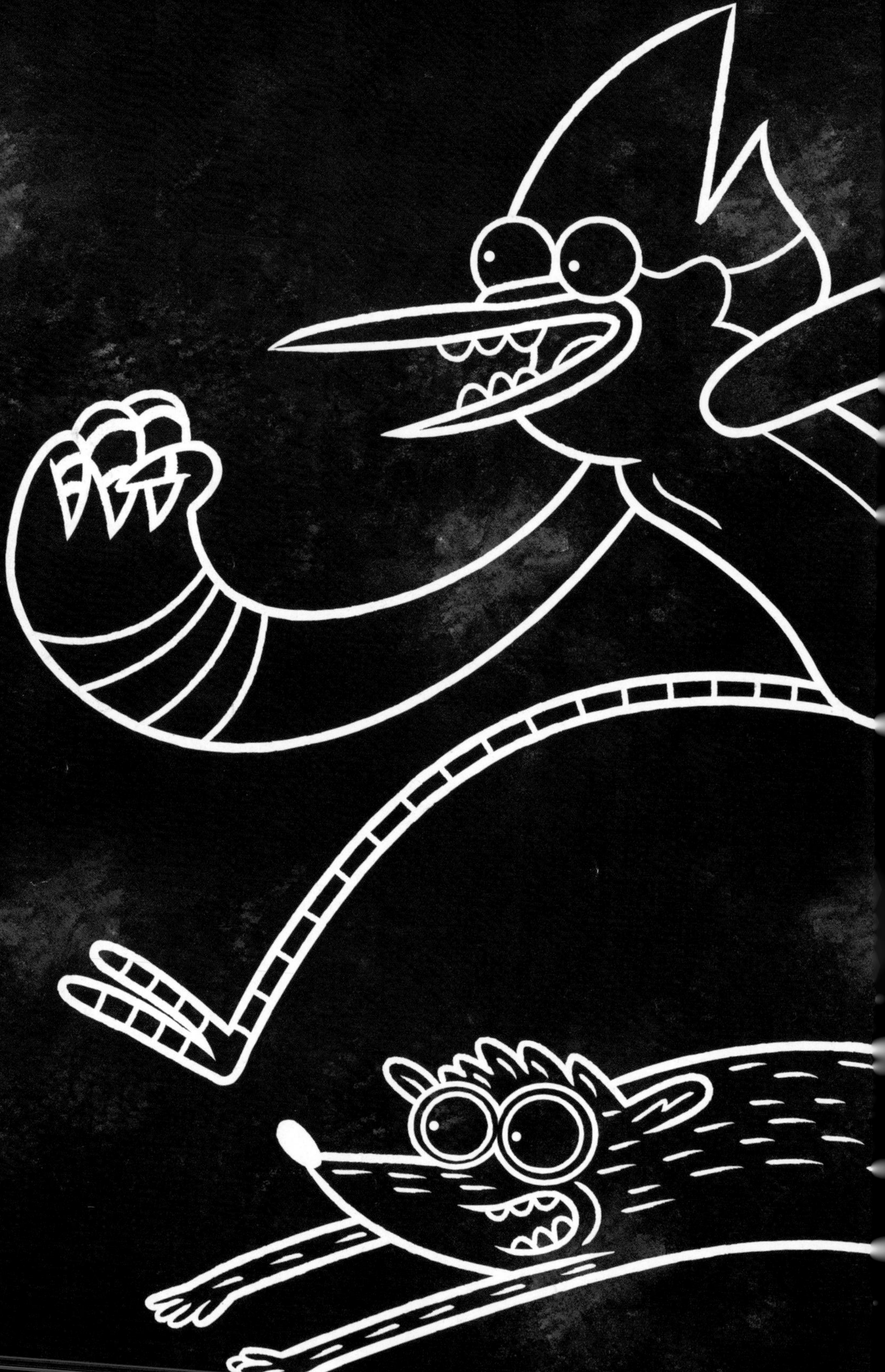

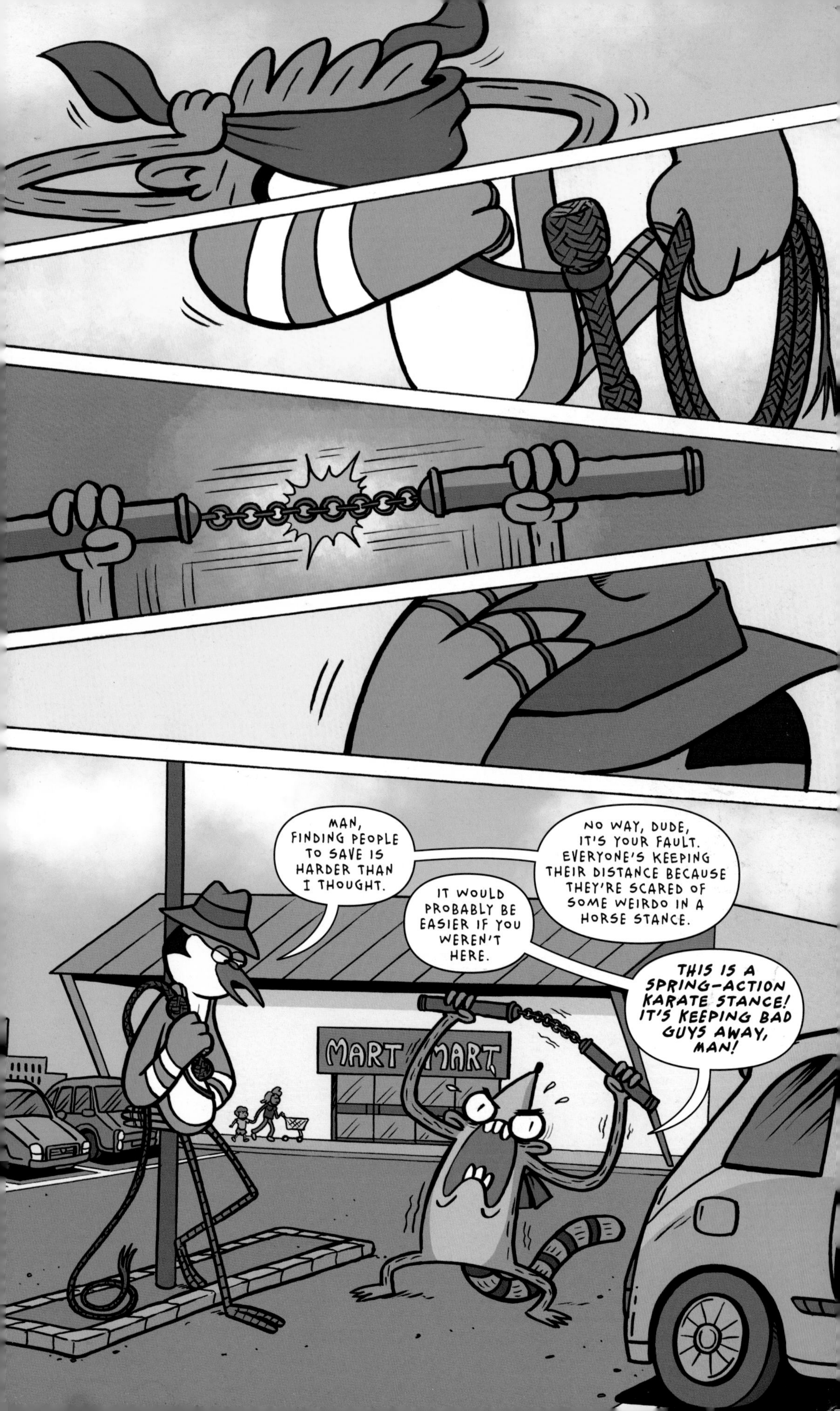

MAN, FINDING PEOPLE TO SAVE IS HARDER THAN I THOUGHT.
NO WAY, DUDE, IT'S YOUR FAULT. EVERYONE'S KEEPING THEIR DISTANCE BECAUSE THEY'RE SCARED OF SOME WEIRDO IN A HORSE STANCE.
IT WOULD PROBABLY BE EASIER IF YOU WEREN'T HERE.
THIS IS A SPRING-ACTION KARATE STANCE! IT'S KEEPING BAD GUYS AWAY, MAN!
MART MART

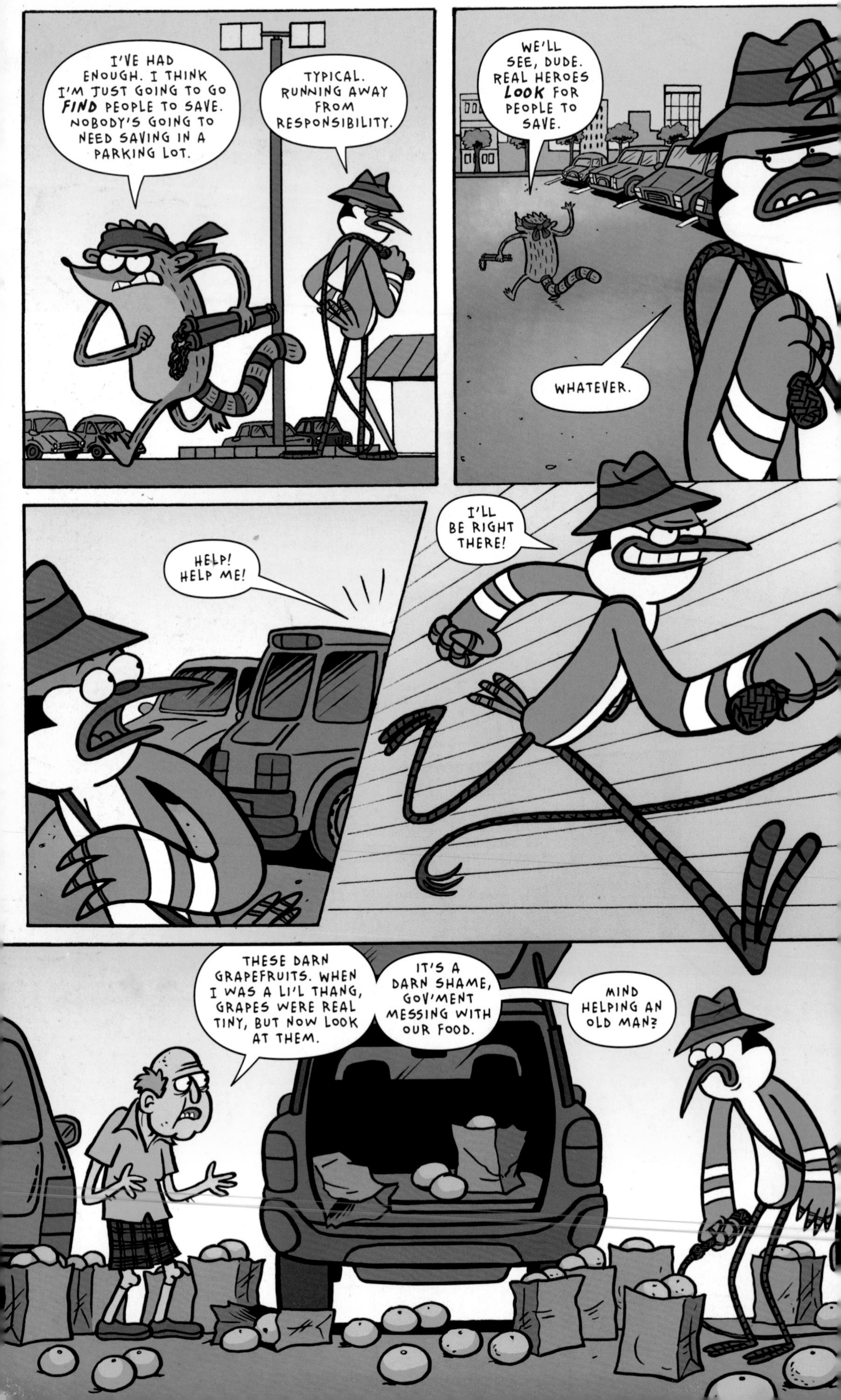

I'VE HAD ENOUGH. I THINK I'M JUST GOING TO GO **FIND** PEOPLE TO SAVE. NOBODY'S GOING TO NEED SAVING IN A PARKING LOT.
TYPICAL. RUNNING AWAY FROM RESPONSIBILITY.
WE'LL SEE, DUDE. REAL HEROES **LOOK** FOR PEOPLE TO SAVE.
WHATEVER.
HELP! HELP ME!
I'LL BE RIGHT THERE!
THESE DARN GRAPEFRUITS. WHEN I WAS A LI'L THANG, GRAPES WERE REAL TINY, BUT NOW LOOK AT THEM.
IT'S A DARN SHAME, GOV'MENT MESSING WITH OUR FOOD.
MIND HELPING AN OLD MAN?

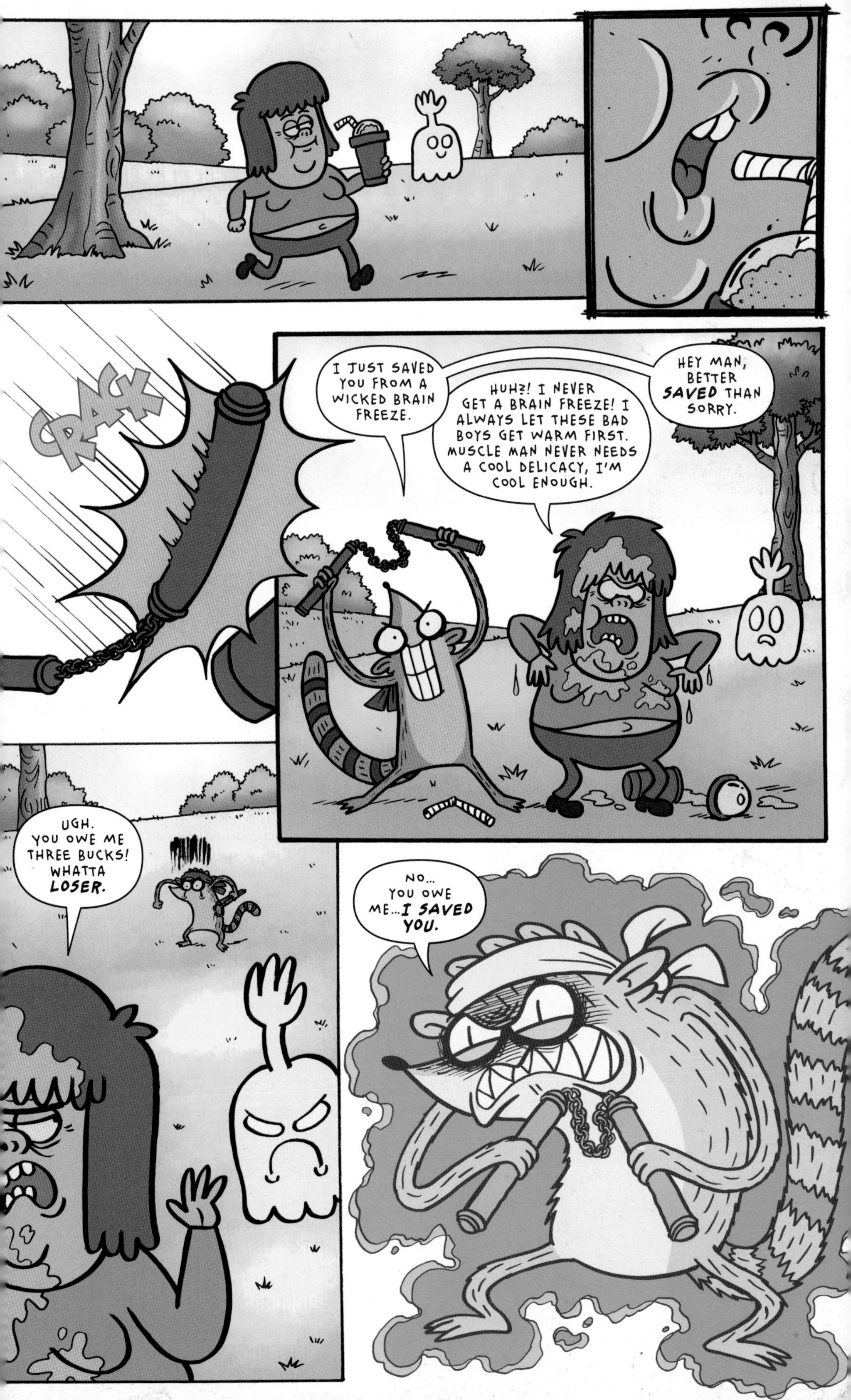
CRACK
I JUST SAVED YOU FROM A WICKED BRAIN FREEZE.
HUH?! I NEVER GET A BRAIN FREEZE! I ALWAYS LET THESE BAD BOYS GET WARM FIRST. MUSCLE MAN NEVER NEEDS A COOL DELICACY, I'M COOL ENOUGH.
HEY MAN, BETTER SAVED THAN SORRY.
UGH. YOU OWE ME THREE BUCKS! WHATTA LOSER.
NO... YOU OWE ME... I SAVED YOU.

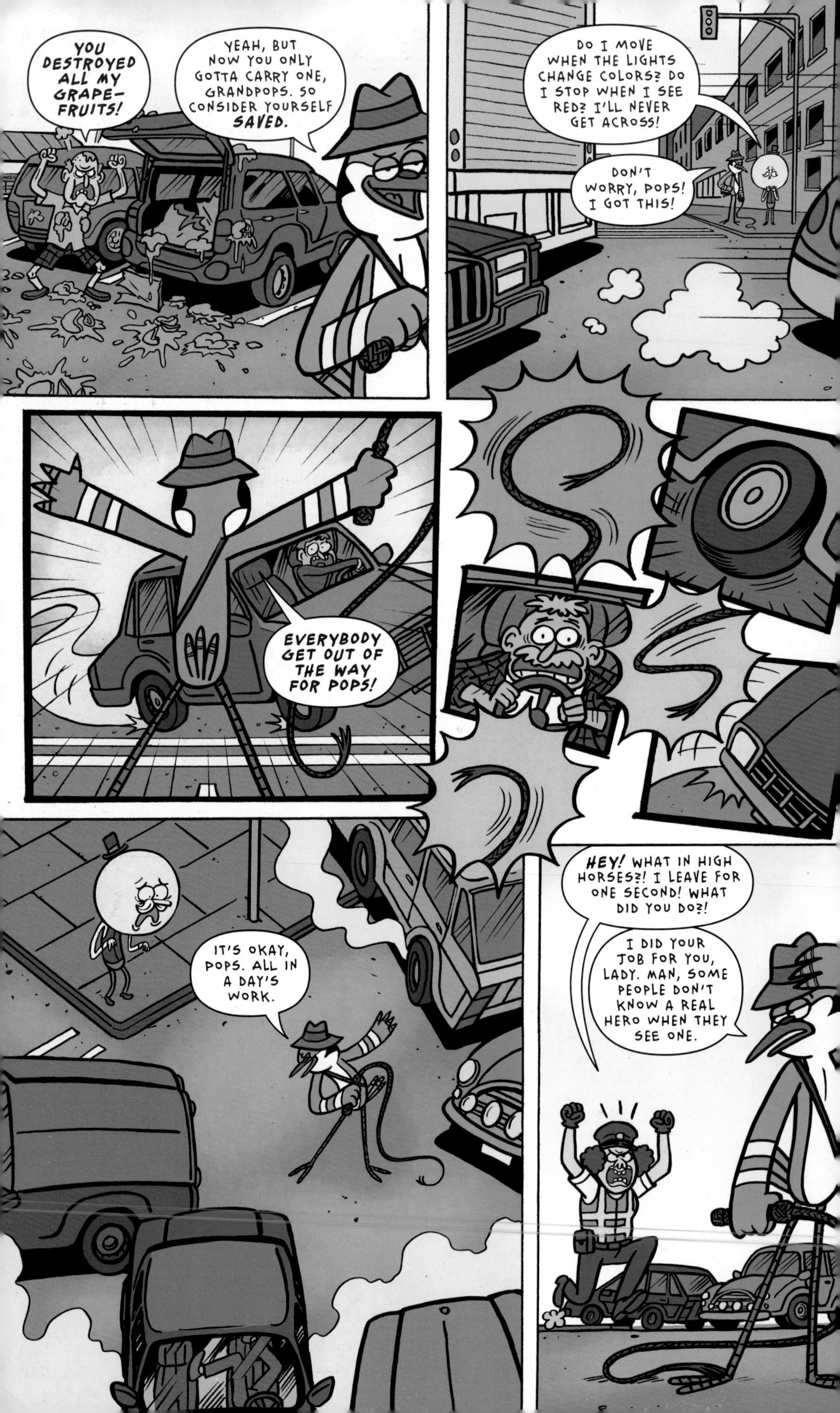
YOU DESTROYED ALL MY GRAPE-FRUITS!
YEAH, BUT NOW YOU ONLY GOTTA CARRY ONE, GRANDPOPS. SO CONSIDER YOURSELF SAVED.
DO I MOVE WHEN THE LIGHTS CHANGE COLORS? DO I STOP WHEN I SEE RED? I'LL NEVER GET ACROSS!
DON'T WORRY, POPS! I GOT THIS!
EVERYBODY GET OUT OF THE WAY FOR POPS!
IT'S OKAY, POPS. ALL IN A DAY'S WORK.
HEY! WHAT IN HIGH HORSES?! I LEAVE FOR ONE SECOND! WHAT DID YOU DO?!
I DID YOUR JOB FOR YOU, LADY. MAN, SOME PEOPLE DON'T KNOW A REAL HERO WHEN THEY SEE ONE.

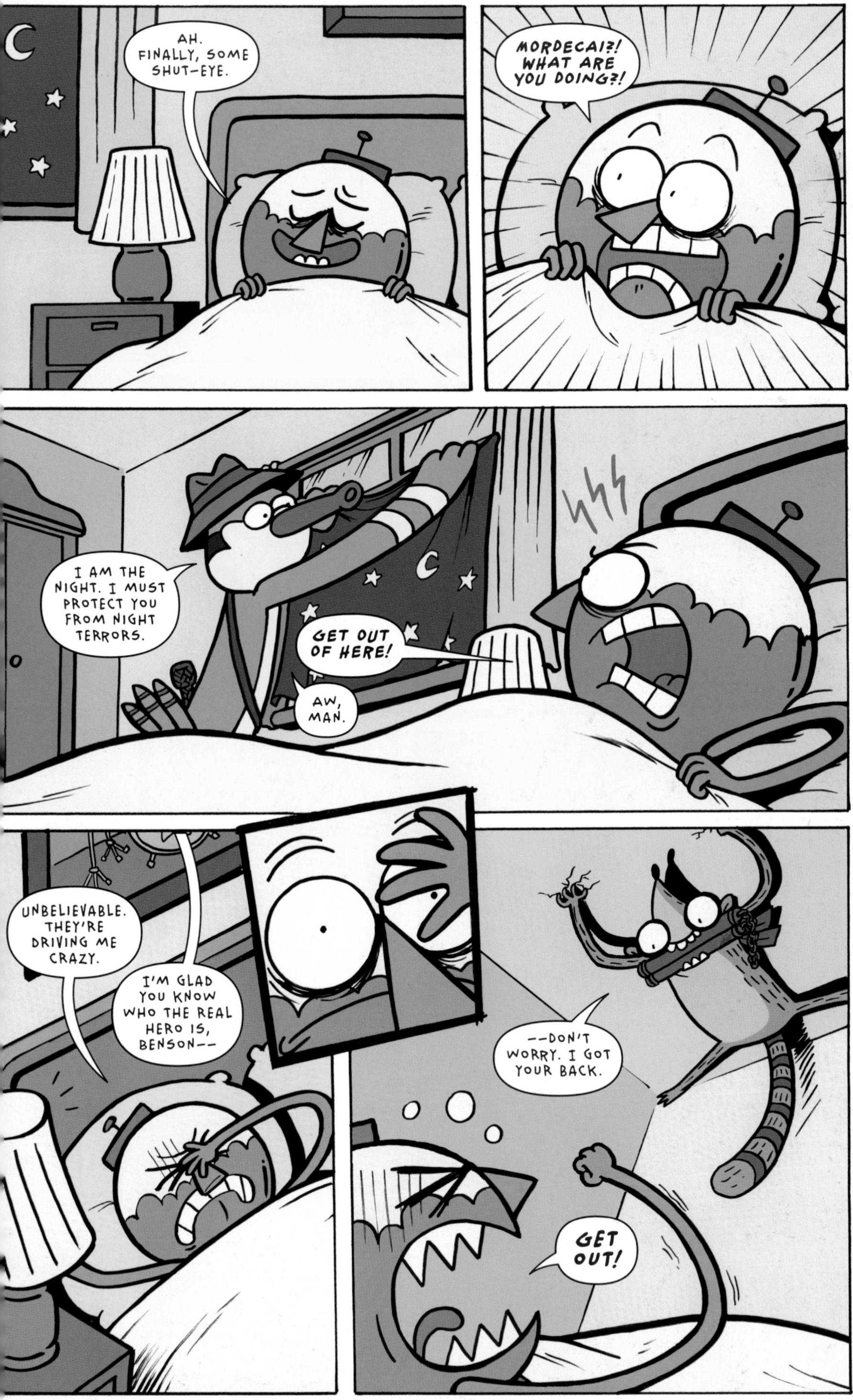
AH. FINALLY, SOME SHUT-EYE.
MORDECAI?! WHAT ARE YOU DOING?!
I AM THE NIGHT. I MUST PROTECT YOU FROM NIGHT TERRORS.
GET OUT OF HERE!
AW, MAN.
UNBELIEVABLE. THEY'RE DRIVING ME CRAZY.
I'M GLAD YOU KNOW WHO THE REAL HERO IS, BENSON--
--DON'T WORRY. I GOT YOUR BACK.
GET OUT!

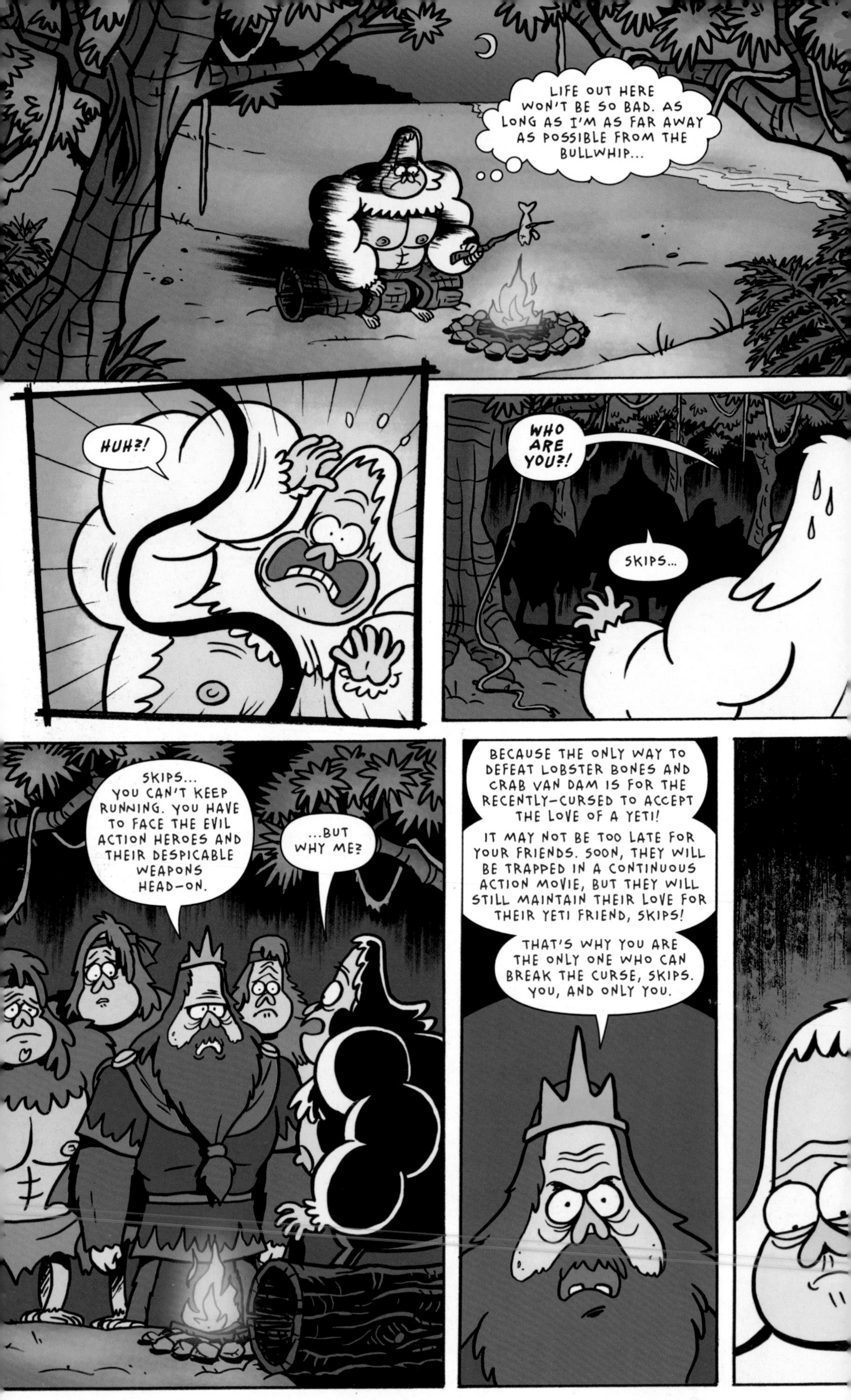
LIFE OUT HERE WON'T BE SO BAD. AS LONG AS I'M AS FAR AWAY AS POSSIBLE FROM THE BULLWHIP...
HUH?!
WHO ARE YOU?!
SKIPS...
SKIPS... YOU CAN'T KEEP RUNNING. YOU HAVE TO FACE THE EVIL ACTION HEROES AND THEIR DESPICABLE WEAPONS HEAD-ON.
...BUT WHY ME?
BECAUSE THE ONLY WAY TO DEFEAT LOBSTER BONES AND CRAB VAN DAM IS FOR THE RECENTLY-CURSED TO ACCEPT THE LOVE OF A YETI!
IT MAY NOT BE TOO LATE FOR YOUR FRIENDS. SOON, THEY WILL BE TRAPPED IN A CONTINUOUS ACTION MOVIE, BUT THEY WILL STILL MAINTAIN THEIR LOVE FOR THEIR YETI FRIEND, SKIPS!
THAT'S WHY YOU ARE THE ONLY ONE WHO CAN BREAK THE CURSE, SKIPS. YOU, AND ONLY YOU.

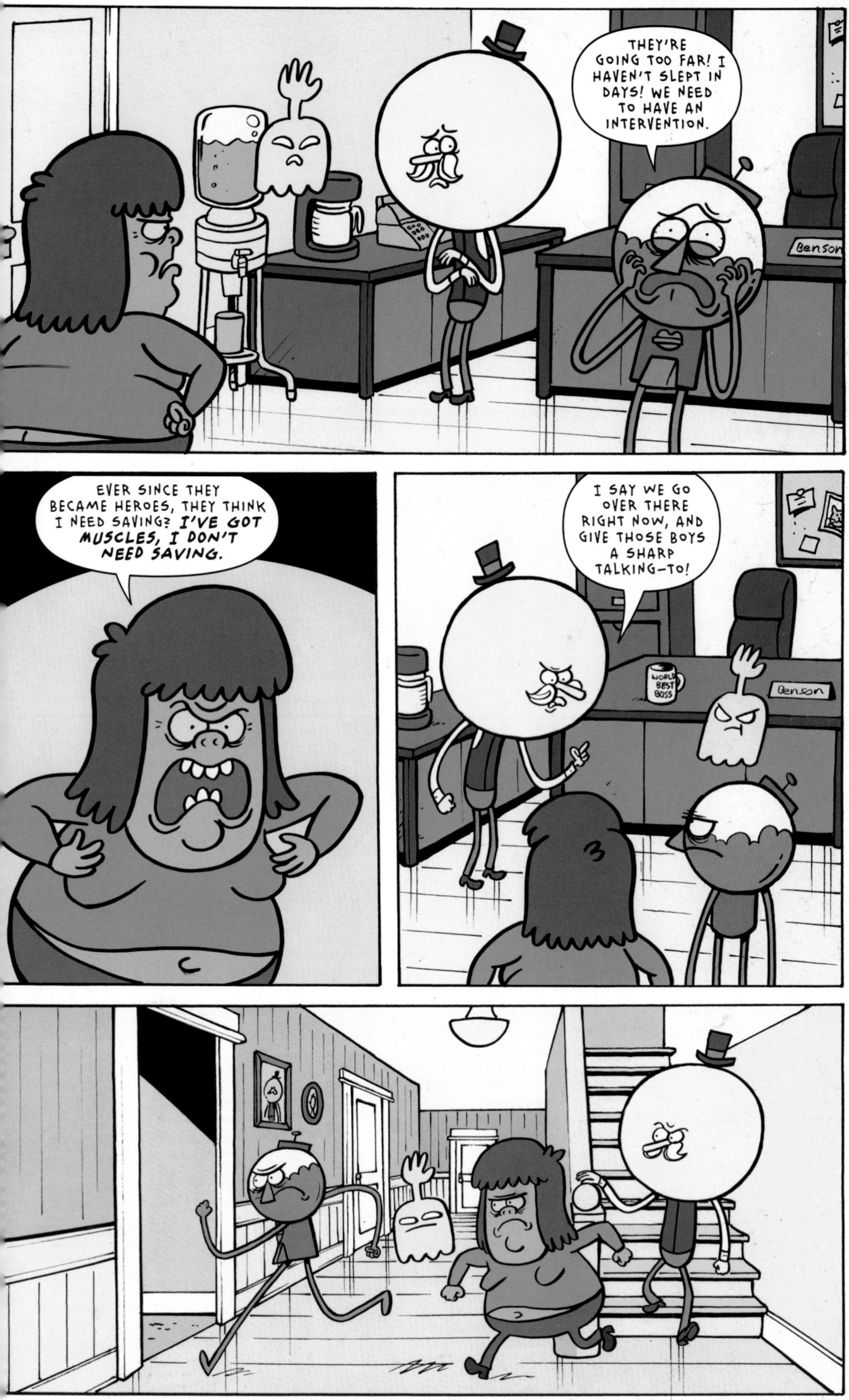
THEY'RE GOING TOO FAR! I HAVEN'T SLEPT IN DAYS! WE NEED TO HAVE AN INTERVENTION.
Benson
EVER SINCE THEY BECAME HEROES, THEY THINK I NEED SAVING? I'VE GOT MUSCLES, I DON'T NEED SAVING.
I SAY WE GO OVER THERE RIGHT NOW, AND GIVE THOSE BOYS A SHARP TALKING-TO!
WORLD BEST BOSS
Benson

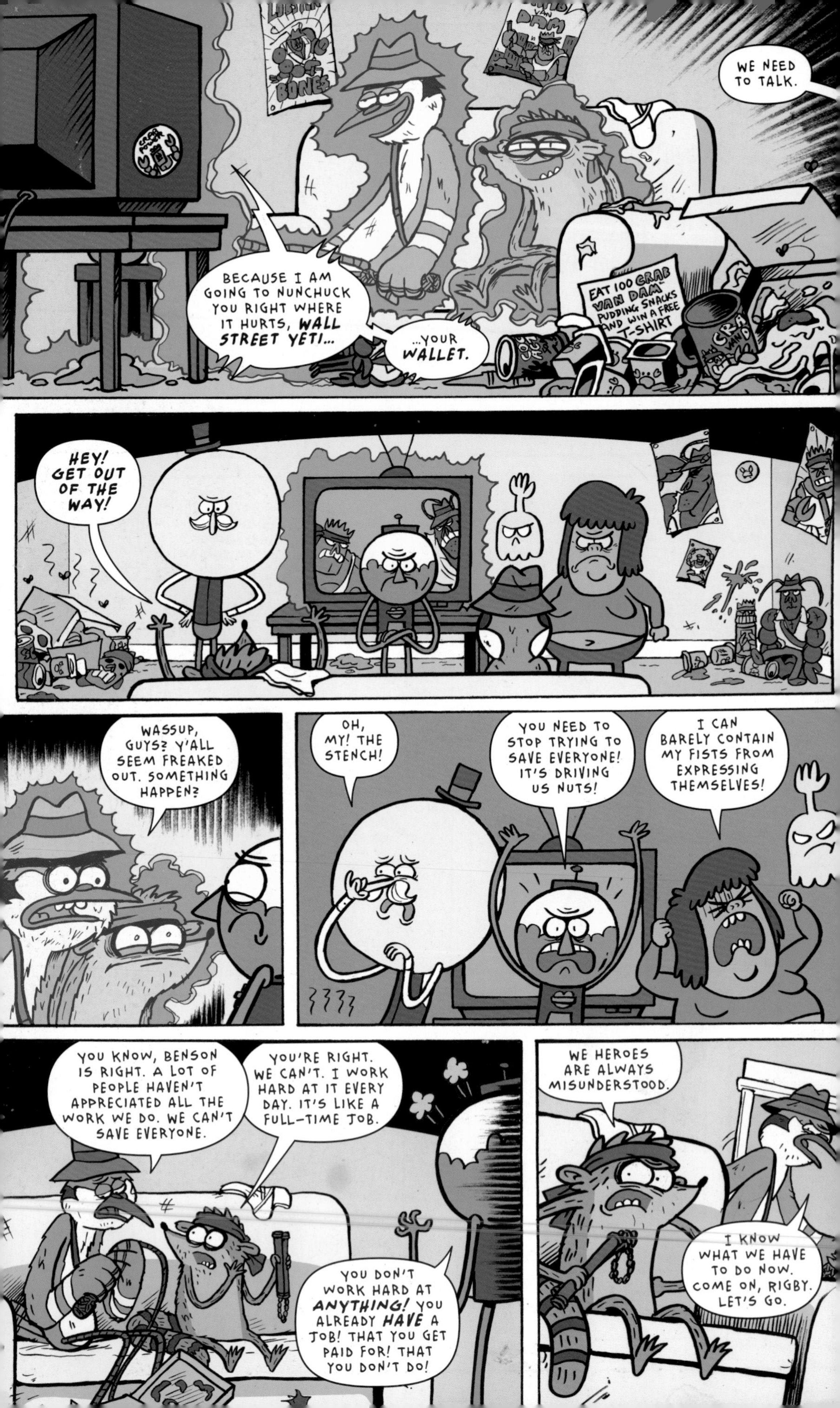
WE NEED TO TALK.
BECAUSE I AM GOING TO NUNCHUCK YOU RIGHT WHERE IT HURTS, WALL STREET YETI...
...YOUR WALLET.
EAT 100 CRAB VAN DAM PUDDING SNACKS AND WIN A FREE T-SHIRT
HEY! GET OUT OF THE WAY!
WASSUP, GUYS? Y'ALL SEEM FREAKED OUT. SOMETHING HAPPEN?
OH, MY! THE STENCH!
YOU NEED TO STOP TRYING TO SAVE EVERYONE! IT'S DRIVING US NUTS!
I CAN BARELY CONTAIN MY FISTS FROM EXPRESSING THEMSELVES!
YOU KNOW, BENSON IS RIGHT. A LOT OF PEOPLE HAVEN'T APPRECIATED ALL THE WORK WE DO. WE CAN'T SAVE EVERYONE.
YOU'RE RIGHT. WE CAN'T. I WORK HARD AT IT EVERY DAY. IT'S LIKE A FULL-TIME JOB.
YOU DON'T WORK HARD AT ANYTHING! YOU ALREADY HAVE A JOB! THAT YOU GET PAID FOR! THAT YOU DON'T DO!
WE HEROES ARE ALWAYS MISUNDERSTOOD.
I KNOW WHAT WE HAVE TO DO NOW. COME ON, RIGBY. LET'S GO.

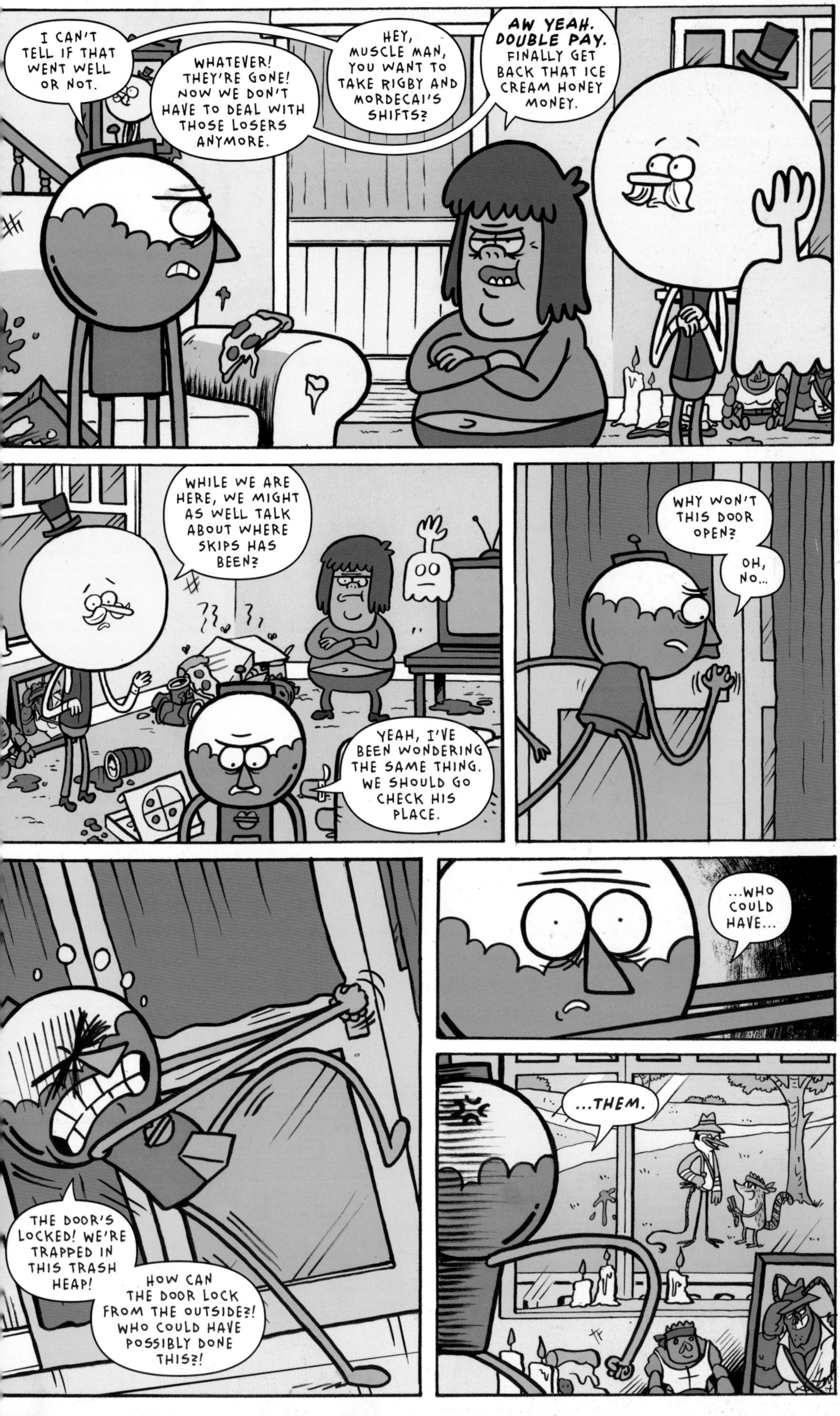
I CAN'T TELL IF THAT WENT WELL OR NOT.
WHATEVER! THEY'RE GONE! NOW WE DON'T HAVE TO DEAL WITH THOSE LOSERS ANYMORE.
HEY, MUSCLE MAN, YOU WANT TO TAKE RIGBY AND MORDECAI'S SHIFTS?
AW YEAH. DOUBLE PAY. FINALLY GET BACK THAT ICE CREAM HONEY MONEY.
WHILE WE ARE HERE, WE MIGHT AS WELL TALK ABOUT WHERE SKIPS HAS BEEN?
YEAH, I'VE BEEN WONDERING THE SAME THING. WE SHOULD GO CHECK HIS PLACE.
WHY WON'T THIS DOOR OPEN?
OH, NO...
THE DOOR'S LOCKED! WE'RE TRAPPED IN THIS TRASH HEAP!
HOW CAN THE DOOR LOCK FROM THE OUTSIDE?! WHO COULD HAVE POSSIBLY DONE THIS?!
...WHO COULD HAVE...
...THEM.

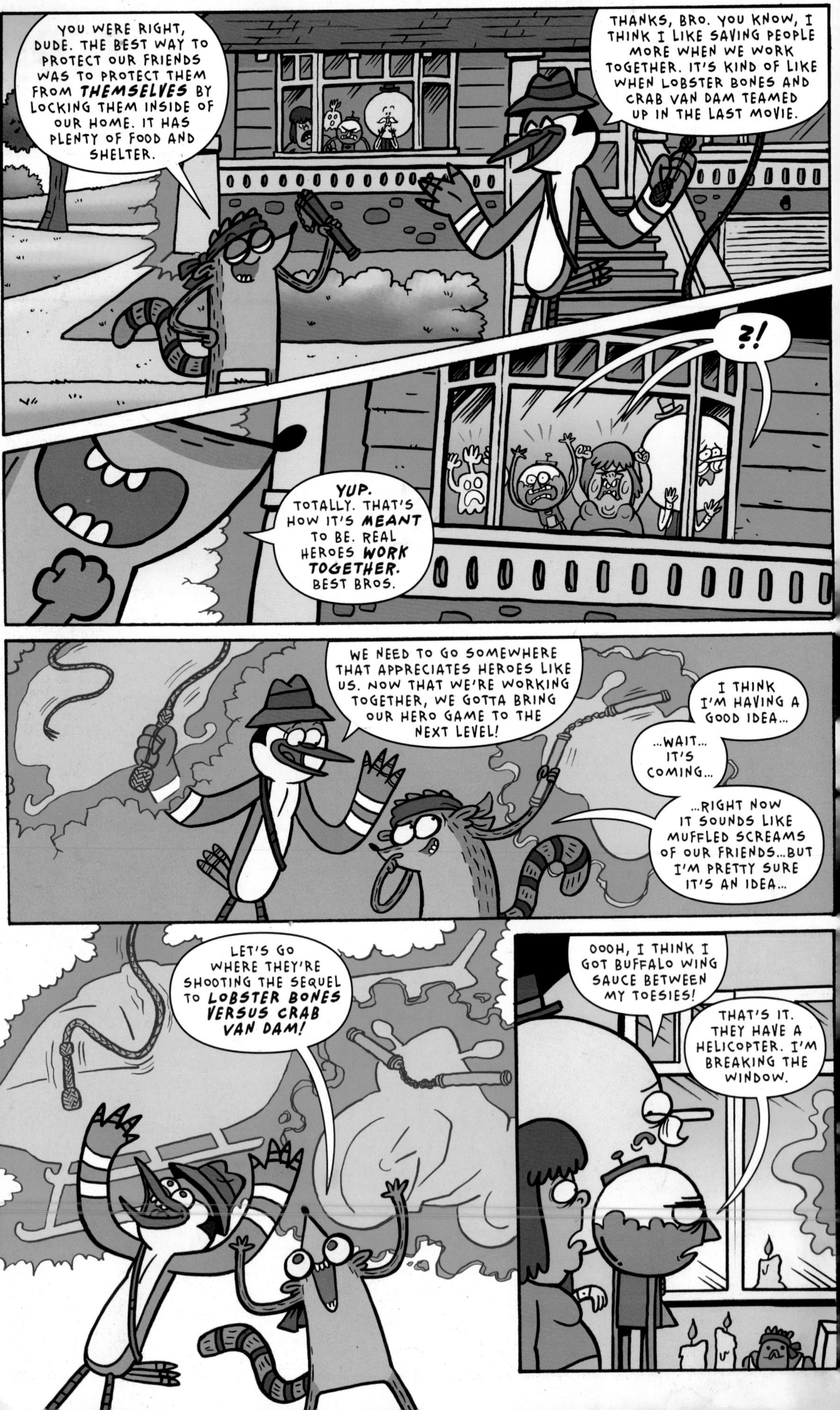
YOU WERE RIGHT, DUDE. THE BEST WAY TO PROTECT OUR FRIENDS WAS TO PROTECT THEM FROM ***THEMSELVES*** BY LOCKING THEM INSIDE OF OUR HOME. IT HAS PLENTY OF FOOD AND SHELTER.
THANKS, BRO. YOU KNOW, I THINK I LIKE SAVING PEOPLE MORE WHEN WE WORK TOGETHER. IT'S KIND OF LIKE WHEN LOBSTER BONES AND CRAB VAN DAM TEAMED UP IN THE LAST MOVIE.
?!
YUP. TOTALLY. THAT'S HOW IT'S ***MEANT*** TO BE. REAL HEROES ***WORK TOGETHER.*** BEST BROS.
WE NEED TO GO SOMEWHERE THAT APPRECIATES HEROES LIKE US. NOW THAT WE'RE WORKING TOGETHER, WE GOTTA BRING OUR HERO GAME TO THE NEXT LEVEL!
I THINK I'M HAVING A GOOD IDEA...
...WAIT... IT'S COMING...
...RIGHT NOW IT SOUNDS LIKE MUFFLED SCREAMS OF OUR FRIENDS...BUT I'M PRETTY SURE IT'S AN IDEA...
LET'S GO WHERE THEY'RE SHOOTING THE SEQUEL TO ***LOBSTER BONES VERSUS CRAB VAN DAM!***
OOOH, I THINK I GOT BUFFALO WING SAUCE BETWEEN MY TOESIES!
THAT'S IT. THEY HAVE A HELICOPTER. I'M BREAKING THE WINDOW.

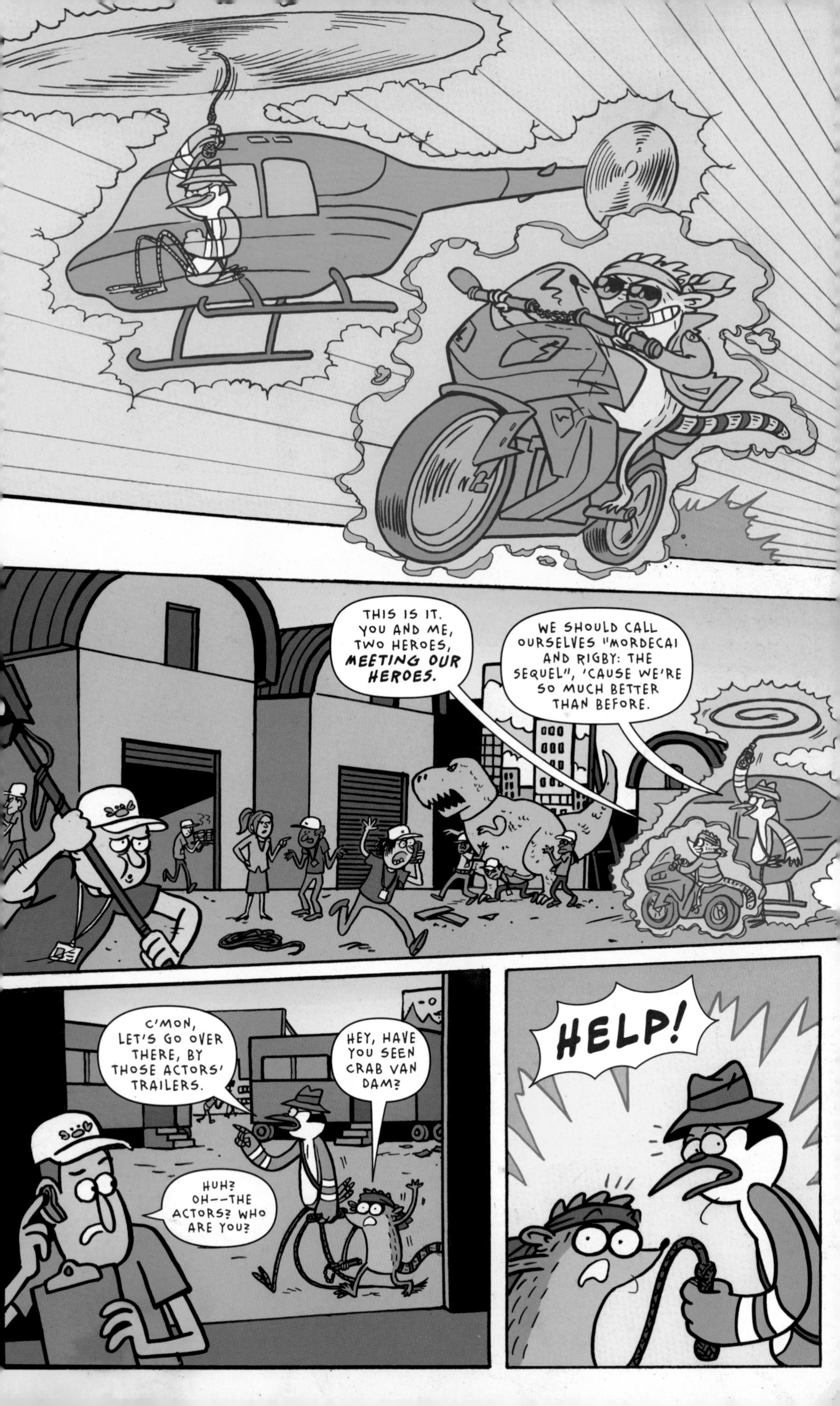
THIS IS IT. YOU AND ME, TWO HEROES, **MEETING OUR HEROES.**
WE SHOULD CALL OURSELVES "MORDECAI AND RIGBY: THE SEQUEL", 'CAUSE WE'RE SO MUCH BETTER THAN BEFORE.
C'MON, LET'S GO OVER THERE, BY THOSE ACTORS' TRAILERS.
HEY, HAVE YOU SEEN CRAB VAN DAM?
HUH? OH--THE ACTORS? WHO ARE YOU?
HELP!

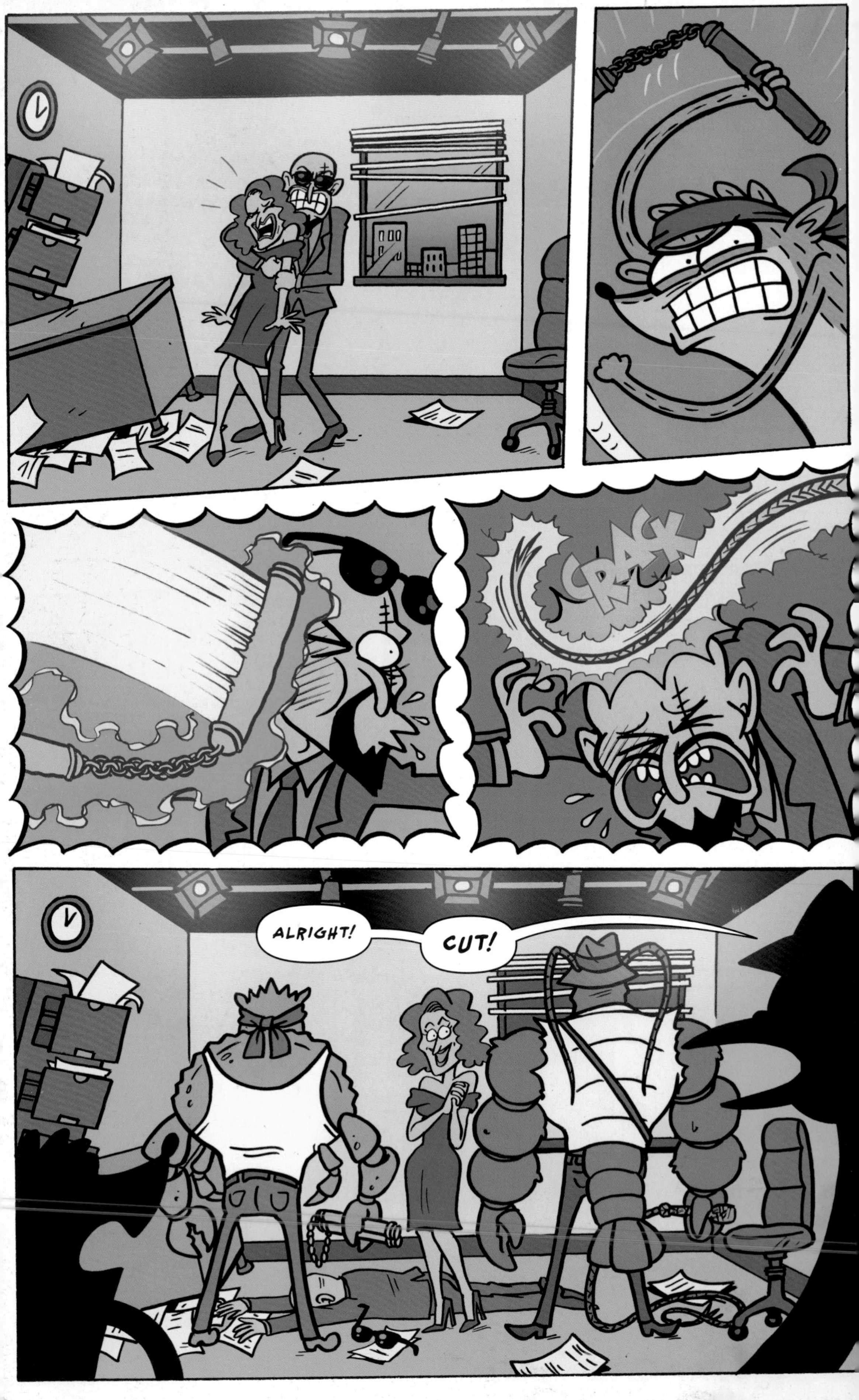
CRACK
ALRIGHT!
CUT!

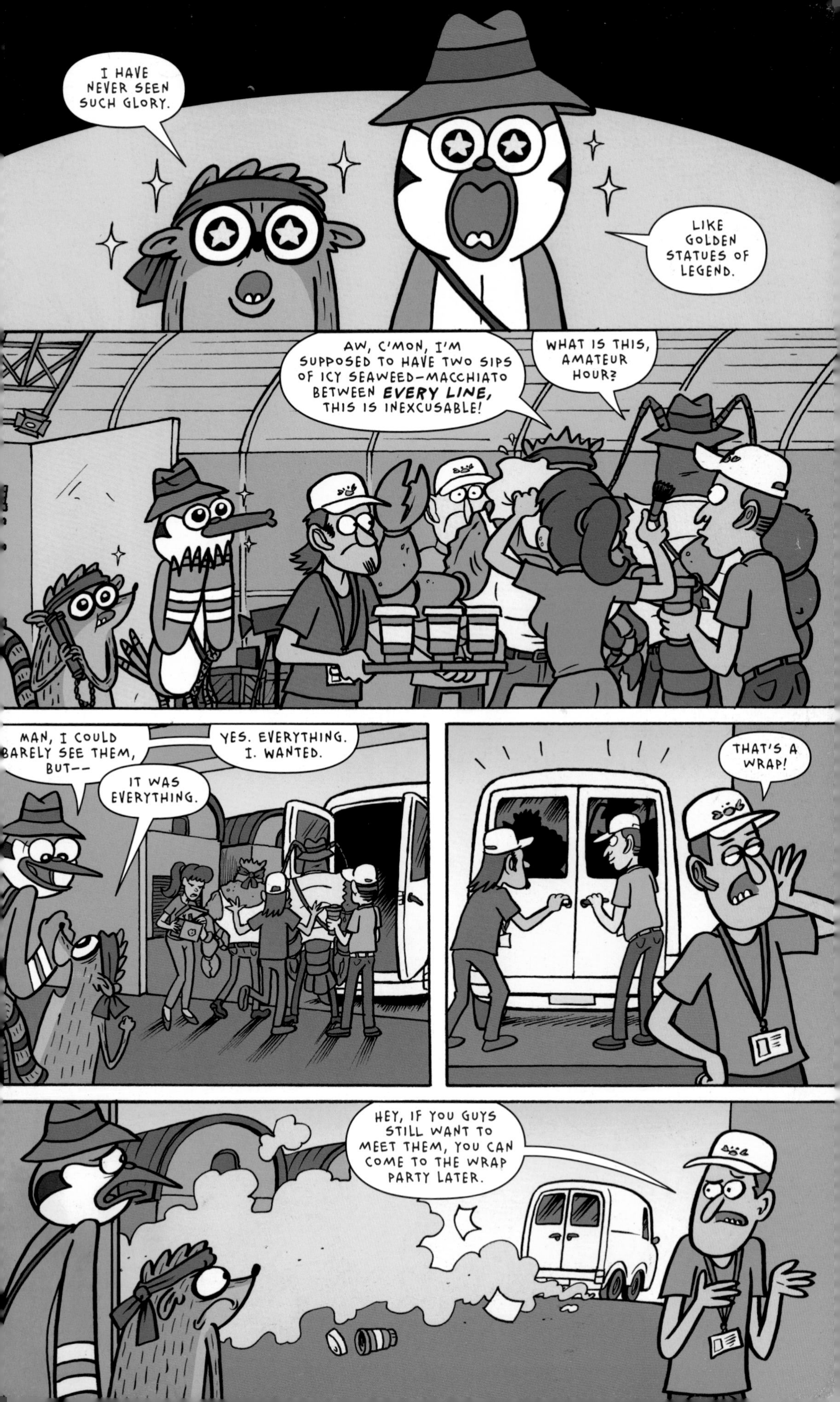
I HAVE NEVER SEEN SUCH GLORY.
LIKE GOLDEN STATUES OF LEGEND.
AW, C'MON, I'M SUPPOSED TO HAVE TWO SIPS OF ICY SEAWEED-MACCHIATO BETWEEN EVERY LINE, THIS IS INEXCUSABLE!
WHAT IS THIS, AMATEUR HOUR?
MAN, I COULD BARELY SEE THEM, BUT--
IT WAS EVERYTHING.
YES. EVERYTHING. I. WANTED.
THAT'S A WRAP!
HEY, IF YOU GUYS STILL WANT TO MEET THEM, YOU CAN COME TO THE WRAP PARTY LATER.

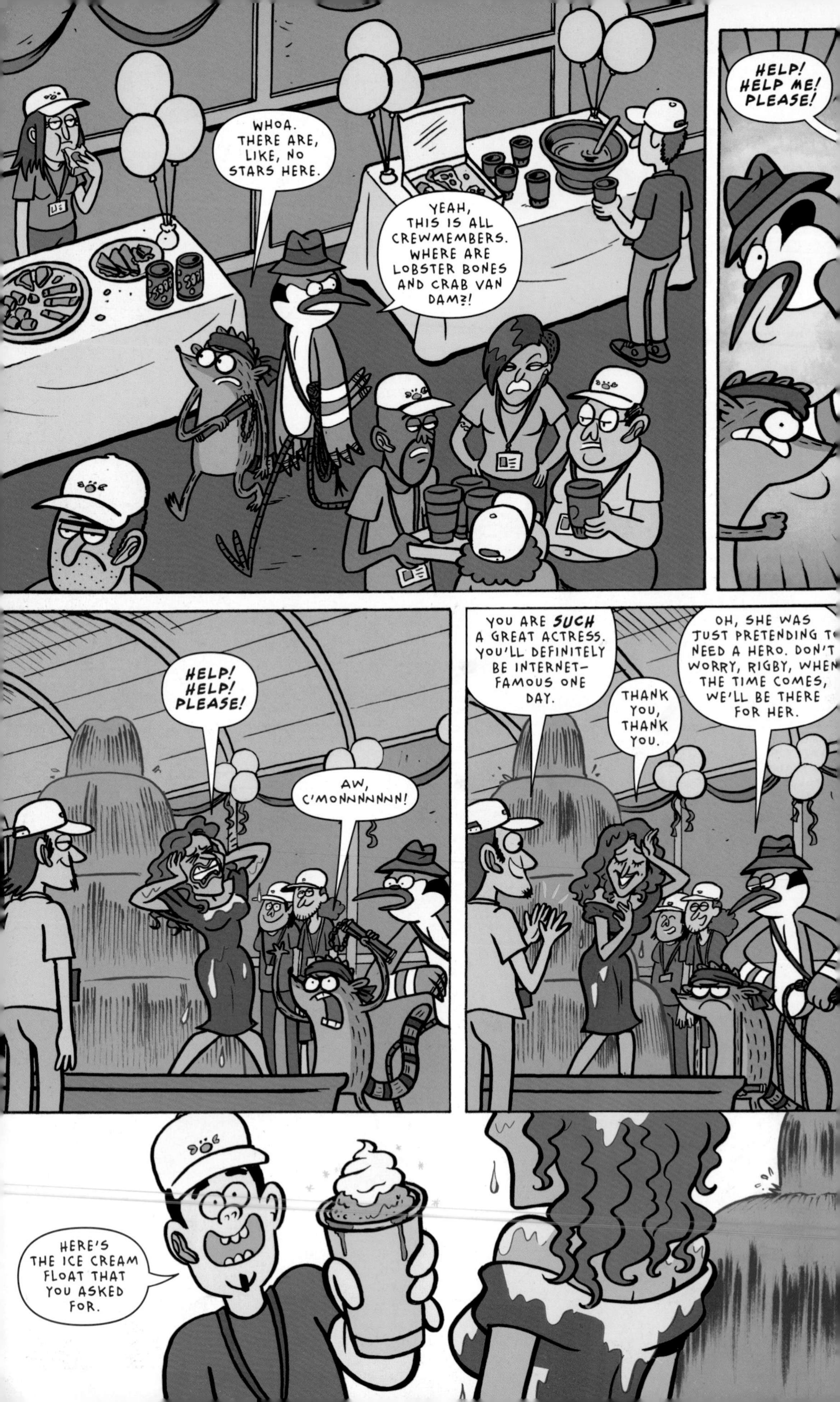
WHOA. THERE ARE, LIKE, NO STARS HERE.
YEAH, THIS IS ALL CREWMEMBERS. WHERE ARE LOBSTER BONES AND CRAB VAN DAM?!
HELP! HELP ME! PLEASE!
HELP! HELP! PLEASE!
AW, C'MONNNNNNN!
YOU ARE SUCH A GREAT ACTRESS. YOU'LL DEFINITELY BE INTERNET-FAMOUS ONE DAY.
THANK YOU, THANK YOU.
OH, SHE WAS JUST PRETENDING TO NEED A HERO. DON'T WORRY, RIGBY, WHEN THE TIME COMES, WE'LL BE THERE FOR HER.
HERE'S THE ICE CREAM FLOAT THAT YOU ASKED FOR.

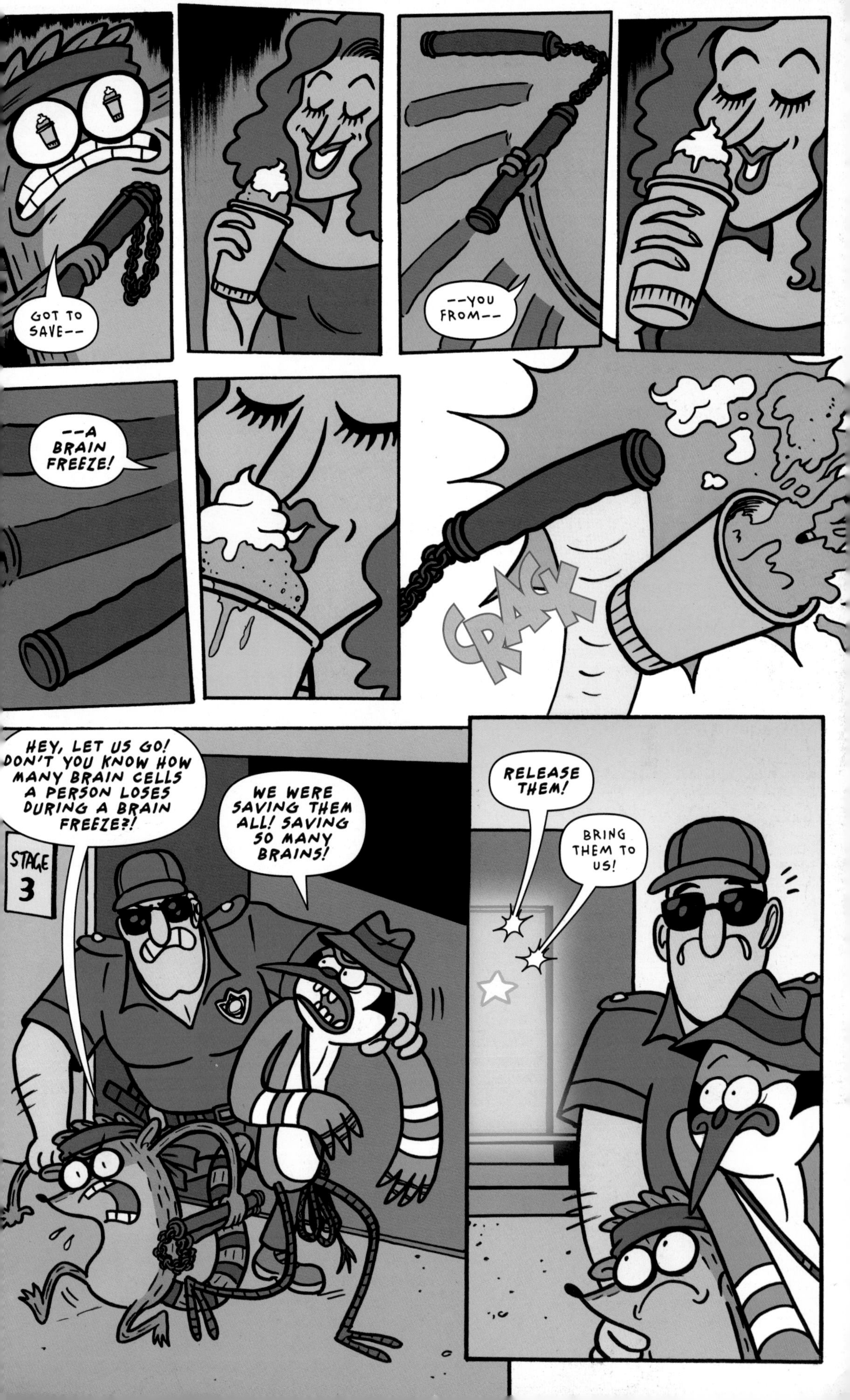
GOT TO SAVE--
--YOU FROM--
--A BRAIN FREEZE!
CRACK
HEY, LET US GO! DON'T YOU KNOW HOW MANY BRAIN CELLS A PERSON LOSES DURING A BRAIN FREEZE?!
WE WERE SAVING THEM ALL! SAVING SO MANY BRAINS!
STAGE 3
RELEASE THEM!
BRING THEM TO US!

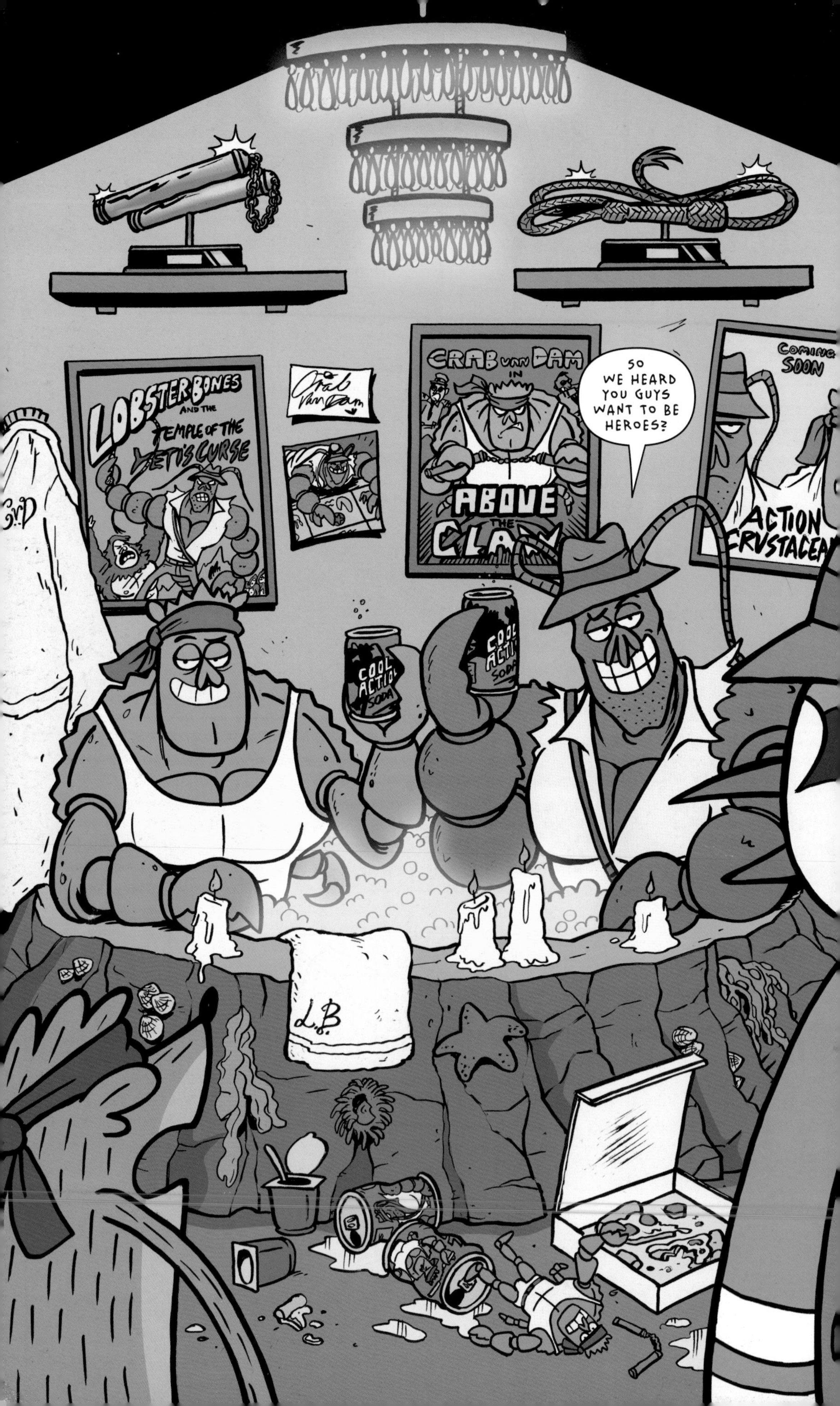
LOBSTER BONES
AND THE
TEMPLE OF THE
YETI'S CURSE
CRAB VAN DAM
IN
ABOVE
THE
COMING SOON
SO WE HEARD YOU GUYS WANT TO BE HEROES?
COOL ACTION SODA

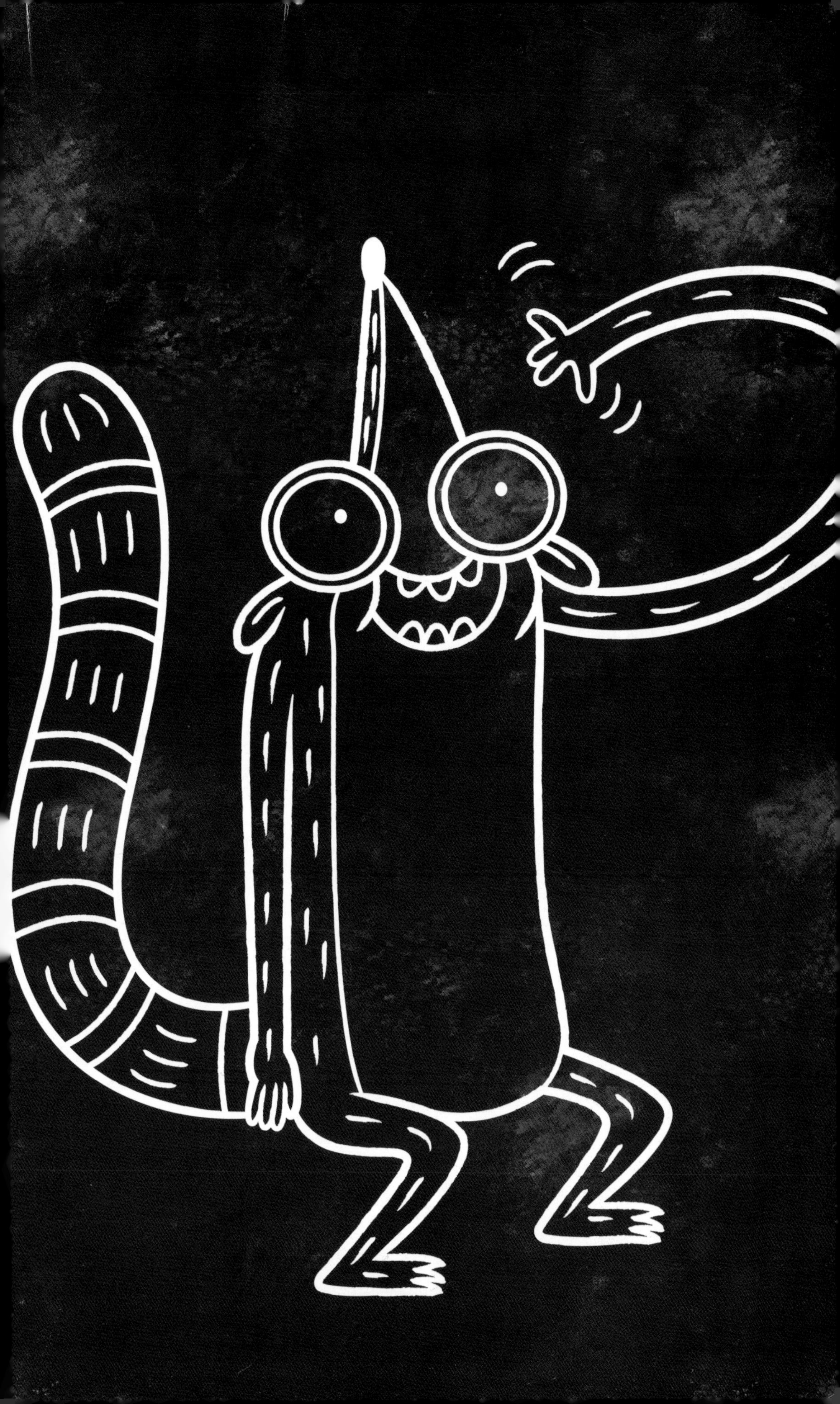

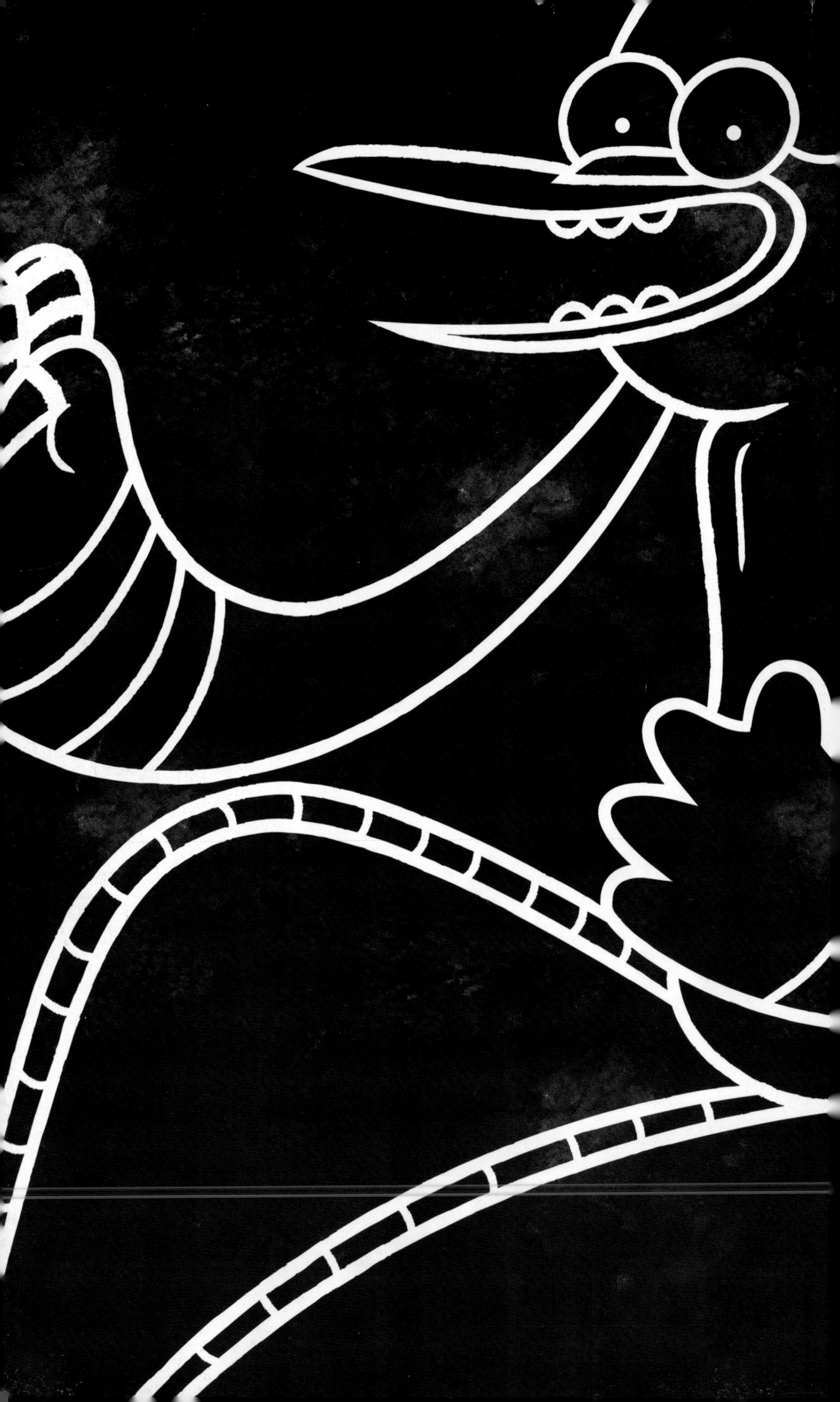

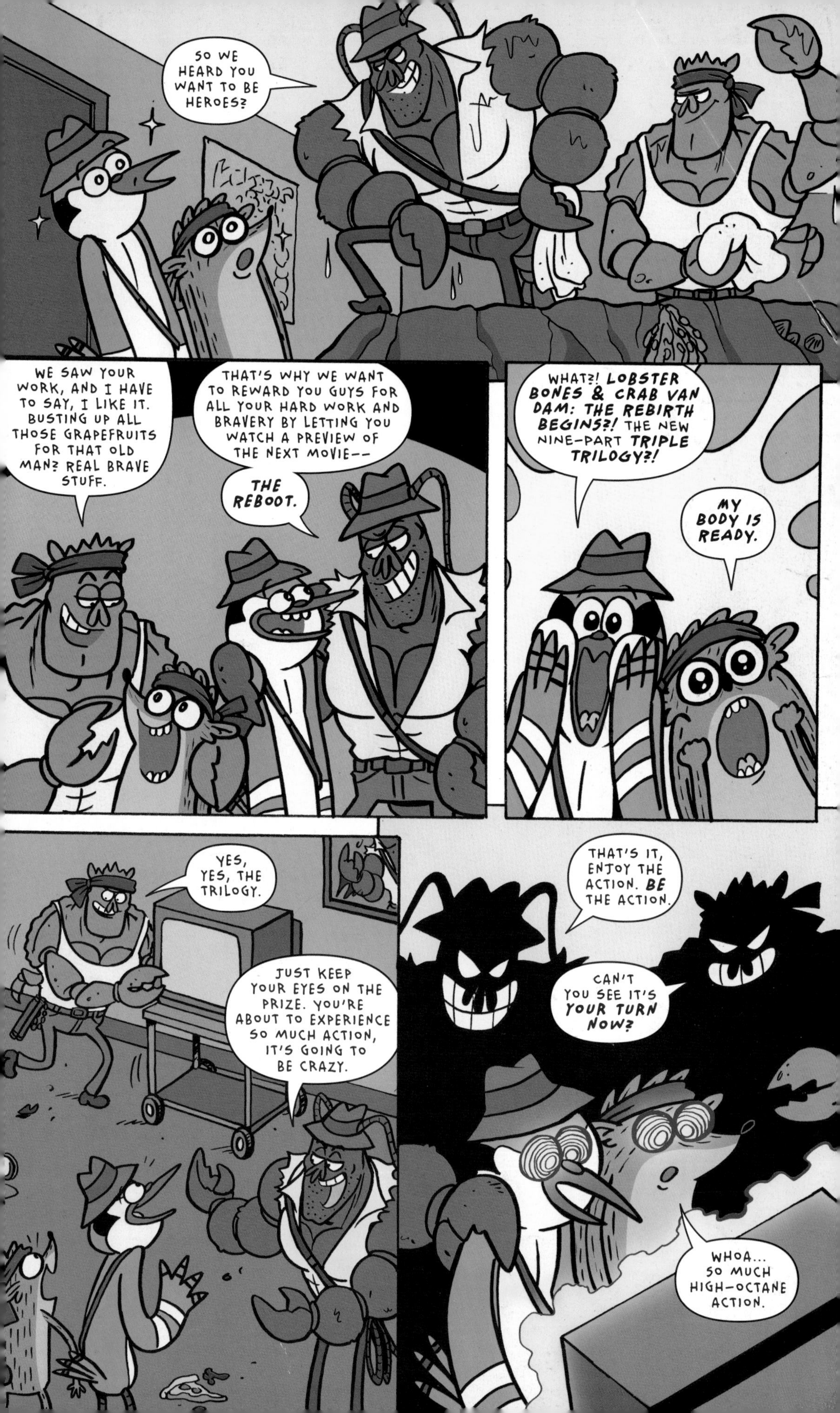
SO WE HEARD YOU WANT TO BE HEROES?
WE SAW YOUR WORK, AND I HAVE TO SAY, I LIKE IT. BUSTING UP ALL THOSE GRAPEFRUITS FOR THAT OLD MAN? REAL BRAVE STUFF.
THAT'S WHY WE WANT TO REWARD YOU GUYS FOR ALL YOUR HARD WORK AND BRAVERY BY LETTING YOU WATCH A PREVIEW OF THE NEXT MOVIE--
THE REBOOT.
WHAT?! LOBSTER BONES & CRAB VAN DAM: THE REBIRTH BEGINS?! THE NEW NINE-PART TRIPLE TRILOGY?!
MY BODY IS READY.
YES, YES, THE TRILOGY.
JUST KEEP YOUR EYES ON THE PRIZE. YOU'RE ABOUT TO EXPERIENCE SO MUCH ACTION, IT'S GOING TO BE CRAZY.
THAT'S IT, ENJOY THE ACTION. BE THE ACTION.
CAN'T YOU SEE IT'S YOUR TURN NOW?
WHOA... SO MUCH HIGH-OCTANE ACTION.

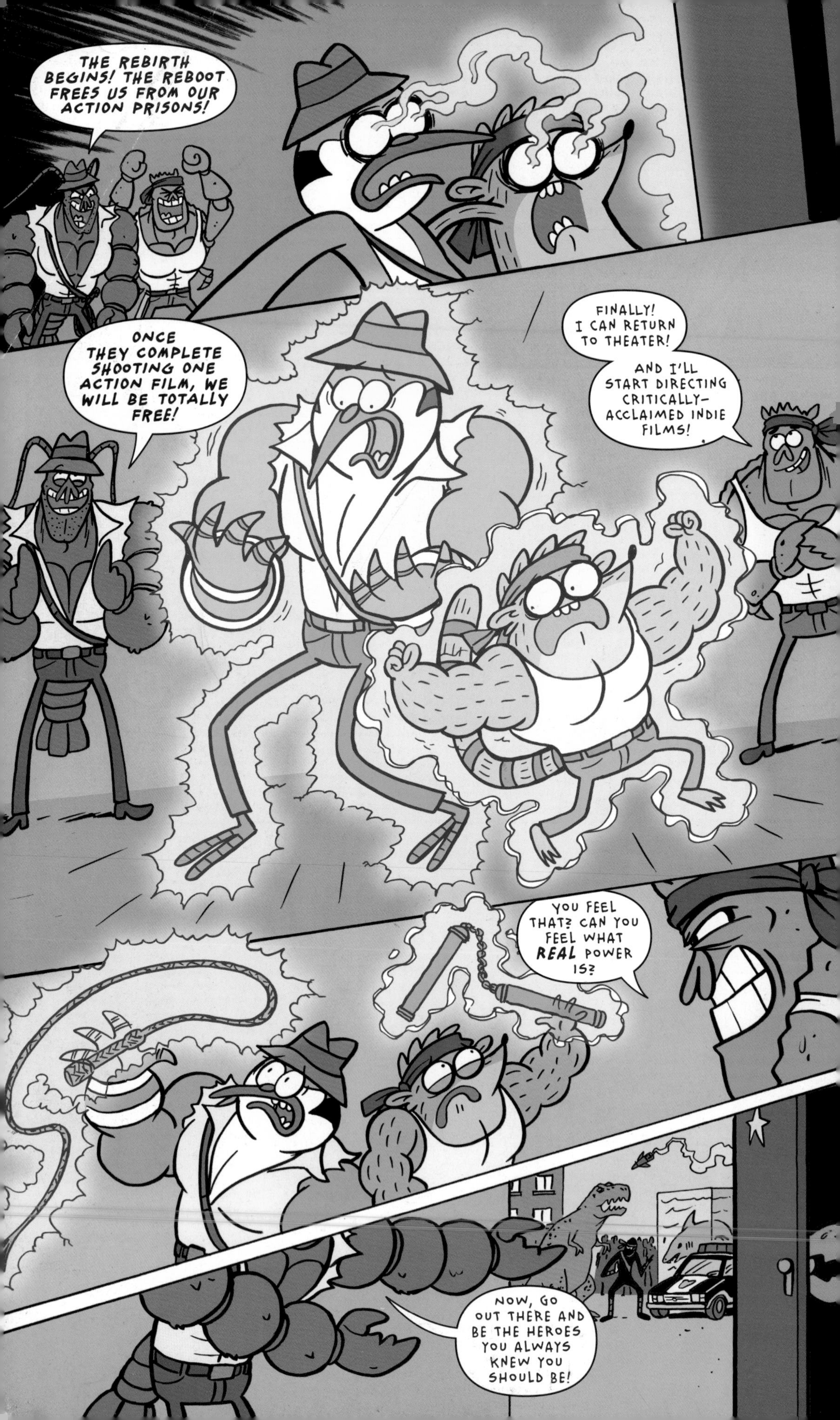
THE REBIRTH BEGINS! THE REBOOT FREES US FROM OUR ACTION PRISONS!
ONCE THEY COMPLETE SHOOTING ONE ACTION FILM, WE WILL BE TOTALLY FREE!
FINALLY! I CAN RETURN TO THEATER!
AND I'LL START DIRECTING CRITICALLY-ACCLAIMED INDIE FILMS!
YOU FEEL THAT? CAN YOU FEEL WHAT REAL POWER IS?
NOW, GO OUT THERE AND BE THE HEROES YOU ALWAYS KNEW YOU SHOULD BE!

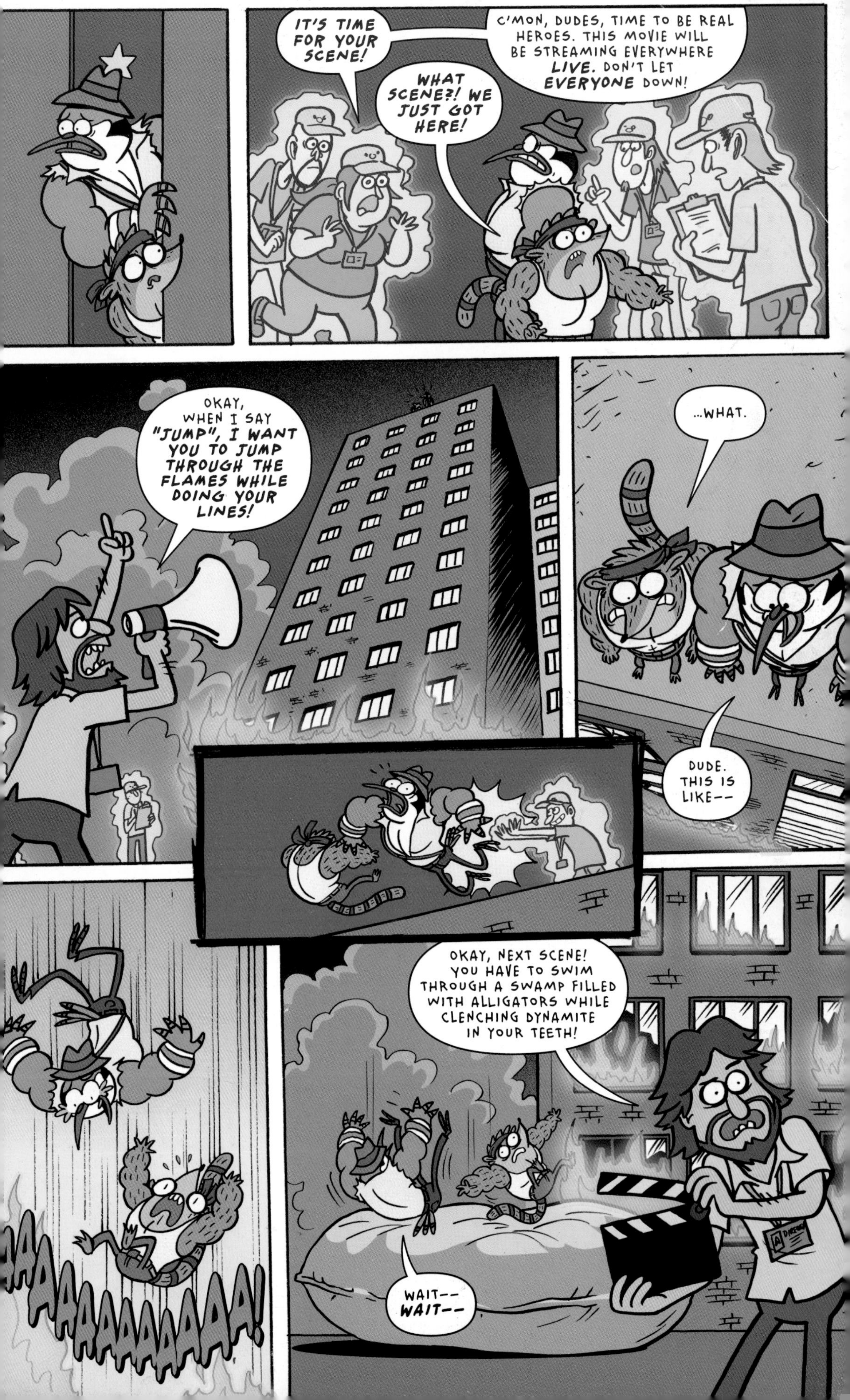

IT'S TIME FOR YOUR SCENE!
C'MON, DUDES, TIME TO BE REAL HEROES. THIS MOVIE WILL BE STREAMING EVERYWHERE LIVE. DON'T LET EVERYONE DOWN!
WHAT SCENE?! WE JUST GOT HERE!
OKAY, WHEN I SAY "JUMP", I WANT YOU TO JUMP THROUGH THE FLAMES WHILE DOING YOUR LINES!
...WHAT.
DUDE. THIS IS LIKE--
AAAAAAAAAAAA!
OKAY, NEXT SCENE! YOU HAVE TO SWIM THROUGH A SWAMP FILLED WITH ALLIGATORS WHILE CLENCHING DYNAMITE IN YOUR TEETH!
WAIT--
WAIT--

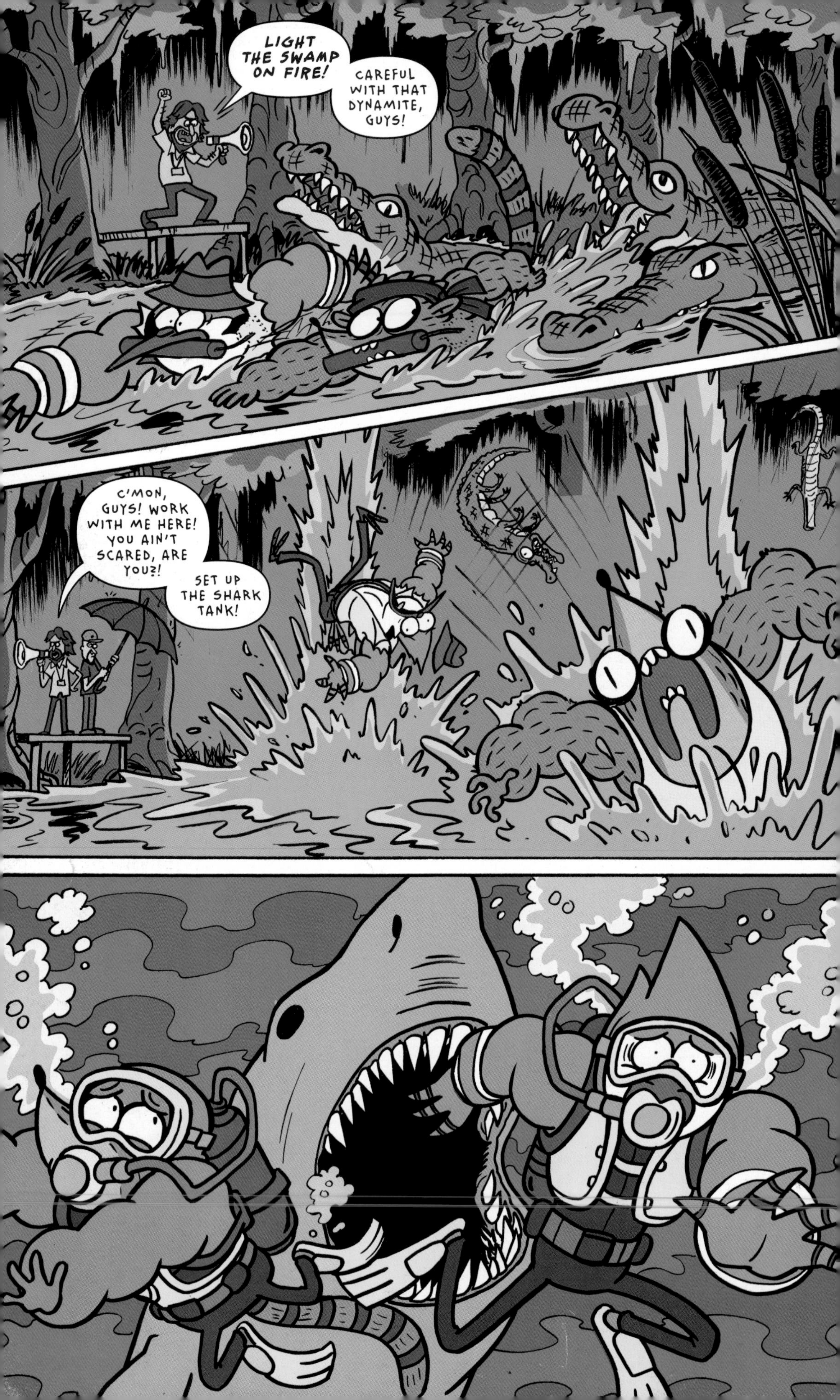

LIGHT THE SWAMP ON FIRE!
CAREFUL WITH THAT DYNAMITE, GUYS!
C'MON, GUYS! WORK WITH ME HERE! YOU AIN'T SCARED, ARE YOU?!
SET UP THE SHARK TANK!

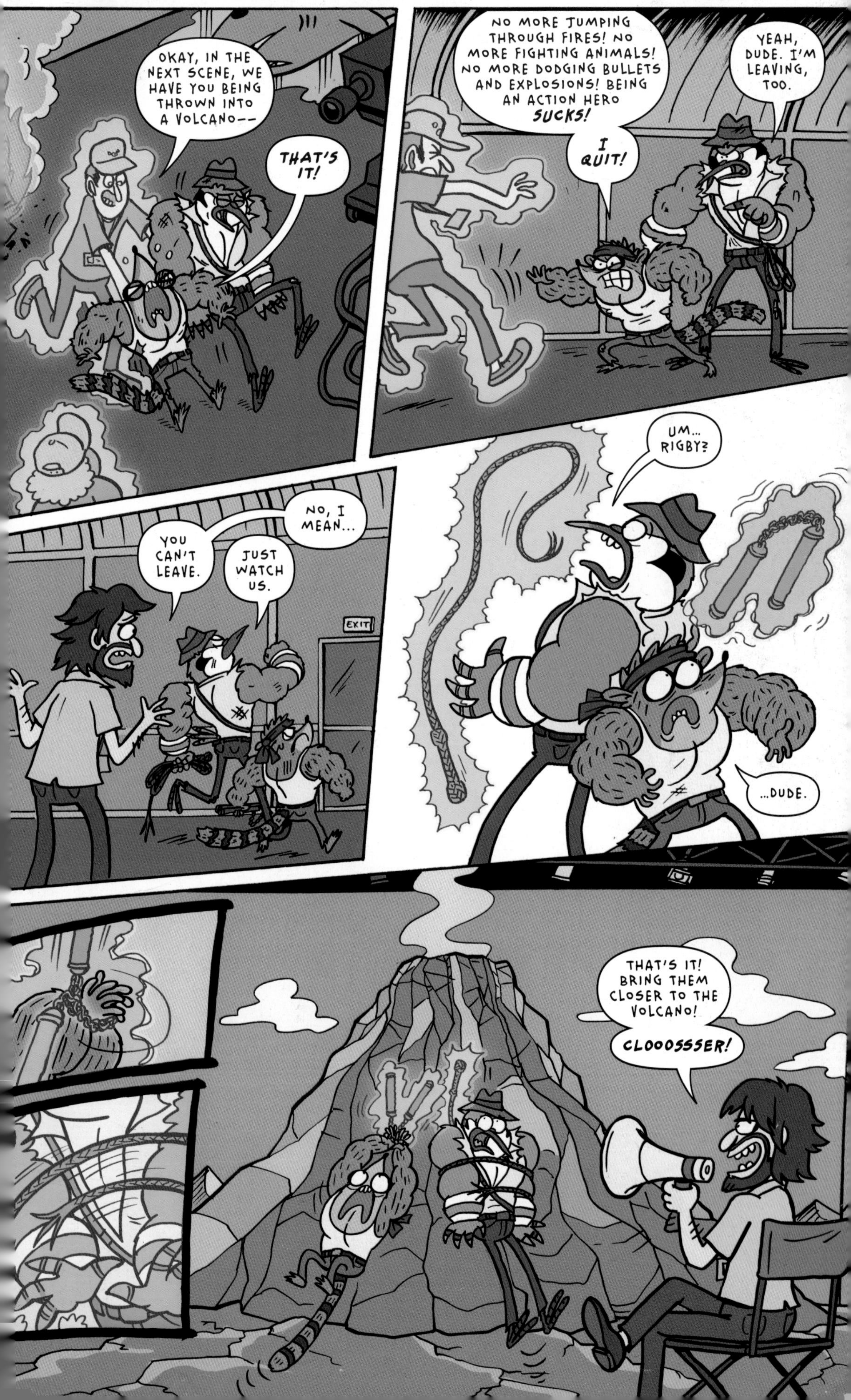
OKAY, IN THE NEXT SCENE, WE HAVE YOU BEING THROWN INTO A VOLCANO--
THAT'S IT!
NO MORE JUMPING THROUGH FIRES! NO MORE FIGHTING ANIMALS! NO MORE DODGING BULLETS AND EXPLOSIONS! BEING AN ACTION HERO SUCKS!
I QUIT!
YEAH, DUDE. I'M LEAVING, TOO.
YOU CAN'T LEAVE.
JUST WATCH US.
NO, I MEAN...
EXIT
UM... RIGBY?
...DUDE.
THAT'S IT! BRING THEM CLOSER TO THE VOLCANO!
CLOOOSSSER!

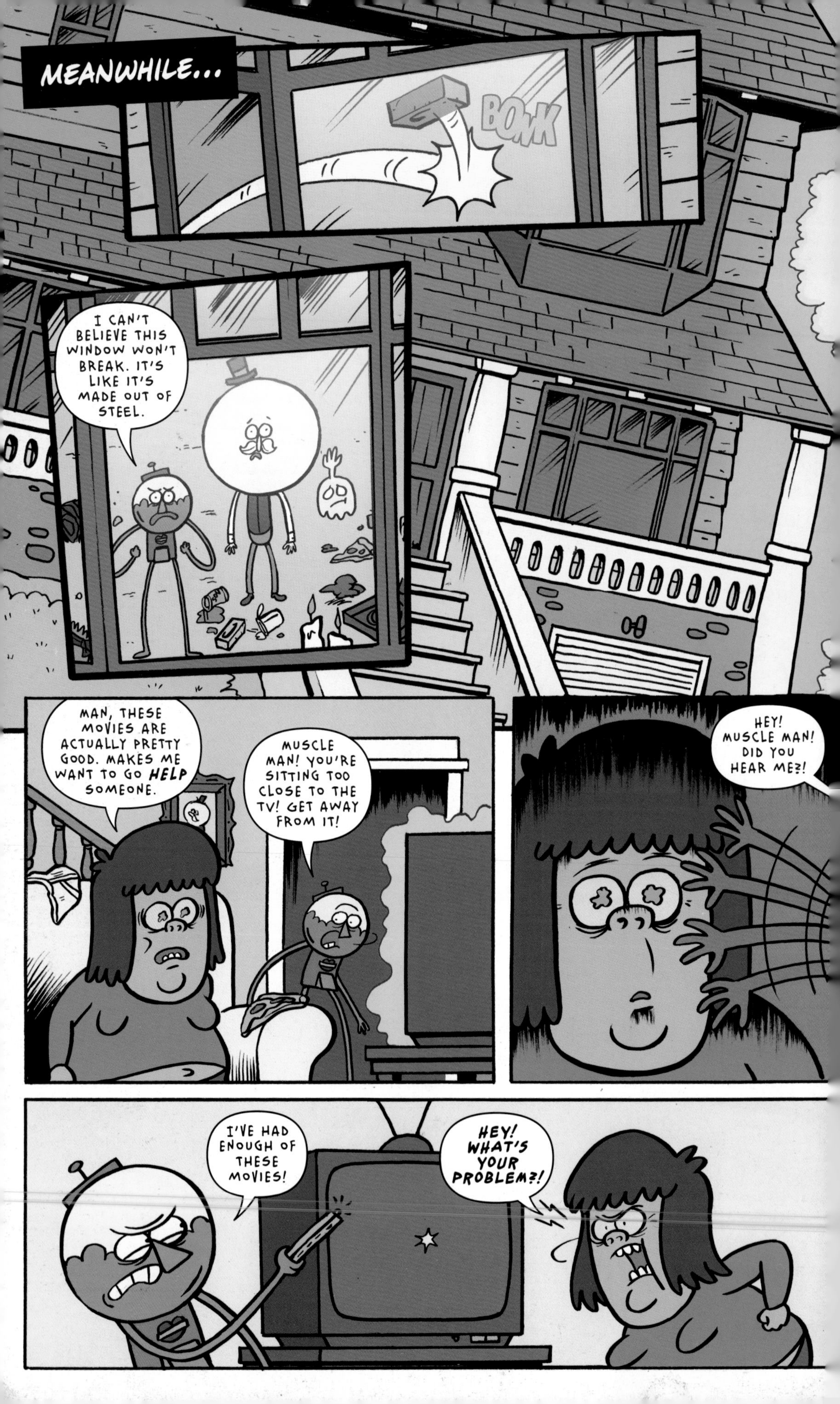
MEANWHILE...
BONK
I CAN'T BELIEVE THIS WINDOW WON'T BREAK. IT'S LIKE IT'S MADE OUT OF STEEL.
MAN, THESE MOVIES ARE ACTUALLY PRETTY GOOD. MAKES ME WANT TO GO **HELP** SOMEONE.
MUSCLE MAN! YOU'RE SITTING TOO CLOSE TO THE TV! GET AWAY FROM IT!
HEY! MUSCLE MAN! DID YOU HEAR ME?!
I'VE HAD ENOUGH OF THESE MOVIES!
HEY! WHAT'S YOUR PROBLEM?!

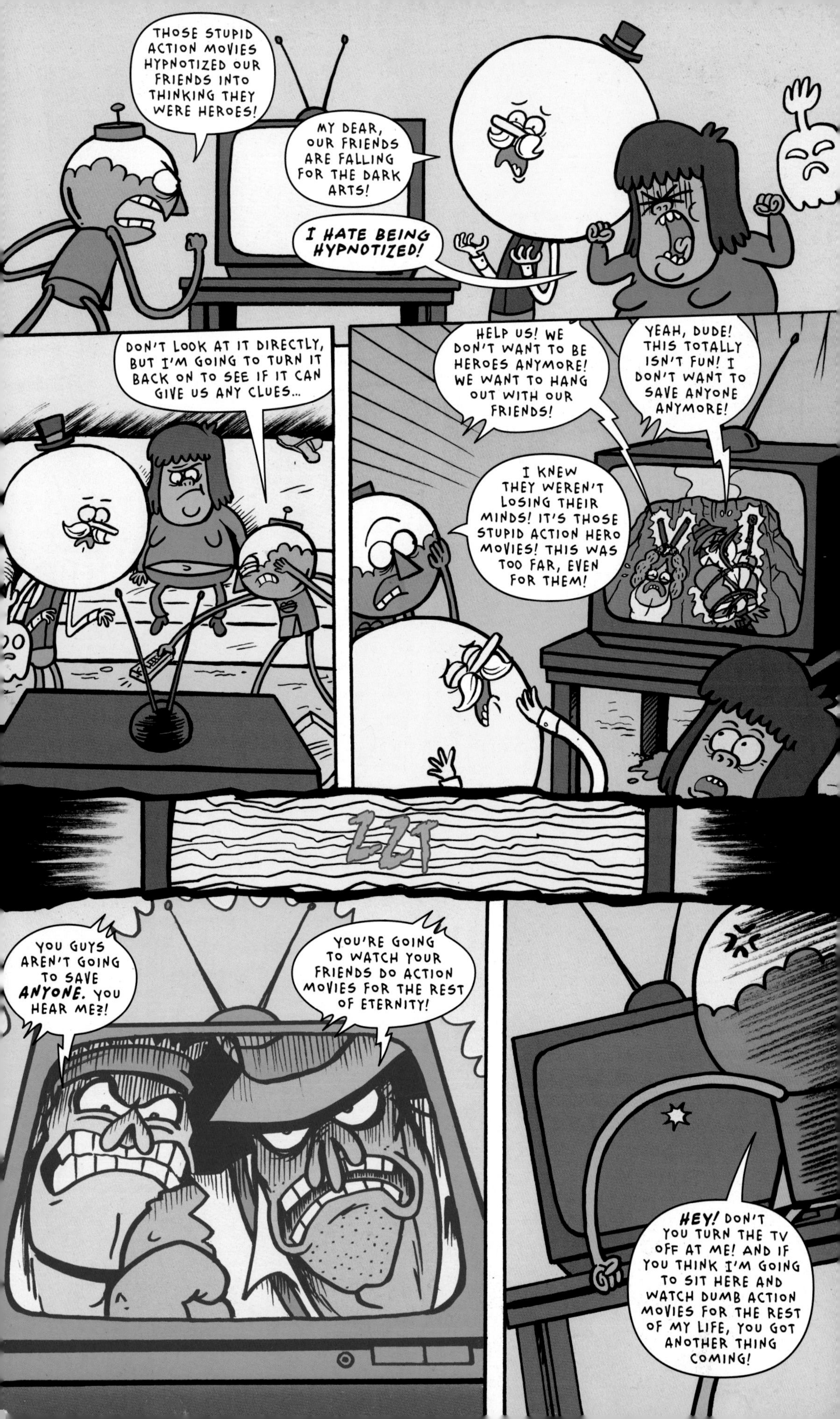

THOSE STUPID ACTION MOVIES HYPNOTIZED OUR FRIENDS INTO THINKING THEY WERE HEROES!
MY DEAR, OUR FRIENDS ARE FALLING FOR THE DARK ARTS!
I HATE BEING HYPNOTIZED!
DON'T LOOK AT IT DIRECTLY, BUT I'M GOING TO TURN IT BACK ON TO SEE IF IT CAN GIVE US ANY CLUES...
HELP US! WE DON'T WANT TO BE HEROES ANYMORE! WE WANT TO HANG OUT WITH OUR FRIENDS!
YEAH, DUDE! THIS TOTALLY ISN'T FUN! I DON'T WANT TO SAVE ANYONE ANYMORE!
I KNEW THEY WEREN'T LOSING THEIR MINDS! IT'S THOSE STUPID ACTION HERO MOVIES! THIS WAS TOO FAR, EVEN FOR THEM!
ZZT
YOU GUYS AREN'T GOING TO SAVE ANYONE. YOU HEAR ME?!
YOU'RE GOING TO WATCH YOUR FRIENDS DO ACTION MOVIES FOR THE REST OF ETERNITY!
HEY! DON'T YOU TURN THE TV OFF AT ME! AND IF YOU THINK I'M GOING TO SIT HERE AND WATCH DUMB ACTION MOVIES FOR THE REST OF MY LIFE, YOU GOT ANOTHER THING COMING!

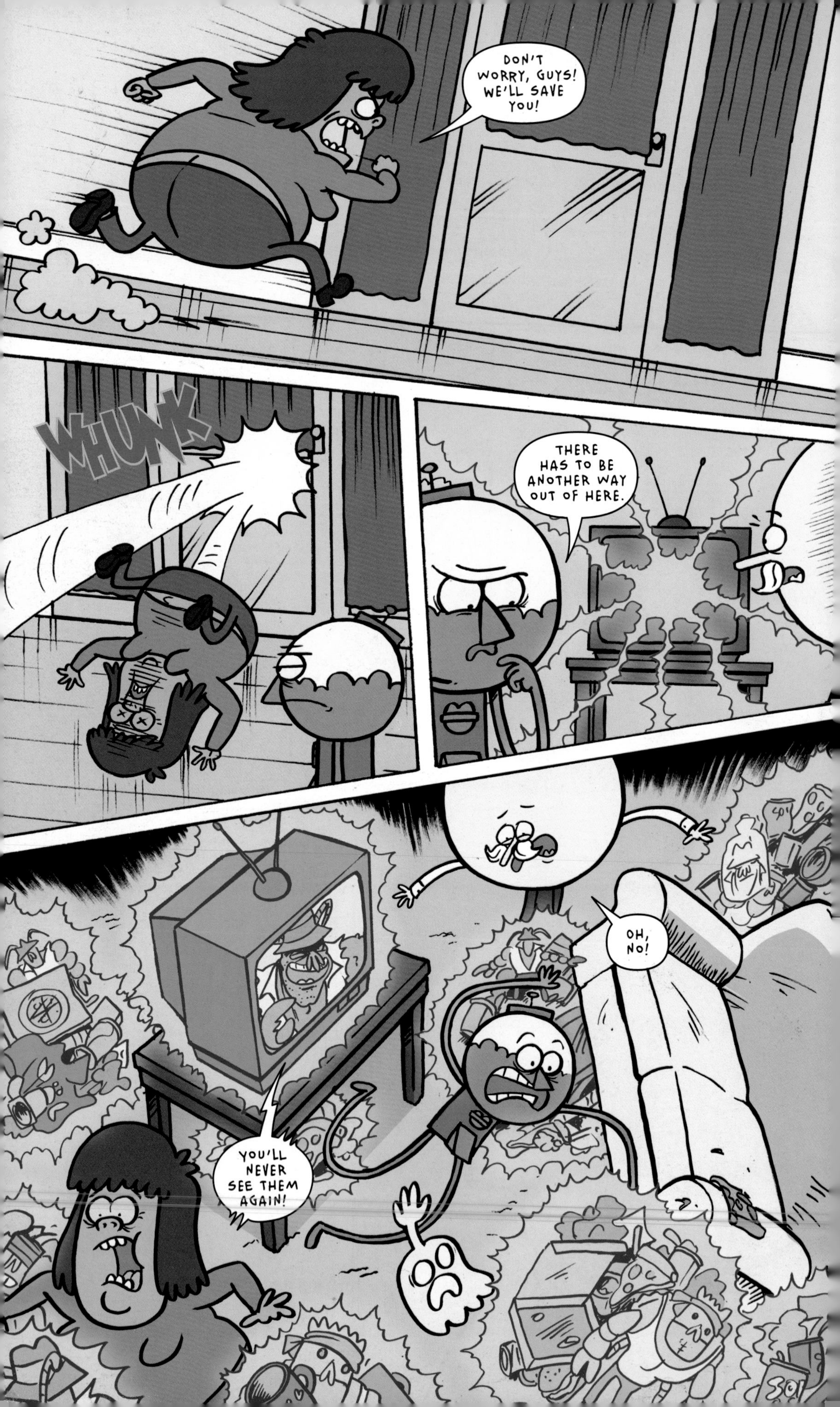
DON'T WORRY, GUYS! WE'LL SAVE YOU!
WHUNK
THERE HAS TO BE ANOTHER WAY OUT OF HERE.
OH, NO!
YOU'LL NEVER SEE THEM AGAIN!

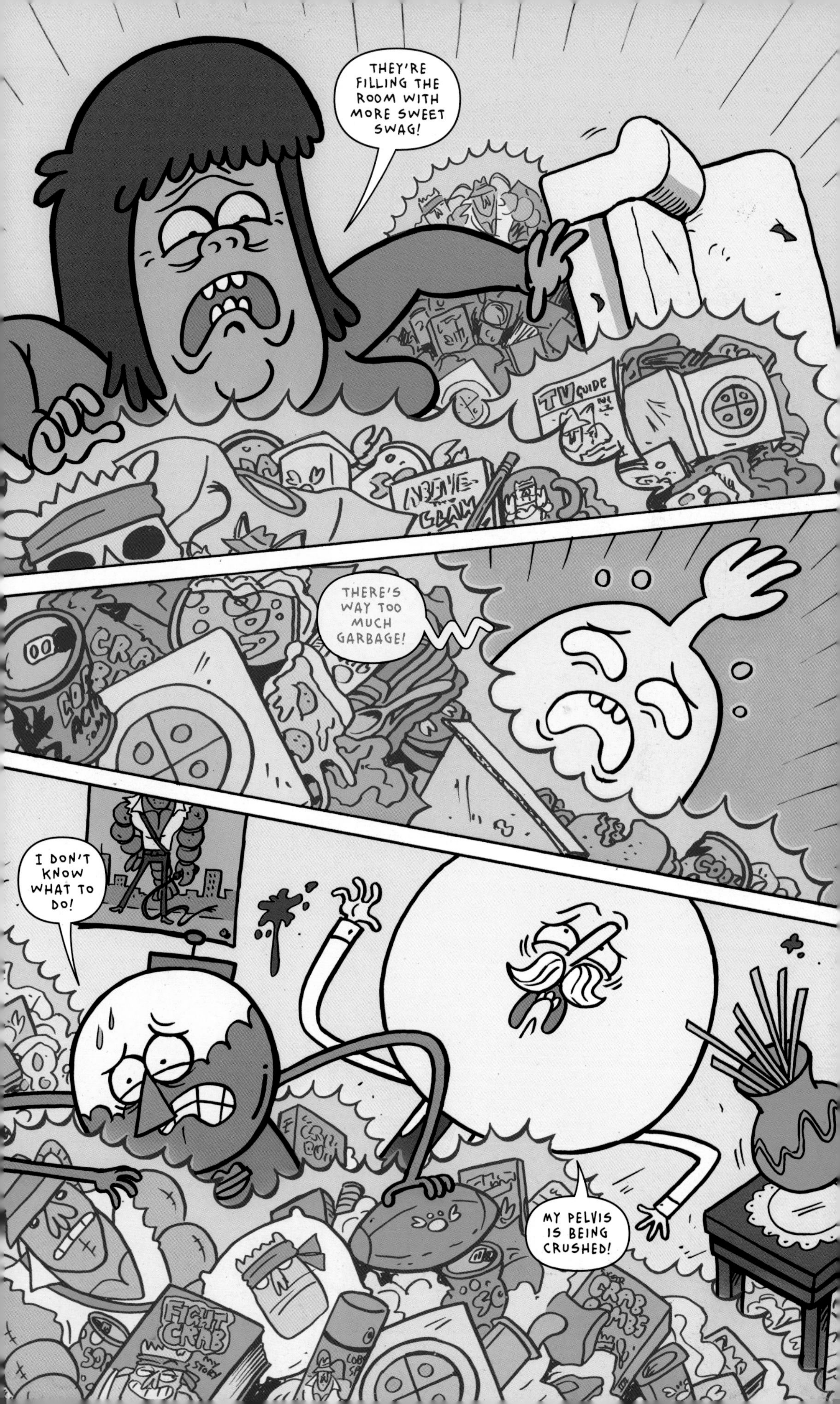
THEY'RE FILLING THE ROOM WITH MORE SWEET SWAG!
THERE'S WAY TOO MUCH GARBAGE!
I DON'T KNOW WHAT TO DO!
MY PELVIS IS BEING CRUSHED!

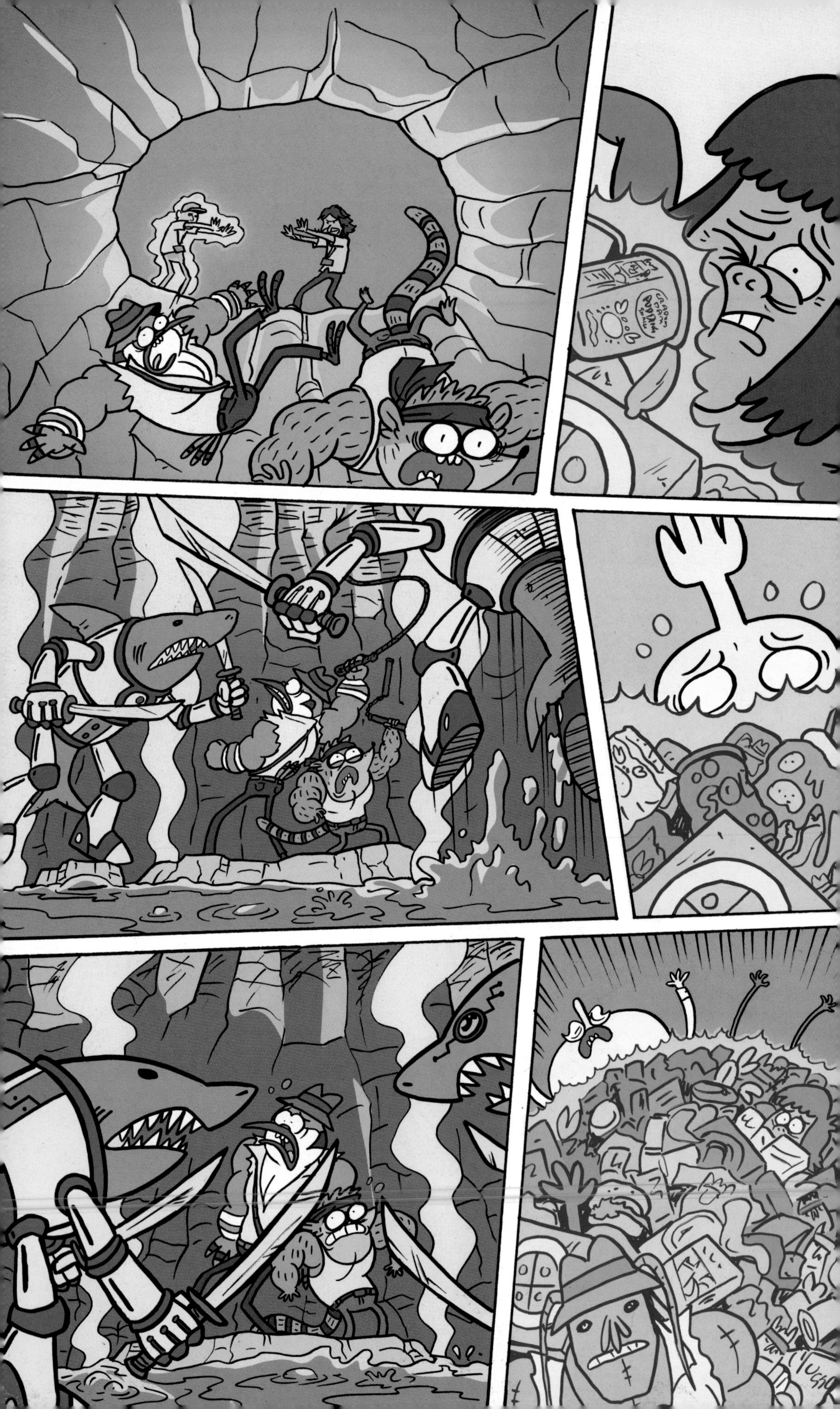

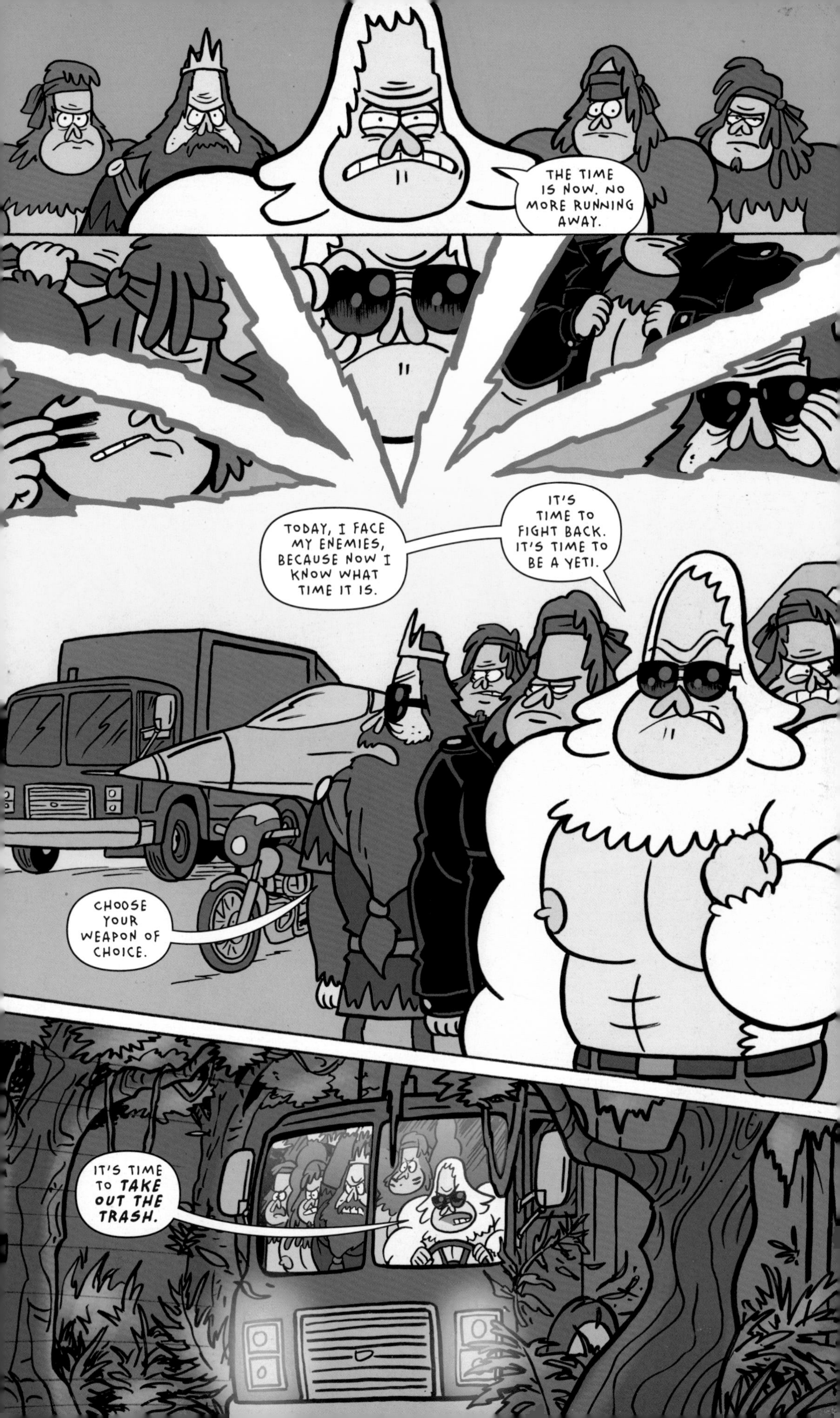
THE TIME IS NOW. NO MORE RUNNING AWAY.
TODAY, I FACE MY ENEMIES, BECAUSE NOW I KNOW WHAT TIME IT IS.
IT'S TIME TO FIGHT BACK. IT'S TIME TO BE A YETI.
CHOOSE YOUR WEAPON OF CHOICE.
IT'S TIME TO TAKE OUT THE TRASH.

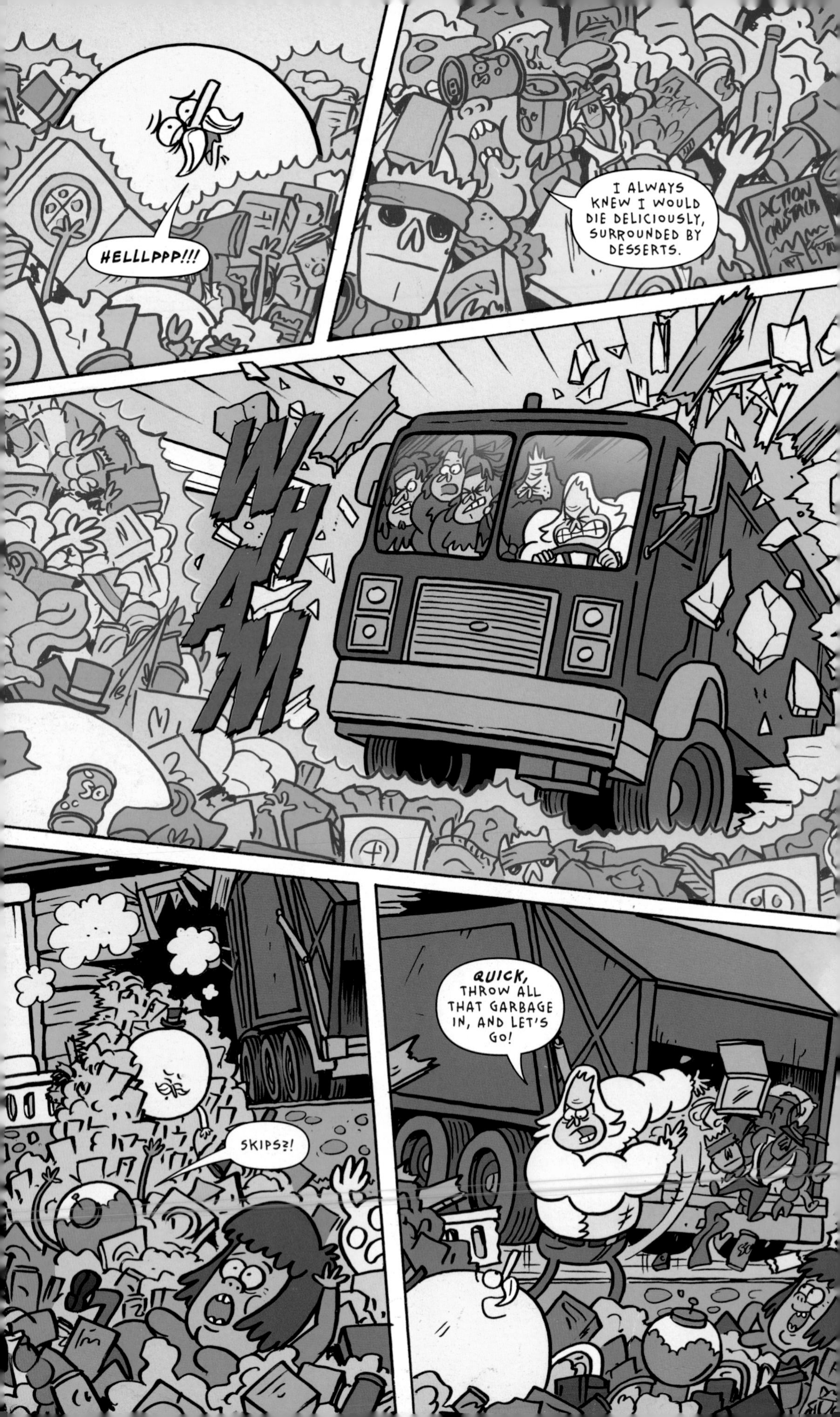
HELLLPPP!!!
I ALWAYS KNEW I WOULD DIE DELICIOUSLY, SURROUNDED BY DESSERTS.
ACTION CRUSTACEANS
WHAM
SKIPS?!
QUICK, THROW ALL THAT GARBAGE IN, AND LET'S GO!

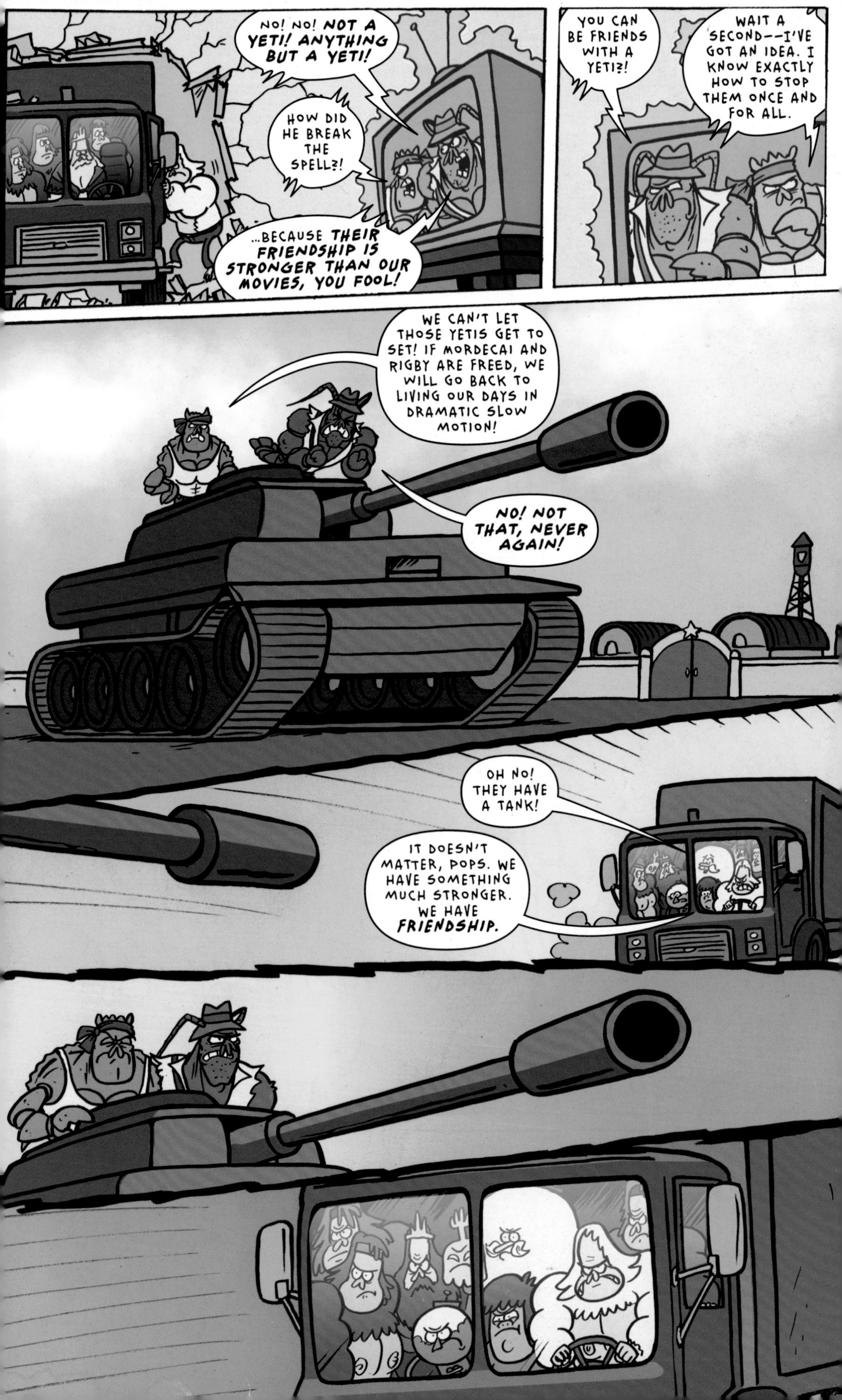

NO! NO! NOT A YETI! ANYTHING BUT A YETI!
HOW DID HE BREAK THE SPELL?!
...BECAUSE THEIR FRIENDSHIP IS STRONGER THAN OUR MOVIES, YOU FOOL!
YOU CAN BE FRIENDS WITH A YETI?!
WAIT A SECOND--I'VE GOT AN IDEA. I KNOW EXACTLY HOW TO STOP THEM ONCE AND FOR ALL.
WE CAN'T LET THOSE YETIS GET TO SET! IF MORDECAI AND RIGBY ARE FREED, WE WILL GO BACK TO LIVING OUR DAYS IN DRAMATIC SLOW MOTION!
NO! NOT THAT, NEVER AGAIN!
OH NO! THEY HAVE A TANK!
IT DOESN'T MATTER, POPS. WE HAVE SOMETHING MUCH STRONGER. WE HAVE FRIENDSHIP.

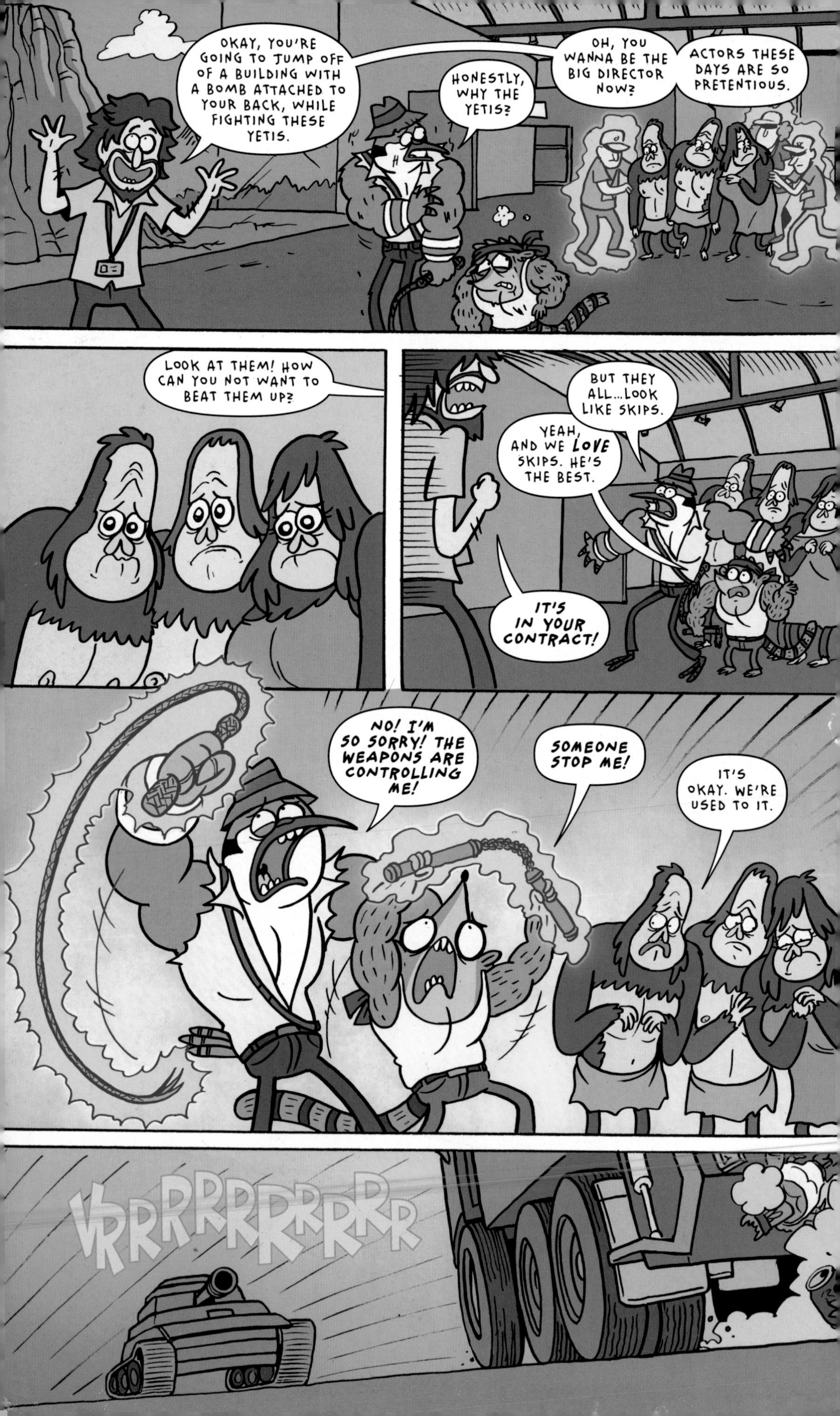
OKAY, YOU'RE GOING TO JUMP OFF OF A BUILDING WITH A BOMB ATTACHED TO YOUR BACK, WHILE FIGHTING THESE YETIS.
HONESTLY, WHY THE YETIS?
OH, YOU WANNA BE THE BIG DIRECTOR NOW?
ACTORS THESE DAYS ARE SO PRETENTIOUS.
LOOK AT THEM! HOW CAN YOU NOT WANT TO BEAT THEM UP?
BUT THEY ALL...LOOK LIKE SKIPS.
YEAH, AND WE LOVE SKIPS. HE'S THE BEST.
IT'S IN YOUR CONTRACT!
NO! I'M SO SORRY! THE WEAPONS ARE CONTROLLING ME!
SOMEONE STOP ME!
IT'S OKAY. WE'RE USED TO IT.
VRRRRRRRRRR

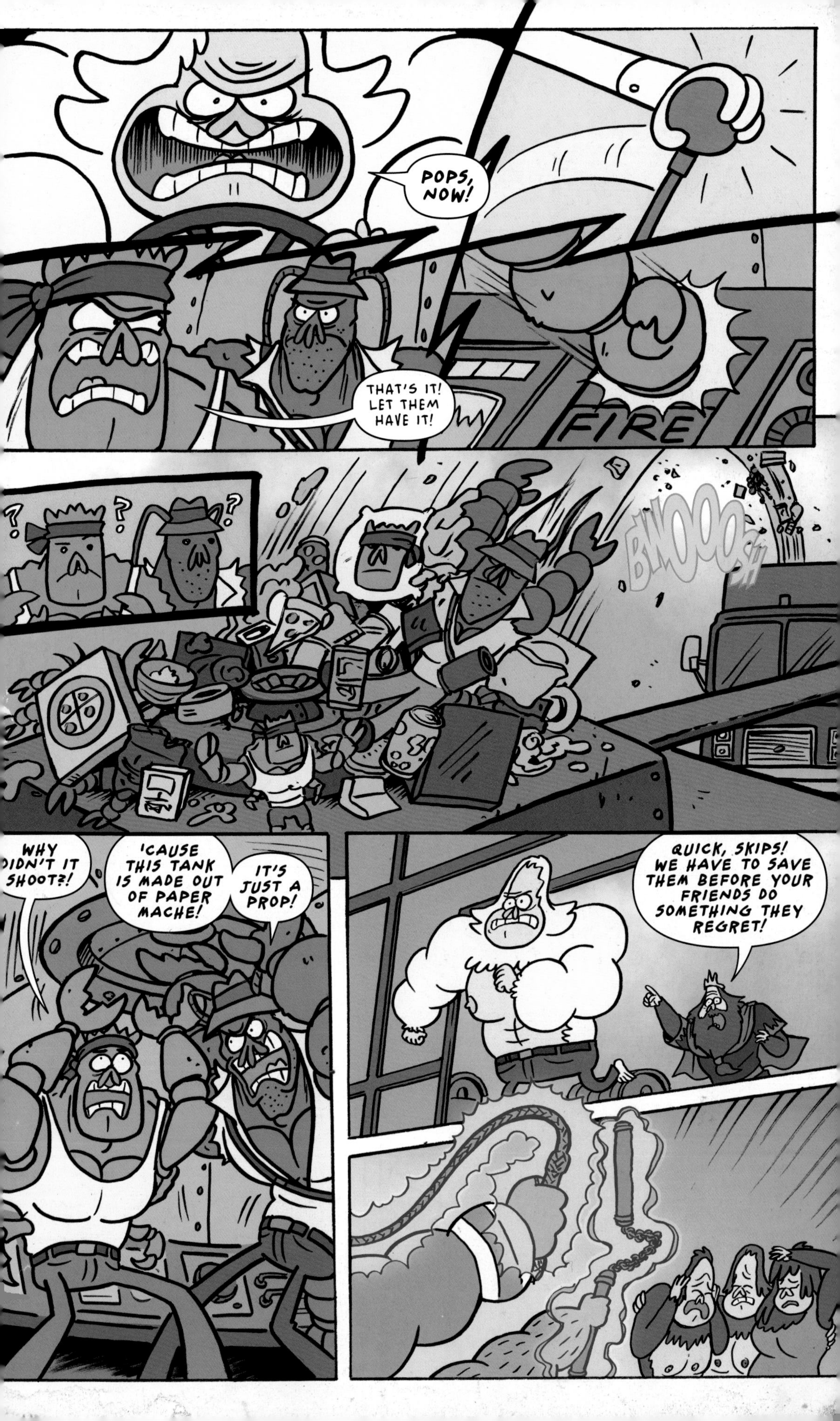
POPS, NOW!
THAT'S IT! LET THEM HAVE IT!
FIRE
BWOOOSH
WHY DIDN'T IT SHOOT?!
'CAUSE THIS TANK IS MADE OUT OF PAPER MACHE!
IT'S JUST A PROP!
QUICK, SKIPS! WE HAVE TO SAVE THEM BEFORE YOUR FRIENDS DO SOMETHING THEY REGRET!

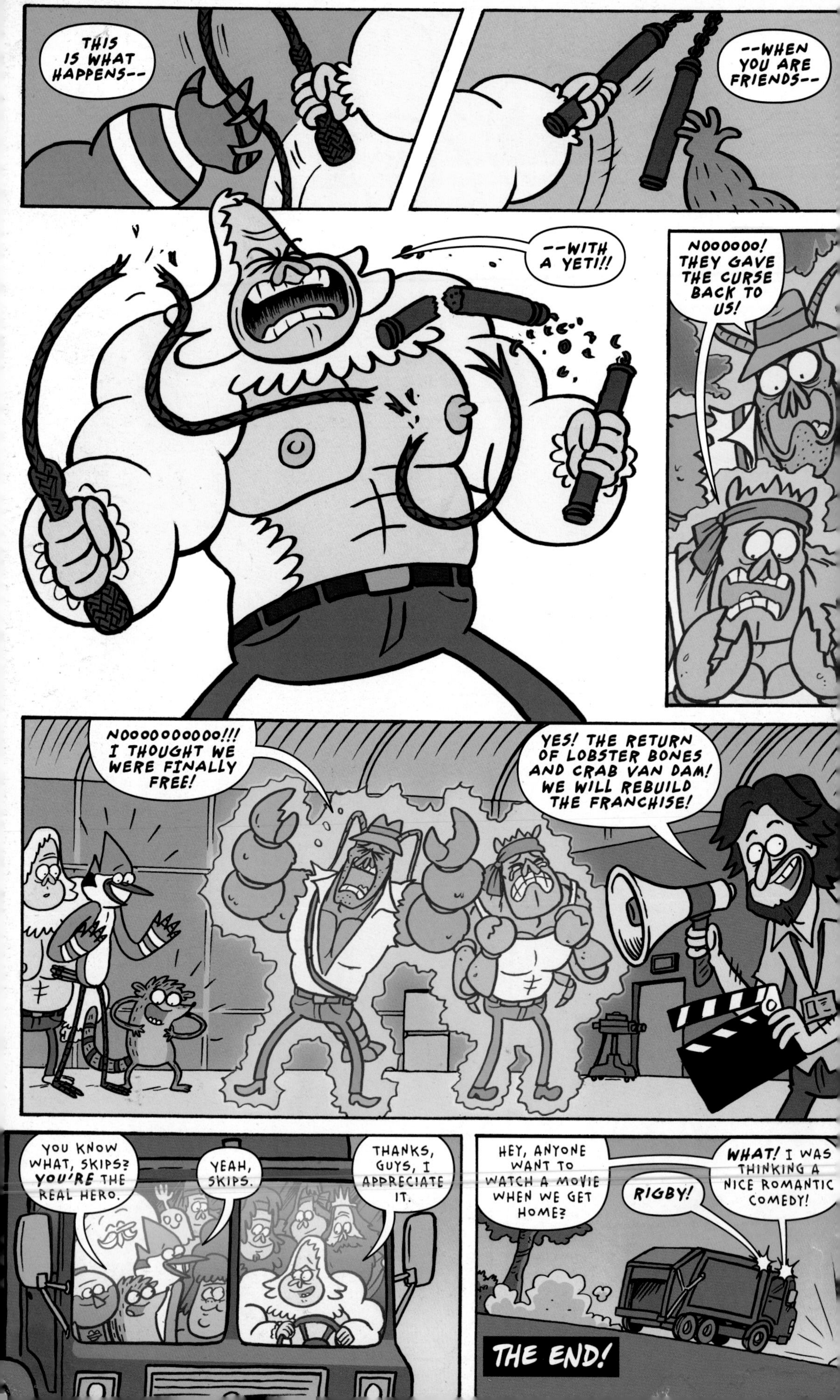
THIS IS WHAT HAPPENS--
--WHEN YOU ARE FRIENDS--
--WITH A YETI!!
NOOOOOO! THEY GAVE THE CURSE BACK TO US!
NOOOOOOOOOO!!! I THOUGHT WE WERE FINALLY FREE!
YES! THE RETURN OF LOBSTER BONES AND CRAB VAN DAM! WE WILL REBUILD THE FRANCHISE!
YOU KNOW WHAT, SKIPS? YOU'RE THE REAL HERO.
YEAH, SKIPS.
THANKS, GUYS, I APPRECIATE IT.
HEY, ANYONE WANT TO WATCH A MOVIE WHEN WE GET HOME?
RIGBY!
WHAT! I WAS THINKING A NICE ROMANTIC COMEDY!
THE END!

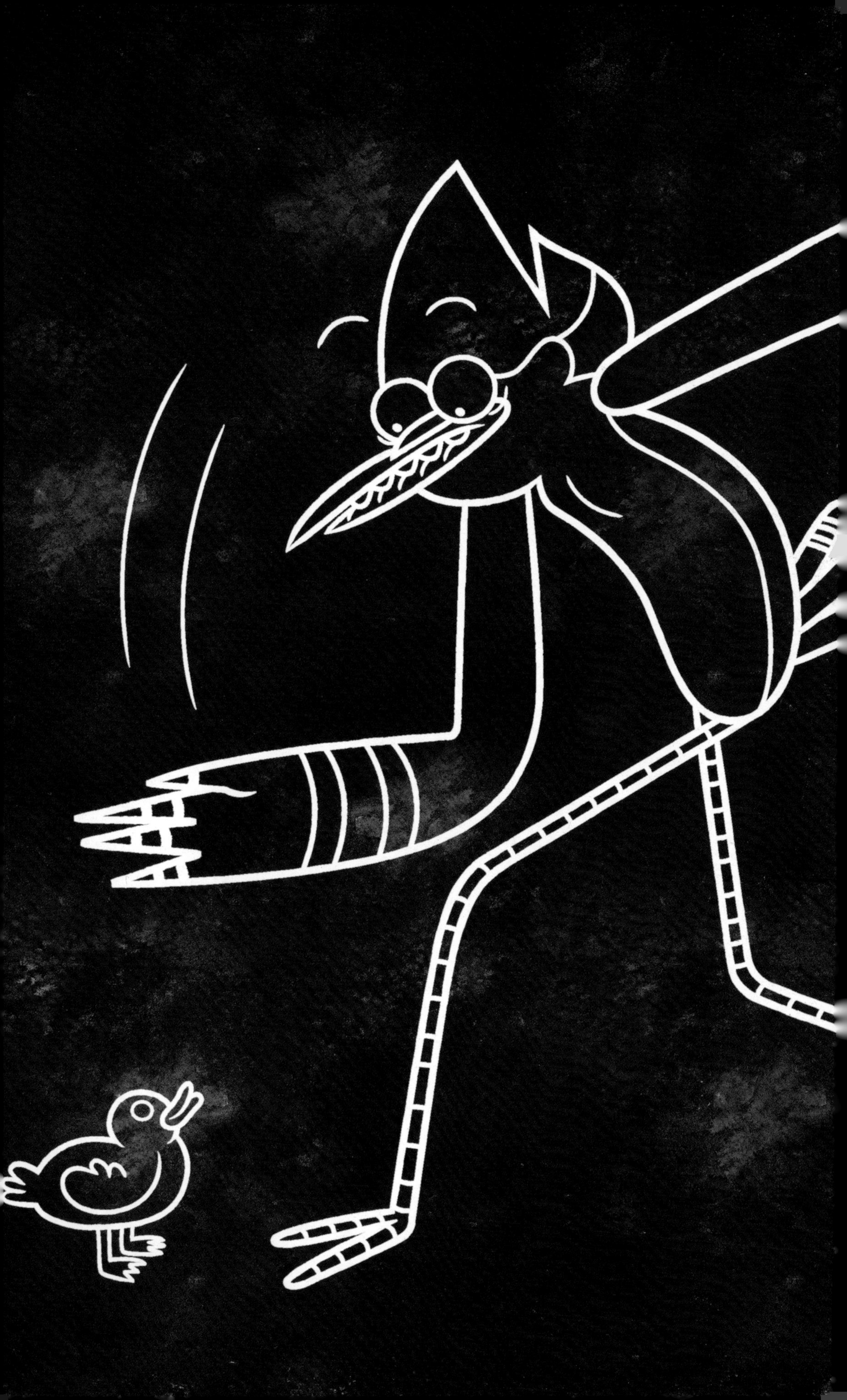

SHORT STORIES, BRO

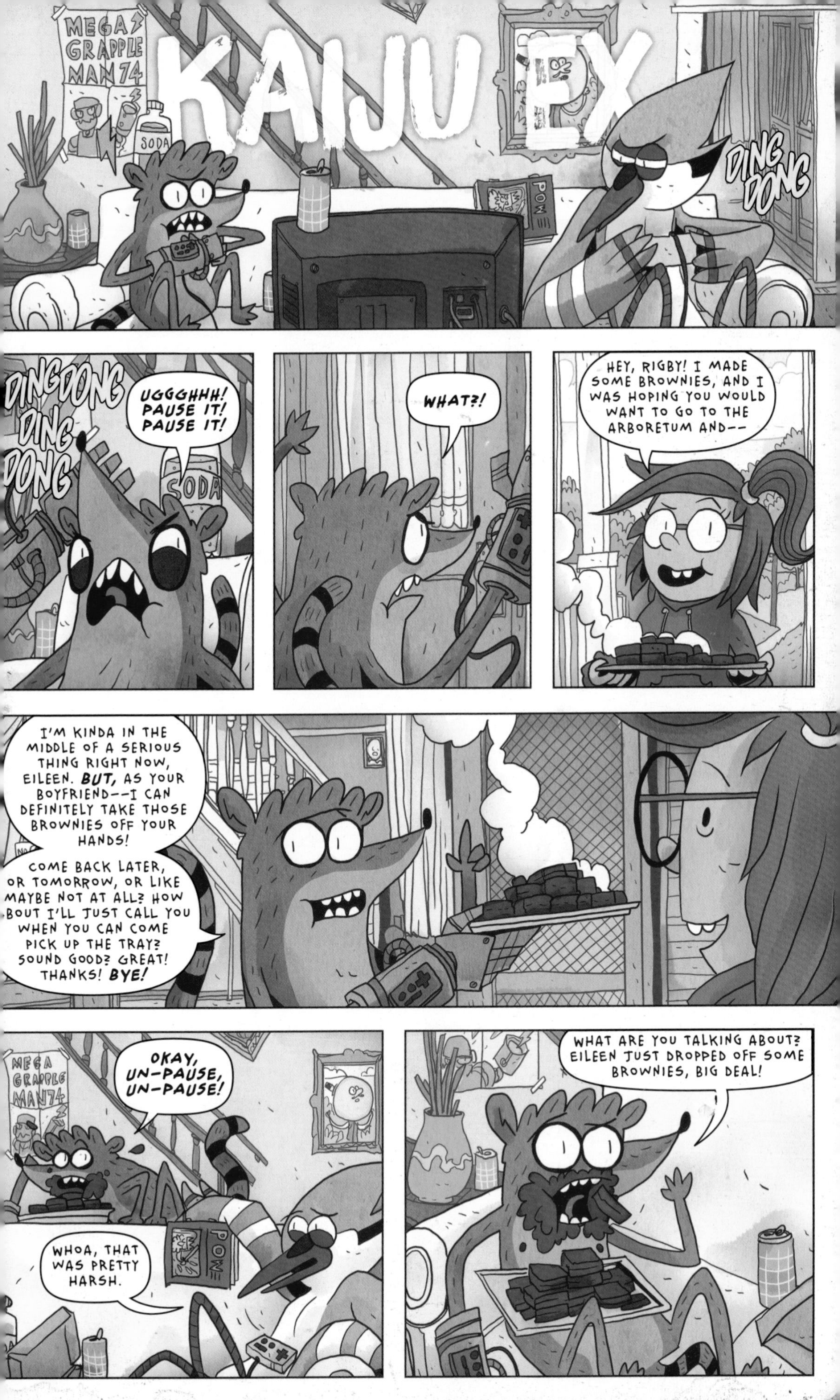
MEGA GRAPPLE MAN 74
SODA
KAIJU EX
POW
DING DONG
DING DONG DING DONG
UGGGHHH! PAUSE IT! PAUSE IT!
SODA
WHAT?!
HEY, RIGBY! I MADE SOME BROWNIES, AND I WAS HOPING YOU WOULD WANT TO GO TO THE ARBORETUM AND--
I'M KINDA IN THE MIDDLE OF A SERIOUS THING RIGHT NOW, EILEEN. BUT, AS YOUR BOYFRIEND--I CAN DEFINITELY TAKE THOSE BROWNIES OFF YOUR HANDS!
COME BACK LATER, OR TOMORROW, OR LIKE MAYBE NOT AT ALL? HOW BOUT I'LL JUST CALL YOU WHEN YOU CAN COME PICK UP THE TRAY? SOUND GOOD? GREAT! THANKS! BYE!
MEGA GRAPPLE MAN 74
OKAY, UN-PAUSE, UN-PAUSE!
WHOA, THAT WAS PRETTY HARSH.
POW
WHAT ARE YOU TALKING ABOUT? EILEEN JUST DROPPED OFF SOME BROWNIES, BIG DEAL!

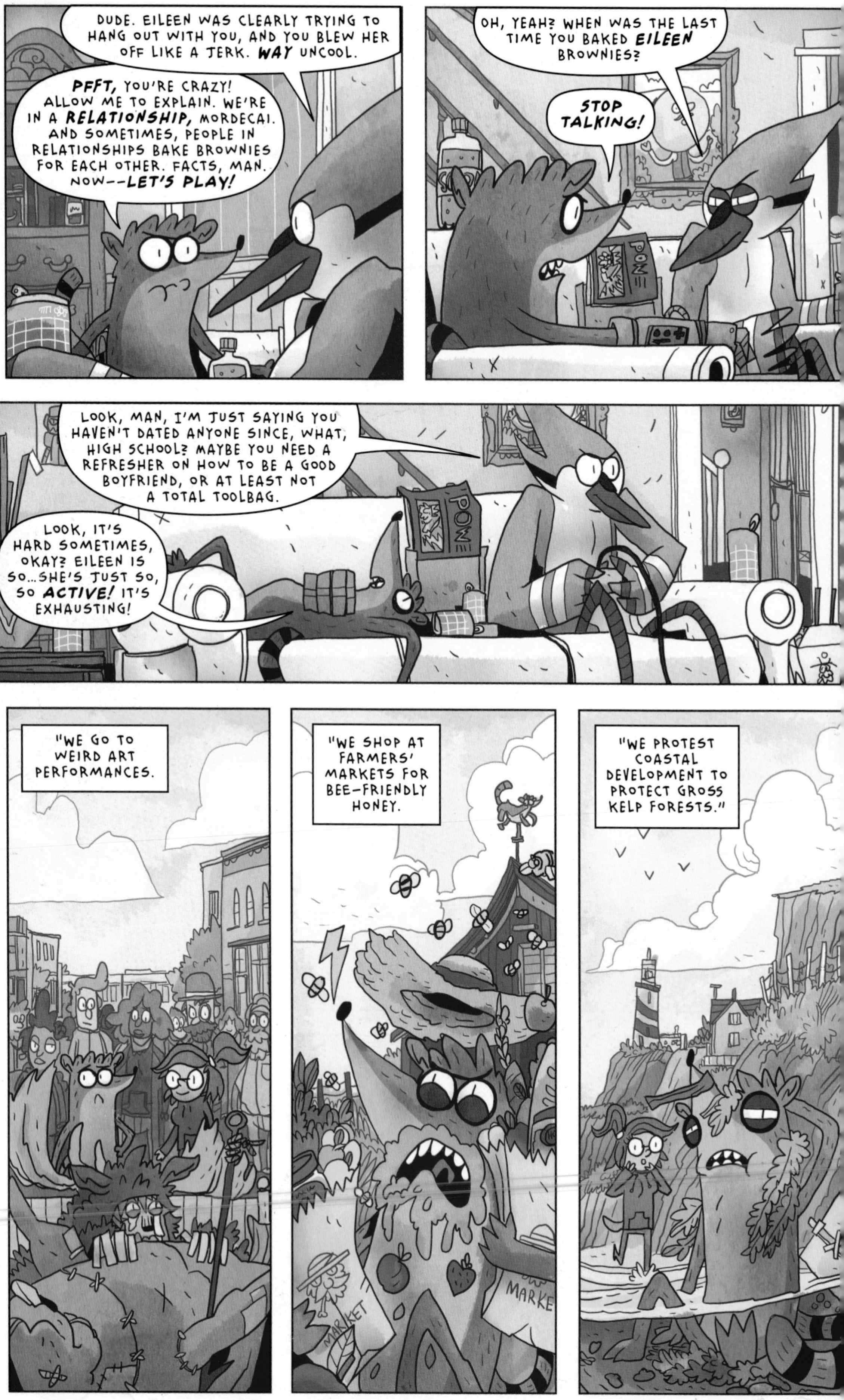
DUDE. EILEEN WAS CLEARLY TRYING TO HANG OUT WITH YOU, AND YOU BLEW HER OFF LIKE A JERK. **WAY** UNCOOL.
PFFT, YOU'RE CRAZY! ALLOW ME TO EXPLAIN. WE'RE IN A **RELATIONSHIP,** MORDECAI. AND SOMETIMES, PEOPLE IN RELATIONSHIPS BAKE BROWNIES FOR EACH OTHER. FACTS, MAN. NOW--**LET'S PLAY!**
OH, YEAH? WHEN WAS THE LAST TIME YOU BAKED **EILEEN** BROWNIES?
STOP TALKING!
LOOK, MAN, I'M JUST SAYING YOU HAVEN'T DATED ANYONE SINCE, WHAT, HIGH SCHOOL? MAYBE YOU NEED A REFRESHER ON HOW TO BE A GOOD BOYFRIEND, OR AT LEAST NOT A TOTAL TOOLBAG.
LOOK, IT'S HARD SOMETIMES, OKAY? EILEEN IS SO...SHE'S JUST SO, SO **ACTIVE!** IT'S EXHAUSTING!
"WE GO TO WEIRD ART PERFORMANCES.
"WE SHOP AT FARMERS' MARKETS FOR BEE-FRIENDLY HONEY.
"WE PROTEST COASTAL DEVELOPMENT TO PROTECT GROSS KELP FORESTS."

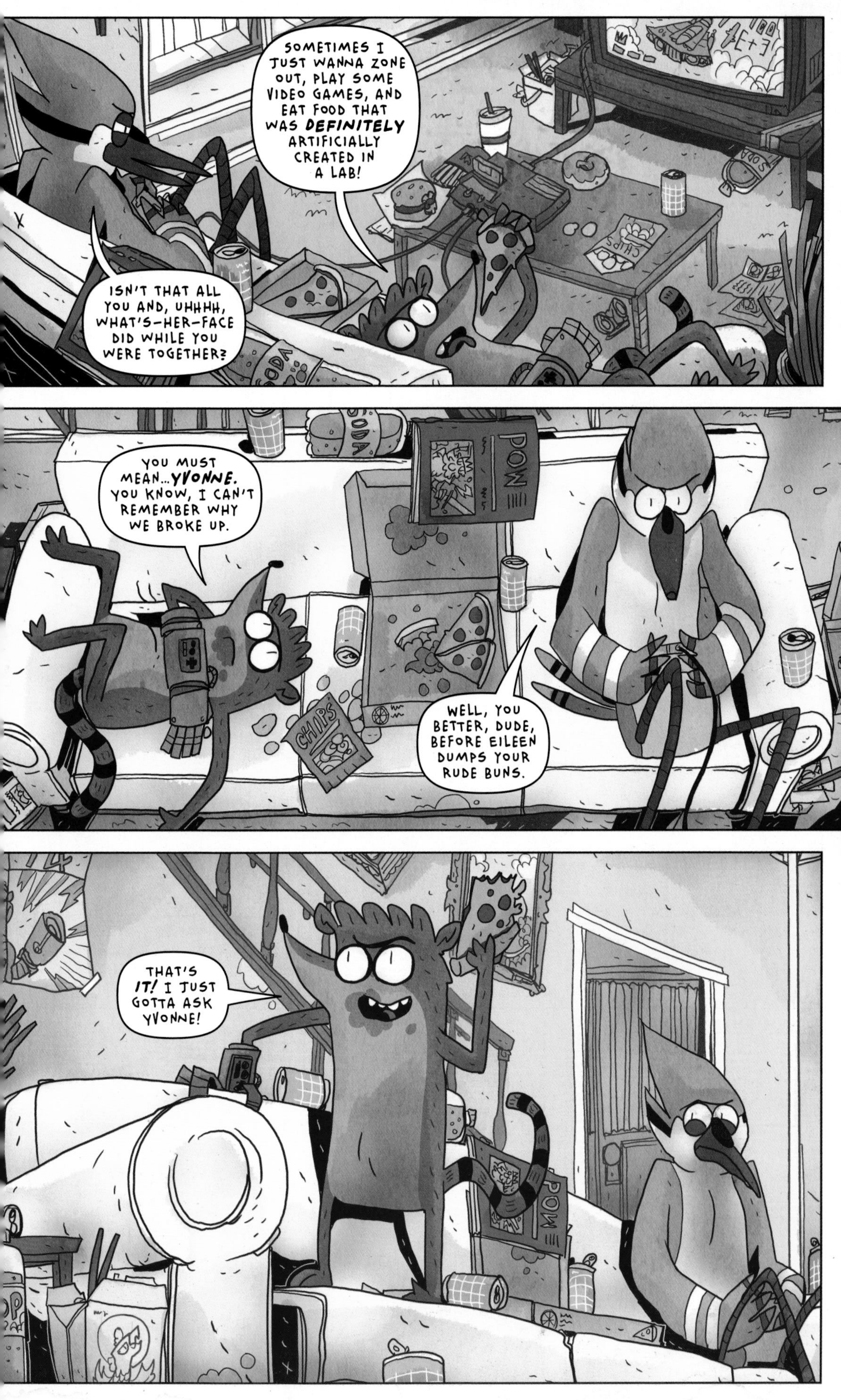
SOMETIMES I JUST WANNA ZONE OUT, PLAY SOME VIDEO GAMES, AND EAT FOOD THAT WAS DEFINITELY ARTIFICIALLY CREATED IN A LAB!
ISN'T THAT ALL YOU AND, UHHHH, WHAT'S-HER-FACE DID WHILE YOU WERE TOGETHER?
SODA
POW
SODA
YOU MUST MEAN...YVONNE. YOU KNOW, I CAN'T REMEMBER WHY WE BROKE UP.
WELL, YOU BETTER, DUDE, BEFORE EILEEN DUMPS YOUR RUDE BUNS.
CHIPS
THAT'S IT! I JUST GOTTA ASK YVONNE!
POW

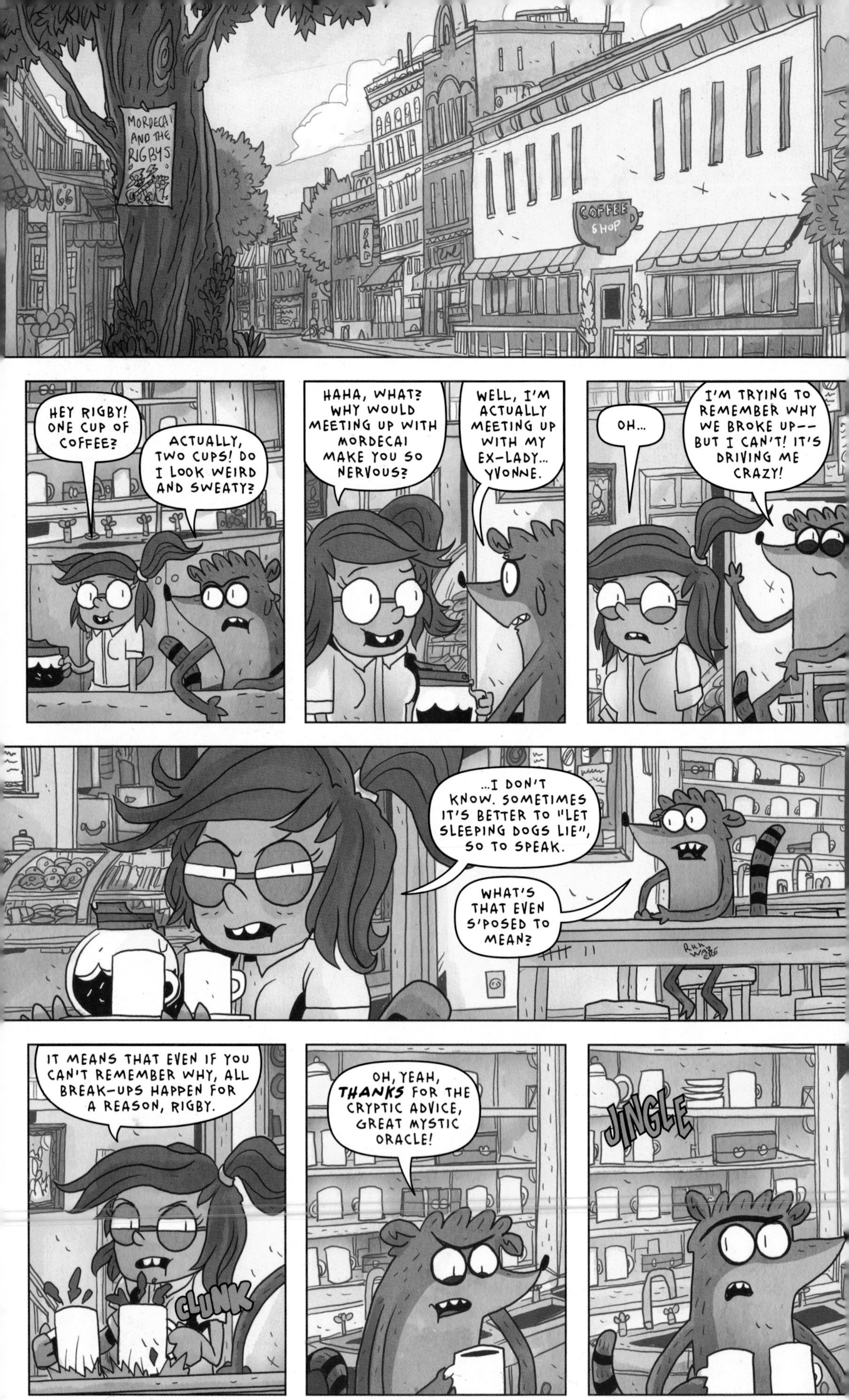
MORDECAI AND THE RIGBYS
66
COFFEE SHOP
HEY RIGBY! ONE CUP OF COFFEE?
ACTUALLY, TWO CUPS! DO I LOOK WEIRD AND SWEATY?
HAHA, WHAT? WHY WOULD MEETING UP WITH MORDECAI MAKE YOU SO NERVOUS?
WELL, I'M ACTUALLY MEETING UP WITH MY EX-LADY... YVONNE.
OH...
I'M TRYING TO REMEMBER WHY WE BROKE UP-- BUT I CAN'T! IT'S DRIVING ME CRAZY!
...I DON'T KNOW. SOMETIMES IT'S BETTER TO "LET SLEEPING DOGS LIE", SO TO SPEAK.
WHAT'S THAT EVEN S'POSED TO MEAN?
IT MEANS THAT EVEN IF YOU CAN'T REMEMBER WHY, ALL BREAK-UPS HAPPEN FOR A REASON, RIGBY.
CLUNK
OH, YEAH, ***THANKS*** FOR THE CRYPTIC ADVICE, GREAT MYSTIC ORACLE!
JINGLE

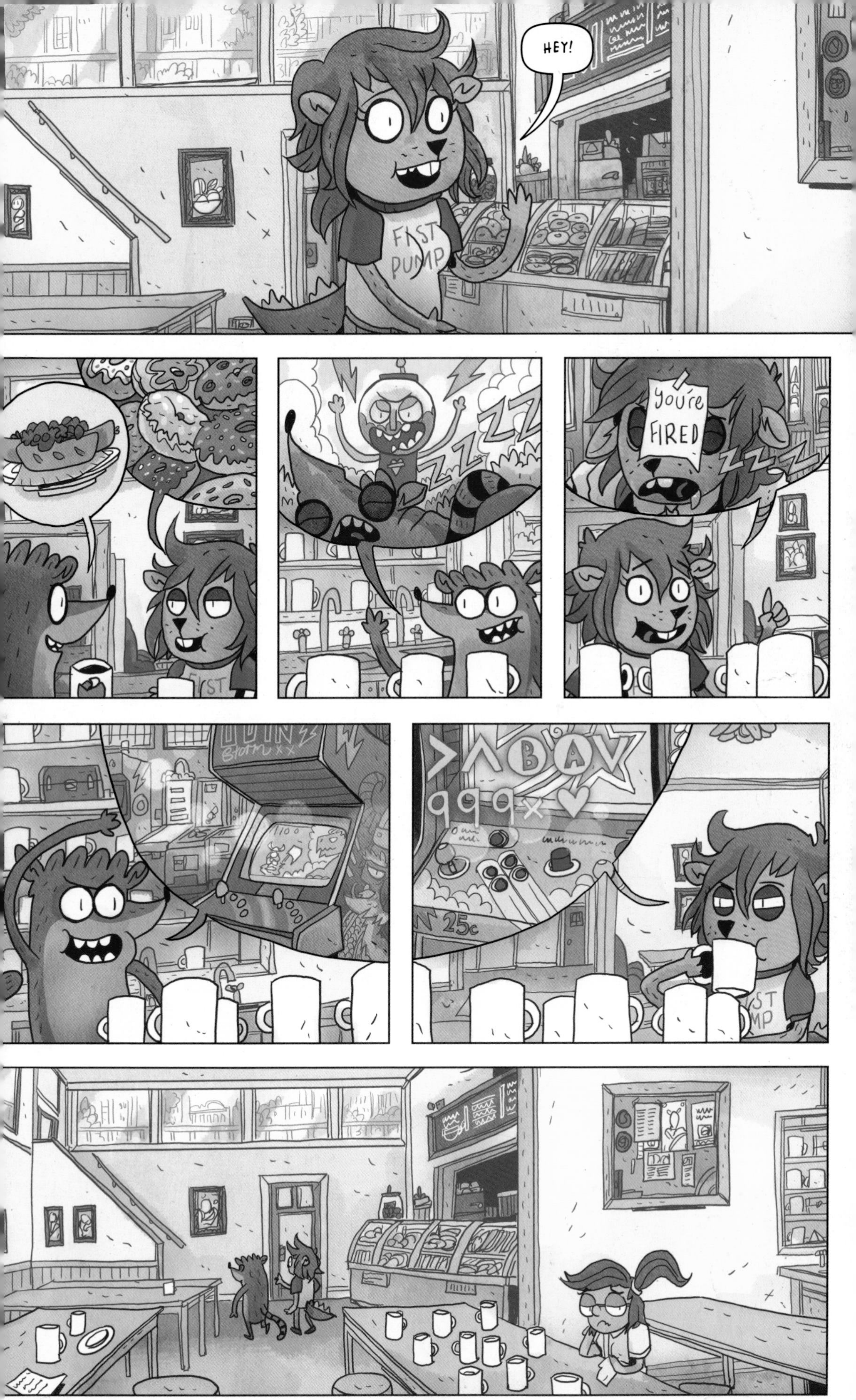
HEY!
FIST PUMP
YOU'RE FIRED
25¢

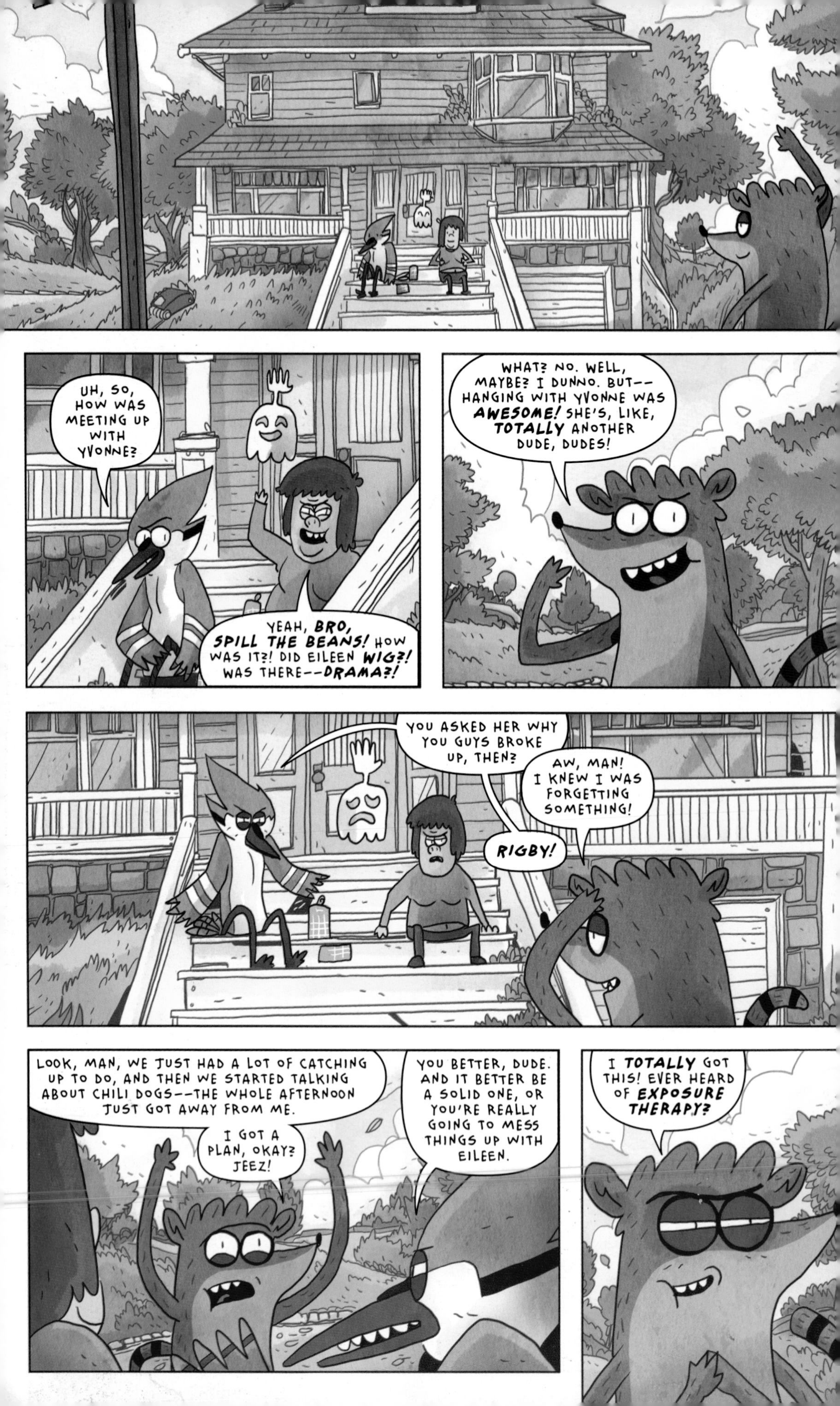
UH, SO, HOW WAS MEETING UP WITH YVONNE?
YEAH, BRO, SPILL THE BEANS! HOW WAS IT?! DID EILEEN WIG?! WAS THERE--DRAMA?!
WHAT? NO. WELL, MAYBE? I DUNNO. BUT-- HANGING WITH YVONNE WAS AWESOME! SHE'S, LIKE, TOTALLY ANOTHER DUDE, DUDES!
YOU ASKED HER WHY YOU GUYS BROKE UP, THEN?
AW, MAN! I KNEW I WAS FORGETTING SOMETHING!
RIGBY!
LOOK, MAN, WE JUST HAD A LOT OF CATCHING UP TO DO, AND THEN WE STARTED TALKING ABOUT CHILI DOGS--THE WHOLE AFTERNOON JUST GOT AWAY FROM ME.
I GOT A PLAN, OKAY? JEEZ!
YOU BETTER, DUDE. AND IT BETTER BE A SOLID ONE, OR YOU'RE REALLY GOING TO MESS THINGS UP WITH EILEEN.
I TOTALLY GOT THIS! EVER HEARD OF EXPOSURE THERAPY?

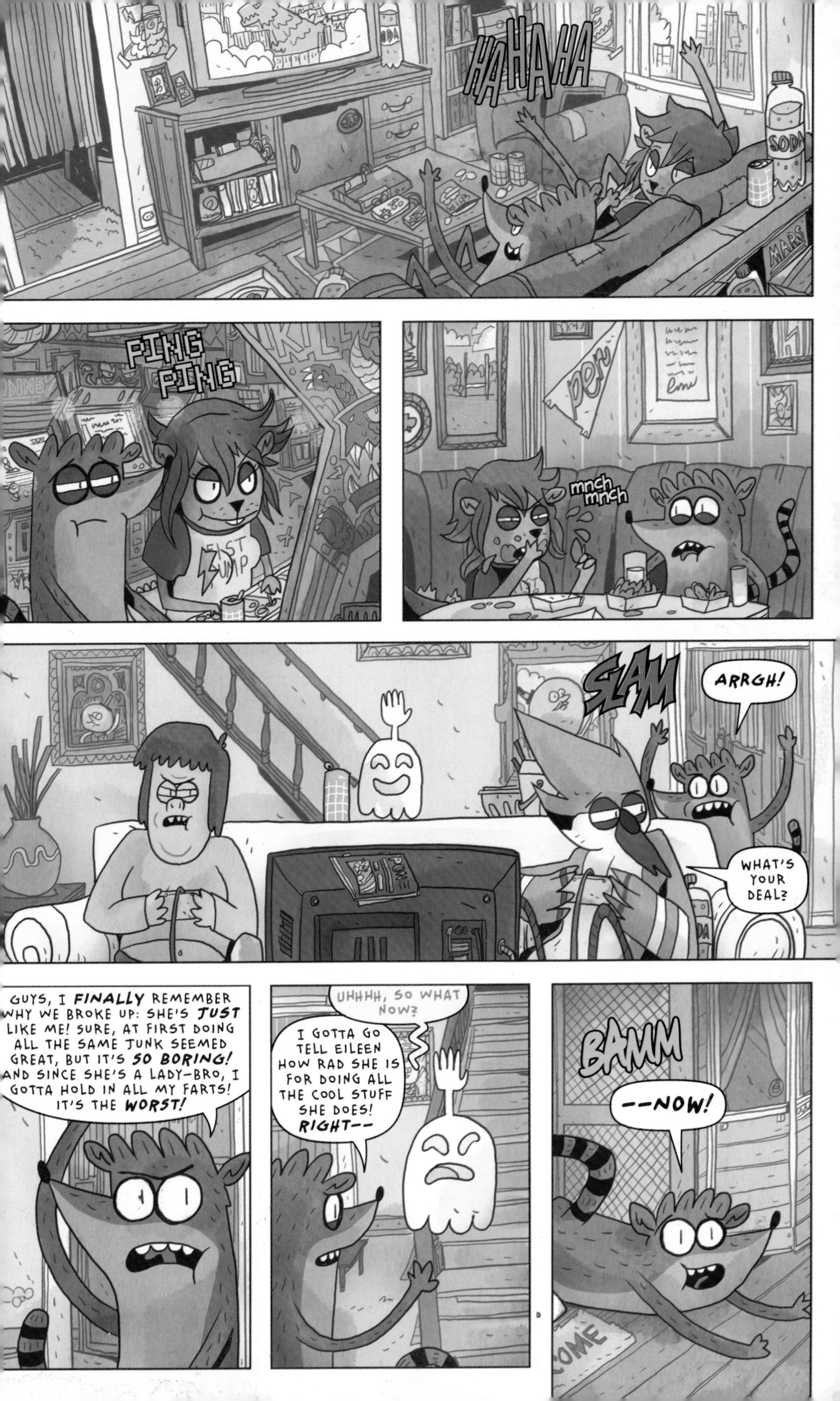
HAHAHAHA
SODA
MARS
PING PING
FIST PUMP
per
mnch mnch
SLAM
ARRGH!
POW
WHAT'S YOUR DEAL?
GUYS, I FINALLY REMEMBER WHY WE BROKE UP: SHE'S JUST LIKE ME! SURE, AT FIRST DOING ALL THE SAME JUNK SEEMED GREAT, BUT IT'S SO BORING! AND SINCE SHE'S A LADY-BRO, I GOTTA HOLD IN ALL MY FARTS! IT'S THE WORST!
UHHHH, SO WHAT NOW?
I GOTTA GO TELL EILEEN HOW RAD SHE IS FOR DOING ALL THE COOL STUFF SHE DOES! RIGHT--
BAMM
--NOW!

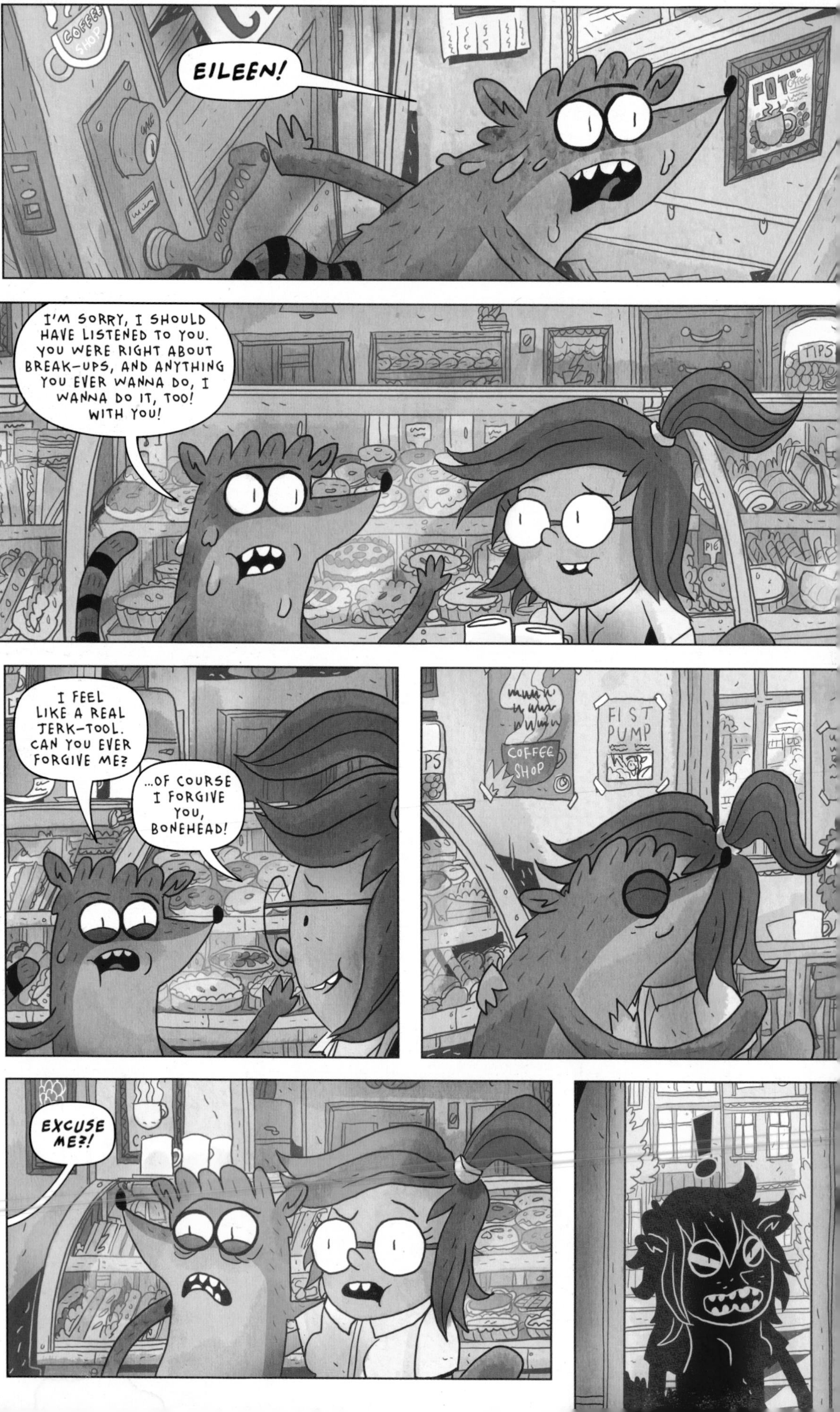
COFFEE SHOP
EILEEN!
I'M SORRY, I SHOULD HAVE LISTENED TO YOU. YOU WERE RIGHT ABOUT BREAK-UPS, AND ANYTHING YOU EVER WANNA DO, I WANNA DO IT, TOO! WITH YOU!
TIPS
PIE
I FEEL LIKE A REAL JERK-TOOL. CAN YOU EVER FORGIVE ME?
...OF COURSE I FORGIVE YOU, BONEHEAD!
COFFEE SHOP
FIST PUMP
EXCUSE ME?!
!

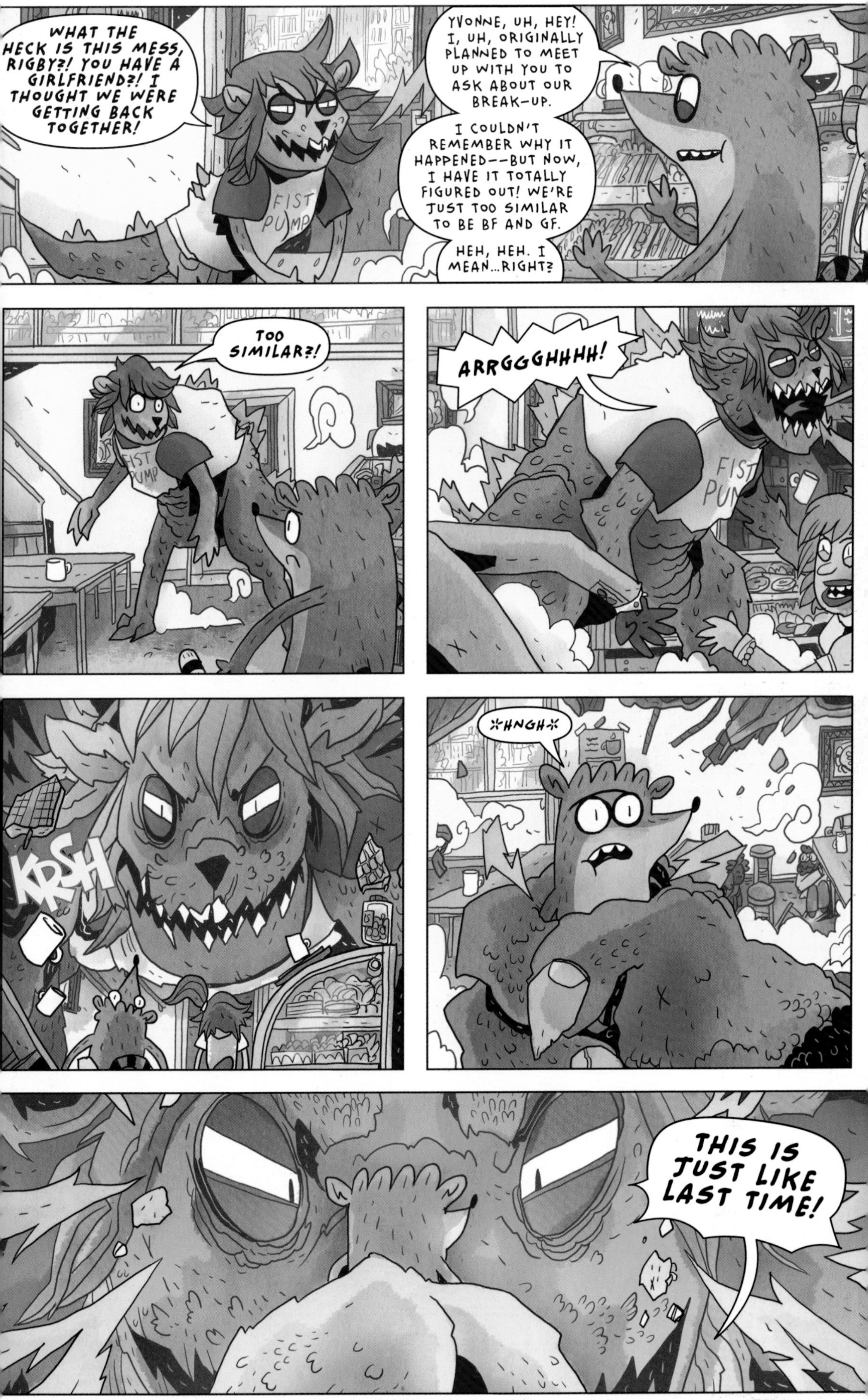
WHAT THE HECK IS THIS MESS, RIGBY?! YOU HAVE A GIRLFRIEND?! I THOUGHT WE WERE GETTING BACK TOGETHER!
YVONNE, UH, HEY! I, UH, ORIGINALLY PLANNED TO MEET UP WITH YOU TO ASK ABOUT OUR BREAK-UP.
I COULDN'T REMEMBER WHY IT HAPPENED--BUT NOW, I HAVE IT TOTALLY FIGURED OUT! WE'RE JUST TOO SIMILAR TO BE BF AND GF.
HEH, HEH. I MEAN...RIGHT?
FIST PUMP
TOO SIMILAR?!
ARRGGGHHHH!
KRSH
HNGH
THIS IS JUST LIKE LAST TIME!

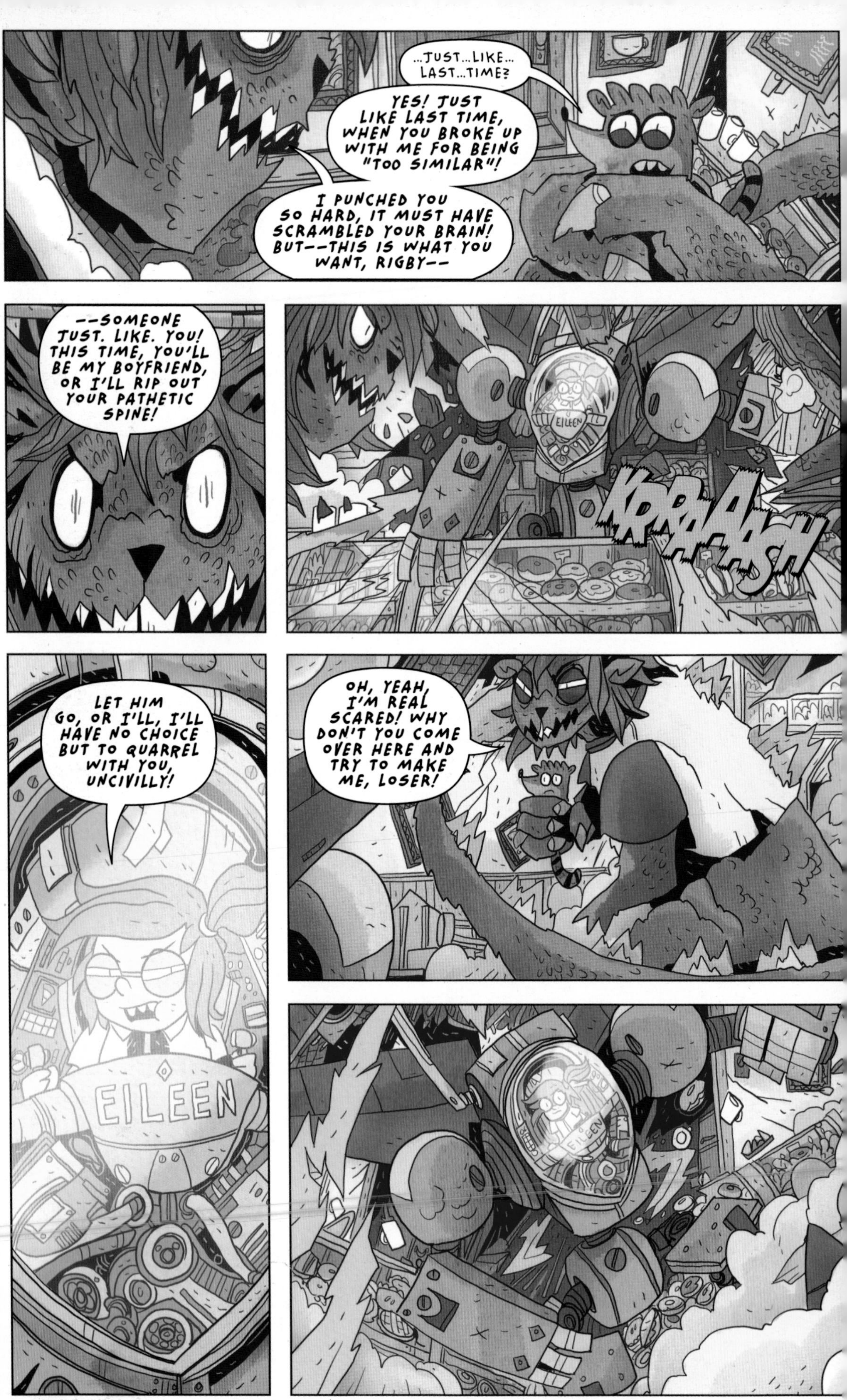

...JUST...LIKE... LAST...TIME?
YES! JUST LIKE LAST TIME, WHEN YOU BROKE UP WITH ME FOR BEING "TOO SIMILAR"!
I PUNCHED YOU SO HARD, IT MUST HAVE SCRAMBLED YOUR BRAIN! BUT--THIS IS WHAT YOU WANT, RIGBY--
--SOMEONE JUST. LIKE. YOU! THIS TIME, YOU'LL BE MY BOYFRIEND, OR I'LL RIP OUT YOUR PATHETIC SPINE!
EILEEN
KRAAASH
LET HIM GO, OR I'LL, I'LL HAVE NO CHOICE BUT TO QUARREL WITH YOU, UNCIVILLY!
EILEEN
OH, YEAH, I'M REAL SCARED! WHY DON'T YOU COME OVER HERE AND TRY TO MAKE ME, LOSER!
EILEEN

WHAM

AAAAAAAAAA!

COFFEE SHOP

ST MP

RIGBY! ARE YOU OKA--

YOU WANNA BUST UP MY RELATIONSHIP, HUH!? I'LL BUST UP YOUR FACE!

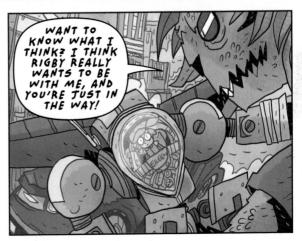

WANT TO KNOW WHAT I THINK? I THINK RIGBY REALLY WANTS TO BE WITH ME, AND YOU'RE JUST IN THE WAY!

WHA--WHAT? NO WAY! IT'S--IT'S NOT LIKE THAT AT ALL!

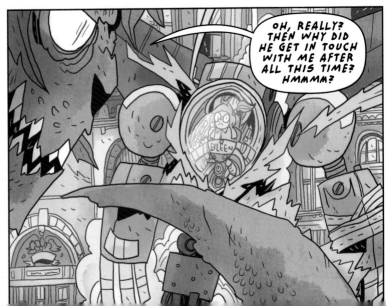

OH, REALLY? THEN WHY DID HE GET IN TOUCH WITH ME AFTER ALL THIS TIME? HMMMM?

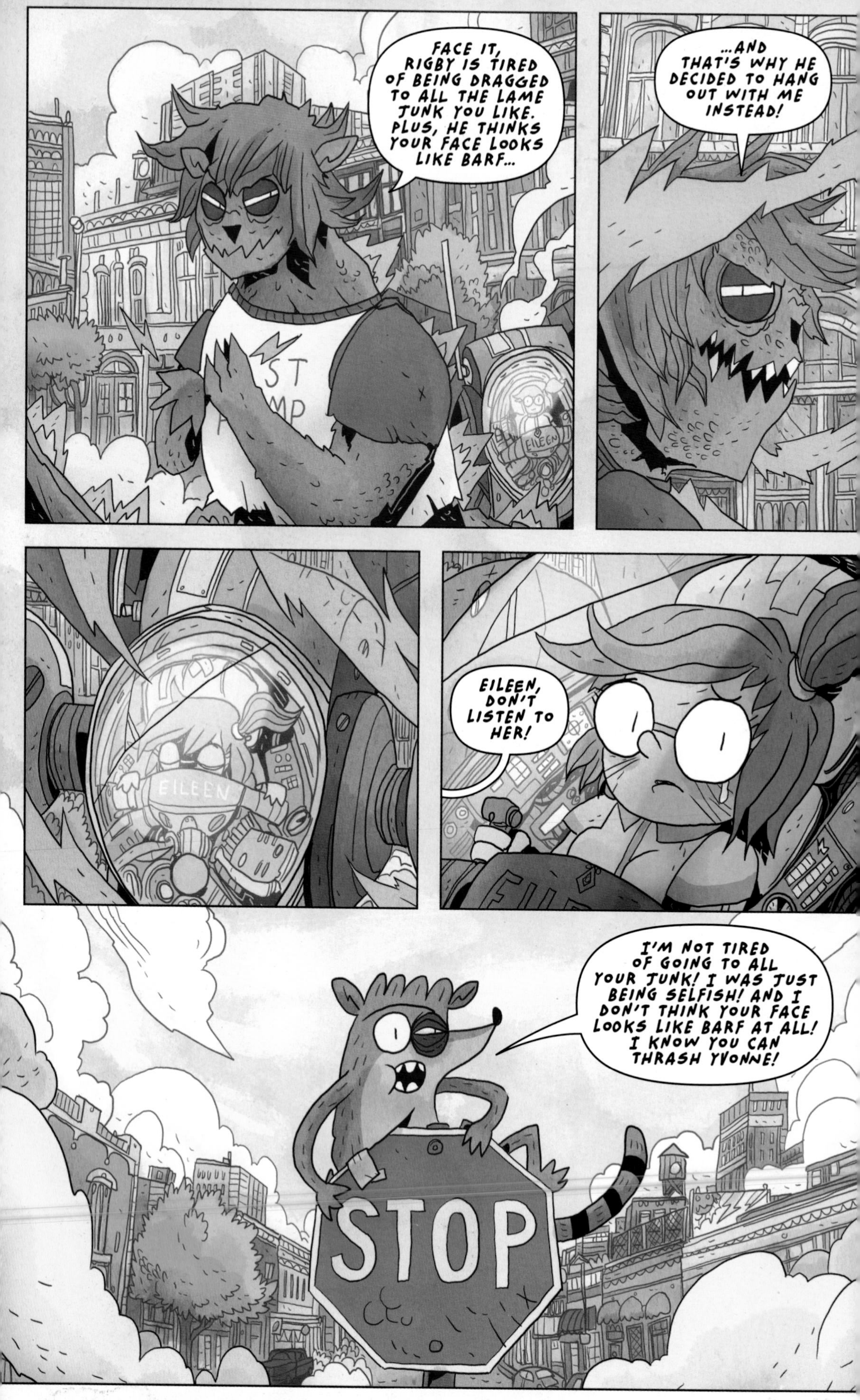
FACE IT, RIGBY IS TIRED OF BEING DRAGGED TO ALL THE LAME JUNK YOU LIKE. PLUS, HE THINKS YOUR FACE LOOKS LIKE BARF...
EILEEN
...AND THAT'S WHY HE DECIDED TO HANG OUT WITH ME INSTEAD!
EILEEN
EILEEN, DON'T LISTEN TO HER!
I'M NOT TIRED OF GOING TO ALL YOUR JUNK! I WAS JUST BEING SELFISH! AND I DON'T THINK YOUR FACE LOOKS LIKE BARF AT ALL! I KNOW YOU CAN THRASH YVONNE!
STOP

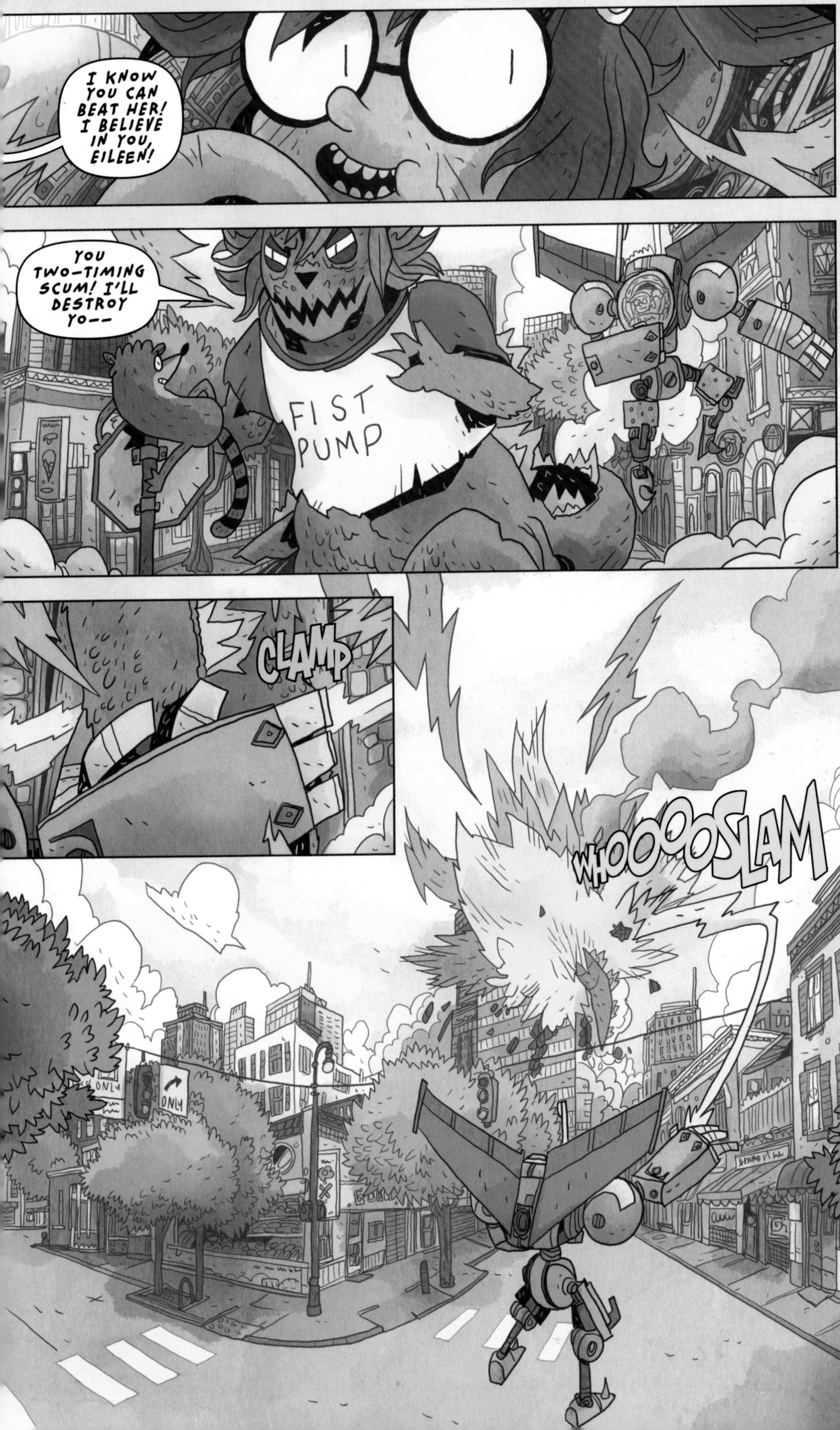
I KNOW YOU CAN BEAT HER! I BELIEVE IN YOU, EILEEN!
YOU TWO-TIMING SCUM! I'LL DESTROY YO--
FIST PUMP
CLAMP
WHOOOOOSLAM
ONLY

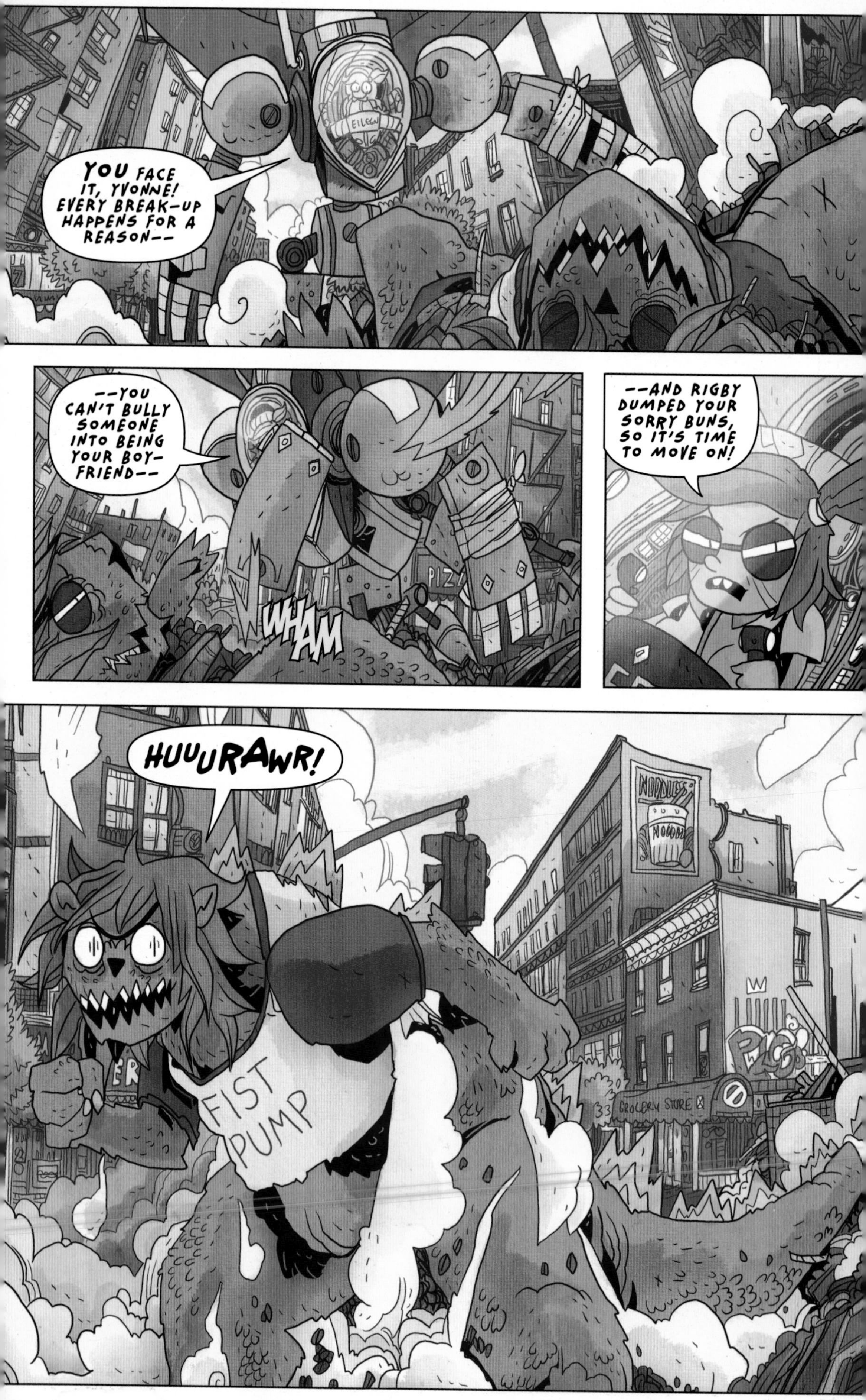
EILEEN
YOU FACE IT, YVONNE! EVERY BREAK-UP HAPPENS FOR A REASON--
--YOU CAN'T BULLY SOMEONE INTO BEING YOUR BOY-FRIEND--
PIZZ
WHAM
--AND RIGBY DUMPED YOUR SORRY BUNS, SO IT'S TIME TO MOVE ON!
HUUURAWR!
NOODLES
FIST PUMP
GROCERY STORE
33

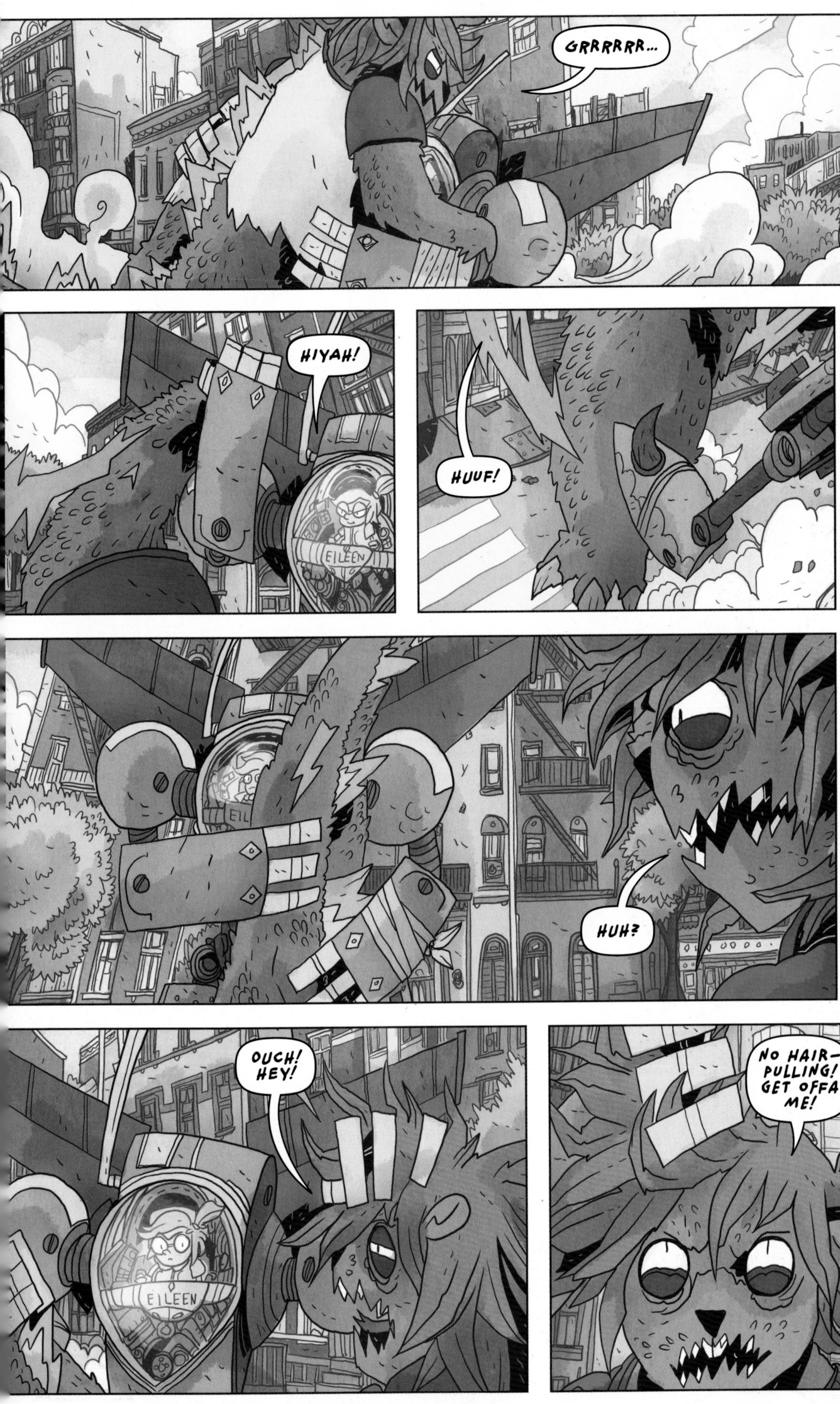
GRRRRRR...
HIYAH!
HUUF!
HUH?
OUCH! HEY!
NO HAIR-PULLING! GET OFFA ME!

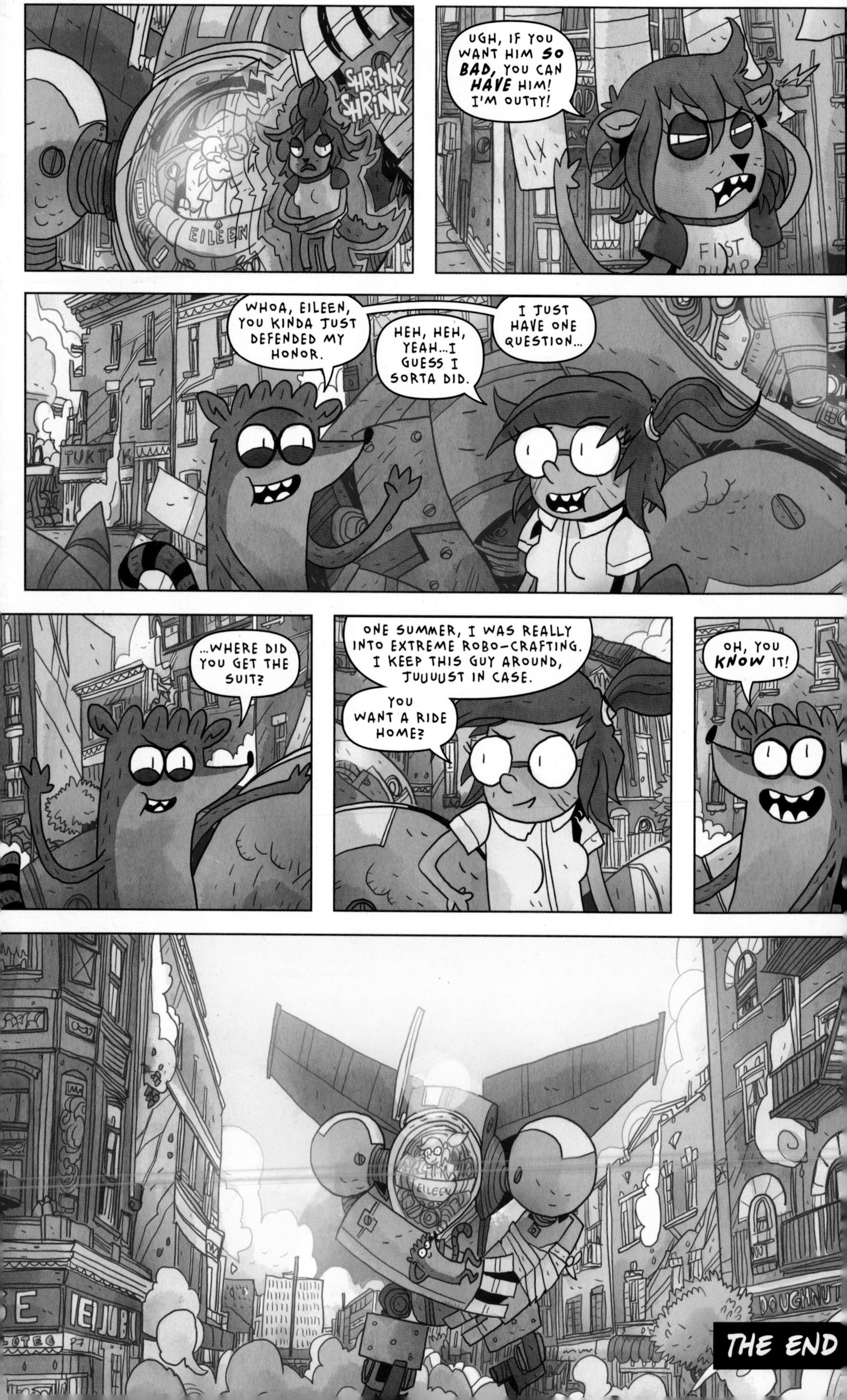
SHRINK SHRINK
EILEEN
UGH, IF YOU WANT HIM SO BAD, YOU CAN HAVE HIM! I'M OUTTY!
FIST PUMP
WHOA, EILEEN, YOU KINDA JUST DEFENDED MY HONOR.
HEH, HEH, YEAH...I GUESS I SORTA DID.
I JUST HAVE ONE QUESTION...
TUKTUK
...WHERE DID YOU GET THE SUIT?
ONE SUMMER, I WAS REALLY INTO EXTREME ROBO-CRAFTING. I KEEP THIS GUY AROUND, JUUUUST IN CASE.
YOU WANT A RIDE HOME?
OH, YOU KNOW IT!
EILEEN
DOUGHNUT
THE END

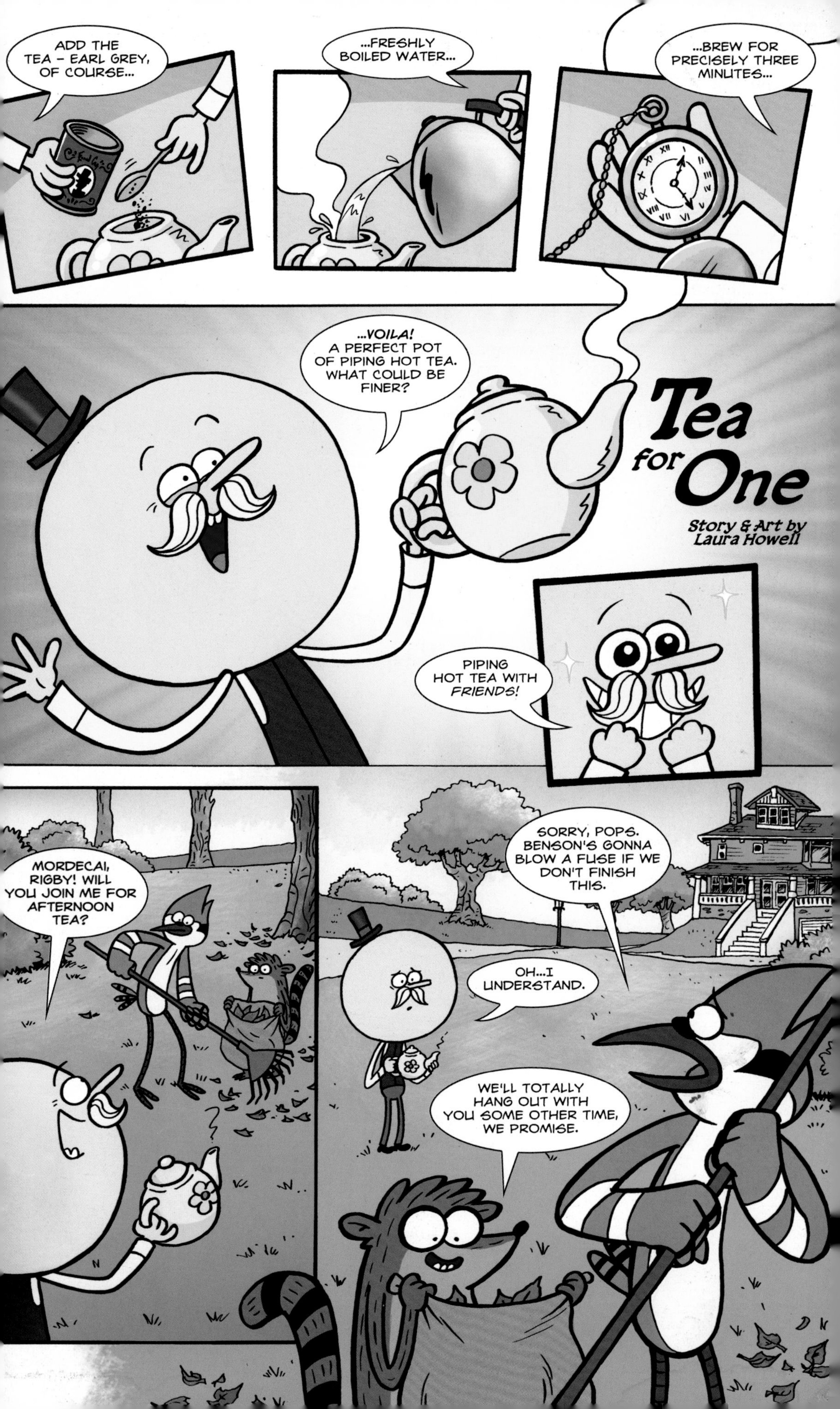

ADD THE TEA – EARL GREY, OF COURSE...
...FRESHLY BOILED WATER...
...BREW FOR PRECISELY THREE MINUTES...
...VOILA! A PERFECT POT OF PIPING HOT TEA. WHAT COULD BE FINER?
Tea for One
Story & Art by Laura Howell
PIPING HOT TEA WITH FRIENDS!
MORDECAI, RIGBY! WILL YOU JOIN ME FOR AFTERNOON TEA?
SORRY, POPS. BENSON'S GONNA BLOW A FUSE IF WE DON'T FINISH THIS.
OH...I UNDERSTAND.
WE'LL TOTALLY HANG OUT WITH YOU SOME OTHER TIME, WE PROMISE.

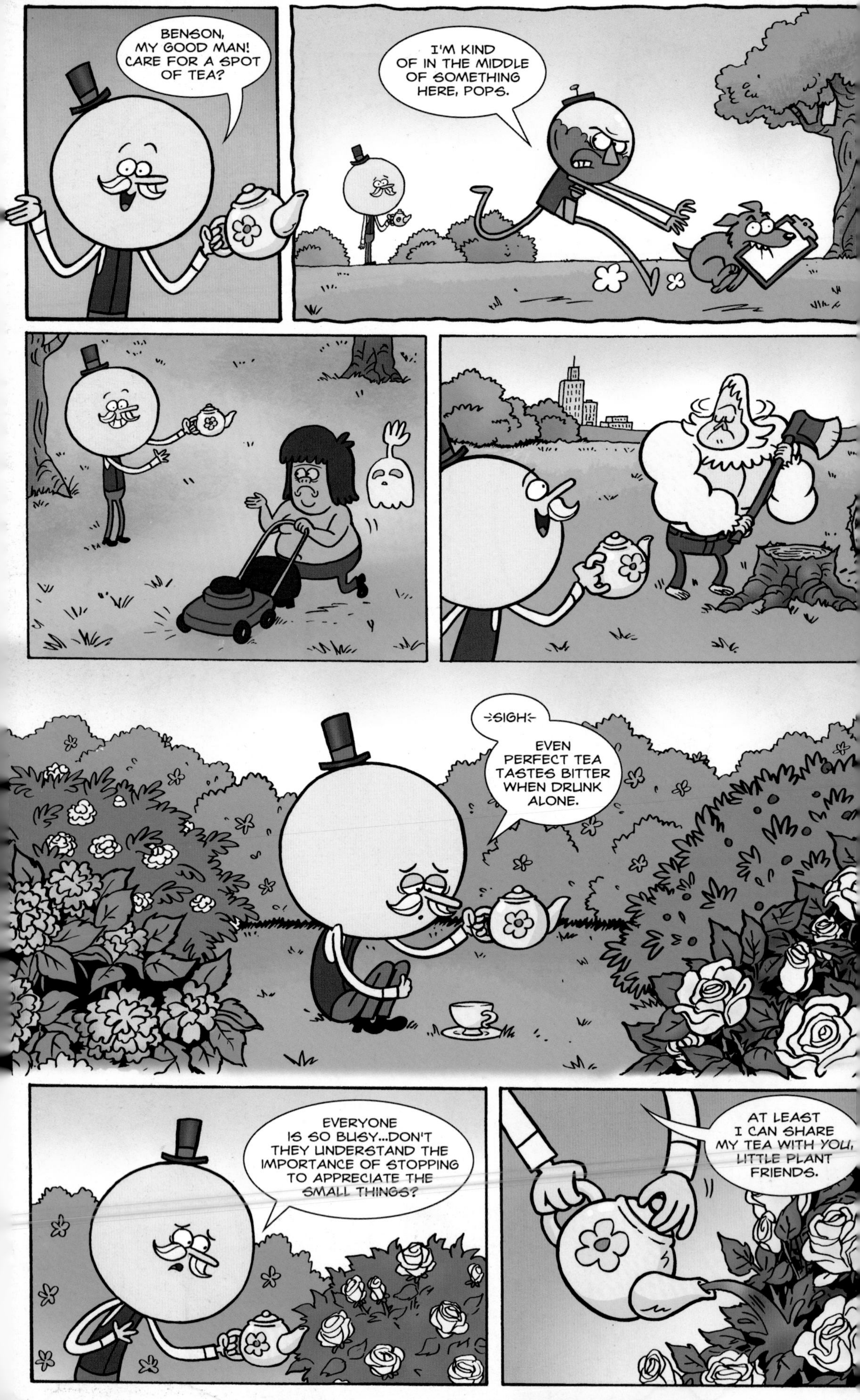
BENSON, MY GOOD MAN! CARE FOR A SPOT OF TEA?
I'M KIND OF IN THE MIDDLE OF SOMETHING HERE, POPS.
SIGH
EVEN PERFECT TEA TASTES BITTER WHEN DRUNK ALONE.
EVERYONE IS SO BUSY...DON'T THEY UNDERSTAND THE IMPORTANCE OF STOPPING TO APPRECIATE THE SMALL THINGS?
AT LEAST I CAN SHARE MY TEA WITH YOU, LITTLE PLANT FRIENDS.

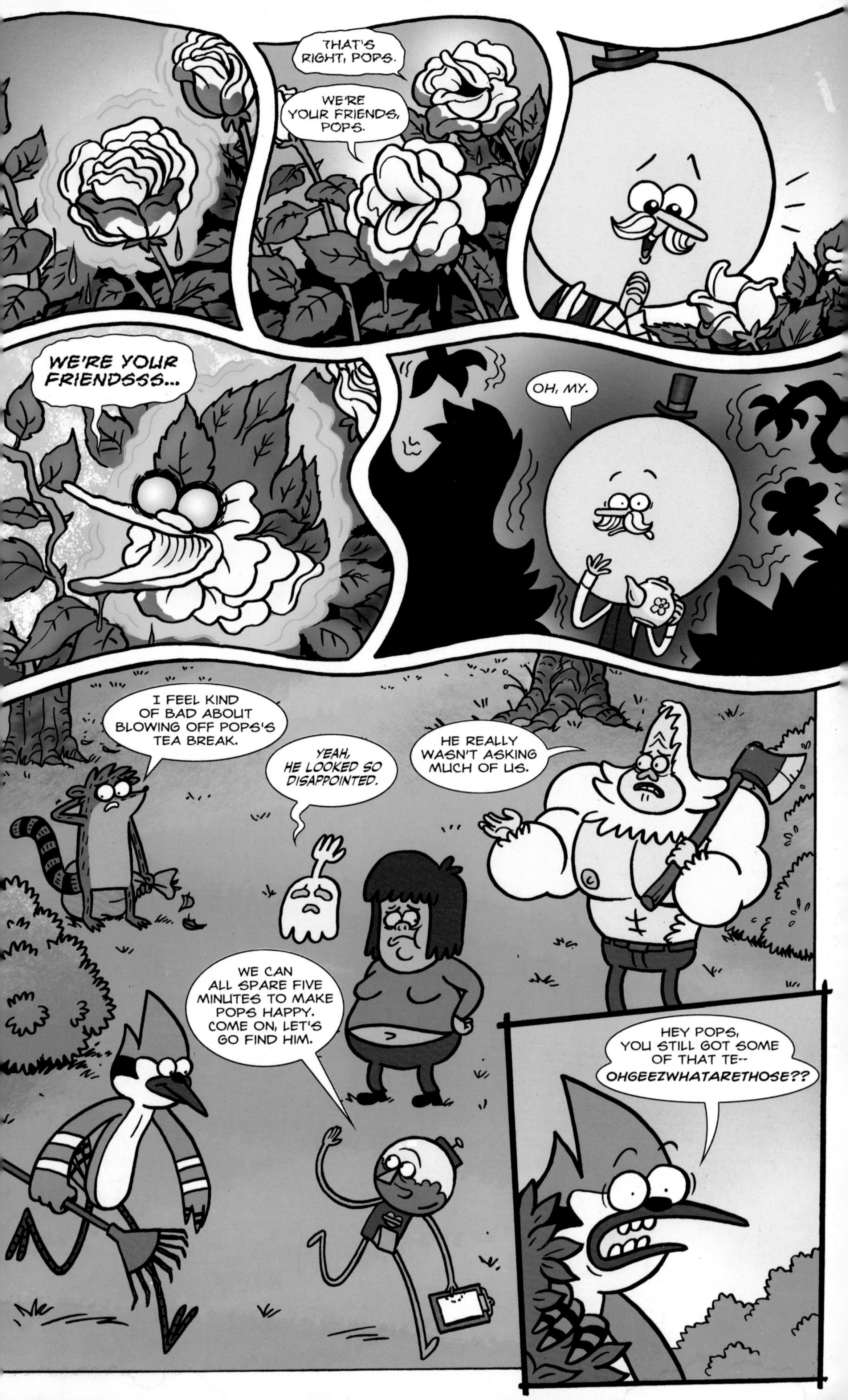

THAT'S RIGHT, POPS.
WE'RE YOUR FRIENDS, POPS.
WE'RE YOUR FRIENDSSS...
OH, MY.
I FEEL KIND OF BAD ABOUT BLOWING OFF POPS'S TEA BREAK.
YEAH, HE LOOKED SO DISAPPOINTED.
HE REALLY WASN'T ASKING MUCH OF US.
WE CAN ALL SPARE FIVE MINUTES TO MAKE POPS HAPPY. COME ON, LET'S GO FIND HIM.
HEY POPS, YOU STILL GOT SOME OF THAT TE-- OHGEEZWHATARETHOSE??

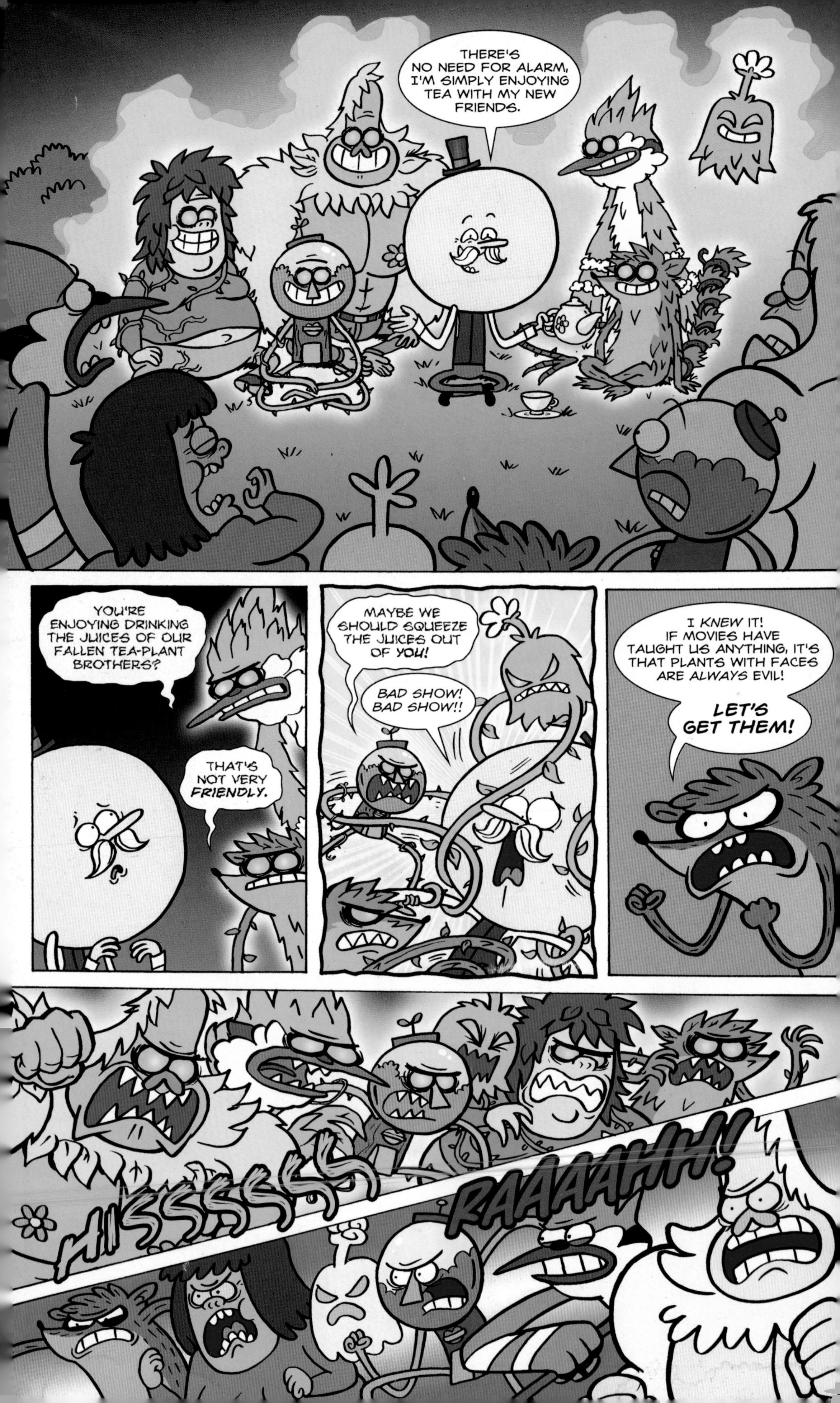
THERE'S NO NEED FOR ALARM, I'M SIMPLY ENJOYING TEA WITH MY NEW FRIENDS.
YOU'RE ENJOYING DRINKING THE JUICES OF OUR FALLEN TEA-PLANT BROTHERS?
THAT'S NOT VERY FRIENDLY.
MAYBE WE SHOULD SQUEEZE THE JUICES OUT OF YOU!
BAD SHOW! BAD SHOW!!
I KNEW IT! IF MOVIES HAVE TAUGHT US ANYTHING, IT'S THAT PLANTS WITH FACES ARE ALWAYS EVIL!
LET'S GET THEM!
HISSSSSS
RAAAAAHH!

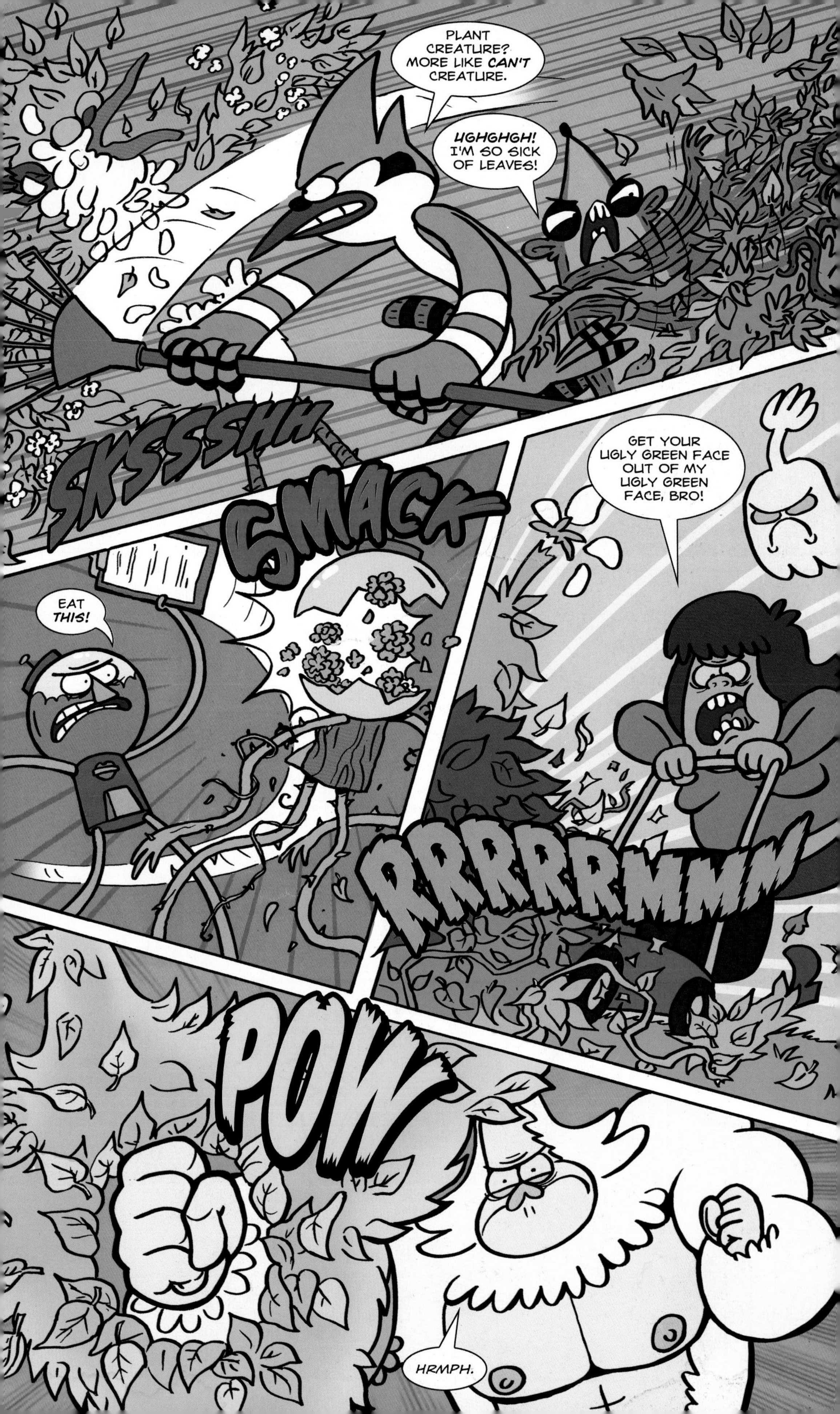
PLANT CREATURE? MORE LIKE CAN'T CREATURE.
UGHGHGH! I'M SO SICK OF LEAVES!
SKSSSHH
SMACK
EAT THIS!
GET YOUR UGLY GREEN FACE OUT OF MY UGLY GREEN FACE, BRO!
RRRRRRMMM
POW
HRMPH.

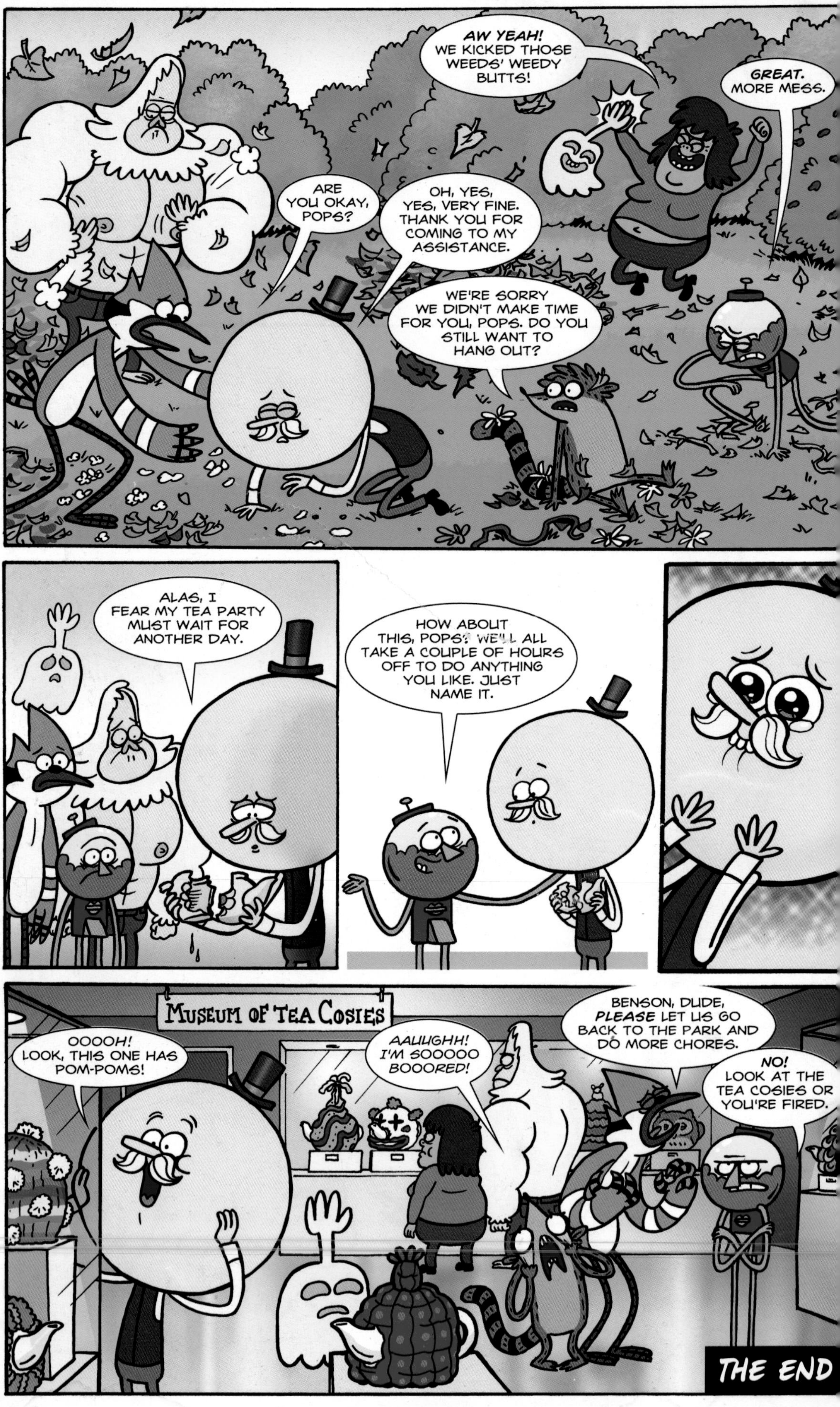
AW YEAH!
WE KICKED THOSE WEEDS' WEEDY BUTTS!
GREAT. MORE MESS.
ARE YOU OKAY, POPS?
OH, YES, YES, VERY FINE. THANK YOU FOR COMING TO MY ASSISTANCE.
WE'RE SORRY WE DIDN'T MAKE TIME FOR YOU, POPS. DO YOU STILL WANT TO HANG OUT?
ALAS, I FEAR MY TEA PARTY MUST WAIT FOR ANOTHER DAY.
HOW ABOUT THIS, POPS? WE'LL ALL TAKE A COUPLE OF HOURS OFF TO DO ANYTHING YOU LIKE. JUST NAME IT.
MUSEUM OF TEA COSIES
OOOOH! LOOK, THIS ONE HAS POM-POMS!
AAUUGHH! I'M SOOOOO BOOORED!
BENSON, DUDE, PLEASE LET US GO BACK TO THE PARK AND DO MORE CHORES.
NO! LOOK AT THE TEA COSIES OR YOU'RE FIRED.
THE END

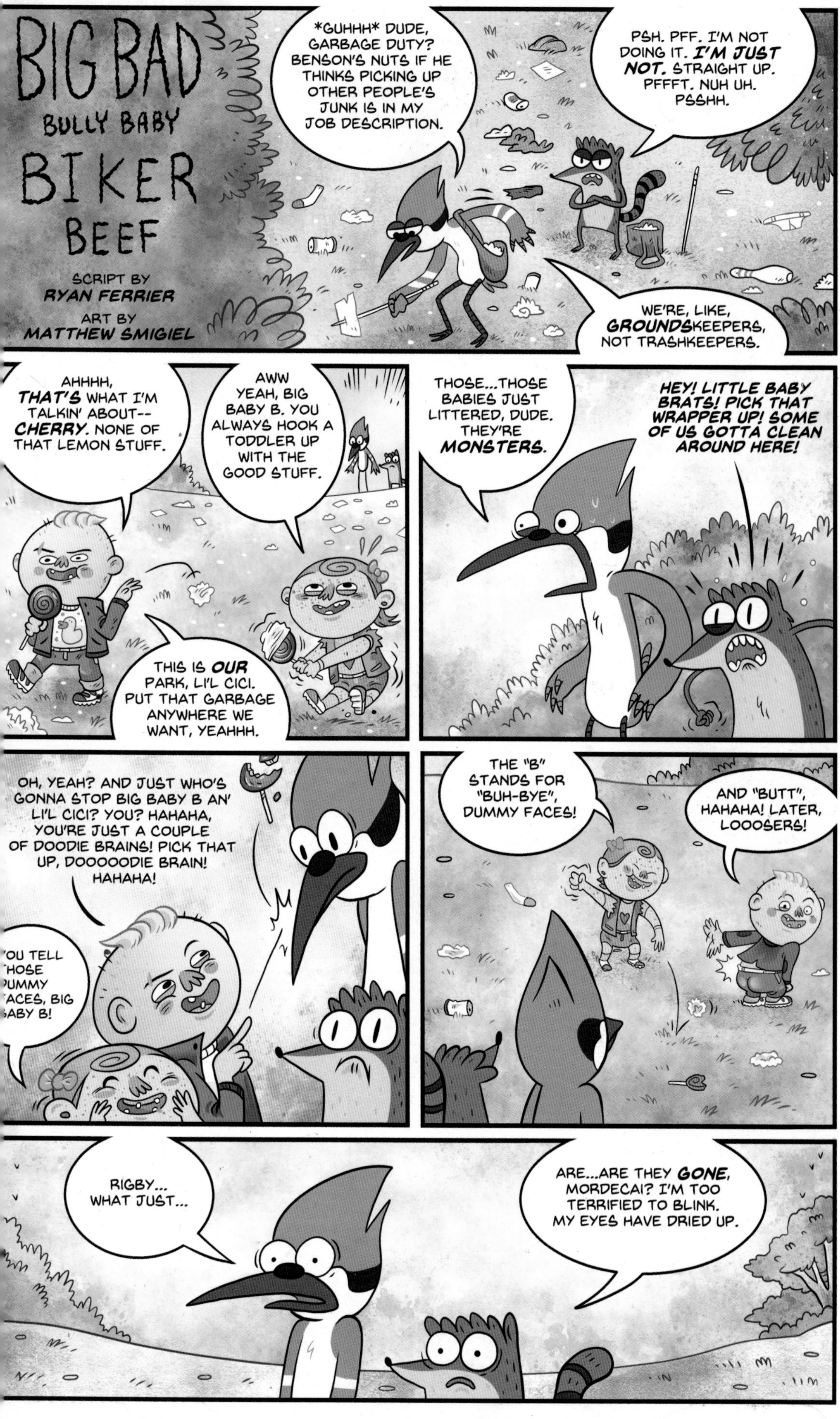

BIG BAD BULLY BABY BIKER BEEF
SCRIPT BY RYAN FERRIER
ART BY MATTHEW SMIGIEL
GUHHH DUDE, GARBAGE DUTY? BENSON'S NUTS IF HE THINKS PICKING UP OTHER PEOPLE'S JUNK IS IN MY JOB DESCRIPTION.
PSH. PFF. I'M NOT DOING IT. I'M JUST NOT. STRAIGHT UP. PFFFT. NUH UH. PSSHH.
WE'RE, LIKE, GROUNDSKEEPERS, NOT TRASHKEEPERS.
AHHHH, THAT'S WHAT I'M TALKIN' ABOUT-- CHERRY. NONE OF THAT LEMON STUFF.
AWW YEAH, BIG BABY B. YOU ALWAYS HOOK A TODDLER UP WITH THE GOOD STUFF.
THIS IS OUR PARK, LI'L CICI. PUT THAT GARBAGE ANYWHERE WE WANT, YEAHHH.
THOSE...THOSE BABIES JUST LITTERED, DUDE. THEY'RE MONSTERS.
HEY! LITTLE BABY BRATS! PICK THAT WRAPPER UP! SOME OF US GOTTA CLEAN AROUND HERE!
OH, YEAH? AND JUST WHO'S GONNA STOP BIG BABY B AN' LI'L CICI? YOU? HAHAHA, YOU'RE JUST A COUPLE OF DOODIE BRAINS! PICK THAT UP, DOOOOODIE BRAIN! HAHAHA!
OU TELL HOSE UMMY ACES, BIG ABY B!
THE "B" STANDS FOR "BUH-BYE", DUMMY FACES!
AND "BUTT", HAHAHA! LATER, LOOOSERS!
RIGBY... WHAT JUST...
ARE...ARE THEY GONE, MORDECAI? I'M TOO TERRIFIED TO BLINK. MY EYES HAVE DRIED UP.

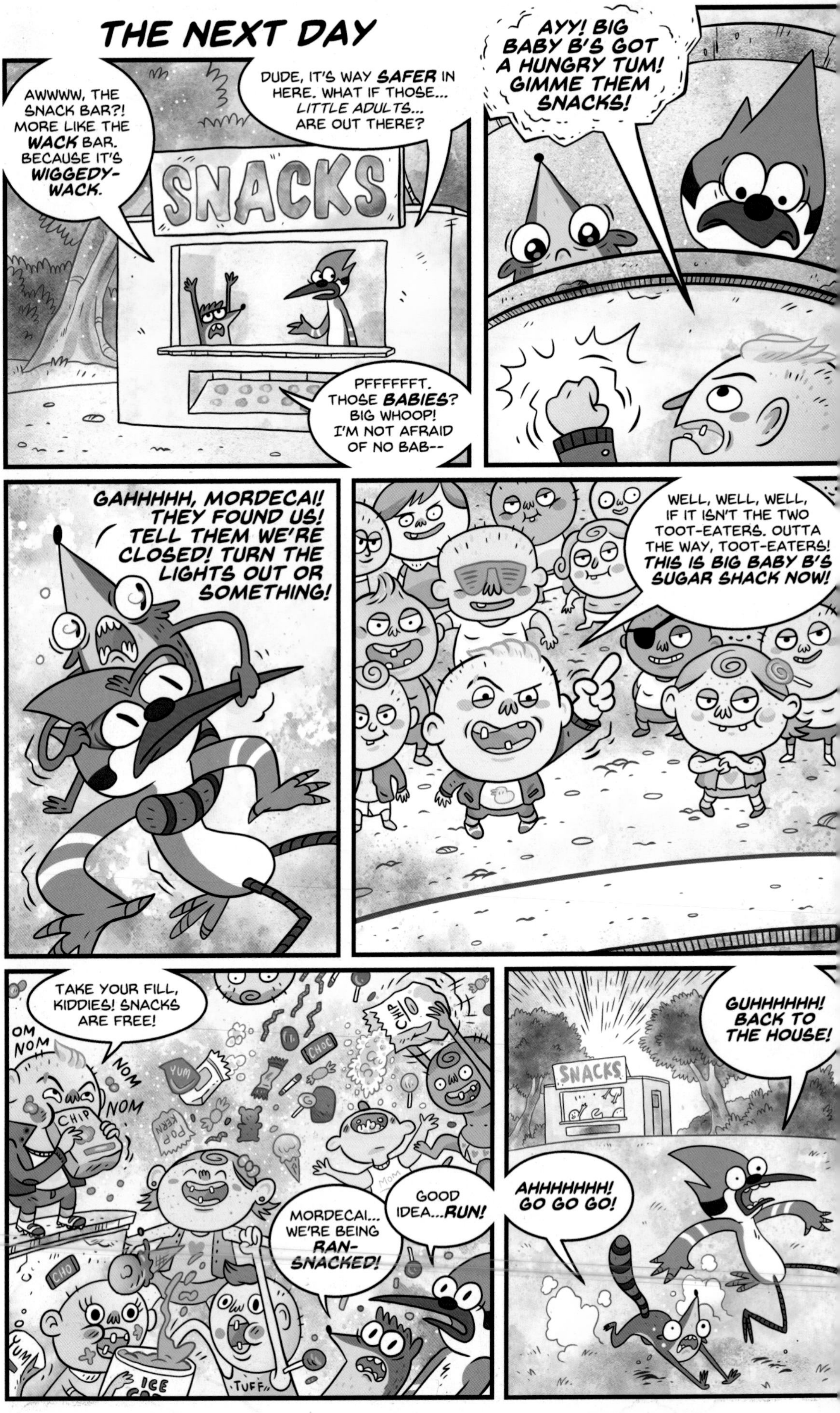

THE NEXT DAY
AWWWW, THE SNACK BAR?! MORE LIKE THE WACK BAR. BECAUSE IT'S WIGGEDY-WACK.
DUDE, IT'S WAY SAFER IN HERE. WHAT IF THOSE... LITTLE ADULTS... ARE OUT THERE?
SNACKS
PFFFFFFT. THOSE BABIES? BIG WHOOP! I'M NOT AFRAID OF NO BAB--
AYY! BIG BABY B'S GOT A HUNGRY TUM! GIMME THEM SNACKS!
GAHHHHH, MORDECAI! THEY FOUND US! TELL THEM WE'RE CLOSED! TURN THE LIGHTS OUT OR SOMETHING!
WELL, WELL, WELL, IF IT ISN'T THE TWO TOOT-EATERS. OUTTA THE WAY, TOOT-EATERS! THIS IS BIG BABY B'S SUGAR SHACK NOW!
TAKE YOUR FILL, KIDDIES! SNACKS ARE FREE!
OM NOM
NOM
NOM
CHIP
CHIP
CHOC
YUM
POP KERN
MOM
MORDECAI... WE'RE BEING RAN-SNACKED!
GOOD IDEA...RUN!
CHO
YUM
ICE
TUFF
GUHHHHHH! BACK TO THE HOUSE!
SNACKS
AHHHHHHH! GO GO GO!

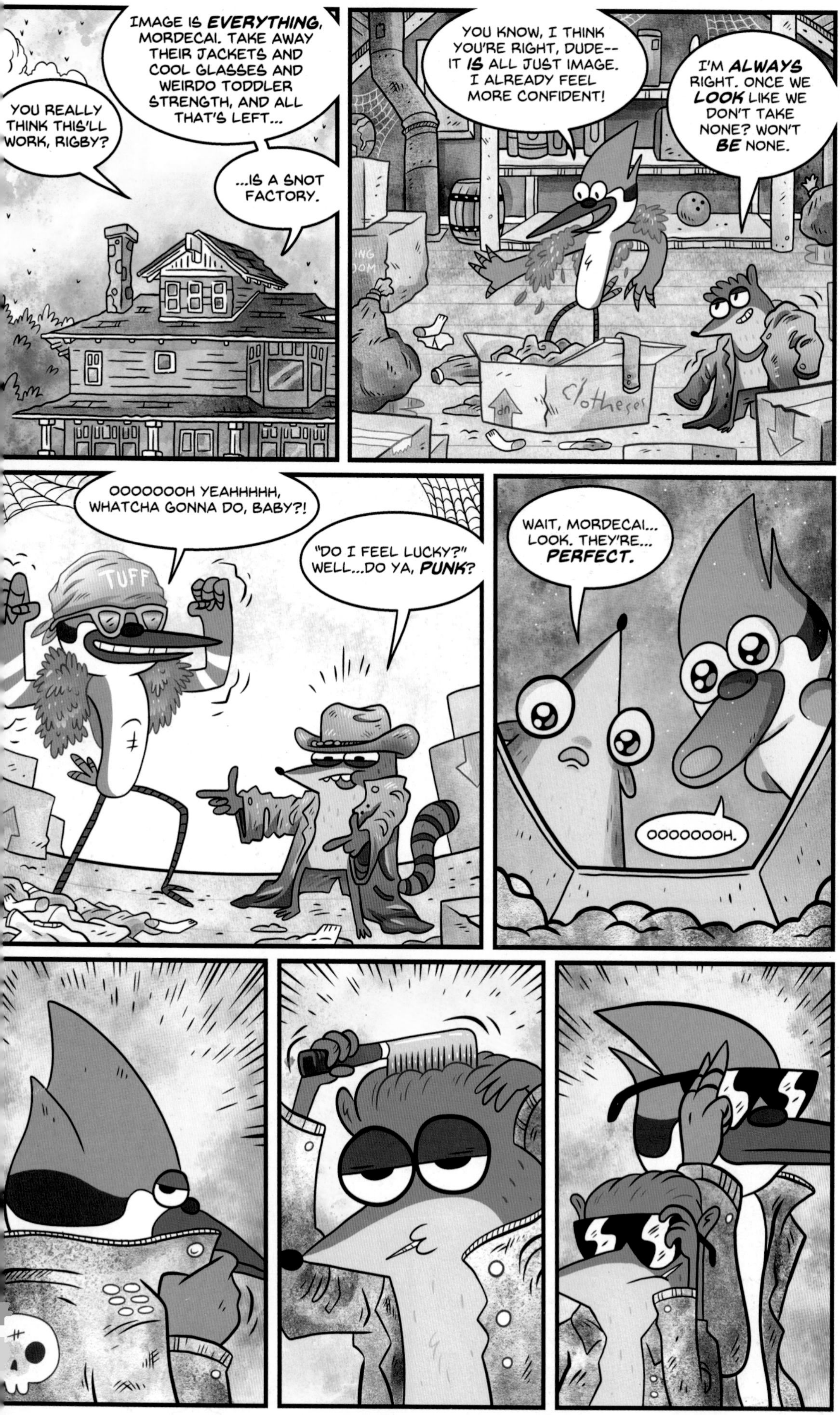

YOU REALLY THINK THIS'LL WORK, RIGBY?
IMAGE IS EVERYTHING, MORDECAI. TAKE AWAY THEIR JACKETS AND COOL GLASSES AND WEIRDO TODDLER STRENGTH, AND ALL THAT'S LEFT...
...IS A SNOT FACTORY.
YOU KNOW, I THINK YOU'RE RIGHT, DUDE-- IT IS ALL JUST IMAGE. I ALREADY FEEL MORE CONFIDENT!
I'M ALWAYS RIGHT. ONCE WE LOOK LIKE WE DON'T TAKE NONE? WON'T BE NONE.
Clotheses
OOOOOOOH YEAHHHHH, WHATCHA GONNA DO, BABY?!
TUFF
"DO I FEEL LUCKY?" WELL...DO YA, PUNK?
WAIT, MORDECAI... LOOK. THEY'RE... PERFECT.
OOOOOOOH.

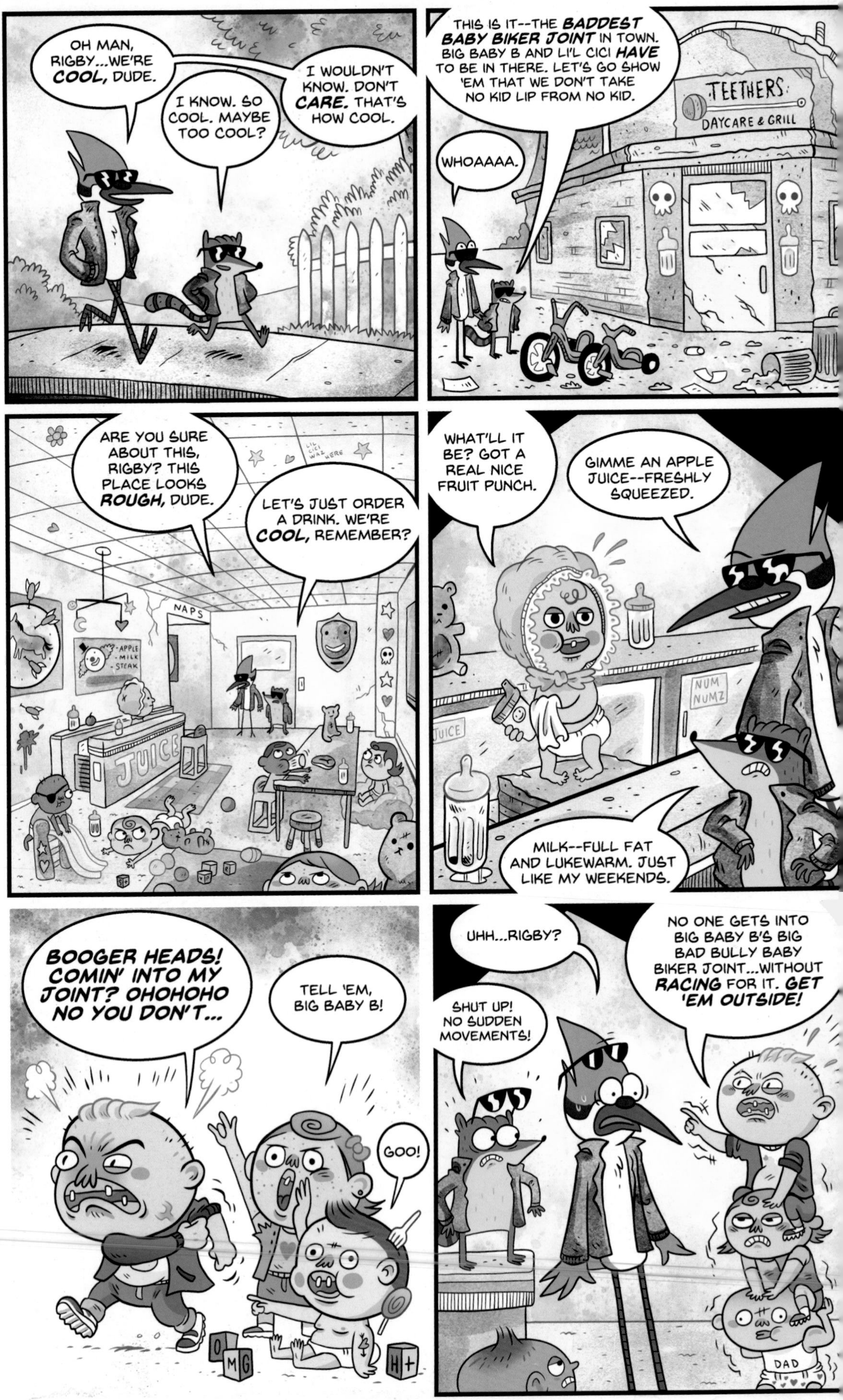
OH MAN, RIGBY...WE'RE COOL, DUDE.
I KNOW. SO COOL. MAYBE TOO COOL?
I WOULDN'T KNOW. DON'T CARE. THAT'S HOW COOL.
THIS IS IT--THE BADDEST BABY BIKER JOINT IN TOWN. BIG BABY B AND LI'L CICI HAVE TO BE IN THERE. LET'S GO SHOW 'EM THAT WE DON'T TAKE NO KID LIP FROM NO KID.
WHOAAAA.
TEETHERS
DAYCARE & GRILL
ARE YOU SURE ABOUT THIS, RIGBY? THIS PLACE LOOKS ROUGH, DUDE.
LET'S JUST ORDER A DRINK. WE'RE COOL, REMEMBER?
LI'L CICI WAZ HERE
NAPS
APPLE MILK STEAK
JUICE
WHAT'LL IT BE? GOT A REAL NICE FRUIT PUNCH.
GIMME AN APPLE JUICE--FRESHLY SQUEEZED.
NUM NUMZ
JUICE
MILK--FULL FAT AND LUKEWARM. JUST LIKE MY WEEKENDS.
BOOGER HEADS! COMIN' INTO MY JOINT? OHOHOHO NO YOU DON'T...
TELL 'EM, BIG BABY B!
GOO!
OMG
UHH...RIGBY?
SHUT UP! NO SUDDEN MOVEMENTS!
NO ONE GETS INTO BIG BABY B'S BIG BAD BULLY BABY BIKER JOINT...WITHOUT RACING FOR IT. GET 'EM OUTSIDE!
DAD

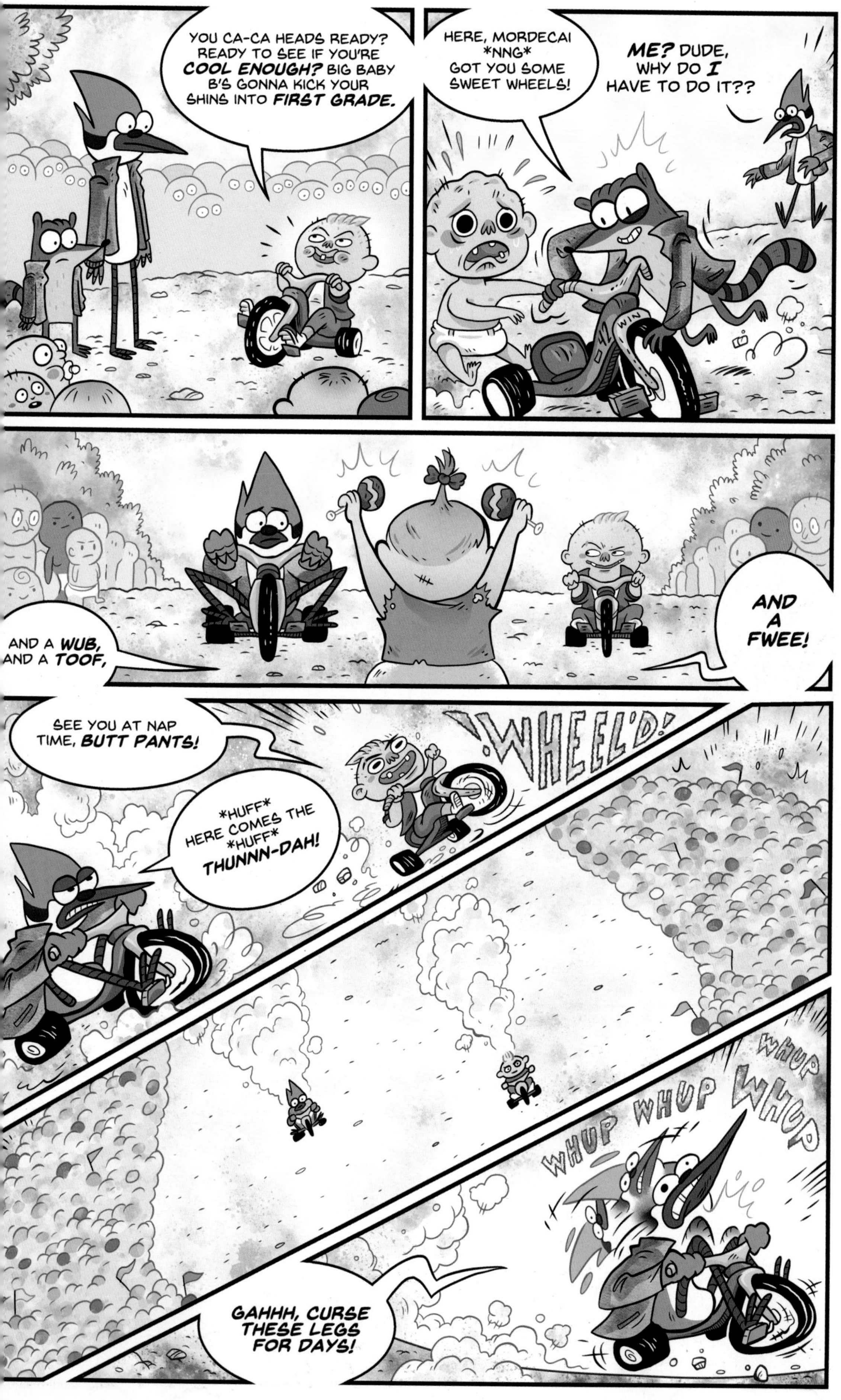

YOU CA-CA HEADS READY? READY TO SEE IF YOU'RE COOL ENOUGH? BIG BABY B'S GONNA KICK YOUR SHINS INTO FIRST GRADE.
HERE, MORDECAI *NNG* GOT YOU SOME SWEET WHEELS!
ME? DUDE, WHY DO I HAVE TO DO IT??
WIN
AND A WUB, AND A TOOF,
AND A FWEE!
SEE YOU AT NAP TIME, BUTT PANTS!
WHEEL'D!
HUFF HERE COMES THE *HUFF* THUNNN-DAH!
WHUP WHUP WHUP WHUP WHUP
GAHHH, CURSE THESE LEGS FOR DAYS!

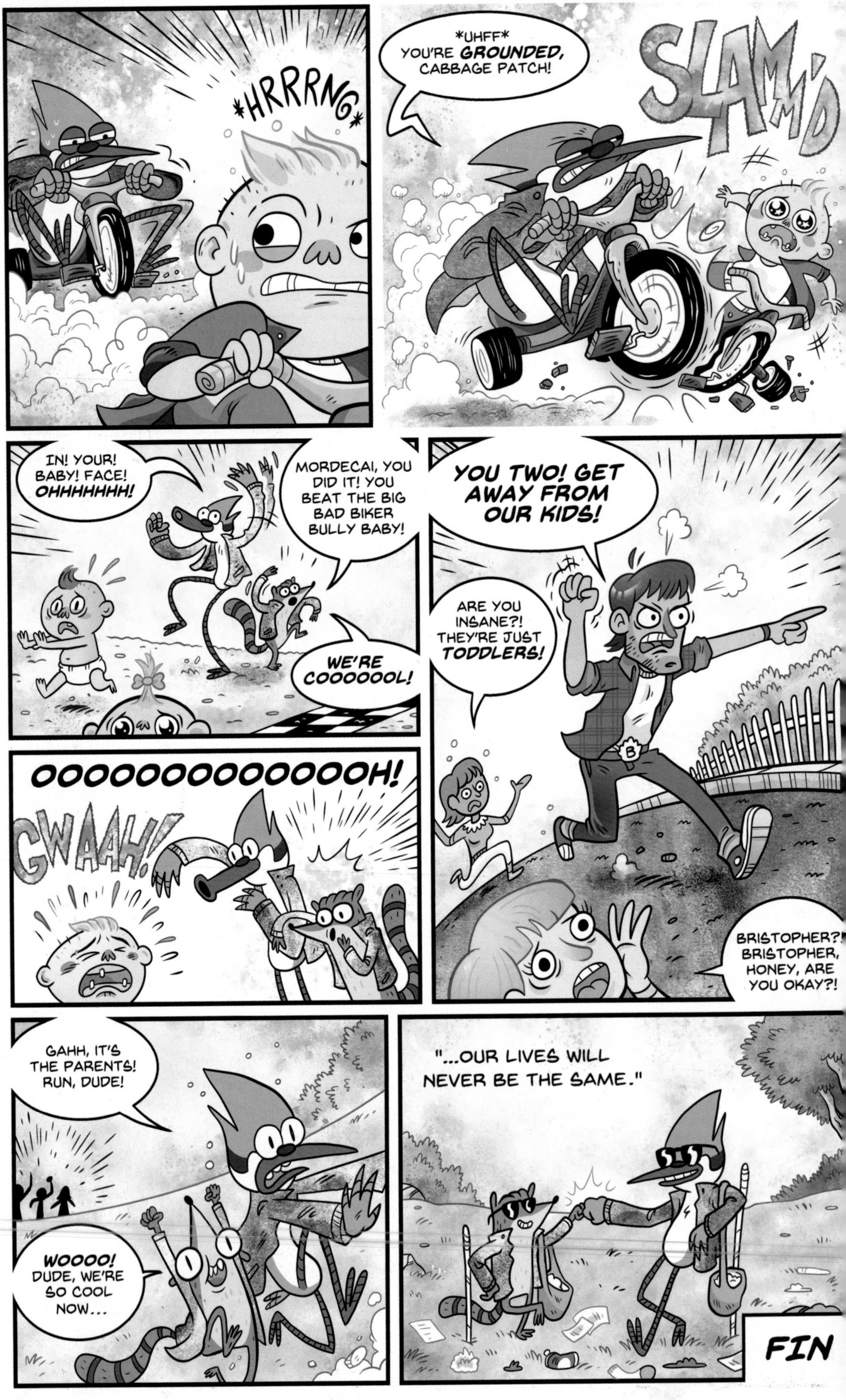

HRRRNG
UHFF YOU'RE GROUNDED, CABBAGE PATCH!
SLAMM'D
IN! YOUR! BABY! FACE! OHHHHHHH!
MORDECAI, YOU DID IT! YOU BEAT THE BIG BAD BIKER BULLY BABY!
WE'RE COOOOOOL!
YOU TWO! GET AWAY FROM OUR KIDS!
ARE YOU INSANE?! THEY'RE JUST TODDLERS!
OOOOOOOOOOOOOOH!
GWAAH!
BRISTOPHER?! BRISTOPHER, HONEY, ARE YOU OKAY?!
GAHH, IT'S THE PARENTS! RUN, DUDE!
WOOOO! DUDE, WE'RE SO COOL NOW...
"...OUR LIVES WILL NEVER BE THE SAME."
FIN

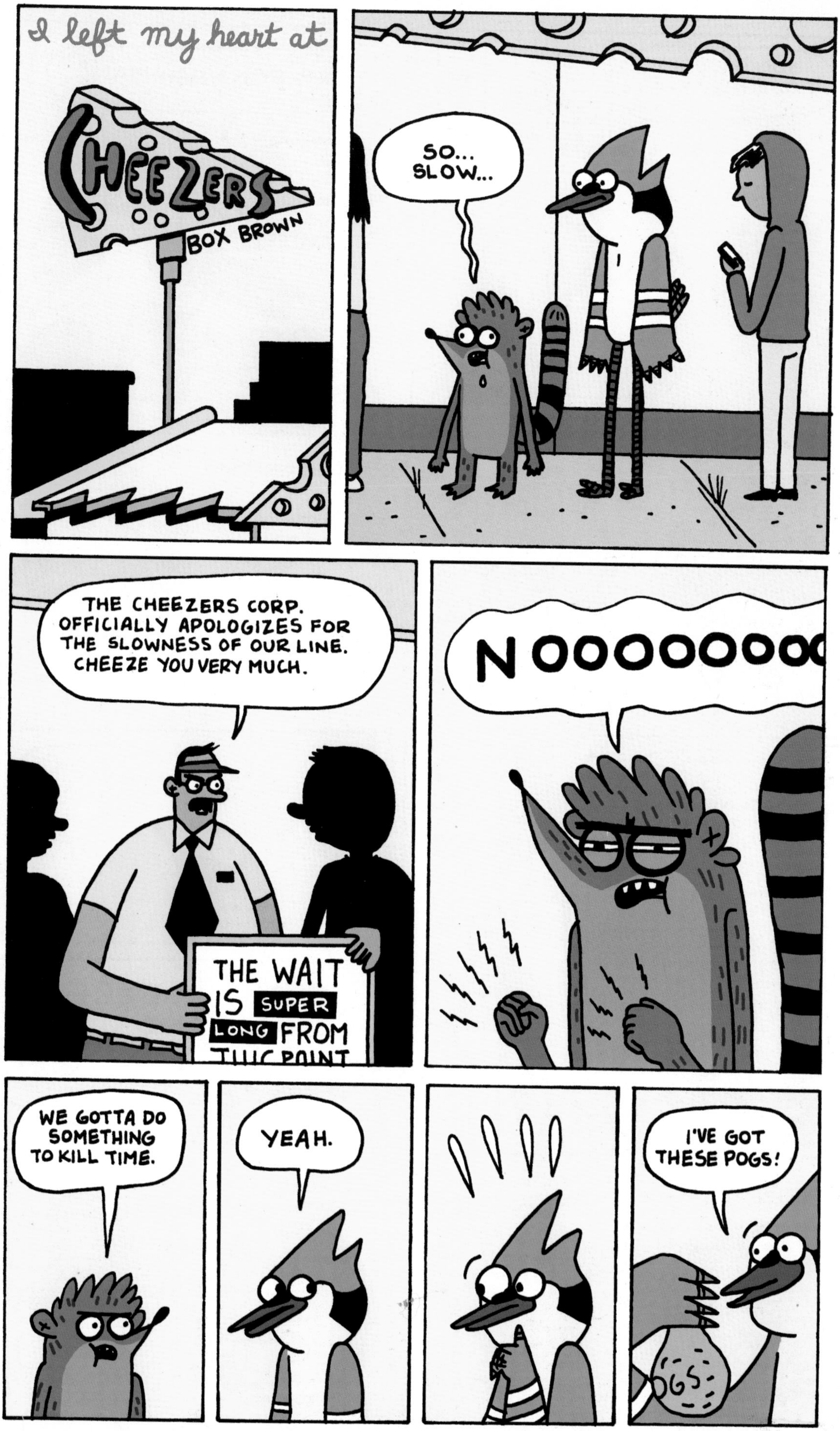
I left my heart at
CHEEZERS
BOX BROWN
SO... SLOW...
THE CHEEZERS CORP. OFFICIALLY APOLOGIZES FOR THE SLOWNESS OF OUR LINE. CHEEZE YOU VERY MUCH.
THE WAIT IS SUPER LONG FROM
NOOOOOOOO
WE GOTTA DO SOMETHING TO KILL TIME.
YEAH.
I'VE GOT THESE POGS!

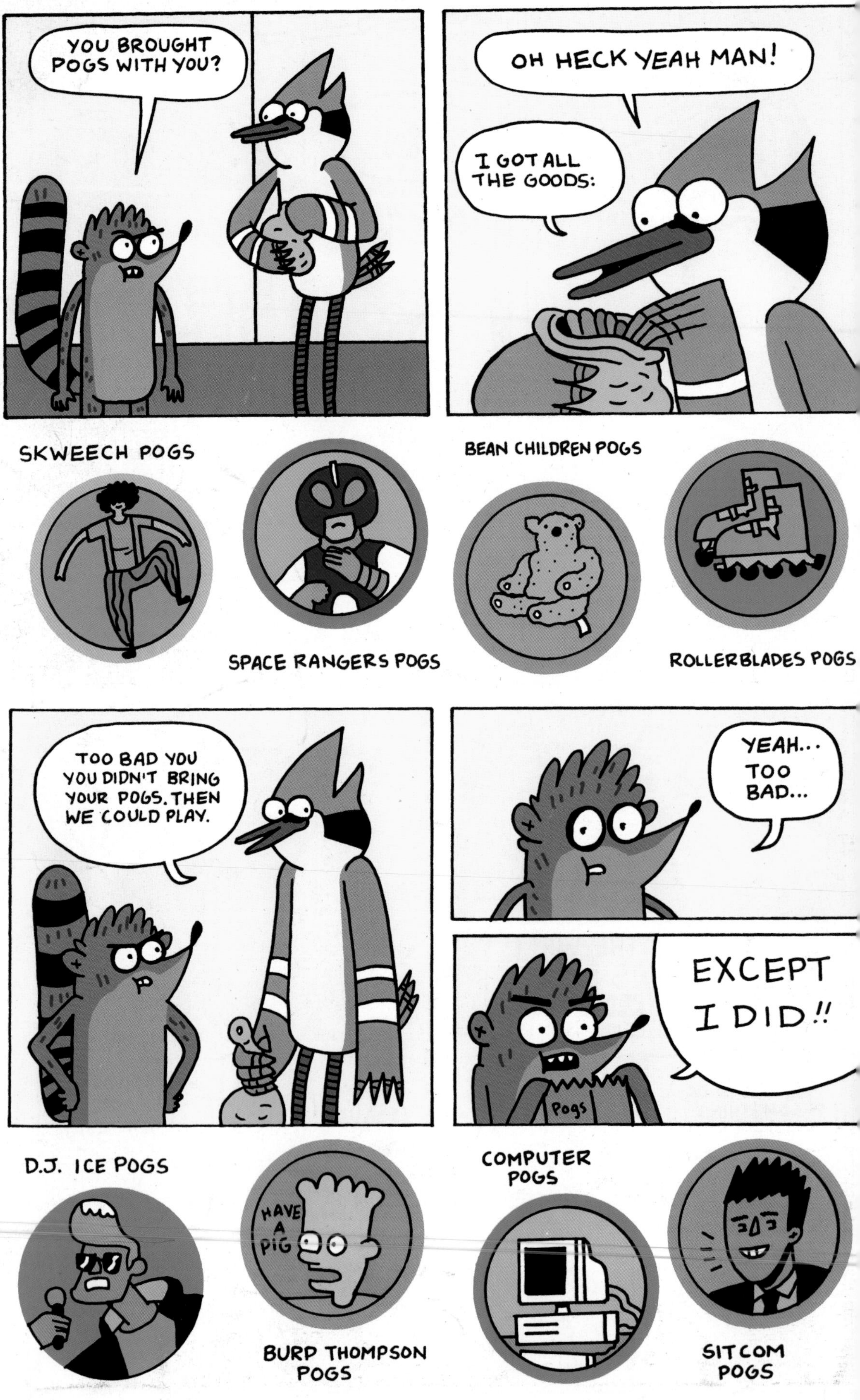
YOU BROUGHT POGS WITH YOU?
OH HECK YEAH MAN!
I GOT ALL THE GOODS:
SKWEECH POGS
SPACE RANGERS POGS
BEAN CHILDREN POGS
ROLLERBLADES POGS
TOO BAD YOU YOU DIDN'T BRING YOUR POGS. THEN WE COULD PLAY.
YEAH... TOO BAD...
EXCEPT I DID!!
Pogs
D.J. ICE POGS
HAVE A PIG
BURP THOMPSON POGS
COMPUTER POGS
SITCOM POGS

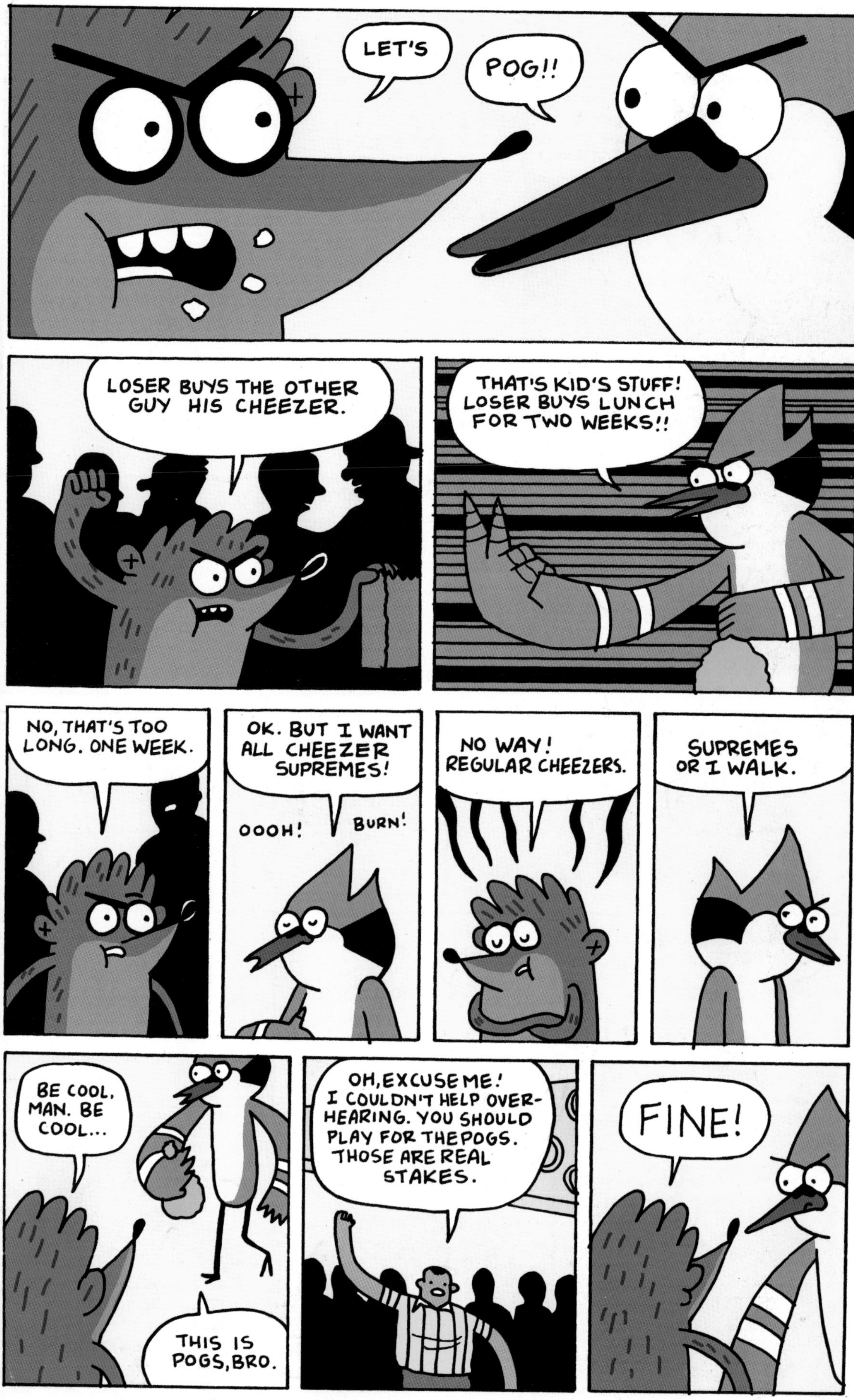
LET'S
POG!!
LOSER BUYS THE OTHER GUY HIS CHEEZER.
THAT'S KID'S STUFF! LOSER BUYS LUNCH FOR TWO WEEKS!!
NO, THAT'S TOO LONG. ONE WEEK.
OK. BUT I WANT ALL CHEEZER SUPREMES!
OOOH!
BURN!
NO WAY! REGULAR CHEEZERS.
SUPREMES OR I WALK.
BE COOL, MAN. BE COOL...
THIS IS POGS, BRO.
OH, EXCUSE ME! I COULDN'T HELP OVER-HEARING. YOU SHOULD PLAY FOR THE POGS. THOSE ARE REAL STAKES.
FINE!

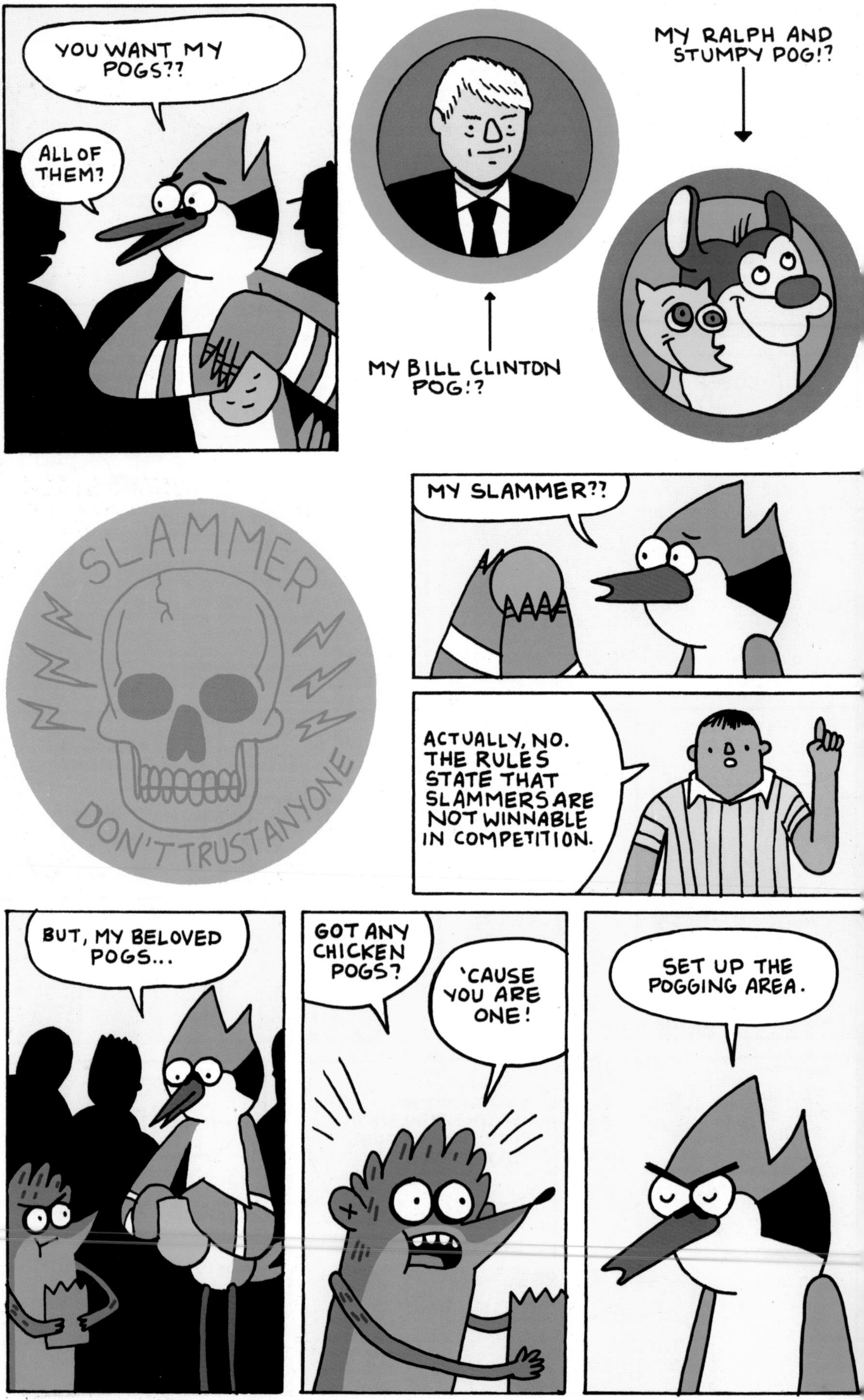
YOU WANT MY POGS??
ALL OF THEM?
MY BILL CLINTON POG!?
MY RALPH AND STUMPY POG!?
SLAMMER
DON'T TRUST ANYONE
MY SLAMMER??
ACTUALLY, NO. THE RULES STATE THAT SLAMMERS ARE NOT WINNABLE IN COMPETITION.
BUT, MY BELOVED POGS...
GOT ANY CHICKEN POGS?
'CAUSE YOU ARE ONE!
SET UP THE POGGING AREA.

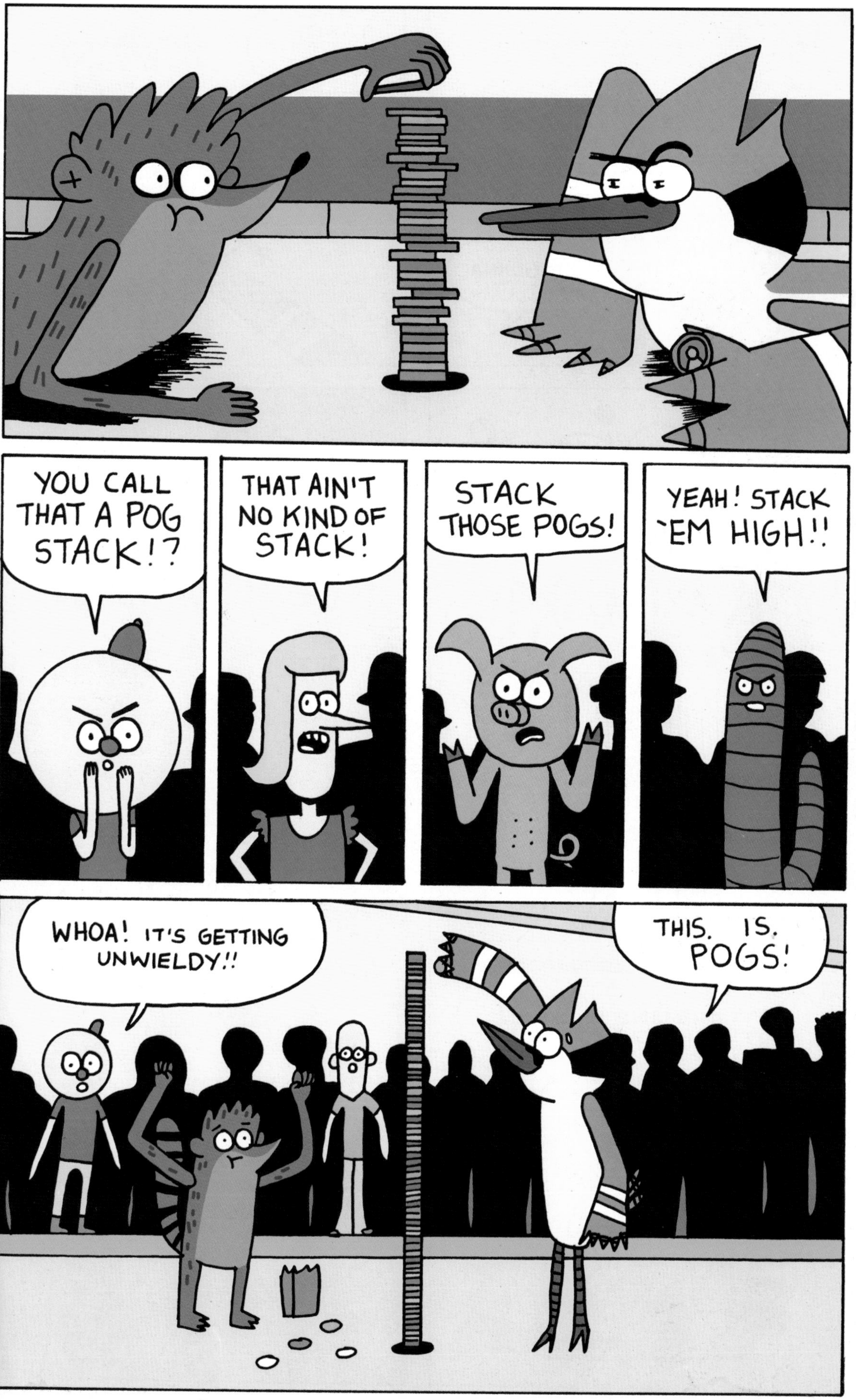
YOU CALL THAT A POG STACK!?
THAT AIN'T NO KIND OF STACK!
STACK THOSE POGS!
YEAH! STACK 'EM HIGH!!
WHOA! IT'S GETTING UNWIELDY!!
THIS. IS. POGS!

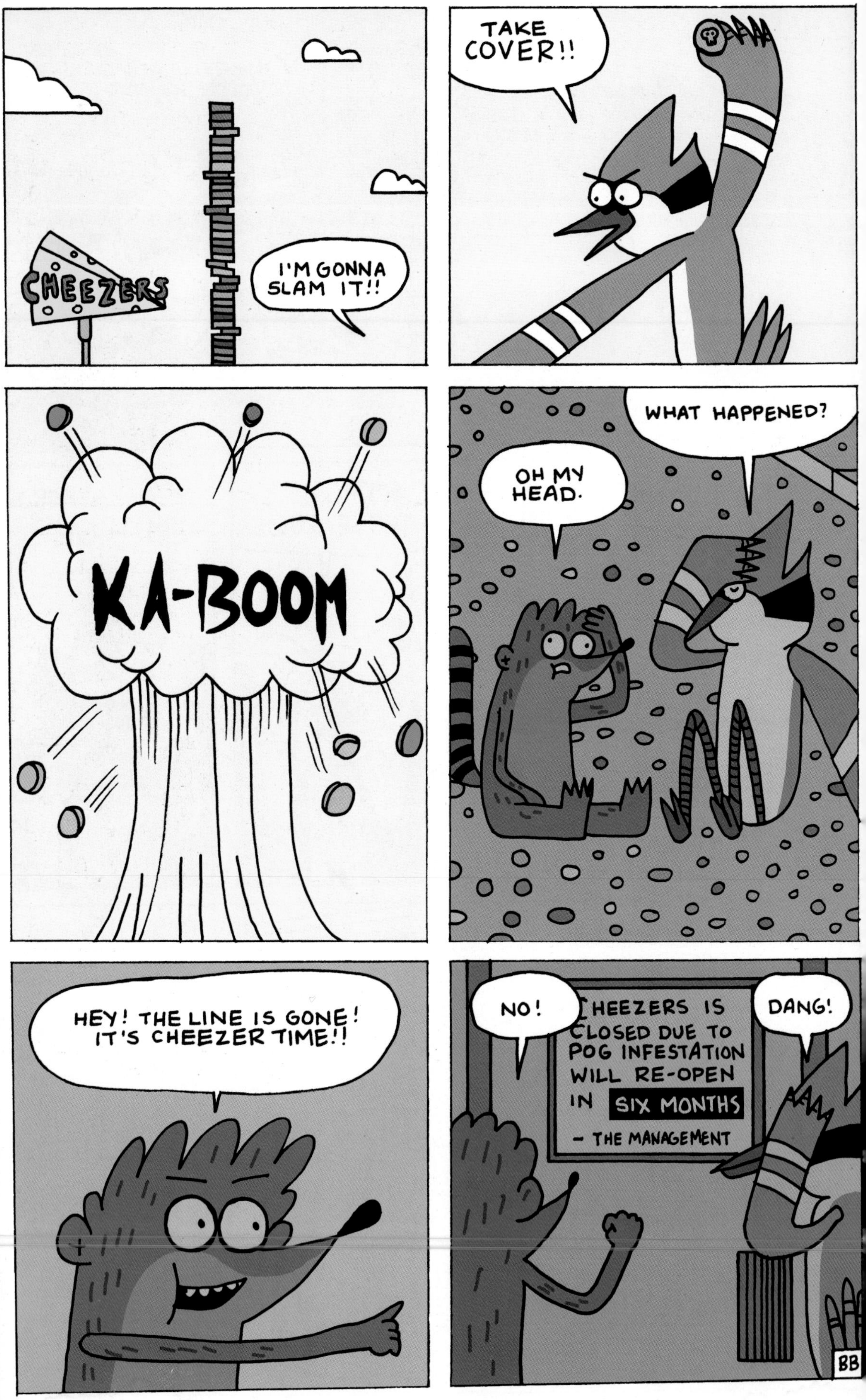
CHEEZERS
I'M GONNA SLAM IT!!
TAKE COVER!!
KA-BOOM
WHAT HAPPENED?
OH MY HEAD.
HEY! THE LINE IS GONE! IT'S CHEEZER TIME!!
NO!
CHEEZERS IS CLOSED DUE TO POG INFESTATION WILL RE-OPEN IN SIX MONTHS
- THE MANAGEMENT
DANG!
BB

EARTH B / SCRIPT BY DEWAYNE FEENSTRA / ART BY JENNA AYOUB

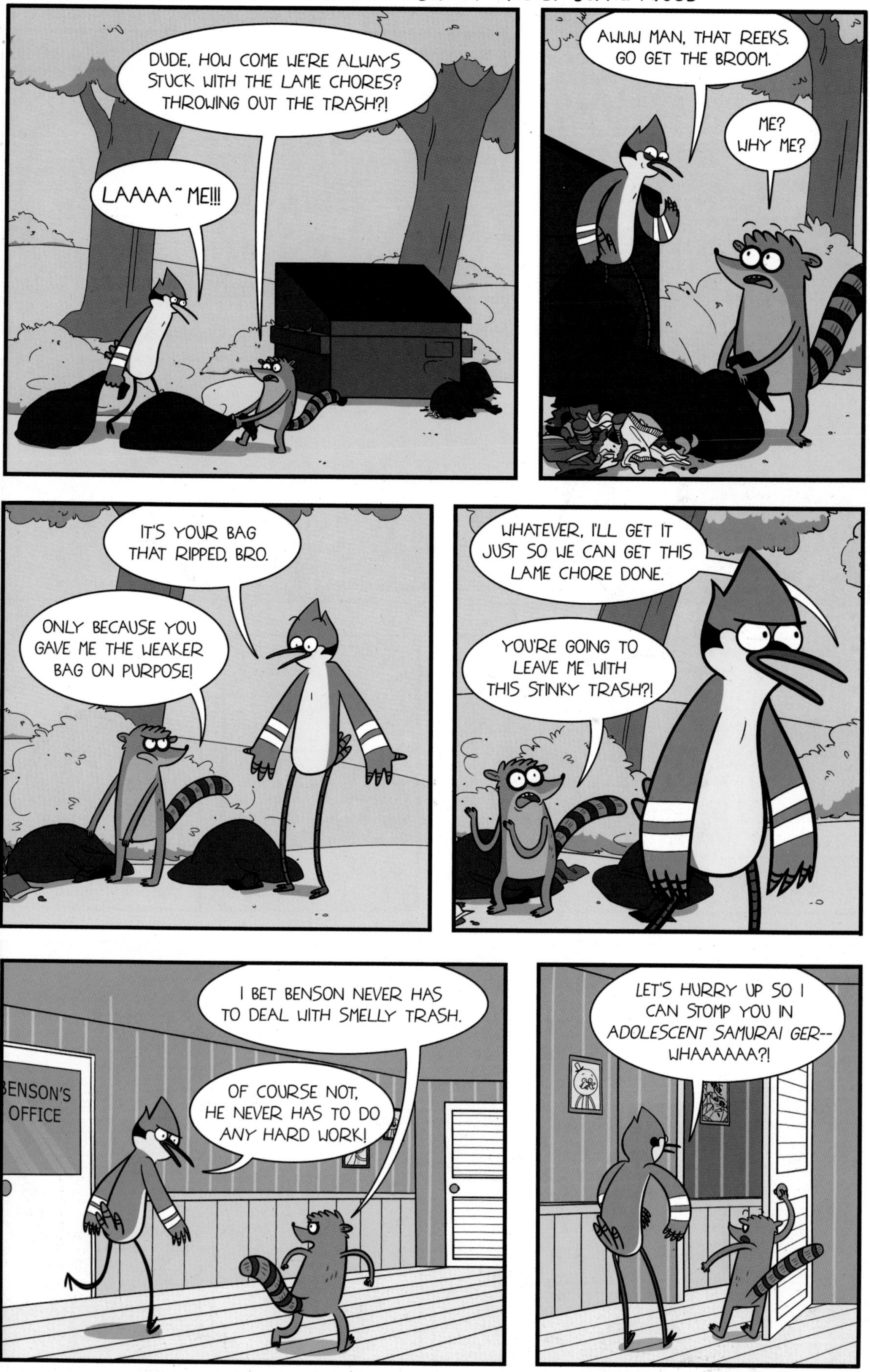
DUDE, HOW COME WE'RE ALWAYS STUCK WITH THE LAME CHORES? THROWING OUT THE TRASH?!
LAAAA~ME!!!
AWWW MAN, THAT REEKS. GO GET THE BROOM.
ME? WHY ME?
IT'S YOUR BAG THAT RIPPED, BRO.
ONLY BECAUSE YOU GAVE ME THE WEAKER BAG ON PURPOSE!
WHATEVER, I'LL GET IT JUST SO WE CAN GET THIS LAME CHORE DONE.
YOU'RE GOING TO LEAVE ME WITH THIS STINKY TRASH?!
I BET BENSON NEVER HAS TO DEAL WITH SMELLY TRASH.
BENSON'S OFFICE
OF COURSE NOT, HE NEVER HAS TO DO ANY HARD WORK!
LET'S HURRY UP SO I CAN STOMP YOU IN ADOLESCENT SAMURAI GER-- WHAAAAAA?!

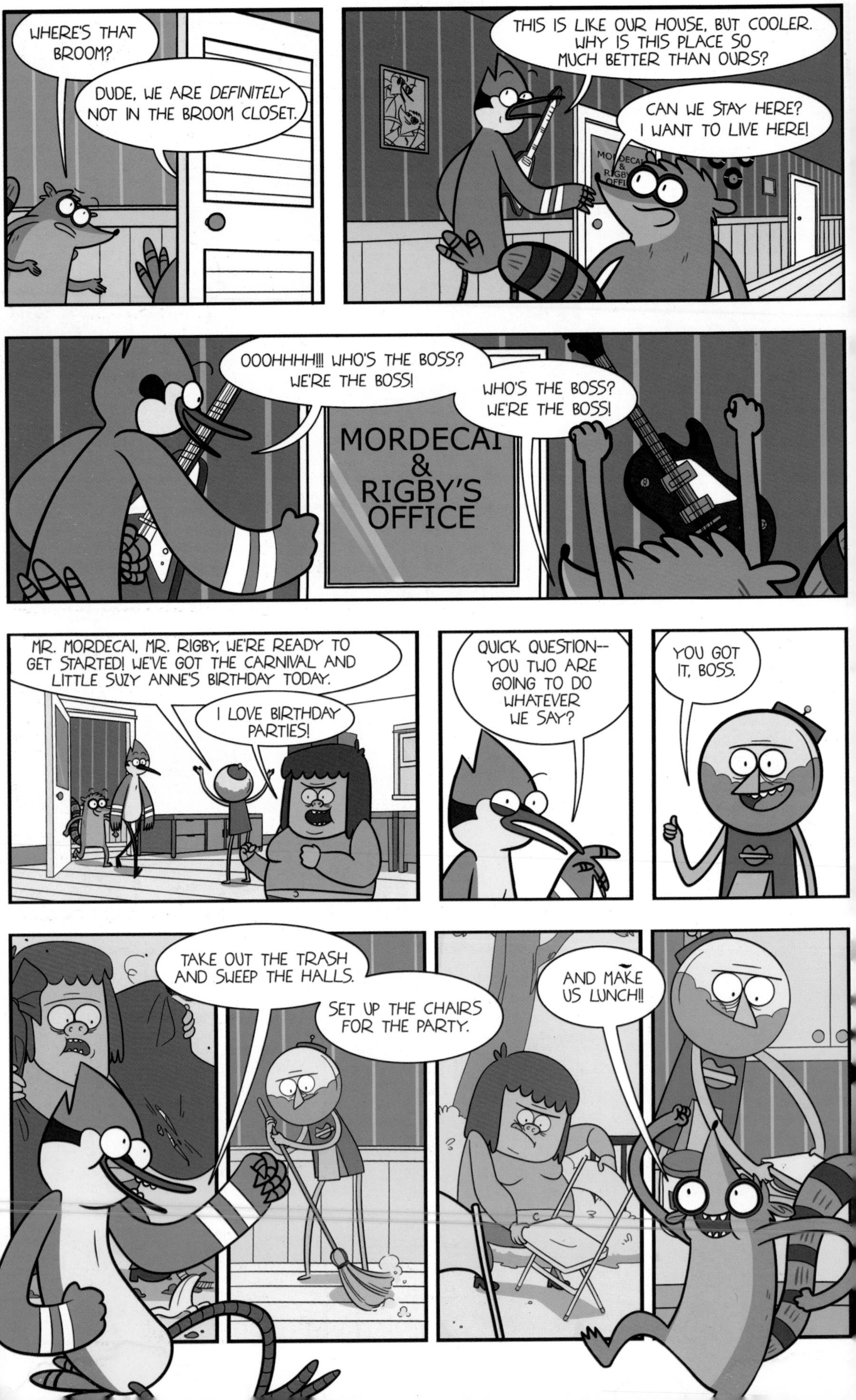

WHERE'S THAT BROOM?
DUDE, WE ARE DEFINITELY NOT IN THE BROOM CLOSET.
THIS IS LIKE OUR HOUSE, BUT COOLER. WHY IS THIS PLACE SO MUCH BETTER THAN OURS?
CAN WE STAY HERE? I WANT TO LIVE HERE!
OOOHHHH!!! WHO'S THE BOSS? WE'RE THE BOSS!
WHO'S THE BOSS? WE'RE THE BOSS!
MORDECAI & RIGBY'S OFFICE
MR. MORDECAI, MR. RIGBY, WE'RE READY TO GET STARTED! WE'VE GOT THE CARNIVAL AND LITTLE SUZY ANNE'S BIRTHDAY TODAY.
I LOVE BIRTHDAY PARTIES!
QUICK QUESTION-- YOU TWO ARE GOING TO DO WHATEVER WE SAY?
YOU GOT IT, BOSS.
TAKE OUT THE TRASH AND SWEEP THE HALLS.
SET UP THE CHAIRS FOR THE PARTY.
AND MAKE US LUNCH!!

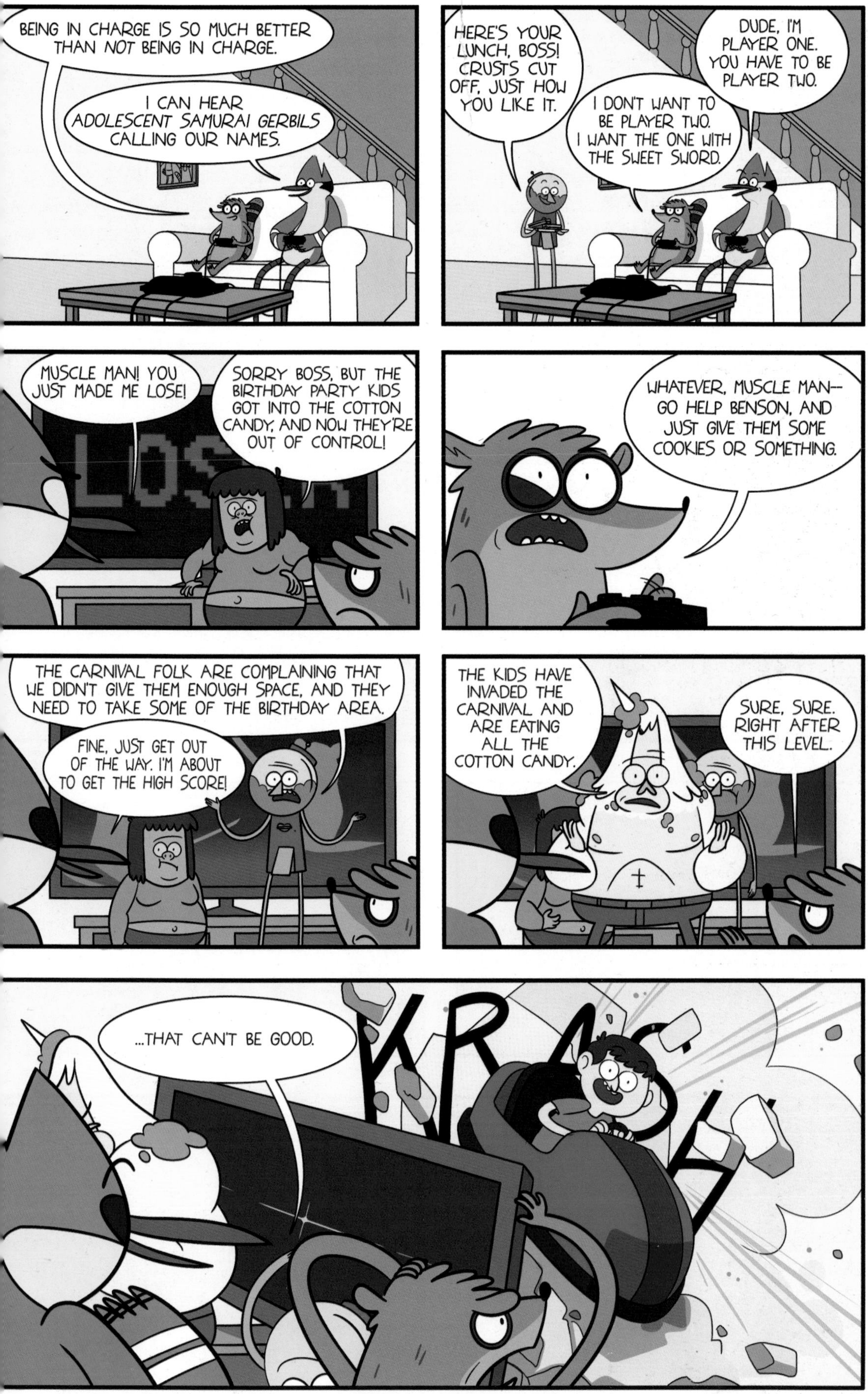
BEING IN CHARGE IS SO MUCH BETTER THAN *NOT* BEING IN CHARGE.
I CAN HEAR *ADOLESCENT SAMURAI GERBILS* CALLING OUR NAMES.
HERE'S YOUR LUNCH, BOSS! CRUSTS CUT OFF, JUST HOW YOU LIKE IT.
DUDE, I'M PLAYER ONE. YOU HAVE TO BE PLAYER TWO.
I DON'T WANT TO BE PLAYER TWO. I WANT THE ONE WITH THE SWEET SWORD.
MUSCLE MAN! YOU JUST MADE ME LOSE!
SORRY BOSS, BUT THE BIRTHDAY PARTY KIDS GOT INTO THE COTTON CANDY, AND NOW THEY'RE OUT OF CONTROL!
WHATEVER, MUSCLE MAN-- GO HELP BENSON, AND JUST GIVE THEM SOME COOKIES OR SOMETHING.
THE CARNIVAL FOLK ARE COMPLAINING THAT WE DIDN'T GIVE THEM ENOUGH SPACE, AND THEY NEED TO TAKE SOME OF THE BIRTHDAY AREA.
FINE, JUST GET OUT OF THE WAY. I'M ABOUT TO GET THE HIGH SCORE!
THE KIDS HAVE INVADED THE CARNIVAL AND ARE EATING ALL THE COTTON CANDY.
SURE, SURE. RIGHT AFTER THIS LEVEL.
...THAT CAN'T BE GOOD.

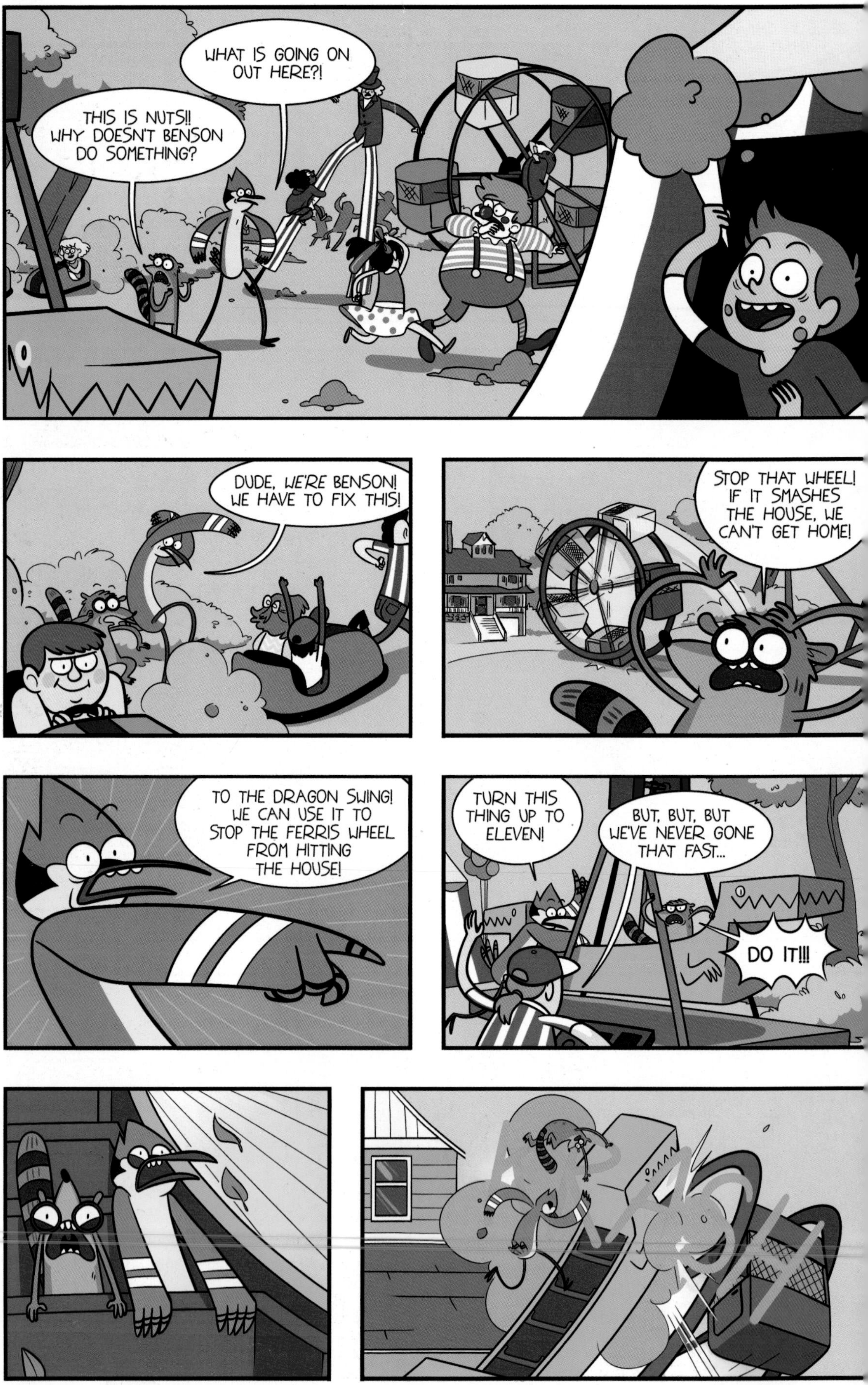
THIS IS NUTS!! WHY DOESN'T BENSON DO SOMETHING?
WHAT IS GOING ON OUT HERE?!
DUDE, WE'RE BENSON! WE HAVE TO FIX THIS!
STOP THAT WHEEL! IF IT SMASHES THE HOUSE, WE CAN'T GET HOME!
TO THE DRAGON SWING! WE CAN USE IT TO STOP THE FERRIS WHEEL FROM HITTING THE HOUSE!
TURN THIS THING UP TO ELEVEN!
BUT, BUT, BUT WE'VE NEVER GONE THAT FAST...
DO IT!!!

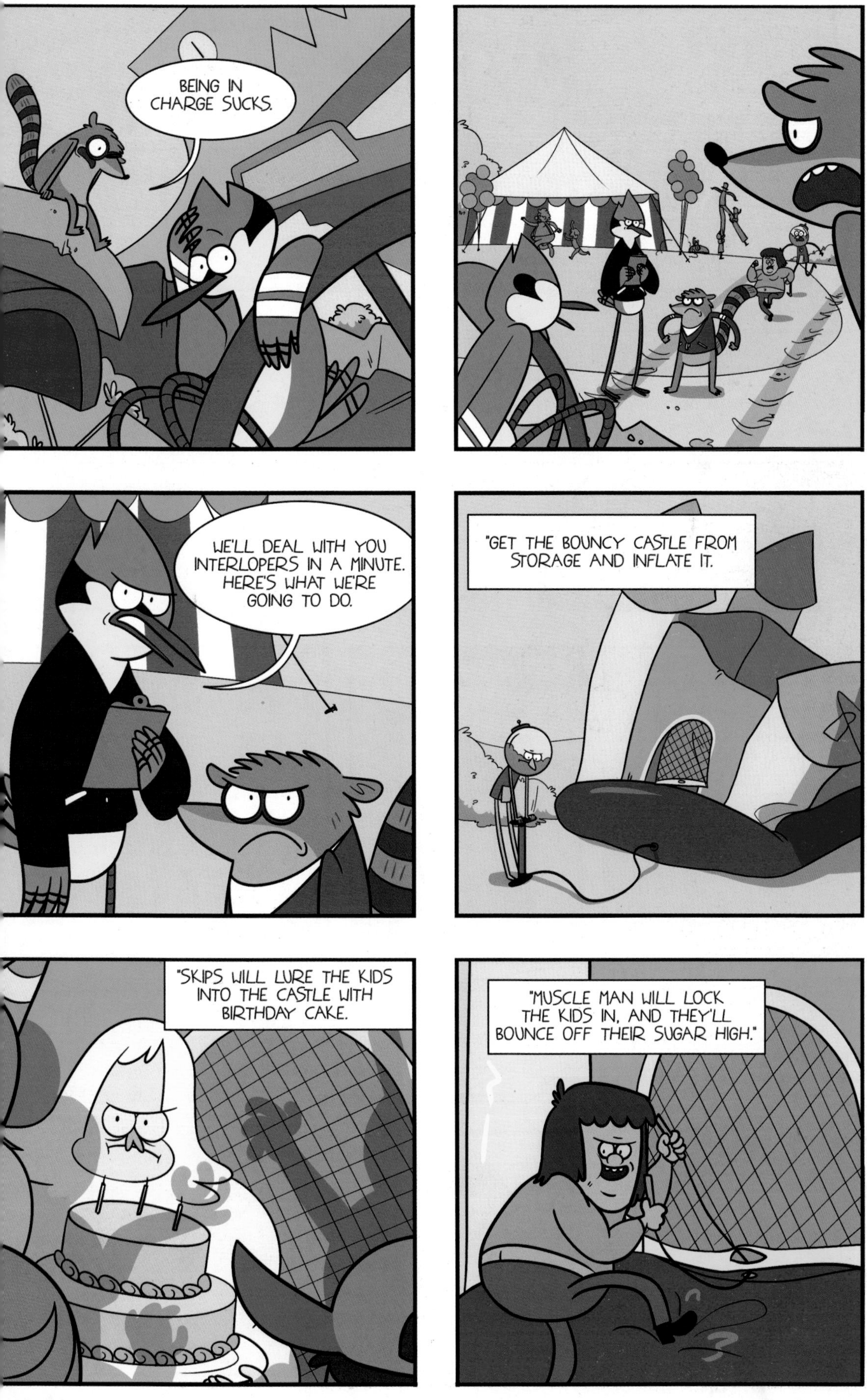
BEING IN CHARGE SUCKS.
WE'LL DEAL WITH YOU INTERLOPERS IN A MINUTE. HERE'S WHAT WE'RE GOING TO DO.
"GET THE BOUNCY CASTLE FROM STORAGE AND INFLATE IT.
"SKIPS WILL LURE THE KIDS INTO THE CASTLE WITH BIRTHDAY CAKE.
"MUSCLE MAN WILL LOCK THE KIDS IN, AND THEY'LL BOUNCE OFF THEIR SUGAR HIGH."

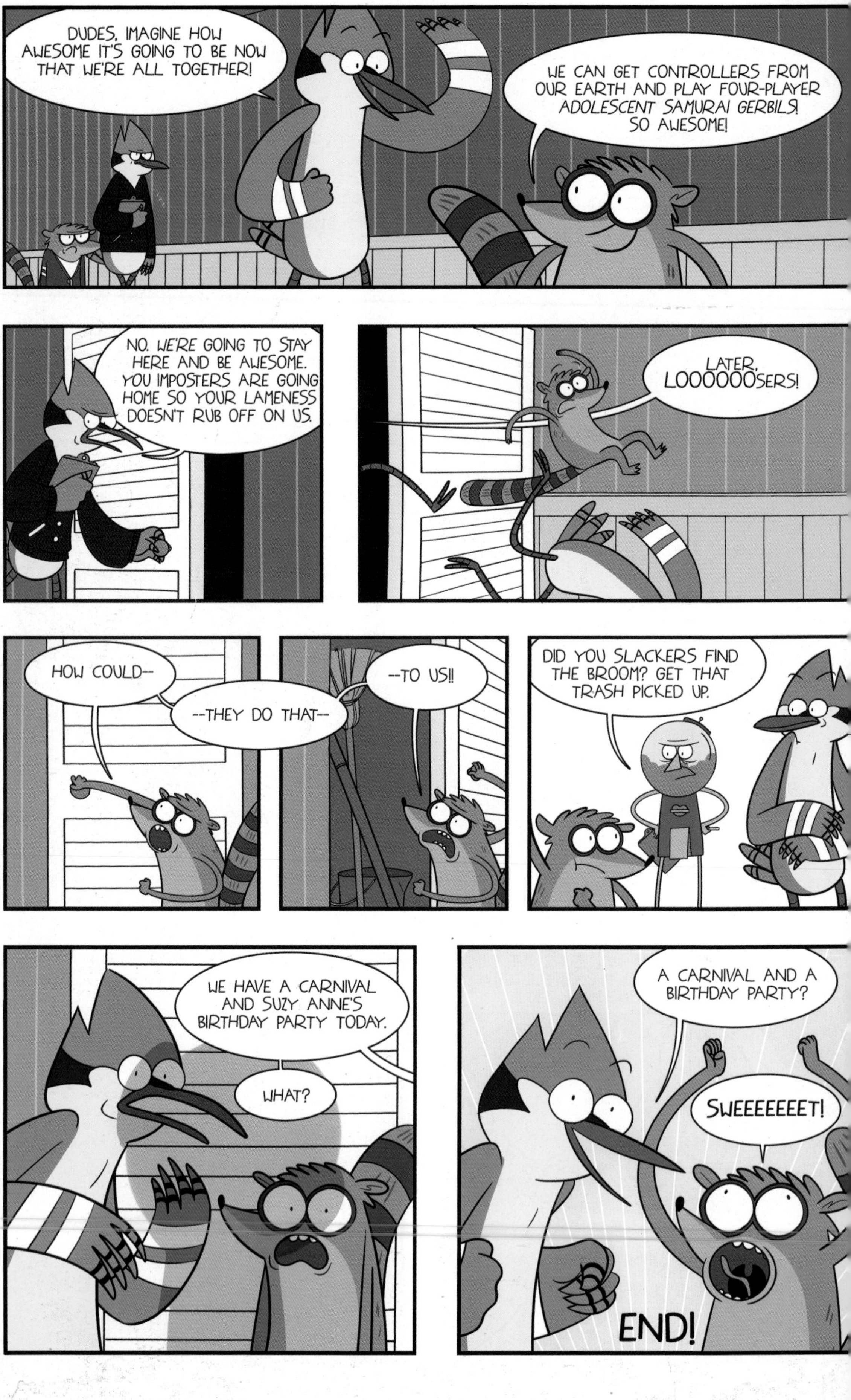
DUDES, IMAGINE HOW AWESOME IT'S GOING TO BE NOW THAT WE'RE ALL TOGETHER!
WE CAN GET CONTROLLERS FROM OUR EARTH AND PLAY FOUR-PLAYER ADOLESCENT SAMURAI GERBILS! SO AWESOME!
NO. *WE'RE* GOING TO STAY HERE AND BE AWESOME. YOU IMPOSTERS ARE GOING HOME SO YOUR LAMENESS DOESN'T RUB OFF ON US.
LATER, LOOOOOOSERS!
HOW COULD--
--THEY DO THAT--
--TO US!!
DID YOU SLACKERS FIND THE BROOM? GET THAT TRASH PICKED UP.
WE HAVE A CARNIVAL AND SUZY ANNE'S BIRTHDAY PARTY TODAY.
WHAT?
A CARNIVAL AND A BIRTHDAY PARTY?
SWEEEEEEET!
END!

COVER GALLERY

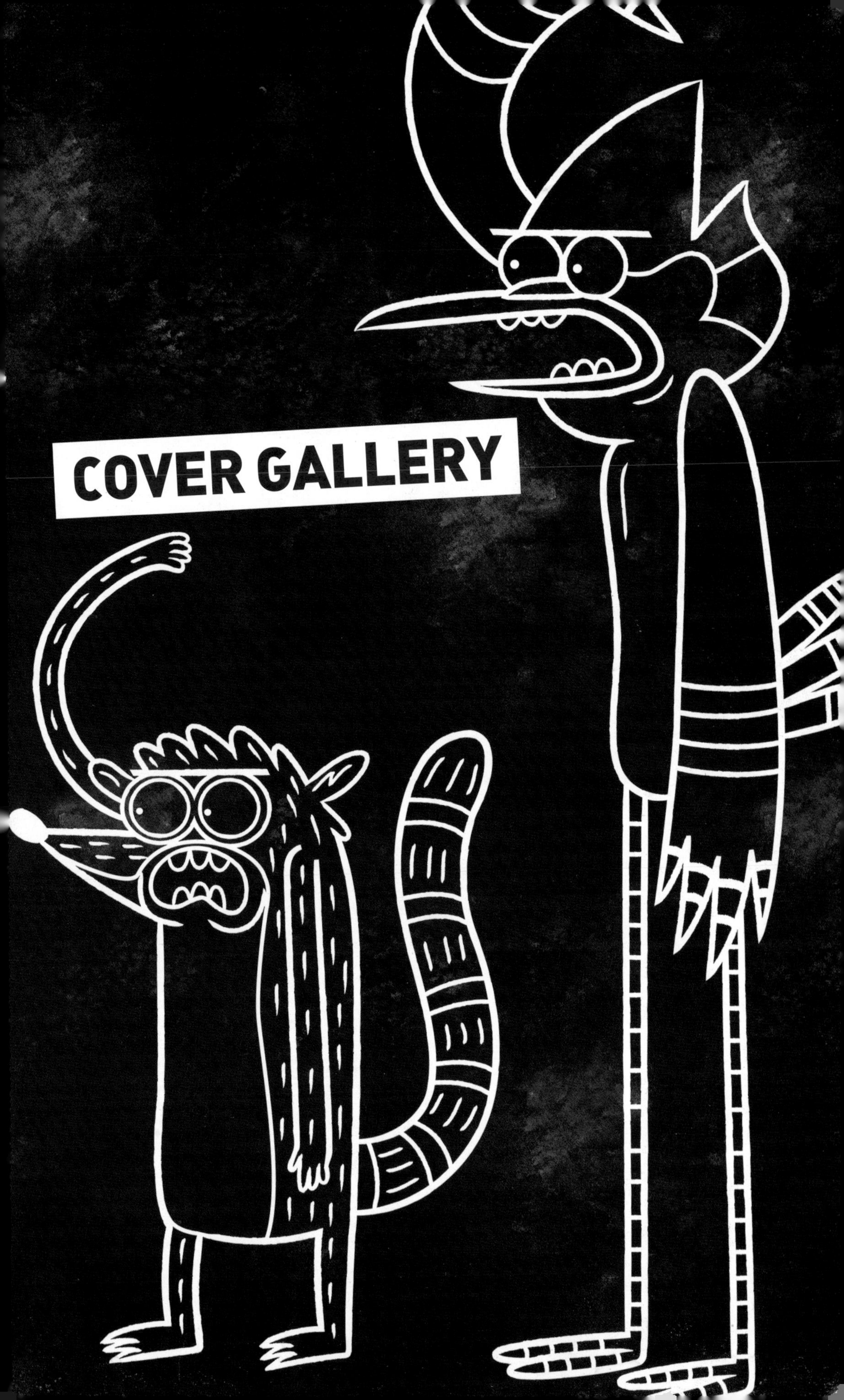

ISSUE THIRTY THREE Main Cover
ALISON STREJLAU

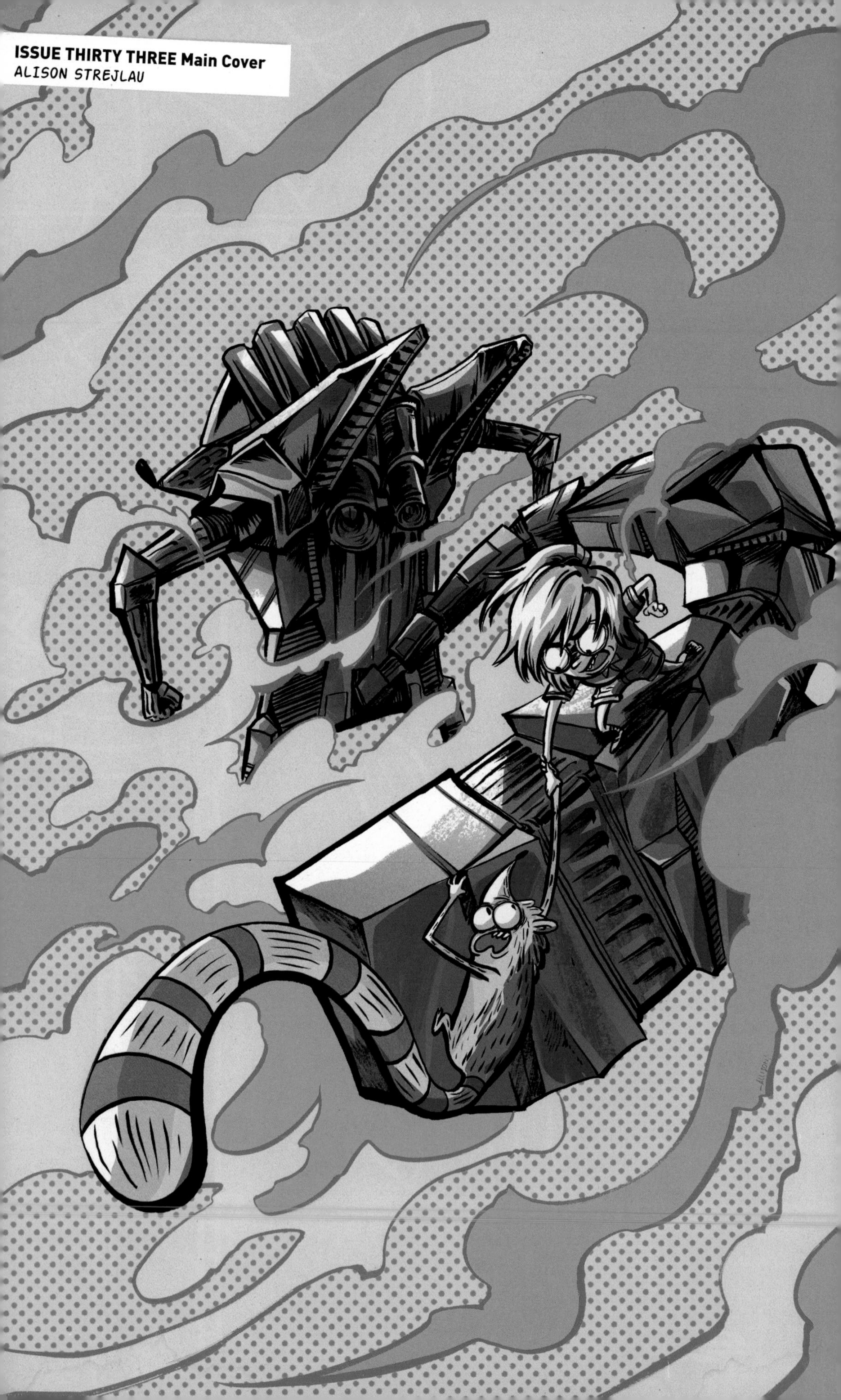

ISSUE THIRTY THREE Subscription Cover
MATTHEW SMIGIEL

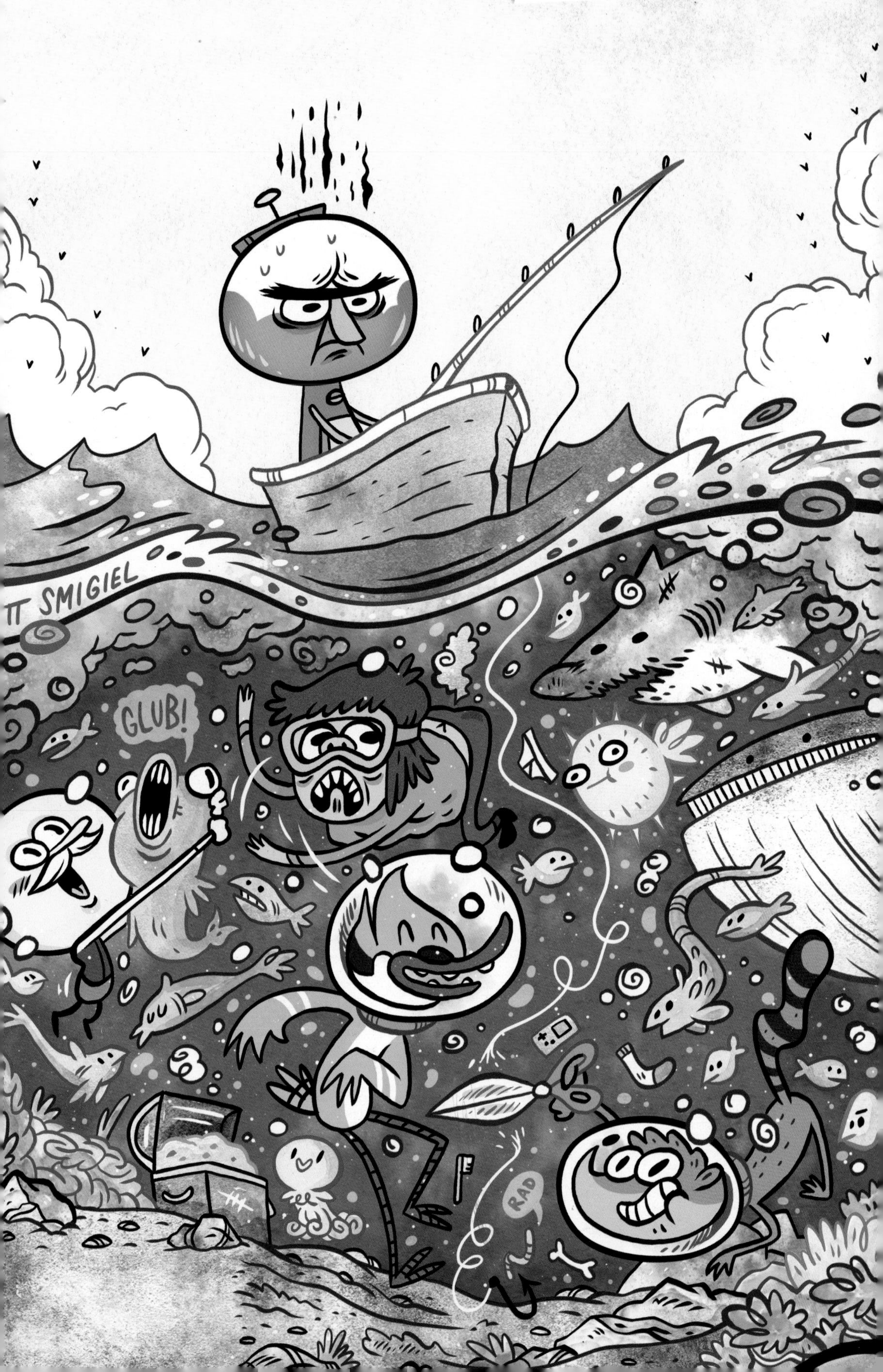

SMIGIEL
GLUB!
RAD

ISSUE THIRTY FOUR Main Cover
MAD RUPERT

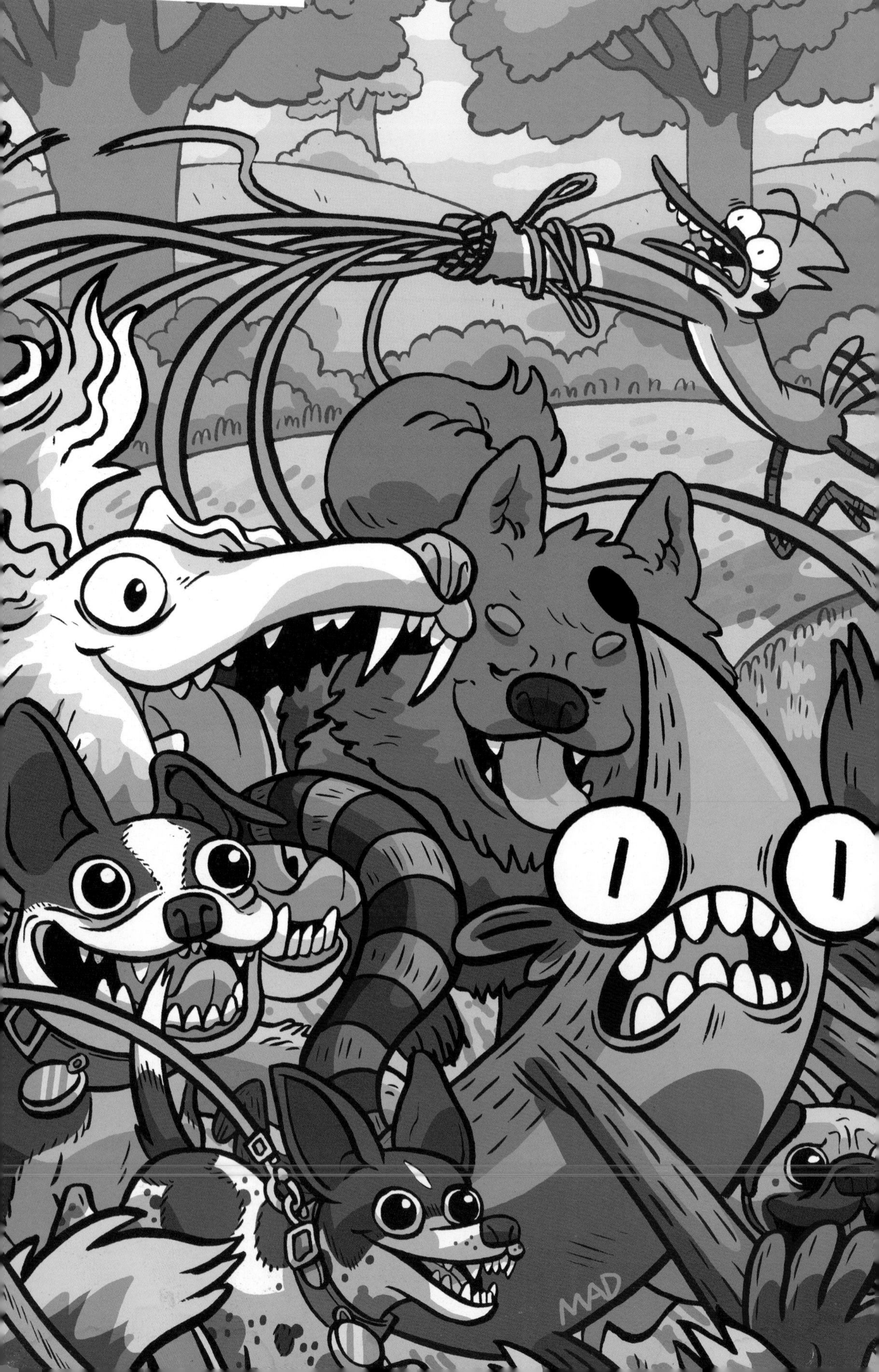
MAD

ISSUE THIRTY FOUR Subscription Cover
PAT KINSELLA

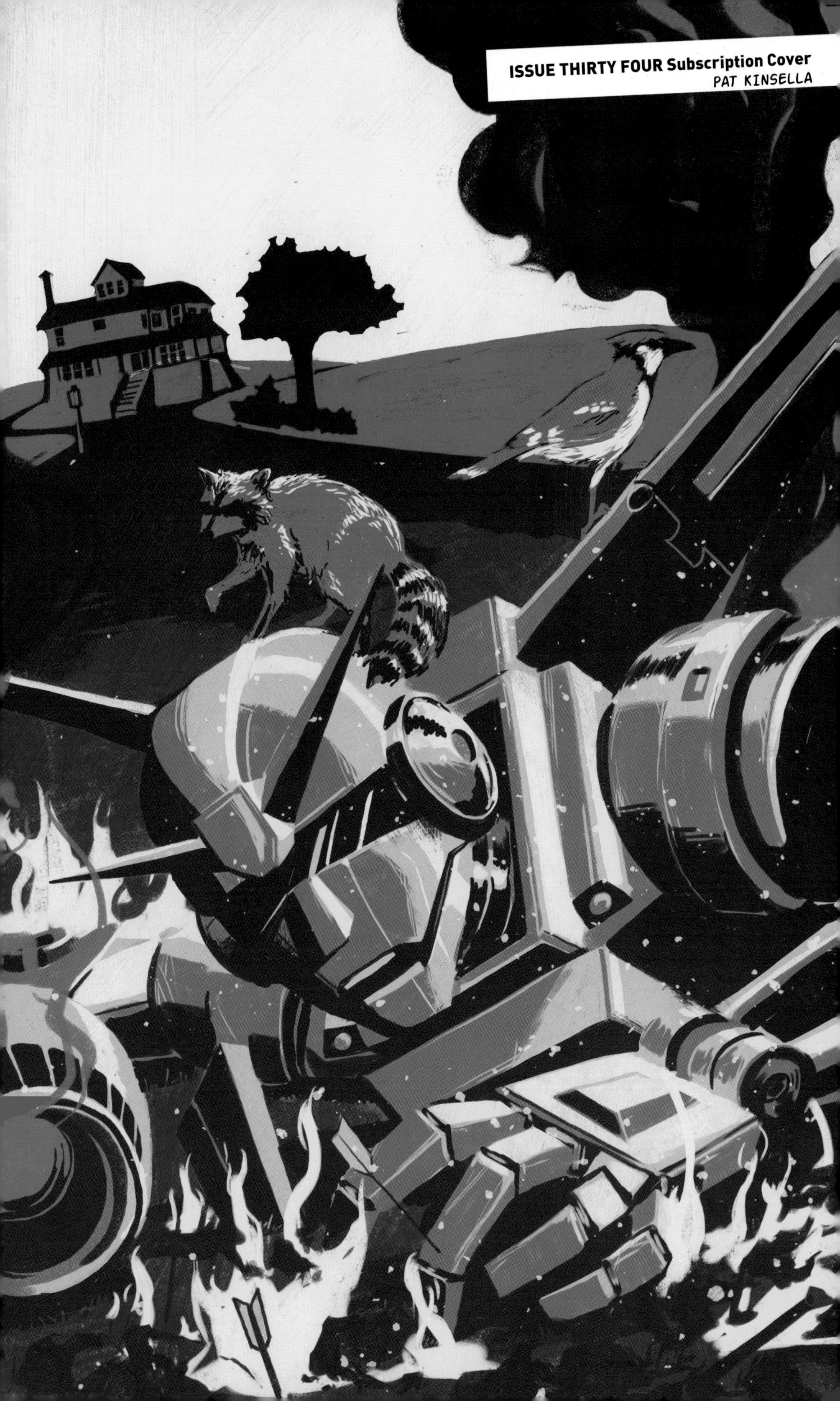

ISSUE THIRTY FIVE Main Cover
PHILIP MURPHY

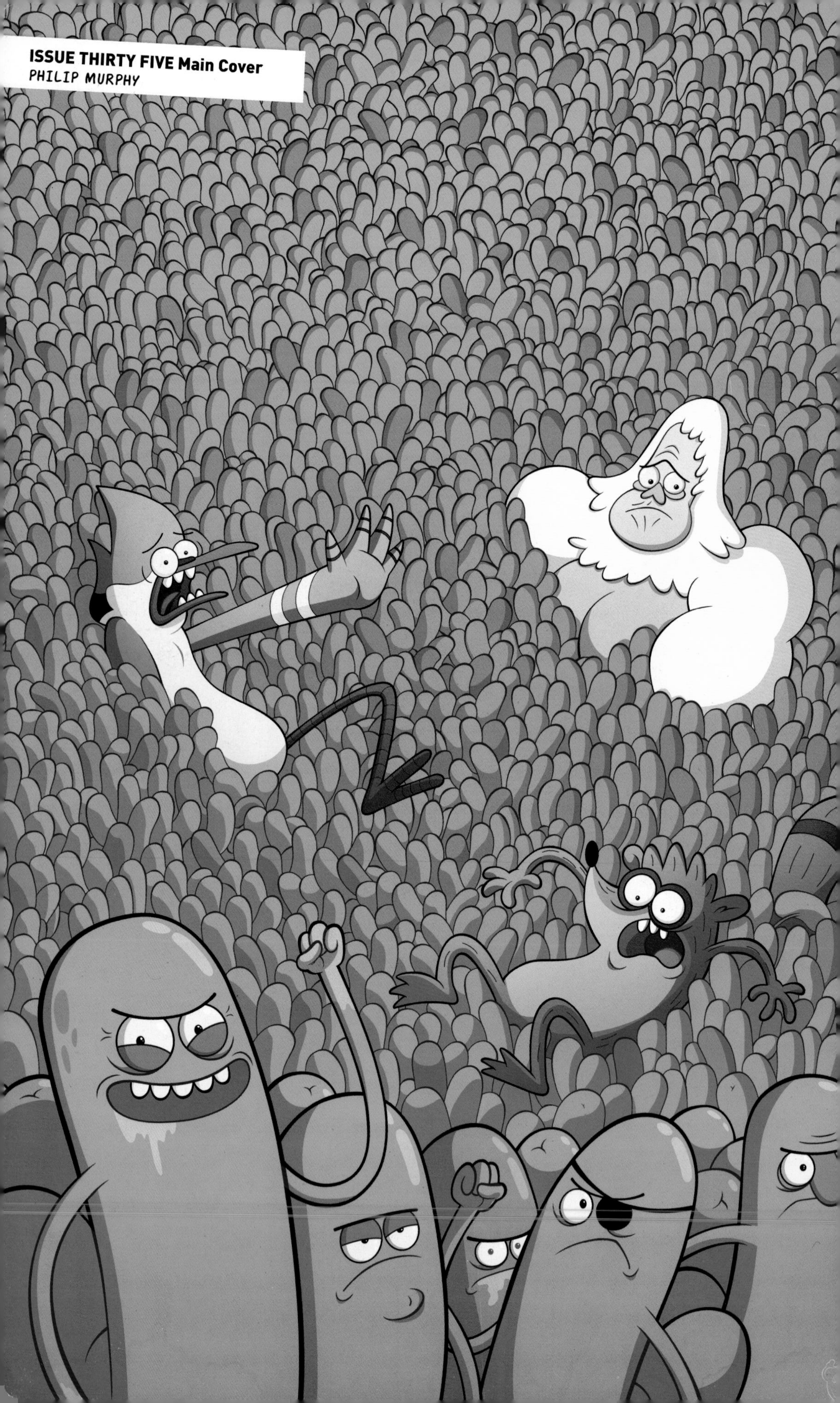

ISSUE THIRTY FIVE Subscription Cover
MATTY NEWTON

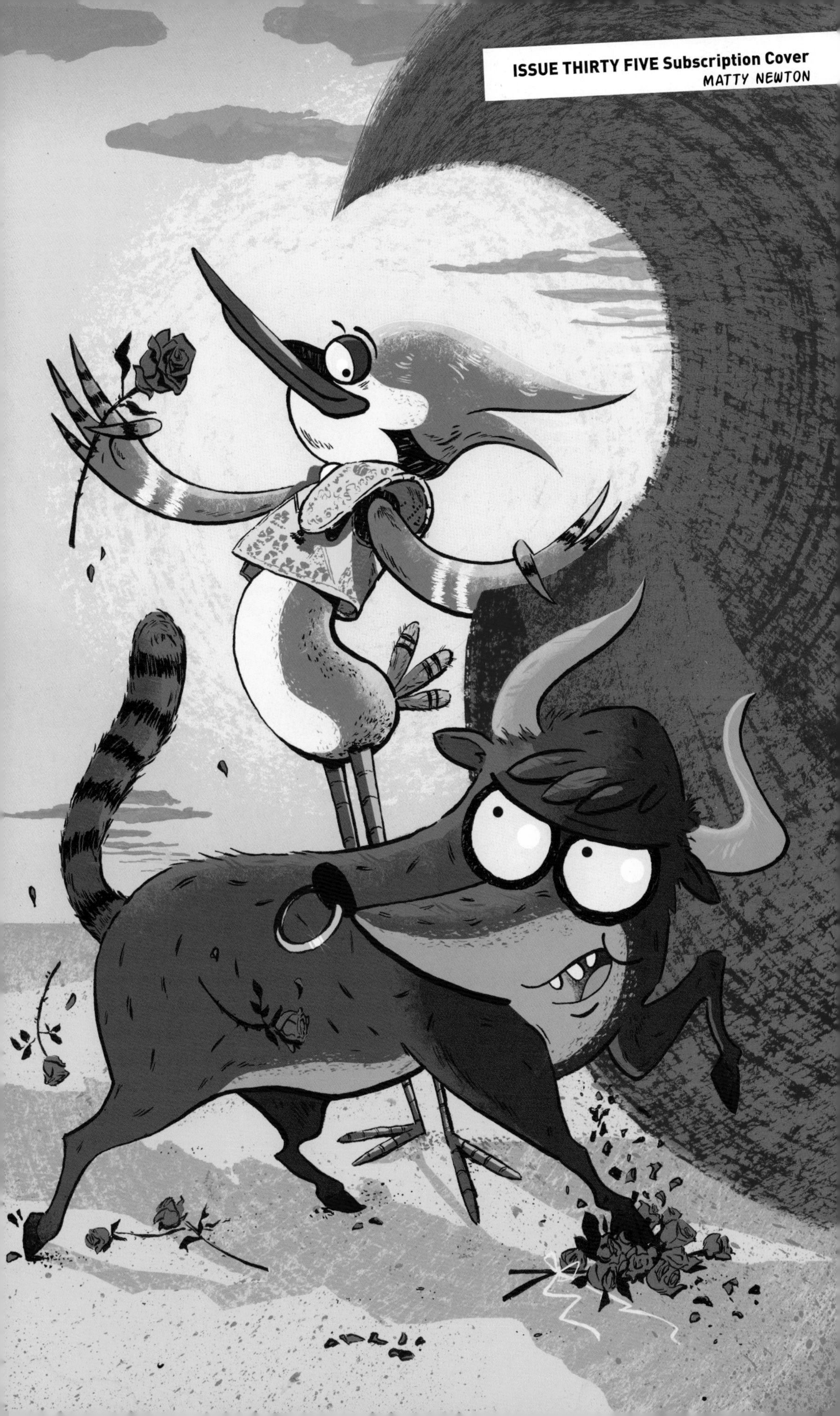

ISSUE THIRTY SIX Main Cover
TERRY BLAS

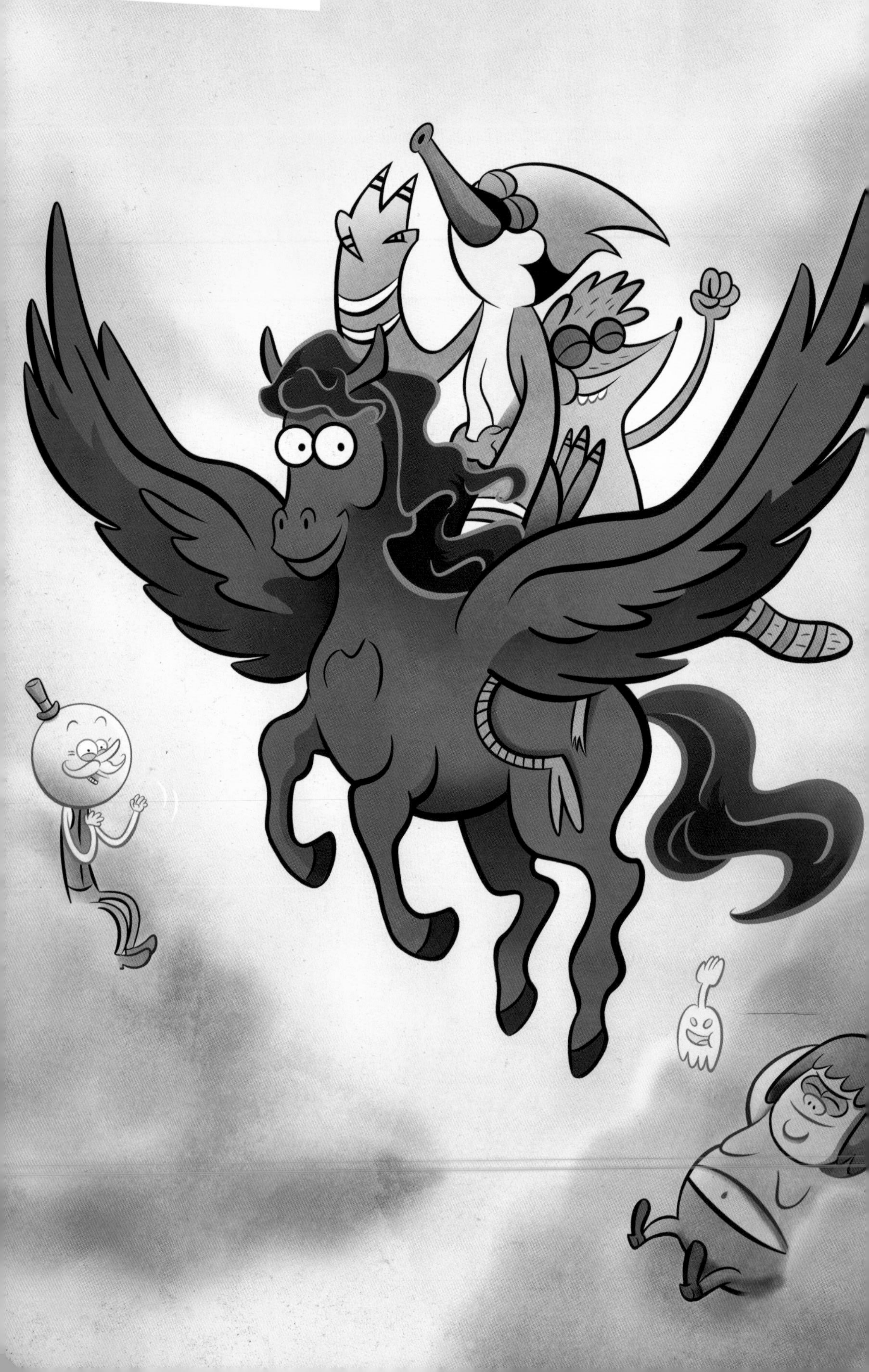

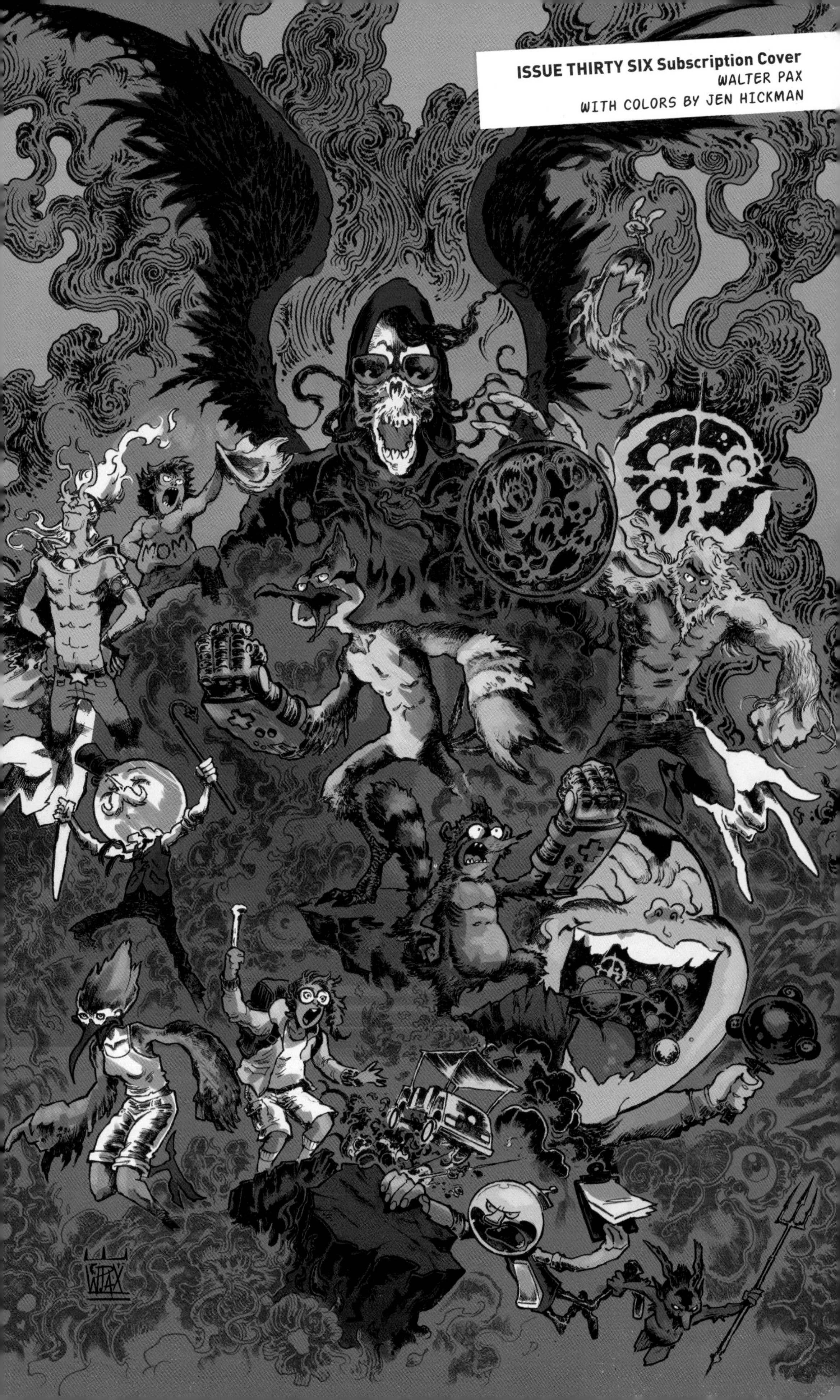
MOM

ISSUE THIRTY SIX Subscription Cover
WALTER PAX
WITH COLORS BY JEN HICKMAN

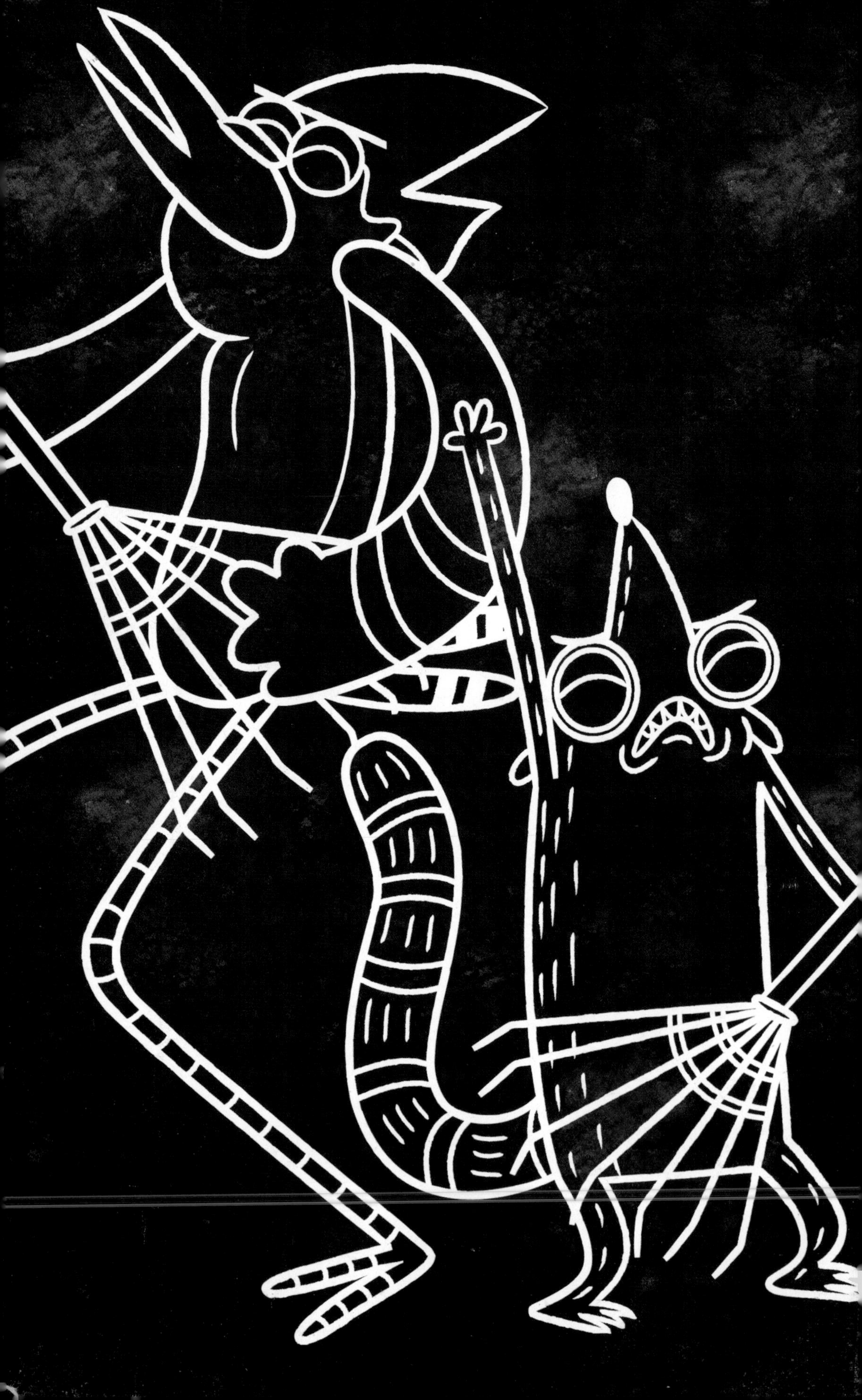

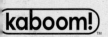

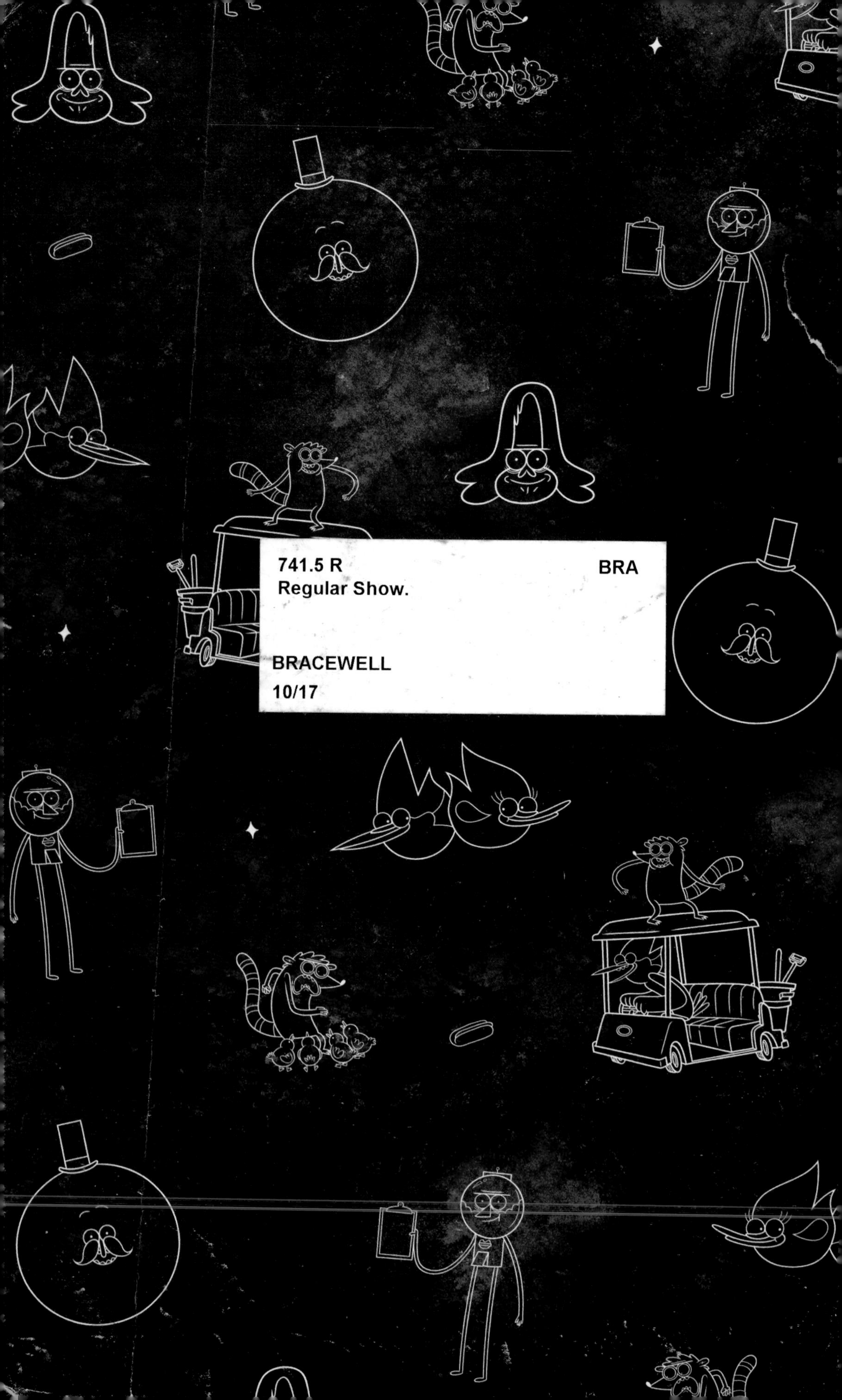